# Just HENRY

# MICHELLE MAGORIAN

EGMONT

## Also by Michelle Magorian

*Goodnight Mister Tom*
*Back Home*
*Cuckoo in the Nest*
*A Spoonful of Jam*
*A Little Love Song*

# EGMONT

*We bring stories to life*

*Just Henry*, first published 2008
by Egmont UK Limited
239 Kensington High Street
London W8 6SA

This edition published 2011

Text copyright © 2008 Michelle Magorian
Design elements © 2008 Nick Keevil

The moral rights of the author have been asserted

ISBN 978 1 4052 6407 5

1 3 5 7 9 10 8 6 4 2

www.egmont.co.uk
www.michellemagorian.com

A CIP catalogue record for this title is available from the British Library

Typeset by Avon DataSet Ltd, Bidford on Avon, Warwickshire
Printed and bound by CPI Group (UK) Ltd, Croydon, CR0 4YY

52680/1

# Contents

*Part Four – Looking for the Diamond*

Dedicated to
my agent Pat White,
and to Cally Poplak,
with thanks.

*In memory of Miriam Hodgson
and Brian Finch.*

# PART ONE

*Ringing in the New*

# 1. Unwelcome news

'WILL YOU PLEASE BE QUIET!'

But the pleas from the usherette were having little effect on the handful of small children who were straddling the backs of the cinema seats and riding them as though they were horses.

Behind them, Henry swayed from left to right in an attempt to see the screen. Above his head, a lone collie was leaping through the flames of a burning orphanage in search of a missing boy who was in bed in the attic. The film music rose to a crescendo, as did the volume of noise from the auditorium. Finally, the wonder dog managed the impossible and the little boy was saved. This was greeted with a roar of approval from a thousand voices in the upper circle and stalls. As soon as the credits began to roll there was the crashing of upturned seats followed by a stampede up the aisles.

The introductory drum roll of *God Save the King*

stopped the ones who hadn't made it through the exit doors and they froze to attention like everyone else. As Henry stood, towering above the noisy group in front of him, he thought yet again that he really was too old for the Saturday Morning Pictures. He had had no intention of going that morning but when the official-looking envelope addressed to his stepfather had plopped through the door he couldn't bear to stay in the house any longer. His mother had looked as if she was about to faint when she spotted it on the mat. He had been tempted to tear it open so that she could find out how stuck-up and stupid his stepfather was there and then, but had stormed out of the house instead.

Once the National Anthem was over he sat down again and gazed up at the screen tabs. Whenever the lights hit the auditorium after the Saturday morning show he was always surprised by the shabbiness of the curtains. In the dark, when red, green and blue lights whirled in circles on them, their age disappeared and it was like being in Hollywood.

Suddenly he was aware of an usherette, peering down at him from the aisle, in her smart brown and gold uniform.

'Hoping to lie low till the main programme?' she enquired. 'Come on, ducks.'

He moved his bare feet along the red carpet and recovered his damp plimsolls with his toes. It was so hot in the cinema that once the lights had dimmed he had kicked them off, as did nearly everyone else he judged, as the smell of hundreds of unwashed feet and hot sweaty rubber had hit the darkened auditorium. He slipped them on and loped towards the exit doors, narrowly missing being sprayed with disinfectant by one of the cleaners. As he stepped into the palatial foyer, hordes of children were still running down the wide carpeted stairway and joining the flood of children pushing their way from the stalls. He stepped to one side and knelt down to tie his laces, sweating profusely, his shirt and baggy shorts clinging to him. It was as stifling in the expansive entrance as it had been in the auditorium. A few yards away, by the Cinema Club table, he observed a smartly dressed man taking down notices advertising the benefits of belonging to the club – cycling groups and handicraft lessons. He was the choirmaster. A girl with long black plaits was hovering beside him.

'And then there's the Carol Competition in December,' the man was saying over his shoulder.

'And I can belong to the choir?' she asked eagerly.

'As long as you're not tone deaf.' And he gave a laugh.

She was very well spoken, thought Henry. He had never heard anyone at Saturday Morning Pictures sounding so lah di dah. He observed the way she stood bolt upright in her blouse and skirt as though her body had never known what the word slouch meant.

'You enjoy singing then?' asked the man.

'I *love* singing.'

Henry turned quickly before he was spotted and wandered over to read the 'Coming Attractions'.

---

### HE'S A FAMILY MAN!

He poisons Uncle Henry . . . drowns Cousin Ascoyne

blows up Uncle Rufus . . . pierces Aunt Agatha

shoots Uncle Ethelred . . . explodes Cousin Henry

Ealing Studios present

### DENNIS PRICE . VALERIE HOBSON

### JOAN GREENWOOD . ALEC GUINNESS in

A hilarious study in the gentle art of murder

### KIND HEARTS and CORONETS

### A BRITISH PICTURE

---

'Blast!' he muttered. It was an A film. That meant he would have to find an adult in the queue willing to take him in.

When he turned, the girl had disappeared. The choirmaster who was clearing the table caught his eye.

'I didn't notice your name among those auditioning for the choir,' he commented. 'You must be about thirteen now?'

'Fourteen, sir. It's my voice, see. It goes a bit up and down now.'

'Ah. Well why not come along to the auditions and

we'll see how you do. I'm sure we can squeeze you in again if you're up to the mark.'

Henry hesitated. He hated performing in public but Gran had told him what a wonderful singer his father had been and it made her feel good knowing he was carrying on the family tradition. Henry had let her think there wasn't a choir any more but she was bound to find out about the competition.

'I'll think about it, sir.'

'Good lad.'

He was about to leave when he spotted the girl again. It was difficult not to. She was the only still figure in the centre of the foyer. Oblivious to the children jostling around her, she stood with her head thrown back. Someone else was also observing her from the foot of the stairway. It was Pip, the smallest boy in his form, almost the smallest in the school. People said he ought to be a jockey and had nicknamed him Pipsqueak. Then it was shortened to Pip and it stuck.

A small, tired-looking woman wearing a faded floral wrap-around overall was dragging an industrial vacuum cleaner towards him. Pip smiled at her. Henry guessed she must be his mother. He looked away out of habit. Pip was nice enough but, as everyone knew, you ignored people like Pip.

The foyer was almost empty now. He glanced back to where he had seen the girl but she had gone. He strolled over to where she had stood and looked up. Heavy dark beams criss-crossed the colossal arched ceilings like something out of a film about the Tudors. It was strange that in all the years he had been coming to the Plaza he had never looked upwards.

'Come on, sonny.'

The commissionaire, a tall imposing man, was waiting patiently for Henry to leave. He was pulling on a large black coat with gold braid and buttons and his smart cap. Henry dawdled past the two box office windows and the chocolate girl. She had just finished wrapping a white overall around her waist and was hanging a tray of chocolates round her neck. Glancing at her, he tried to think of yet another excuse to stay so that he could avoid going home, but one look at the commissionaire's raised eyebrows and he quickly pushed open the nearest foyer door. Out on the stone steps, the August heat nearly knocked him sideways. Two queues for the matinee had already formed on the pavement and were beginning to trail down Victoria Road. It often struck Henry as strange how two roads that joined each other could be so different. Victoria Road had been untouched by the bombing but all that remained in Henry's street were nine small houses clustered in front of a bombsite. A fence had been put up in front of it after the war to prevent children playing in the rubble but it had been broken for years and everyone used it as a shortcut to Hatton Road and the railway station.

He was hopping down the steps when he spotted a familiar figure in khaki having a smoke.

'Charlie!' he yelled.

The nineteen-year-old turned and gave him a wave. Henry gaped at him in astonishment, for Charlie's luxuriant mop of ginger curls had been shorn off. All that remained was a carrot-coloured blur on his scalp. Charlie sprang to his feet, put on his black beret and slowly turned round in his Army uniform, as if in a fashion parade. Henry took in the huge polished black boots, gaiters and white blanco'd belt.

'Smart, eh?'

'Yeah. They didn't leave much hair on your head, did they? What's it like?'

'It'll get better now I've finished Basic Training.'

'That bad, eh?'

'I survived.' He shook his head and gave a short laugh. 'I dunno. One minute Dad says doing National Service will make a man out of me. The next minute he says don't volunteer for anything.' He took out a packet of Woodbines from his pocket. 'I expect you'll get on better than me when it's your turn, your dad being a hero and all that.'

'That was nine years ago.'

'Makes no difference. He sacrificed his life for another man.'

He pushed the packet of cigarettes in Henry's direction. Henry shook his head.

'Still think it's like burning money?'

'Burning cinema tickets,' said Henry.

'So what was it like?' asked Charlie, indicating the cinema. 'They still have the sing-song with the Wurlitzer organ?'

'Yeah *and* the short films *and* the news *and* the cartoons *and* the serial *and* a bell-ringing concert on stage. I had five Hopalong Cassidys in front of me as well.'

'Why d'you still go?'

'It's cheap and sometimes they have a good film.'

'Roy Rogers?'

They grinned at one another. Henry couldn't stand Roy Rogers, a singing cowboy who was always immaculately dressed even at the end of a gun battle.

'That too. But last week they had a film with Errol Flynn in it, *Sea Hawk*. It was good.'

'I dunno how you can stand the racket.'

'I can't,' said Henry, smiling.

'So, have you found someone else in the street to take you into the A films?'

He shook his head. He had missed Charlie's company in the queues. Charlie didn't mind him talking about the films. But he wasn't going to tell him that. He'd sound soft.

'When d'you get back?'

'Late last night. I got a seventy-two.'

'What's that?'

'Seventy-two hours' leave. So far, most of it's been used up, gettin' 'ere. So,' he added, dragging on his cigarette, 'where you off to?'

'Home,' said Henry quietly.

'You don't sound too cheerful about it.'

They stared across the bombed landscape towards Hatton Railway Station, where his stepfather worked. A ring of smoke rose above Charlie's head.

'When do you have to go back?' Henry asked, changing the subject. He didn't let anyone know about the rows at home, not even Charlie.

'Tomorrow. I'll either get the coach from London just after midnight or get the one-thirty milk train.'

'Not long then?'

'Nah. Got to make the most of what I got left.'

'Yeah,' agreed Henry quietly.

'Good to see you, mate.'

Henry took that as his cue to go. He gave a casual nod, turned the corner into his street past Number 2 and headed for the broken fence. For a while he burrowed around in the long stretch of rubble for broken floorboards or scraps of material his mother could wash and use for making swathes of patchwork material, but his heart wasn't in it. He knew he was just filling in time to avoid walking into Number 6.

He crossed back over the road past half a dozen girls playing hopscotch and glanced through the front window. His gran was sitting, flopped back in her armchair, fanning herself with a magazine. As he opened the front door a screeching sound erupted from the kitchen followed by high-pitched laughter. He pressed his hands to his ears. How his mother could put up with it for a day let alone weeks mystified him. The kitchen door had been flung open and he caught sight of his half-sister running in circles at top speed round the kitchen table, shrieking her head off, her blonde curls bobbing up and down. He wondered how so much sound could emerge from someone so small.

His mother was closing the range door. She looked over her shoulder, her face flushed with the heat.

'She just needs to get out,' she said, smiling.

'I didn't say anything,' he protested.

'You didn't have to,' she said, 'your face! You look like you've walked into a horror film.'

He wanted to talk to her about going to see *Kind Hearts and Coronets* but it was impossible to think straight with Molly making such a racket. He wished he could be alone with his mum, like they used to be before Molly was born. He glanced up at the shelves on the wall opposite the range, crammed with books. Sticking out between a Latin primer and a geometry textbook on the top shelf was the unopened envelope. His mother turned hurriedly away.

*

'Auntie cross!' yelled Molly from her highchair and she pointed her spoon at Henry's gran and banged it on the tray.

'She needs a good slap, that girl,' snapped Gran, who sat slumped opposite her, scowling.

'It's just high spirits!' said Henry's mother nervously. 'You keep forgetting. She's only two.'

'Too noisy. Too messy. Too spoilt for her own good.'

Henry's mother gave a laugh.

'Now, Mrs Dodge, you don't mean that, do you?'

'Don't I just?' she muttered.

'Now, let's enjoy the meal, shall we?' said his mother brightly. The atmosphere in the room was so tense that Henry thought his backbone would snap. Only Molly seemed not to notice the tension in the room. As soon as his mother had begun stacking the dirty dishes and had placed a pan of potatoes on the range ready for when his stepfather returned home from the morning shift, his grandmother shuffled back to the front room.

It was at about half past two when the door in the yard opened and Henry spotted a tall gangly figure in blue overalls and a black cap through the back window. His mother visibly jumped. Molly froze for an instant and then started jumping up and down, shouting, 'Daddy! Daddy!'

No sooner had he opened the scullery door into the

kitchen than she flung herself at him. Within seconds she was in his arms. Struggling, he managed to put his tea can on the table.

'Hello, love,' he said, turning to Henry's mother and kissing her on the cheek.

This display of affection still embarrassed Henry, even though his mother and Uncle Bill had been married for three years.

'Had a good day?' she asked automatically.

'Yes. I was on a steam engine. They needed extra trains for the holidaymakers so they had to use them as well as the electric ones.' He stopped and stared at her. 'It's come, hasn't it?'

She nodded.

*Now he'll get his come-uppance*, Henry thought.

'And you haven't opened it?' he asked, struggling with Molly, who was bouncing energetically in his arms.

'No.'

'Shall I take Molly into the yard?' Henry heard himself say.

'Molly not go!' she screamed. 'Molly STAY!'

His mother glanced at the wall, which divided his gran's room from the kitchen.

'Molly, you don't want Auntie coming in here and telling you off again, do you?'

'And watching Uncle Bill open the envelope,' murmured Henry, under his breath.

His mother shot him a pleading look as if to say, *Don't you start too*. She scooped Molly from her father's arms and handed her a wooden spoon. 'Come and do some stirring for me, Molly.'

By now Henry was fighting down the urge to smile. He knew that the letter would upset his mother but it was worth it to see his stepfather put in his place.

Uncle Bill took the envelope down and stared at it as though it was an unexploded bomb.

'Do you want me to . . .?' began his mother.

He shook his head and tore it open. He unfolded the letter and sat down slowly.

*Trounced*, thought Henry.

'I don't understand,' Uncle Bill murmured shakily.

*But I do, Mister High and Mighty*, thought Henry. *Now Mum will see you for what you really are.*

'Bill?'

'I've done it. I've got the Higher School Certificate. Advanced French. Advanced History. Advanced English.'

'Oh, Bill!' she cried and she stepped over Molly and flung her arms round him, her eyes filling.

Henry froze. *It must be a mistake. His stepfather was stupid. He couldn't have passed the examinations. He was all talk. Had ideas above his station. That's what Gran said.*

There was a loud hammering at the front door.

'I'll get it,' said Henry, needing to escape, and he stumbled into the hall.

Through the long windows at the top of the door he saw a bald head bobbing up and down. He had hardly opened it when a short portly man in a threadbare tweed suit and bow tie rocketed past him and flew into the kitchen.

'Mr Cuthbertson!' his mother exclaimed.

Uncle Bill stood up.

'Don't keep me in suspense, man,' he said.

Speechless, Uncle Bill handed him the letter.

'By heaven, you've done it!' he exclaimed. 'I knew you would. Doors will be opened to you now.'

Uncle Bill gave a weary smile. 'Don't mention university again,' he began.

'No, no, no! Not university, old chap. I'm talking about teaching. Because of the shortage of teachers, there's an Emergency Training Scheme. It only takes a year to train and you are more than qualified.'

'I'm a railwayman,' protested Uncle Bill.

'Smoke! Smoke!' yelled Molly, pointing to the potatoes which had begun to make a crackling sound.

'Oh, no!' gasped his mother. As she grabbed the saucepan handle, Mr Cuthbertson suddenly dashed out of the kitchen crying, 'Stay there!' over his shoulder.

Minutes later he re-appeared, flanked by two pasty-looking men. A cigarette was dangling from the mouth of one man and his companion was carrying a camera.

'*Sternsea Evening News*,' the photographer announced.

'Is that the letter?' asked the one with the cigarette, glancing at it on the table.

'The very one,' said Mr Cuthbertson and he handed it to him. 'He's been to classes with me, studied between shifts.'

'You're right, Mr Cuthbertson. It is a scoop. Working-class man up there with the grammar school lot.'

'I'll take a shot of him outside the front door with the family,' commented the photographer.

'But I'm still in my overalls,' protested Bill.

'That's good. Now let's get outside into the light. And put your cap back on.'

As they walked through the hall to the front door, Henry tried to linger behind.

'What's going on?' said Gran, opening her bedroom door. 'Oh, hello, Mr Cuthbertson. Come to commiserate have you, dear?'

'Not to commiserate,' said Mr Cuthbertson, wiping his glistening head with a handkerchief. 'To celebrate, Mrs Dodge. To celebrate!' And he dashed out of the doorway.

Her face fell.

'He's got it,' said Henry numbly.

'What! He never has?' she whispered.

Henry nodded.

At that moment Henry's mother appeared, carrying Molly. 'Henry?' and then she spotted Gran.

'I'm not coming out without Gran,' said Henry firmly.

'I thought you were having a nap, Mrs Dodge. I didn't want to disturb you,' and she reddened. 'I expect Henry's told you the news.' And she darted outside.

Gran took his arm.

'Come on,' she said. 'We Dodges will show 'em, eh?'

Henry smiled. His gran always made him feel better.

They found his mother and Uncle Bill huddled by the front door, holding Molly's hands between them like gingerbread men.

'If you'd just close the door,' said the photographer cheerily.

By now the next-door neighbours had appeared and Henry was so embarrassed he wanted to disappear.

'Hold the little girl in your arms,' said the photographer to Henry's mother and he placed Gran next to her.

'And if you could just stand next to your dad,' he said, waving at Henry.

'He's not my dad!' Henry said fiercely.

'*His* dad's a hero,' said Gran. 'Gave up his life to save another man's life. Pushed him aside during a bombing raid and took the blast. He should have been decorated.'

'Henry is my stepson,' Uncle Bill explained.

'Righti-ho,' said the photographer, 'so, if you could stand next to your *stepfather*.'

A short dumpy woman, who lived next door at Number 8, suddenly appeared with a collection of clothes pegs wedged in her mouth, a bundle of nappies in her arms.

'What's goin' on, Maureen?' she asked, through the pegs.

'Bill's passed some examinations, Mrs Henson.'

'All eyes on me and cheese!' interrupted the photographer. 'And move a bit closer.'

They shuffled awkwardly towards one another.

'Cheer up, Mrs Carpenter,' he added, winking at Henry's gran.

'I am not Mr Carpenter's or Mrs Carpenter's mother,' she snapped.

'Mrs Dodge is my previous husband's mother,' explained Henry's mum hurriedly. 'She moved in with us when she was bombed out.'

'And then *he* moved in with his grand ideas,' Gran said.

'Give me strength!' Henry heard the reporter murmur.

'Cheese again!' sang out the photographer, at which point Molly suddenly stretched an arm upwards and laughed. 'That's my girl!'

Afterwards his grandmother escaped into her room.

'He'll make our lives even more of a misery now,' she complained.

Uncle Bill strode back in, smiling. Henry wanted to hit him.

'I see there's a Dick Barton film on at the Gaiety,' he said jovially.

'I know,' murmured Henry, looking away.

Henry was annoyed to see his mother placing three tiny glasses filled with sherry on the table. His mother only brought out the sherry at Christmas. She handed one to Uncle Bill.

'Congratulations, love.'

'I couldn't have done it without you,' he said, beaming.

Henry clenched his fists, remembering how he and his mother had to keep Molly away from him so that he could study upstairs in peace. Suddenly the door swung open and his gran stood there, her face rigid. Henry picked up the third sherry glass and handed it to her.

'And about time,' she said, her lips pursed. 'I wondered if you'd remember, Maureen.'

'Of course I remembered you. That's why I poured you a glass.'

'I'm not talking about me. You do know what day it is today, don't you?'

There was an uncomfortable silence.

She had forgotten, thought Henry bitterly. But he wasn't surprised. All she ever thought about now was his sissie stepfather.

'Seems not,' said his gran. She flung her head back dramatically. 'Had he lived, it would be the birthday of Henry's father.' She raised her glass, 'To my beloved Alfred. Lest we forget,' she added pointedly.

# 2. Escape

'AT LEAST I TALK ABOUT HIS FATHER. YOU HAVEN'T FOR YEARS.'

'I leave that to you, Mother.'

'I've had to put up with a strange man moving into the house . . .'

'A strange man! How can you talk about Bill like that? If it hadn't been for him . . .'

Henry was sawing wood in the old air-raid shelter the following afternoon when he overheard his mother and Gran in the kitchen.

'Well, what man spends all his time with books? Not like Henry. He's always doing odd jobs, deliveries, sawin' up wood, scavenging. Out in all weathers.'

'As is Bill at work,' added his mother, 'and he pays the rent and puts food on the table.'

'P'raps you don't talk about Henry's dad because you feel guilty. You married pretty quickly after his death.'

'I was a widow for five years!'

'Five years is nothing.'

Henry didn't like being around when they argued. He slipped out of the shelter, bolted through the door at the back of the yard and along the alley behind the houses, climbed over the pile of bricks next to Number 18 and headed for the bombsite opposite. Aside from a motorbike with its sidecar outside Number 14 and a few kids sitting on their front steps in their Sunday best, the road was deserted. He made his way to the Plaza to see *Kind Hearts and Coronets*.

Hovering at the foot of the cinema steps he watched the queues grow. He hated having to ask an adult to take him in to see an A film. Asking favours from anyone was embarrassing and he was shy of strangers. His attention was suddenly caught by a thin woman in her thirties who was waiting with a boy in his form called Jeffries, a boy whose company he had done his best to avoid for years. He recognised her instantly. She was Jeffries' mother. Why couldn't they leave Sternsea? No one wanted to know them so why did they stay? Why didn't they get the message? Gran said she thought Mrs Jeffries had sent her son to Henry's school out of spite and it did seem that way. He moved further away from them and spotted a short middle-aged woman wearing glasses, her hair pinned back into a dishevelled bun under a wide-brimmed hat. She was absorbed in an orange paperback. He watched her absently scooping strands of hair behind her ears so that they trailed along her shoulders. He hesitated for a moment and then slowly drew nearer. He was about to speak when she turned a page with such speed that he changed his mind. It was obvious she had got to the exciting bit and wouldn't want to be interrupted. It was then that he noticed Charlie heading towards the back of the stalls' queue. He waved frantically.

'Will you take me in?' he called out.

'Yeah, 'course.'

Henry sauntered towards him, relieved.

'So, spill the beans,' said Charlie when he had reached him.

'About what?' asked Henry puzzled.

'Come on, mystery boy, everyone's talkin' about it. The *Sternsea Evening News*?' And he pulled a half-smoked cigarette out of his pack of Woodbines.

'Oh, that.'

'Yeah, that,' he said, lighting the stub.

'It's my stepfather,' said Henry wearily. 'He's been learning from these books and going to classes between shifts.'

'And?' said Charlie, taking a drag from the stub.

'He's just passed some exams.'

'What sort of exams?'

Henry sighed.

'Higher School Certificate,' he said, putting on a snooty accent.

Charlie gave a long, low whistle.

'He must be really brainy!' he said. 'Like you.'

'I am not,' Henry protested. 'I'm nothing like him. I'm like my dad.'

'You should have gone to the grammar school.'

'I'm happy where I am.'

What Charlie didn't know was that when Henry had taken the eleven plus examination for the grammar school, he had written his name, put down his pen and folded his arms. He was determined to show in whose footsteps he was going to follow. His mother had been upset but his gran had understood.

'Henry's going to grow up to be a proper man who goes out and does things,' she had said. 'Not someone who reads about it in some book. He's his father's son,' she had added proudly.

'Is he goin' to leave the railways, then?' asked Charlie.

Henry shook his head.

'So why did he take the examinations?'

'Because he's stupid,' Henry muttered.

As they reached the bottom step, Charlie asked suddenly, 'Do you mind if we sit apart?'

'No, course not,' said Henry, minding a lot. He liked being with Charlie, in spite of his awkward questions. 'Is it because of my stepfather getting this certificate?'

'Nah,' laughed Charlie. 'It's . . .' He hesitated. 'It's a girl, see. One of the usherettes.'

'Do I know her?'

'Yeah. She lives in our street. Lily Bridges.'

Henry knew all about Lily Bridges. She was nineteen and *divorced*.

'You know she's . . .'

'Divorced? Yeah. And I can hardly get two words out of her.'

It was all the talk of the street. Henry's mum said she didn't know how she could bear it. She would rather put up with anything than end up as a divorced woman.

'Don't you mind?'

'Nope. She married someone who didn't deserve her. And now she's shot of him. And one day she'll marry me. But don't tell her that. She's scared enough of people as it is. All I want to do right now is to make her smile.'

Halfway up the steps, Henry was just sorting out his ticket money when he spotted the middle-aged woman with the hat by the foyer doors. But she was no longer alone. The girl with the black plaits he had heard asking about the Cinema Club choir was with her. She had such a clear voice that he couldn't help overhearing their conversation.

'It's her first film,' she was saying excitedly.

'But why did you want to see it three times?' asked the woman.

'To hear her sing *It's Magic*.'

'What's her name?'

'Doris Day.'

'Here,' he said, turning to Charlie and handing him a handful of coins.

Not long now, he thought, and he could forget about the argument he had overheard at home.

As *Kind Hearts and Coronets* began, he felt disappointed. It looked like one of those films where posh people laughed a lot at things he didn't find the least bit funny, but before long he was enjoying the story. He smiled as a man called Mazzini methodically bumped off every member of his mother's snobbish family, out of revenge for them letting her die in poverty because she had married his Italian father. If he was Mazzini and his stepfather was a snobby D'Ascoyne, how would he kill him? He grinned. He would remove a nail from one of his stepfather's bookshelves and the whole shelf would tumble on his head and knock him out for good.

When he left the cinema, the girl with the black plaits was walking down Victoria Road with the middle-aged woman, still chatting to her non-stop. He couldn't help watching her. There was something about her that caught your attention. Suddenly it struck him as odd that she had to hunt for an adult on her own. Unlike him, she looked like the sort of girl who would have lots of friends. Not that someone like her would ever be friendly with him. She was too posh.

*

'Now tell me all about it while you have your bath,' said his mother. 'I want to know every detail.'

Henry gazed down at the murky water in the tub in front of the range.

'Yes, I know everyone else has been in it but once I top it up with hot water,' she said, lifting a large iron kettle from the range, 'it'll be lovely.'

'If I keep my eyes shut.'

She laughed.

He could hear *Bandbox* on the wireless coming through the wall from Gran's room.

'Uncle Bill's upstairs reading a story to Molly,' said his mother, noticing him glance round the kitchen. 'Now tell me all about it.'

'There's this actor called Alec Guinness,' said Henry, pulling off his plimsolls, 'and he plays eight parts.'

'Eight! But how could you understand what was going on?'

'He walks and speaks and looks different when he plays each one. He's really funny.'

'Are you going to see it again?'

'Yeah! Why don't you come with me?'

'I'd love to but what with Molly and . . .' She paused, 'One day soon, I promise.'

Henry nodded. It was Uncle Bill who stopped her but she wouldn't let on. He could see he'd better change the subject and then he remembered something else.

'I saw Jeffries and his mum in the queue.'

They looked at one another for a moment.

'Did they see you?'

'I don't think so.'

'It won't be for long. Just three more terms.'

'Why does she stay? She can't believe Private Jeffries will come back now.'

'Well, obviously she still does.'

'But even if he did turn up, why would they want to have anything to do with him after what he's done? And what about us?'

'We've managed so far. Don't tell Gran you've seen them. She'll only get upset.'

He placed the clothes horse with his towel on it round the bath tub to give himself privacy and his mother turned her back on him so that he could undress.

'You're early!' Mr Jenkins said, unlocking the shop door on Wednesday morning,

Henry noticed he was already wearing his white coat.

'Come on in, lad.'

Behind Henry two men were wheeling large sacks of flour and sugar on grocery trolleys. Henry stepped out of their way and leaned against the wooden counter on the left where the shelves of tinned food, biscuits, Oxo cubes and large squares of green soap were stacked. The men lifted up a section of the counter facing them and pushed the two sacks through to the room at the back.

'There's dog mess on the pavement,' said Mr Jenkins. 'You know the drill. Chuck a bucket of soapy water over it and sweep it all down. You can clean the brass plate on the door as well. And after you've done that and washed your hands,' he continued, 'I'll need those dozen jars I mentioned yesterday filled with pickling vinegar and then you can help Miss Moira with the weighing and bagging up.'

'Hello, Henry!' sang elderly Miss Deardon, her white hair only just visible from behind the cash register at the end of the counter. The drawer shot out towards her with a ringing ping as she pulled down the lever at the side.

'We're a bit short of change in the sixpenny bit and farthing compartments, Mr Jenkins,' she announced.

Miss Moira came staggering between the gap in the two counters, a large round cheese in her arms, its skin removed. She swung it on to a marble slab on the left counter by the wire cutter and smiled over the scales beside it, her new National Health glasses misting over. She was always pleased when Henry helped her because he was quick.

'Mr Jenkins,' Henry started hesitantly. 'I know my mother ain't on your delivery list but she was wondering if I could buy her groceries for her today instead of her having to queue. It's just that she needs to collect something . . .'

'This won't become a habit, will it?'

'No, Mr Jenkins.'

'When does school start, by the way?'

Henry's heart fell. He had deliberately avoided thinking about the new autumn term. The article and photograph about his stepfather would be out that afternoon in the *Sternsea Evening News* for all to see. He was sure to be teased about it. Or ignored even more than usual.

*You don't need friends*, his gran had said to him one day, trying to comfort him.

*What do you need friends for when you've got yer old gran?*

'Monday, Mr Jenkins.'

'I don't know why the government wants you youngsters to stay on till you're fifteen. I know lots of lads who want to be out, learning a trade. But then even the ones who've learned a trade are called up for National Service! We've thousands of homeless people, desperate for a decent roof over their heads, living in train carriages and Army huts. And where are all our newly trained electricians, plumbers and builders, I ask you? They're out in the middle of nowhere polishing boots and marching up and down.'

'Yes, Mr Jenkins,' said Henry politely.

The bell above the door began ringing. A tall gangly sixteen-year-old boy with a scrub of curly hair perched on top of a severe short back and sides was hovering outside. Mr Jenkins let him in. The boy glanced at Henry in a manner that was far from friendly.

Mr Jenkins gave a weary sigh.

'You can wipe that look off yer face, Frank.'

'Pardon, Mr Jenkins?'

'You've got a scowl on you that'd frighten the horses. I've told you, he's not trying to steal your job. And anyway he's back at school next week.'

Frank loped over to a peg on the wall behind the counter where a long white apron was hanging.

'Now, Henry,' continued Mr Jenkins, 'you'd best get that pavement cleaned and swept. And after all those other jobs you can help with deliveries.'

'But I do the deliveries!' protested Frank.

'And you'll still be doing the ones that are a bike ride away. Henry can do the ones within walking distance. Don't worry, he won't be taking all your tips.'

Frank reddened.

'Any complaints?'

'No, Mr Jenkins,' muttered Frank.

After work, Henry headed for the Plaza. The middle-aged woman was in the queue again, her hair still tucked up untidily under the same hat, only this time the paper-back she was reading had a green cover on it. She looked so comfortable standing there and appeared to be completely unaware of the people around her. He moved closer but still felt too tongue-tied to talk to her. Just then the commissionaire appeared on the steps.

'There's two seats left in the one and nine's,' he announced.

Henry couldn't afford one and nine pence. And he wasn't allowed to stay for the second programme as it was too late. It looked as though he would have to go home, which he was dreading. His mother would have bought copies of today's *Sternsea Evening News* by now.

'Millions of 'em,' he muttered. 'With pictures of him in them.'

And then he remembered Uncle Bill mentioning the Dick Barton film the day the newspapermen had dropped in on them.

'The Gaiety!' he whispered. The film with it was a Randolph Scott western. '*And* they're both "U"s,' he blurted out with relief.

The woman in the hat whirled round and glanced at him. He hesitated for a moment and then began running.

He found the kitchen door wide open when he arrived back from the Gaiety. His mother, Mrs Henson from next door and young Mrs Wilkins from Number 12 were peering excitedly at a page in the *Sternsea Evening News*.

'Electrifying results,' read Mrs Wilkins, 'as Hatton railwayman steams ahead to success. William Carpenter, a

Duel Link driver who drives both steam and electric trains, astounded his teacher, Mr Hubert Cuthbertson of . . .' She suddenly noticed Henry and stopped. 'Hello, Henry. The photograph's above the grammar school results.'

'You and Gran have been cut out, love,' said his mother, 'but don't take it to heart. I expect they ran out of room.'

At the top of the page he saw a photograph of his stepfather and mother standing together with Molly. *The Carpenter family*. Through the window he saw Molly happily playing in the yard with two of the Wilkins' girls and he was aware of a flicker of jealousy.

'I'll go and keep Gran company,' he said abruptly.

'Ain't you goin' to read it?' asked Mrs Henson.

'Later,' he said, heading for Gran's room.

'I haven't even had my tea yet,' she complained, switching off the wireless.

'Have you seen the photograph?'

'Oh, yes,' and she pursed her lips.

'Mum thinks it was because they didn't have enough room.'

'Don't you believe it. It was your stepfather's doing. He stayed outside with the reporter when we went indoors. Remember? Bit of a coincidence, don't you think?'

'Yeah,' said Henry slowly, his fists clenched.

'We was happy before he came along, weren't we?'

'Yeah.'

'I wish yer dad were 'ere.'

'Me too.'

Sounds of laughter came from the next room.

'Tell me about him,' he said. He had heard it all before many times but it comforted him to hear it again.

'The best footballer in the street he was, and he had a beautiful voice on him. When people heard him sing you could have heard a pin drop. A real gentleman. Anyone in a fix, he'd be the first one there. I know I keep saying it, but he should have been decorated.' They were interrupted by small hurrying footsteps out in the hall and the rattling of the doorknob. 'Not her again,' muttered Gran.

'No, Molly,' they heard Henry's mother cry, 'you know you're not allowed into Auntie's room.'

'Little brat!' Gran added.

Henry stared intently at the photograph of his uniformed father on the mantelpiece.

'Tell me more, Gran.'

# 3. Mr Finch & The Third Man

'AND NOW FORM IVA,' BOOMED THE HEADMASTER ACROSS THE school hall, 'let me introduce you to your new form master, a man who has survived typhoons in the China Seas, was in the Russian convoys and has served both in the Arctic and in India.' He indicated a man with a full head of dark brown hair and a generous moustache, standing beside him on the stage. 'Mr Finch!'

Mr Finch gazed directly down at them, his eyes never wavering. Out of the corner of his eye Henry noticed three girls giggling. Wearing the usual teacher's uniform of a tweed jacket and flannel trousers, he stood almost to attention, unlike their other white-haired teachers who had been bent over books for so many years they had a permanent stoop.

He gave his class a brief nod, and after six-foot-tall Miss Plimsoll had thundered out their school song on the piano, they followed him out in single file in stunned silence. This new man had authority, thought Henry. A clip round the ear from him, he guessed, would hurt more than usual.

They headed across the rough pitted playground towards the year-old prefab classrooms. He glanced swiftly from side to side but everyone was ignoring him, as usual. It seemed as though no one had seen the photograph in the *Sternsea Evening News*, much to his relief.

Pip was sprinting on ahead, trying to keep up with Mr Finch's forceful stride and grinning up at him like an organ grinder's monkey.

*He hasn't got a hope of getting round him*, thought Henry. *He's wasting his time*.

As soon as they stepped into the makeshift classroom, a sense of oppression hit Henry. The building was like an oven.

'You, you and you,' said Mr Finch, pointing to three pupils, 'open the windows or you'll be starting your first cookery lesson of the term earlier than planned.'

To Henry's amazement they jumped to it with no smart-aleck backchat. Suddenly he realised that while he had been staring at Mr Finch all the others had been quickly grabbing a desk.

'Where's Woods?' he asked a boy behind him.

'His dad got him an apprenticeship,' the boy said. 'He had his fifteenth birthday in the holidays and Mr Barratt said he didn't have to come back.'

Henry had to think quickly. He couldn't risk having someone he didn't like sitting next to him for the rest of the year. Already there were only three double desks empty. Two were in the front row, the other in the row behind. He slipped into the one in the second row. To his alarm he saw Jeffries heading in his direction. He kept his head down and avoided looking at him.

'You'd best sit in the front row, lad,' Mr Finch said to Pip. 'You'll be able to see more easily, being on the small side.' This was unusual. The other teachers usually put Pip in the back row out of sight. Out of the corner of his eye Henry could see Jeffries hovering.

'You,' said Mr Finch, 'what's your name?'

'Jeffries, sir.'

'Why don't you join . . .?' He turned to Pip.

'Morgan, sir.'

Jeffries nodded and slid into the seat beside Pip, and Henry felt safe.

Although Mr Finch was their form master, he only took them for French, English and History, the very subjects Uncle Bill had taken for his Higher School Certificate. It made Henry feel uncomfortable at first but Mr Finch was so different from his stepfather it didn't seem to matter. Uncle Bill had never left England, he had worked on the railways during the war, whereas Mr Finch had been all over the world.

After the inkwells had been filled and their pens were

in the grooves at the front of their desks, Mr Finch gave Pip forty pieces of paper to be handed out to the class.

'Before you get the idea that I'm going to ask you to write an essay on what you did in the holidays, I'm not,' began Mr Finch. 'However, I'm still going to ask you what you did.' This was greeted by a stifled groan. 'But I want a list. I won't mind if you prefer to draw pictures rather than write. Put your name at the top of the page and only write on one side of the paper. When you've finished, put your pens down and turn your papers over. If you went to any matches or cricket fixtures, I'd like to know who won. If you went fishing, I'd like to know what you caught. If you were working or had to help out at home, put it down.'

This wasn't like school at all, thought Henry. Eagerly he listed every film he could remember having seen and who had appeared in them, then his favourite ones and what kinds of films they were and why he liked them. After a while he became aware that there was less scratching of nibs around him. He looked up and put his pen down. Jeffries, he noticed, was still writing and Pip looked as if he had drawn diagrams with labels.

Henry leaned back with his arms folded. Eventually everyone's paper was turned over.

'Now,' said Mr Finch, 'if you could wave a magic wand and wish for something you would really like to *do* now or in the future, write it down.'

Several of the girls flung up their arms. Mr Finch picked a girl in the front.

'I want to walk down an aisle in a white dress. Does that count?'

'And I want to be a bridesmaid,' said the girl next to her.

'So soon?' murmured Mr Finch gazing at them intently. He sighed. 'All right. But tell me where you'd like to be married and what you might wear. I want details.'

'Sir!' blurted out another girl. 'I'd like to work in a sweet shop.'

'In one where sweets are plentiful and there are no queues?'

The girl smiled. 'Yes, sir.'

'Write down what you'd like to have in the shop.'

More arms shot up.

'Yes, Wilson,' he said to a lanky freckled-faced boy in the back row.

'I want to be a cowboy.'

This was greeted by laughter.

'Dealing with cattle or horses? And what kind of horse would you ride?'

'We can wish for anything?' said the boy next to him.

'Anything. It's a magic wand, remember.'

'Even go to the moon?' asked a boy called Johnson, who wore spectacles with lenses so thick they looked like marbles.

'Or train a winning greyhound?' added another boy.

'Anything, but I'd like details. It can be now or in the future.'

Henry thought hard. And then he knew. He would be with a film crew, he wrote. He would travel with them all over the country, standing in the background, watching and listening, observing the technicians and actors.

An image suddenly sprang into his head. He saw himself slamming a clapperboard shut and a voice from somewhere yelling, 'Action!'

'I need you to weigh and bag up fourteen bags of raisins and fourteen bags of sultanas,' said Miss Moira, smiling at Henry over the counter. 'And then after you've finished those I need you to fill fourteen one-pound bags with sugar.'

'And mind you weigh them *meticulously*,' added Mr Jenkins with raised eyebrows.

'Oh, Mr Jenkins,' scolded Miss Moira, 'he always does.'

'Are there any jobs for me tomorrow, Mr Jenkins?' Henry asked.

'Providing you don't mind coming in before school.'

'No, Mr Jenkins.'

'Usual jobs then. Windows, pavement and door handle. And you can pop back after school to sweep the yard.'

'Mr Jenkins,' said Miss Moira hesitantly, 'what about the flour delivery on Thursday?'

'Frank can help you with that, can't he?'

'Of course, Mr Jenkins.' She cleared her throat. 'Of course there'll be fewer spillages with Henry,' she added quietly.

'And we don't want Mrs Jenkins on the warpath, is that it, Miss Moira?'

Miss Moira gave a girlish laugh.

'Point taken. He can help you fill the bags with flour. But not a word to Frank.' And he winked at Henry. 'I take it you won't be coming round on Friday afternoon though.'

'No, Mr Jenkins.'

'I don't know how we put up with him, Miss Moira,' he said, smiling. 'So, which cinema is it to be?'

'The Plaza.'

'The Plaza. Ah, Youth! Now go and wash your hands. And don't forget, Miss Moira will be checking your fingernails!'

It was going to be a good week, thought Henry. More jobs meant more money, which meant more visits to the cinema and less time at home.

History was the first lesson on Friday. As soon as Henry entered the classroom he noticed a picture on the wall of a short fat woman in a long black dress with what appeared to be a white handkerchief on her head. She didn't look too happy. Above her was written QUEEN VICTORIA.

'In three months' time it will be 1950,' began Mr Finch. 'To mark this passage through the half century we are going to be looking at life fifty years ago. In addition to what we'll be doing in the lessons I will be expecting you all to do a bit of detective work.'

A hand shot up in the front.

'Yes, Mavis.'

'Do you mean homework, sir?'

'In a sense, yes.'

There was a smothered groan of protest.

'But not on your own. And you'll have plenty of time. The presentations won't be till the end of term.'

'Presentations?' muttered Henry.

'On Monday I asked you to write down what you did in the holidays and what you might wish for if you had a magic wand. That was my way of getting to know you a little better. I am putting you into twelve groups of three and one group of four. The first group will be Jane, Ivy and Doris. You expressed an interest in nursing and looking after babies. Your project is to find out about nursing in 1899. You three,' he said, pointing to three friends in the front, 'you will look into marriage in 1899. I want to know about weddings for the rich and the poor.

'Davis, Kemp and Roberts, I want you to look into the lives of people who settled in America fifty years ago. One of you said he would like to live with the Indians. Which Indians? Sioux, Cherokee, Mohican? Find out about their customs and how they were treated then.'

He then picked a football trio and a greyhound racing trio. Another group of three had to find out about sweet shops.

'Dodge, you will be looking at films. You will be working with Jeffries and Morgan.'

Henry heard some of his classmates gasp.

'Morgan,' continued Mr Finch, 'you expressed interest in being a projectionist, so maybe you could concentrate on how they *showed* the films then.'

Pip was nodding and smiling. Henry could hardly make out what Mr Finch said next. The teacher's voice seemed muffled and a great acid gob of nausea had risen into Henry's mouth, burning the back of his throat. Through the blur, he heard Mr Finch talking to the other groups.

'Every Friday I'll see how you're getting on,' he said. 'In December each group will give a short presentation to the class. Raise your arms those of you with grand-parents or great-aunts or uncles.'

Henry slowly raised his hand. He noticed that Jeffries and Morgan didn't.

'Ask them what fourteen-year-old girls and boys were doing in 1899. And remember, if you listen to what people say, you'll discover that history lies not only in books but is all around you.'

At the end of the lesson Henry was slow to put his

books away. He watched Mr Finch tidy up, but instead of following the others out, he remained seated.

'Out you go, Dodge,' said Mr Finch.

'Sir,' Henry began quickly, 'can you put me with another group?'

'I'm quite happy with the groups I've chosen. Now off you go.'

'But I can't be put with Jeffries, sir.'

'Why not?'

'It's family business, sir.'

'You're going to have to tell me more than that, Dodge.'

Henry took a deep breath.

'My dad saved his father's life, but his dad never even turned up to my father's funeral. And he's a deserter.'

'And this happened when?'

'Nine years ago.'

'And did Jeffries fail to report to his unit?'

'No, sir,' said Henry puzzled. 'He was only five, sir.'

'Exactly. In other words whatever his father is guilty of, he is not guilty of the same crime.'

'But my grandmother would be upset.'

'I'm sorry about that, Dodge.'

'And we don't talk to one another.'

'Perhaps it's time you started.'

Henry couldn't think of anything to say.

'Is that all, Dodge?'

'No, sir. There's Pip.'

'Pip?'

'Morgan. We don't mix with boys like him.'

'Oh? Why is that?'

'It's just one of those things. No one does.'

'Does he have impetigo?'

'No, sir.'

'Or any other infectious disease?'

'No, sir. It's just my grandmother says that because he was born on the wrong side of the blanket it means . . .' he paused. 'Well, he's unlucky and if you're seen with him, you'll be unlucky too with jobs and things.'

Mr Finch stared silently at him for so long that it was unnerving.

'Do you know what being born on the wrong side of the blanket means?' he said eventually.

Henry felt indignant. Of course he knew.

'It's the way you're born, sir. It's like a superstition.'

'Ah.' He gave a weary sigh. 'I think it's about time someone told you.'

'But I know, sir!' protested Henry.

'No you don't. Being born on the wrong side of the blanket means being illegitimate.'

'You mean he's a *bastard*?' said Henry, shocked.

'I believe that is the term. Unfortunately it often means that children like Morgan are stigmatised. But that will not happen in my form. I chose you to work together because you all have an interest in the cinema. Morgan is a pupil in my class and as such he will be treated equally. Is that understood?'

'Yes, Mr Finch,' Henry murmured.

'Now go along with you.'

As soon as school was over Henry ran home, head down. 'I'm not hungry!' he yelled when he burst into the kitchen.

'Take it with you,' his mother said, holding out a slice of bread and jam.

He snatched it from her, avoiding her eyes.

'Something's happened, hasn't it?' she said.

'I don't want to talk about it,' he muttered and fled out into the yard.

Fists clenched, he sprinted down the back alley to the street, crawled under his gran's window so that she wouldn't call out for him to come in and have a chat, and headed for the Plaza. The queues were already round the corner and halfway down the next street. If he was quick, he might make it to the Apollo. The first feature film began just before four o'clock. He started running again, praying he would find an adult willing to take him in. Both films showing at the Apollo were A films.

Five minutes later, yards from the Apollo, he spotted the middle-aged woman he had seen queuing for *Kind Hearts and Coronets* stepping out of the Kings Theatre. She turned and walked on ahead of him to join the queue at the Apollo. Breathless and with no time to think, Henry gasped out, 'Please would you take me in?'

The woman beamed. 'Of course,' she said.

He'd heard her talk to the girl with black plaits and knew she was well spoken, and her blue-green eyes seemed amused by something. He nodded his thank you between gasps, his shirt now glued to his body with sweat.

'And, yes, I am going for the cheaper seats,' she said, reading his thoughts, 'though you take your life in your hands sitting in them here. And don't believe them when they tell you they're *all* broken. They just want you to pay the extra for the next price up.'

Henry nodded again and handed her his collection of coins.

After the usherette had torn their tickets in half, she pulled aside the curtain and they entered a world of dust, disinfectant and carbolic soap. Silently they followed another usherette to the front of the stalls. She shone her torch along the floor of the second row and Henry and the woman excused their way past the packed seats in an effort to find ones that were safe to sit on. She had ignored one perfectly good seat so Henry understood that she meant him to take it. She chose a seat at the end of the row, well away from him. Relieved, he sat down, grateful to be alone.

*

*The Third Man* was like nothing he had ever seen before, yet it felt unnervingly familiar. It was about an American writer called Holly who had travelled to Vienna to look for his friend, Harry Lime, only to discover that he had just missed his funeral. As Henry watched Holly try to find out what events had led to his friend's death, he was drawn into a night-time world of dark empty squares and alleyways and wary faces peering out of shadowy doorways. It was a world of police and black marketeering, of late-night bars and coffee houses and murder.

Much later, when Henry stumbled out of the cinema, he was so lost in his thoughts that he didn't hear the woman speak to him at first.

'So what did you think of it?'

He whirled round.

'He was evil!'

'Harry Lime?'

'Yeah. But that man Holly was his friend. How could anyone want to be his friend? I don't understand it. And that Miss Schmidt.'

They began walking.

'The one who loved Harry Lime?'

'Yeah. She seemed really nice but . . .' He struggled to find the right words.

'You can't understand why she still loved him even after she'd been told about the terrible things he'd done?'

'No.'

Suddenly he realised why the film was so familiar to him. It was Mrs Jeffries. She was waiting for Private Jeffries to return, even though he was a deserter, even though he hadn't turned up to the funeral of Henry's father – the man who had saved his life.

'There's a saying that love is blind,' said the woman.

They passed the Kings Theatre and headed in the direction of the police station.

'Yeah,' said Henry thoughtfully, 'you could say that about my mother.'

'You're not that bad are you?' remarked the woman.

'Not me,' he said. 'My stepfather. He thinks he's Lord Snooty. *And* he stops my mother going to the Pictures.'

'That's sad.' They crossed the road. 'Do you ever go back and see films again?'

'Sometimes.'

'I'm going again, tomorrow. First show. I'll take you in if you want.'

Henry felt embarrassed.

'This boy Charlie used to take me into A films all the time. He already looked sixteen when he was my age. But he's in the Army now.'

'I take it that's a roundabout way of saying yes, then?'

Henry couldn't help smiling. He nodded.

'Thanks.' There was a brief silence. 'I saw you the other day,' he said, 'outside the Plaza.'

'*Kind Hearts and Coronets*?'

'Yeah. I was going to see it again but I left it too late so I went to the Gaiety.'

'To see *Dick Barton Strikes Back*?'

'Yeah.'

Henry was astonished at how easy he found it to talk to her. They chatted amiably about films until she stopped outside one of the enormous Victorian houses in Victoria Road.

'This is where I live,' she said.

*She must rent a room there*, thought Henry. It was too big for one person.

'I presume you'll be scouring the *Sternsea Evening News* tomorrow for next week's films. Let me know if there are any A films you want to see. If I'm going to the same ones, I can look out for you.'

Henry felt awkward.

'And no, I'm not a lonely old dear who wants you to sit with me,' she said. 'Once we're in, you do what you like. Agreed?'

He grinned.

'Agreed.'

'And my name's Hettie, short for Henrietta, but you might be more comfortable calling me Mrs Beaumont. And your name?'

'Henry.'

'Same as mine!' she said smiling. 'Well, almost.'

*

The next day they met as arranged outside the Apollo. She was only yards from one of the box offices when he ran up to her.

'Quick! Tell me what you want to see next week before we separate,' she said.

'*Train of Events*,' he panted. 'It's four stories about four different people on a train but they don't know one another and they're all on the train for different reasons. And there's a crash.'

'Is next Saturday matinee the best time?'

'Yeah.'

Once inside the Apollo, Henry was impatient for *The Third Man* to begin. As soon as he heard the strange zither music he could feel his back straightening. His senses alert, he found himself once again being sucked into the murky world of racketeering and blood money.

And still the film disturbed him. Try as he might, he still could not understand the loyalty of Miss Schmidt for Harry Lime. Neither could he understand Mrs Jeffries' loyalty for her cowardly husband.

He slipped into the crowd of people leaving, keeping his head lowered in case any of the usherettes spotted him and cottoned on that he had stayed to watch two programmes for the price of one ticket. Outside, he was about to cross the road when someone caught his eye.

Walking briskly down a small road which broke off from Princes Road, he saw the back of a figure he recognised, this time unaccompanied by his mother. Henry realised that he must have seen the film too.

It was Jeffries.

# 4. The presentations

ON MONDAY MORNING HARDLY HAD HENRY REACHED THE SCHOOL playground when Pip appeared, skipping along beside him and waving his arms around. This was what Henry had been dreading. Not only did he not want to speak to Pip but he didn't want to be seen with him either.

'Good idea, eh?' Pip said.

'What's a good idea?' Henry snapped.

'If I see how a projector works, then I can . . .'

'No projectionist is going to let you anywhere near him.'

There was a moment's silence.

'You're right,' he said brightly. 'He won't.'

Suddenly Pip spotted Mr Finch and ran off to join him.

Embarrassed, Henry glanced round quickly to see if anyone had seen them together but no one had even noticed he was in the playground, let alone who was with him. He waved at a group of boys in his class but it was as though he was invisible. He put on a smile. He was back in the world of school, where only teachers noticed him.

In the lessons, Henry was even more conscious of the empty seat beside him. He missed Woods. The time dragged slowly because he always finished his work before anyone else and had usually covered up the fact by swapping exercise books with Woods and doing his work for him. Now, after his usual ploy of deliberately making a few mistakes so that he wouldn't look too clever, he had to resign himself to staring at the blackboard or out of the window or at the dreams inside his head.

Henry wasn't the only one who finished early. Pip did too. One afternoon Henry made a surprising discovery. Someone had accidentally knocked Pip's jotter to the floor during Geography. Henry could see that the margins on the exposed pages were filled with intricate drawings of machinery. They looked like plane engines. It was then that he remembered countless incidents when the teachers had thrown Pip's jotter back at him complaining about the mess in them. Maybe the 'mess' was his drawings.

As soon as the bell rang he moved briskly out of the classroom and slunk away from everyone to the corner of the playground. He was still afraid he would be approached by Pip. He knew he would be safe from Jeffries. Jeffries knew better than to come anywhere near him. In desperation he hit on the idea of asking Sergeant, the caretaker, if there was a job he could do for him at break times. Sergeant, an ex-Army man with a neat white moustache, stared at him in astonishment.

'You must be a mind-reader, Dodge. Are you sure you want to help?'

'Yes, sir.'

Sergeant took him to a tiny room at the corner of the school where he struggled to open the door. Under a bare light bulb, stacked almost to the ceiling, were assorted boxes of every size, old discarded gas masks, tin helmets, a paraffin stove and battered textbooks. It looked like a salvage drive that had been abandoned.

'I have to empty this room out completely. Still willing to help?'

'Yes, sir.'

'Once it's clear it needs to be scrubbed from top to bottom. After that we've got to find out if the tap buried under that mound,' he said, indicating a pile of boxes balanced precariously in the sink and on the wooden draining board, 'still works. Then I suppose I'll have to get hold of some black paint.' At this point he scratched his head. 'Where I'm goin' to find black paint, I don't know, but I'll worry about that later.'

'Why do you need black paint, sir?' Henry asked.

'For the walls and ceiling. Didn't I tell you? It's to be a darkroom.'

'For developing photographs in?' exclaimed Henry.

'That's right. It's for you lot. Getting photographs developed is expensive, Mr Finch says, so he reckons it's a good idea for you to learn to develop your own. Your science teacher is all for it too.'

Henry had to suppress a strong desire to leap into the air.

'When can I begin?' he asked enthusiastically.

'Before we look at the kind of work children in Victorian times were expected to do, I'd like to know how you're all getting on in your groups.'

Henry quickly looked down at his desk. This was the lesson he had been dreading all week.

'So,' Mr Finch said, rubbing his hands together, 'let's start with group one. Cowboys.'

There was an embarrassed mumble from the back.

'We're going to see a cowboy film, sir,' said one hesitantly.

'What's the film?'

'*The Dead Don't Dream*, sir,' muttered the first boy, 'it's a Hopalong Cassidy film, sir.'

'It's about a gold mine,' added his friend. 'And murder.'

'Well, it's a start. I take it he'll round up the villains.'

The boys laughed and Henry could tell it was with relief.

'He don't mind us goin' to the Pictures!' he heard Davis whisper from behind. 'Now that's the kind of homework I like.'

'Ever heard of Zane Grey?' Mr Finch asked.

Henry had. In *The Third Man* the American who was searching for Harry Lime had mentioned Zane Grey. He noticed Jeffries' arm was up.

'Yes, Jeffries.'

'He wrote westerns didn't he, Mr Finch?'

'That's right. Maybe you boys should get hold of one of his books from the library.'

The boys were shaking their heads.

'We don't go to the library, sir.'

'Why not?'

'We're boys, sir,' said the boy called Riley.

'We'd be laughed at, sir,' said his friend.

'Called a sissie, sir,' said Daniels, a boy in the aeroplane group.

He looked directly at Jeffries, who had a history of having books he was reading surreptitiously under his desk confiscated.

'Zane Grey is a man,' said Mr Finch, 'and is usually read by men.'

'Is he, sir?' said Riley, astonished.

'I'll get hold of one of his books for you to borrow and you can make up your own mind. Now for group two. Weddings.'

There was an awkward silence as Mr Finch gazed at three girls in the front row.

'Ethel?'

'We didn't have time, sir. We have to help out at home and we're always being sent out to the shops.'

'Yeah, Mr Finch. Sometimes I'm in a queue for two hours,' added her friend Glenda.

'Notice any old people?' he asked.

'Yes, sir,' they chorused, looking puzzled.

'Who can work this out?' he said, looking at the class. 'If someone was twenty-five in 1899, how old would they be now?'

Before Henry realised what he was doing he had raised his arm.

'Yes, Dodge.'

'Seventy-five, sir.'

Mr Finch turned back to Glenda.

'Ever noticed anyone in the queues in her seventies?'

'Sometimes, Mr Finch.'

'Hands up the group doing sweets?'

Three girls raised their arms.

'A ten-year-old customer in 1899 would now be . . .'

'Sixty!' chorused half the class.

'So look out for anyone who is sixty.'

'Why, sir?' asked Ethel.

She was immediately nudged by Madge.

'Don't be soft, gel.'

'Madge, why do you think I'm talking about people's ages?'

'We can ask them questions, sir.'

'Exactly. So when you find yourself stuck in a queue, always have a pencil and paper on you.'

'Please, sir, we don't have that at home,' said Glenda.

'You can take your jotters home.'

'But isn't that homework? Only grammar school swots do homework.'

'Haven't you seen a reporter use a notebook? That's what I'd like you to be. Interview them. Be polite and write down what they say. You may even find that your wait in the queue is less boring.'

'I'd be too shy,' said Ethel. 'I wouldn't know what to say, sir.'

'You don't have to do much in the way of talking. In fact the less you talk the better. You just need to listen. Try it.'

He glanced down at his list again and called Henry's group.

Pip flung his arm up.

'I got an idea, sir, but it's a bit tricky.'

'Go on, Morgan.'

'I thought it would be a good idea to see a cinema projector.'

Mr Finch looked puzzled.

'Why do you want to see a projector now when I want you to find out about films fifty years ago?'

'I thought if I could see a 1949 projector and then see a Victorian one . . .'

'Ah,' said Mr Finch, 'compare the two to see how projectors have developed in the last fifty years?'

'Yes, sir. But I haven't been able to see one yet. My mum, she works at the Plaza, she says no one goes upstairs, not even the usherettes.'

'I'm sure you'll find a way to get permission to go up there, Morgan.'

'He'll have no chance,' said a loud voice from the back.

Mr Finch looked up sharply.

'Oh, yes, Riley, and why is that?'

''Cos he's not kosher, sir.'

'Meaning?'

'You know, sir,' said the boy, grinning.

'I don't. That's why I'm asking.'

No one spoke.

'Would anyone like to explain?'

No one did.

'Morgan,' he said, 'I like your approach and your ideas. Perhaps others might like to take a leaf out of your book.'

Pip was beaming. Henry had never seen a teacher praise Pip.

'How about the rest of your team?'

Henry swallowed.

'I know this second-hand bookshop,' said Jeffries, 'and I've been to see the man who runs it and he says I can look through his books and magazines. I've found an old magazine about silent films but it's all about ones in the 1920s.'

'Never mind. You're developing an eye while looking.'

'I'll help,' said Pip excitedly.

Jeffries smiled at him.

'You'll have to keep your arm gestures down a bit, Pip, or you'll knock the shelves over.'

To Henry's surprise some of the people in the class laughed.

'You're right,' said Pip, and they grinned at each other.

Henry expected Mr Finch's attention to be turned on to him. Instead he went on to the next group.

'Group ten,' he said. 'Aeroplanes. I heard on the grapevine that one of you has a father who works in the aeroplane factory.'

It was as if he didn't exist. He was used to people in his class ignoring him but not a teacher.

After the bell rang, Henry waited to see if Mr Finch would call him up or glance in his direction but nothing happened. All week he had been dreading his attention in the History lesson. Now, instead of feeling relieved that Mr Finch had taken no notice of him, he felt acutely uncomfortable.

On Sunday, even though it was pouring outside, the kitchen windows, scullery door and door into the yard were flung open. Henry's mother had been preparing steak and kidney pudding for Sunday dinner and because it took three hours to cook, the kitchen was tropical.

'I feel sorry for the day trippers,' said Uncle Bill as Henry's mother served out the dinner. 'Sternsea Front is going to be deserted.'

'See the boats,' said Molly, waving her spoon.

'That spoon's fer eatin' with,' Gran muttered. 'It ain't a Union Jack.'

'We could go on the bus, Maureen, and sit in one of the shelters on the beach.'

'Why not?' said Henry's mother. 'It'll be nice to get out of the house. Henry, do you want to come with us? Or are you going to the Pictures?'

'Pictures,' said Henry.

'What's on?' asked Uncle Bill.

'*Words and Music.*'

'I didn't know you liked musicals.'

'I like some,' he said defensively. 'I want to see the other film too, *Who Shot Jesse James?*'

'You'd better wear your raincoat,' said his mother.

'He can't do that,' said Gran. 'It don't fit any more.'

'I'll hold it over my head,' said Henry.

'You can get him a new one now,' said Gran, looking pointedly at Henry's mother.

'Mrs Dodge, just because clothes have come off rationing . . .' She paused as if trying to control her temper. 'You still need money to buy them,' she added quietly.

'Get one on tick,' said his gran.

'You know we don't get anything on tick, Mrs Dodge. That's the road to debt.'

'I heard from your mother you saw *The Third Man* again,' said Uncle Bill.

There was an uncomfortable silence. Henry could see he was trying to change the subject, but he wasn't going to help him out and he refused to speak.

'Tell Uncle Bill about the darkroom,' his mother said brightly, 'how you're helping the caretaker clear a room out for it.'

'What's this?' said Uncle Bill, looking interested.

'Mr Finch has got permission for us to have a darkroom,' said Henry wearily.

'Silly man,' said Gran. 'Where are you goin' to find cameras?'

'I dunno. Maybe he's goin' to have us develop his film.'

'Anyone want some more cabbage?' asked his mother.

His stepfather held out his plate. 'Please,' he said.

'Mrs Harris at Number 14 was telling me your Mr Finch wants you to do a History presentation at the end of term,' she said, handing back Uncle Bill's plate. 'Why didn't you tell us?'

'Do I have to talk about school?' said Henry.

'You don't have to, love. I'm just interested. What is it you have to do?'

'Look at life fifty years ago,' he mumbled. 'We've all been given different subjects.'

'Oh, yes?' said Uncle Bill, his mouth full of potato. 'What have you been given?'

'Films,' said Henry.

'Well, that's good!' exclaimed his mother.

'Lumière brothers. French,' said his stepfather. 'They made the first films, I think.'

'And you have to do this all on yer own?' said his gran. 'Sounds like you're doin' the teacher's job.'

'You've all been put into groups. That's right, isn't it?' said his mother.

Henry sighed.

'There's no call for rudeness,' said Uncle Bill.

'Sorry,' he muttered.

'Who have you been put with?' his mother asked.

Henry didn't answer.

'Henry?' Uncle Bill leaned across towards him. 'Your mother asked you who you've been put with.'

'Two other boys,' said Henry evasively.

'Do I know them?' his mother asked.

'Not to speak to.'

'Oh. So who are they?'

'Why do you need to know? It's not very interesting.'

'Is there some reason you don't want your mother to know?' asked Uncle Bill.

Henry froze for a moment and then nodded. His

mother sat back in her chair and stared at him.

'Well, I'd like to know if you don't mind.'

Henry swallowed.

'Morgan.'

His grandmother gave a gasp.

'Oh,' said his mother. 'I'm not sure . . .' She stopped. 'I mean, I'm sure he's a nice enough boy.'

'Nice!' said his grandmother.

'But people do talk, don't they?' added Henry's mother.

'Of course they talk,' said his gran. 'A man is judged by the company he keeps.'

'I asked if I could be put with someone else.'

'You did what?' Uncle Bill asked quietly.

'But Mr Finch wouldn't change his mind.'

'Did you tell him why?' said his gran.

'Yeah. And he told me what being born on the wrong side of the blanket means.'

His mother reddened.

'So he knows?' said his gran.

'What did he say?' asked Uncle Bill.

'He said he would be treated the same as everybody else in the class.'

He saw his stepfather suppress a smile. Henry felt like hitting him.

'So you still have to be in a group with him?' said his mother.

'Yeah.'

'Well, if that's what Mr Finch wants, you must do as you're told.'

'Yes, Mum.'

'So who's the other boy?' asked his gran.

Henry turned away from her and looked out the window.

'Henry,' added his mother. Henry looked across at her. 'I think I know,' she said slowly.

'Jeffries,' said Uncle Bill.

Henry nodded.

'No!' cried his grandmother.

Molly began banging her tray with her spoon.

'Auntie red! Auntie red!'

'But didn't you tell him?' Gran demanded.

'Yeah.'

'Well, what did he say?'

'That he's not his dad.'

'What about the sins of the father . . .?'

'He doesn't believe that.'

His stepfather glanced briefly at Henry's mother and then scraped another forkful of steak and kidney pudding into his mouth.

'Maureen,' said his gran, 'you gotta get up to that school and put a stop to it straight away.'

'I don't think there's any point. It sounds as if I won't be taken much notice of.'

'You should be ashamed of yerself!'

'Auntie cross!' shrieked Molly.

With that, Gran rose to her feet and stalked out of the kitchen. After the loud slam of her door they heard the wireless at full blast.

'Auntie gone!' yelled Molly, jubilant.

'I'll get the plums and custard,' said Henry's mother quietly.

As soon as his mother had left the house with Molly and Uncle Bill to catch a bus to the seafront, Henry knocked on his gran's door. At first there had been no response. Eventually he heard her mutter, 'Come in.'

She was sitting hunched over in her armchair, wringing her hands. He could see she was still upset.

'I'm sorry, Gran. I really tried not to be in a group with them.'

She nodded and gave a tight smile.

'Of course you did,' she said, 'you're a good boy. But I've been havin' a bit of a think. And there's a way round this, yer know.' She looked at him intently. 'You don't have to find out about films together, do you?'

'No, but we have to do this presentation thing together.'

'But you could keep yourself separate till then, couldn't you?'

'That's what I'm doing.'

To Henry's relief she gave a broad smile.

'Atta boy!' she said.

Being a U film, Henry could join the queue for

*Words and Music* without having to ask an adult to take him in. As he held his raincoat over his head, he noticed the three 'western' boys in his class. They were huddled together, talking and laughing. He felt a pang of envy. He had seen loads of westerns. He could easily have been in their group. Not that he wanted to talk to anyone just then. He was still smarting from the scene at home.

Hidden under his raincoat, mulling over what Gran had said, he suddenly spotted the posh girl with the black plaits, but then she disappeared, swallowed up by the crowd. It wasn't until later that he caught sight of her again. He had been sitting in the dark, watching the usherettes moving down the aisles showing people to their seats, when he discovered she was sitting in the same row.

And then the music began, the screen flickered and blazing hugely in front of them was *Words and Music*. Judy Garland, who had played Dorothy in *The Wizard of Oz*, was in the film. She sang a song called *Johnnie One Note*, which had everyone laughing. Henry glanced down the row and saw the girl beaming.

And then a beautiful black woman in a nightclub took his attention away. She sang two numbers. The one Henry liked best was called *The Lady is a Tramp*. He peered in the dark down the row again. The girl was leaning forward, almost off her seat with excitement.

During one song, when a man sang *Blue Moon*, Henry watched her the whole time. She looked as though she wanted to dive into the film and join in.

He returned to the screen, where a man and a woman were dancing. The man was stocky and muscular and looked more like someone who worked in Sternsea Dockyard than a dancer. He danced right into the ground, moving gracefully round the girl as if his body was liquid. Henry didn't like ballet but this kind of dancing was different. It was jazzy. The dance even had its own name, *Slaughter on Tenth Avenue*, and the music was so powerful, it made Henry want to leap to his feet.

When the credits came up he looked for the name of the black singer.

'Lena Horne,' he whispered in the dark.

The Pathé news flickered above his head and he found himself thinking back to what his gran had said. It was silly not to find out anything for the presentation just because he didn't want to work with Pip and Jeffries, and if he carried on doing nothing, Mr Finch might think he was stupid. But how was he going to find out about films in 1899?

He couldn't ask Gran. She hadn't started going to the cinema until much later and then didn't go very often.

And then he remembered Mrs Beaumont. She would be too young to help him but her parents would be the right age. Maybe he could ask them questions. He sat back relieved.

There *was* a way out.

## 5. Mrs Beaumont and the mystery girl

HENRY'S CHANCE TO MEET MRS BEAUMONT CAME THE FOLLOWING Sunday as he made his way to see a film at the Classic. He took the usual route to the cinema towards the town centre, past decimated houses, dust, rubble and jagged walls. He was so used to these deserted spaces that he couldn't imagine them with proper buildings on them but the greyness of his surroundings still left him feeling as flat as the landscape. Tumbleweed drifting down the road wouldn't have looked out of place.

He walked swiftly past a railway station, the new C&A department store, the empty shops and the deserted stalls in the street market. And then he heard voices and laughing. He broke into a run and turned a corner to where the towering Classic loomed. Immediately, he spotted Mrs Beaumont in the queue, opening her umbrella. She waved to him and he strolled casually in her direction.

'Are you going to see the Errol Flynn film, *Silver River*, at the Majestic? It's only on till Wednesday.'

'I can't,' he said, 'I wouldn't have enough time to get there from school for the first showing. And I work at a shop till six if I can. And the Majestic is a bus ride away and once I've paid the fare . . .'

'You've used up money you could have spent on a cinema ticket. Yes, I see what you mean. What about *Joan of Arc*?'

He shrugged.

'Do come. Ingrid Bergman's in it.'

He hesitated. 'It's not . . .'

'Soppily romantic?'

He grinned.

'Yeah.'

'And if you're wondering how I guessed, I brought up two boys, which is how I know you're itching to ask me something but don't quite know how to pitch it. Am I right?'

Henry nodded, smiling.

'Fire away.'

Mr Finch was right. The most important thing about getting information from people was to listen and let them do the talking. And she talked. Unfortunately the more she did, the gloomier he felt. She had hardly any relatives left. Her husband had been killed in the Great War, as had two of her brothers.

'And I've only been in Sternsea for the last three years, since 1946,' she explained. 'I moved down here from London to nurse my mother, but she died and then I stayed to look after my father.'

'Could I speak to him?' asked Henry.

'I'm afraid not. He died in June. And my one remaining brother died five months before him. The only relatives I have are my two sons and they're too young to be of any use to you. I'm so sorry. But my brother's collection of cameras is here,' she said.

'Cameras?' Henry repeated, suddenly alert.

'Yes. He was mad about films and photography. After he died all his belongings were sent from his flat to my parents' address here. He had friends in London who are involved in all that too. I could get in touch with them if you like. And then there's my younger son, Max. He knows a lot about cameras.'

'So you live on your own in that big house?' Henry blurted out.

'Yes. Disgraceful, isn't it? With so many homeless people.'

Henry felt his face grow hot.

'I'm sorry,' he stammered, realising he must have sounded rude.

'No, you're quite right. But the house isn't mine. Not yet anyway. Since my father died there's been trouble finding the deeds and a lot of bureaucratic red tape, which I won't bore you with. So I sit in it to avoid squatters moving in. Anyway,' she said, 'enough of that. Come and see *Joan of Arc* next Saturday afternoon and afterwards we'll go back to the house and we can look for the cameras.'

'Can I come too?' said a voice.

Henry swung round. It was the girl with the black plaits.

'How long have you been there?' asked the woman.

'Long enough,' said the girl cheekily. 'If there was a certificate in eavesdropping . . .'

'You'd get a distinction,' the woman finished off for her.

She smiled.

'So can I?'

'Can you what? See *Joan of Arc*?'

'No. I mean, yes. I mean can I come back to your house too?'

'On one condition, that you both let me pay for you to see *Joan of Arc*, as I know neither of you is too keen. What about it?'

'I earn my money,' Henry said firmly.

'And I've been told by my great-aunt never to take money from strangers.'

'That's easily sorted. You do a job for me,' Mrs Beaumont said, turning to Henry. 'And I'll come and speak to your great-aunt. Agreed?'

'Agreed,' said the girl.

They looked at Henry.

'Agreed,' he said slowly.

'And now,' said the woman and she turned to the girl, 'I think we ought to introduce ourselves. You already know who I am, but you neglected to tell me who you were when we last met because you were talking so much.'

The girl burst out laughing. Henry envied her confidence. Then, to his embarrassment, he found them both staring at him.

'Henry,' he mumbled to the girl.

'And I'm Grace. *Grace, Grace, the family disgrace,*' the girl chanted. 'That's why I've come here to live with my Great-Aunt Florence. My other aunts have washed their hands of me. So here I am.'

'Well, I'm glad you are,' said Mrs Beaumont, 'or maybe I shouldn't be. Have you robbed a bank?'

'Worse,' said the girl.

Henry looked suspiciously at her. She didn't look the violent type.

'Tried to burn down the Houses of Parliament?' asked Mrs Beaumont.

'Even worse than that, I'm afraid.' She turned suddenly to Henry. 'How many schools have you been to?'

'Two,' said Henry.

'I've been to twelve.'

'Ah,' said Mrs Beaumont, 'are we talking expulsions here?'

'Yes. Or polite letters to my parents, asking them to remove me. I just thought I ought to warn you.'

'Well, thank you for that, Grace,' said Mrs Beaumont, 'but will these expulsions interfere with our enjoyment of *The Lady Vanishes*?'

'Not at all,' said Grace. 'At least I don't think so.'

The queue began moving again.

'Now tell me about this great-aunt of yours.'

Henry was relieved Grace was such a chatterbox. It meant that neither she nor Mrs Beaumont would notice how shy he was to be so close to Grace after secretly watching her.

'So she lives in the same road as I do,' he heard Mrs Beaumont exclaim.

'Yes. With an old maid. I moved there a few weeks ago. My parents live abroad. My father's a diplomat. I've got three brothers but they're much older than me and they live all over the place too, so I don't see much of any of them really,' she said cheerfully.

They had almost reached the box office by now.

'What does that say?' she asked, pointing to a large placard.

Henry was puzzled. It was in huge letters. She obviously needed glasses.

Mrs Beaumont looked at her for a moment in surprise

and then read out, 'Margaret Lockwood, Michael Redgrave, Paul Lukas in *The Lady Vanishes*. For four days.'

'Thank you.'

Henry handed over his ticket money to Mrs Beaumont, as did Grace, and they stepped into the Grecian portals of the Classic.

Although Henry sat apart from them throughout the two films, they were waiting for him in the foyer afterwards. Without discussion they walked back together past the fenced-off, unlit bombsites. It wasn't until they had reached his street and were about to walk past his house that he plucked up the courage to speak.

'I live here,' he said, awkwardly.

'Now remember. Next week. Odeon cinema,' announced Mrs Beaumont. 'I shall be there from one o'clock to make sure I get a seat for the one-forty programme. You can pop round one evening this week after you've finished at the grocers to do a job for me in exchange for a ticket. How about Wednesday?'

'Yeah. All right,' said Henry shyly.

And then they were off. When they reached the end of his street they turned and waved.

'See you Wednesday night!' Mrs Beaumont called out.

Henry waved back and watched them till they disappeared round the corner.

He didn't tell his family where he was going on

Wednesday night, not even his gran. For some reason, he wanted to keep his friendship with Mrs Beaumont private. He let them think he was going to the Pictures. After supper he headed down Victoria Road to her house, pushed open the large wooden gate and walked up the tiled path to her front steps. He paused for a moment and peered down a deep stone trench at the side, where steps led down to a heavy front door leading to what looked like a basement flat. Above him at the top of the steps, inside the open porch, were two doors and they were both open. The inside one was an imposing carved wooden door with stained glass windows, the vivid patterns outlined in black. He hesitated, not feeling he could walk in or call out. He raised a heavy doorknob in the shape of a lion's head on the outer storm door and knocked loudly. Within seconds he heard footsteps coming from downstairs. Mrs Beaumont peered round the door.

'Come in,' she said eagerly, and beckoned him to follow her up a wide stairway. He let his hand drift along the largest banister he had ever seen. It was smooth and the wood was a rich, dark brown. Supporting it were heavy ornate rails, which looked like a series of table legs.

At the top of a second flight of stairs was a large landing with four doors leading off it and even more stairs going upwards. She stopped outside the door on the left and stared at it as if gathering strength.

'This is something I've avoided looking at for months,' she said. 'I hope you're feeling strong,' and she swung open the door.

They stepped into an enormous room with two high windows and a tiled fireplace, packed with furniture, boxes, trunks, suitcases and crates of books. There was more in the room than in the whole of Henry's house.

Two single beds, which had been taken apart, were spread out in sections. An armchair was stuck in the middle with four oriental rugs piled on top of it, and a wooden table was submerged beneath suitcases and boxes. In the alcove by the fireplace nearest one of the windows was a massive mahogany wardrobe. A cupboard over a deep drawer was built into the alcove on the other side of the fireplace, unreachable behind a pile of chairs and a chest of drawers. Mrs Beaumont looked thoughtful for a moment and then climbed over some boxes to the centre of the room.

'Right, she said, 'let's start.'

Between them they put the two beds together and cleared the area by the wall opposite the fireplace. They heaped most of the boxes and suitcases on to the beds and stacked the rest up against the wall next to them. Once the table was cleared, they carried it through the door and out on to the landing, and returned to stack more of her brother's belongings up by the fireplace.

Henry noticed Mrs Beaumont gazing sadly through the doorway.

'So many people used to come and visit my brother and sit round that table: writers, actors and actresses, photographers, musicians. He was a shy man but a good listener, and he liked to feed hungry people. There's been a lot of laughter round it. I kept it up here because I thought it would be a bit silly sitting at it on my own. It seats eight, you see.'

'Do you want it back in the bedroom?'

'No. Let's take it down to the kitchen.'

As they picked it up, Mrs Beaumont suddenly smiled. 'I wonder which seven people will join me round it.'

Henry crept past his gran's room and slowly turned the kitchen doorknob. Uncle Bill was sitting at the table reading one of his Penguin New Writing paperbacks. Henry suddenly became aware of his stepfather's hands. His skin was so rough and blemished from working in railway cabs that they looked dark against the pages of the book. He glanced up at Henry.

'Your mother's gone to bed. Good film, was it?'

Henry nodded.

'Those cinema seats must be very neglected,' he remarked casually.

Henry glanced down at his jersey and trousers. They were covered in dust. He removed the remains of a cobweb from his sleeve and quickly slipped into the scullery to clean his teeth.

Knowing that on Friday morning Mr Finch would be asking them about their research, Henry called again at Mrs Beaumont's house on Thursday evening.

'You must come upstairs immediately,' she insisted as she opened the front door. She seemed very excited.

Henry was staggered when he walked into the huge junk room, only it wasn't a junk room any longer.

'It looks like a proper bedroom now,' she stated, and she threw open the doors of the large fitted cupboard on the left of the fireplace. Behind it the rows of deep shelves were now neatly filled with books and magazines. 'I've unpacked all his books,' she declared. 'And put his film magazines on the bottom shelf.'

The shelves reached the ceiling. Henry was surprised to see some of the Penguin paperbacks that Uncle Bill had read, on the top shelf. The magazines were stacked horizontally. Beside them was a black case.

'His typewriter,' she said. 'He used to type up my stories.'

'Do you write stories?' Henry asked, surprised.

'Did. But since I moved here, I've done no writing at all.'

'What kind of stories?'

'Not westerns or thrillers, I'm afraid. Children's

stories. For annuals. That sort of thing.'

'I've never met a writer before,' said Henry.

'Well, now you have,' she said. 'Now, this is what I want to show you,' and she walked over to a trunk, snapped open the lock and eased back the lid. 'They're not movie cameras. You're looking at 1899, aren't you? Most of them will probably be too old for your presentation. The zoetrope!' she exclaimed. 'That might be fun.'

'What's a zoetrope?'

'It's a machine that makes a set of almost identical picture cards look as if the images are moving when it spins round. Oh, my goodness!' she cried, picking up a small tan leather camera case, 'I remember him buying this just before he died.' She unbuckled it and drew out a slim black camera.

Henry gasped. It was a beauty.

She pressed a silver button at the side and it flew open, the lens springing forward from bellows. Surrounding the lens was a circular silver dial with numbers etched into it, a little silver lever at its side. Behind it was another dial in black, which also had numbers on.

'It still has film in it.' She looked at him for a moment. 'Here,' she said and held it out to him.

As he took it, Henry noticed that his hands were shaking.

'Finish it.'

Henry stared at her, puzzled. *Finish what?* he thought.

'The film. Finish it.'

'But don't you want to do that?'

'I'm not in love with it. You are,' she said simply.

He couldn't help smiling.

'Then I can get it developed,' she added.

And that's when Henry told her about the darkroom.

'But the school caretaker doesn't think we'll be able to get hold of any black paint.'

'He doesn't, eh?' she said thoughtfully. 'Well, I'll just have to put on my thinking cap, won't I? By the way, what do you have to do with all this research?'

'Give a presentation. In groups.'

'How many are there in your group?'

'Three.'

'And your fellow information collectors are pulling their weight, are they?'

Henry nodded awkwardly.

'Well, if you want to bring them round here, they'd be very welcome.'

No sooner had he stepped into the hall than Gran's door flew open. She was in her nightdress.

'Where've you been?' she asked. 'You didn't come and kiss me goodnight last night.' She glanced at the camera case. 'What's in there?'

'A camera.'

'Oh, yeah? What you doin' with it, then?'

'Someone's lent it to me. She's helping me with the Victorian presentation.'

Her face lit up.

'Ah ha! That'll show that Mr Finch, eh?'

'Yeah,' said Henry quietly.

# 6. The audition

'COULD YOU ALL COME TO THE FRONT PLEASE,' SAID THE usherette.

The children who were auditioning for the choir had been asked to stay behind after the Cinema Club. Henry had been dreading this moment all week. Singing in a choir was kid's stuff, but he knew Gran would get upset if he didn't turn up. Out of the corner of his eye he spotted Grace. She turned and smiled at him. Henry pretended not to see her. Boys who were seen being friendly with girls were called sissies.

The choirmaster walked on to the stage and stood next to the pianist.

'I'll hear the girls first,' he said. 'Don't worry if you can't think of a song. *Happy Birthday* or *God Save the King* will suit the purpose. Now I need you to call out your names in a nice loud voice, please,' and he nodded at Grace.

'Grace, Grace, the family disgrace,' she chanted.

'I hope you won't be disgraceful here,' the man said firmly and went on to the next girl.

Henry wondered why she did it. It was almost as if she did it without thinking. As the girls were called up to sing solo in groups of three, he slid further down into his seat in an attempt to make himself invisible. After listening to several renditions of *Cherry Ripe*, *Molly Malone* and *Bobby Shaftoe* among high-pitched versions of *God Save the King*, he watched Grace go up with the final three, knowing it would soon be time for him to humiliate himself on stage.

'And how old are you?' the choirmaster asked Grace.

'Thirteen. Almost.'

'Have you prepared something or would you like the pianist to play *God Save the King*?'

'I've prepared something,' she said excitedly.

'Another English folk song, is it?'

'No. It's called *It's Magic*. It was sung by Doris Day in the film.'

'Well, that sounds interesting,' said the man, 'I don't know it, I'm afraid, but I'm sure you'll sing it in tune.'

'Do you mind if I find the right note to start with?' she asked.

Before the man could answer, she walked over to the pianist and said, 'May I?'

She looked so comfortable up there, Henry thought.

He would never have had the nerve to speak up there, let alone ask for a favour. The pianist looked a bit ruffled. Then he nodded and allowed her to find the note she wanted.

'That's the one,' she said.

'It's a little low, isn't it?' he commented.

'Oh, no. It's just perfect.'

She strode to the centre of the stage and gazed up at the dress circle.

'*You sigh, the song begins*
*You speak and I hear violins*
*It's magic,*' she sang.

Henry was aware of giggling from the girls. Unlike the high, piping sounds of the ones who had auditioned before her, Grace's voice was deep. By now their smothered laughter had reached the boys. Henry couldn't understand why she didn't stop. It was so embarrassing.

'She's got a voice like a man!' one of the boys muttered and they exploded into laughter.

By now the choirmaster was looking flustered. Grace suddenly began humming the melody, interspersing it with the occasional, '*It's Magic.*'

'I'm doing the orchestra's bits,' she explained mid-flight.

Before she could be stopped, she was singing the verses again, only now it was difficult to hear the words.

'*Why do I tell myself*

*These things that happen are all really true,'* she sang above the noise,

*'When, in my heart I know,*

*The magic is my love for you.'*

She stopped, looked at the man and smiled.

'Thank you, Grace,' he said stiffly.

And then she glanced down into the auditorium.

'Why are they laughing?' she said in surprise.

When the choirmaster announced which girls had been chosen, there was no Grace among the names. What made it worse was that she was the only one not on the list.

'All the girls may now leave,' he said. 'I will send rehearsal details to your parents.'

Henry looked across at her. He couldn't see her face because her head was bowed.

'Now for the boys. Anyone here whose voice is breaking?'

Henry raised his arm.

'We'll have you first.'

As Henry dragged his burning body up to the stage he consoled himself with the thought that it would be all over soon. He was halfway through yodelling *Happy Birthday* when the man stopped him.

'I see what you mean,' he said.

At least no one was laughing at him, Henry thought, as he returned to his seat.

When the list of chosen boys was read out, to Henry's relief, he wasn't on it. He could now at least tell Gran that he had tried.

The boys couldn't get out of the auditorium fast enough. Henry took his time. He liked being in the auditorium and he was in no hurry to leave. But then he spotted Pip's mother clearing away the debris of the children's matinee from behind the seats and he walked quickly towards the foyer.

As he was passing the Ladies he heard sobbing. Before he realised what he was doing, he found himself walking back down the aisle.

'Hello, love. Have you lost something?' asked Mrs Morgan.

'No. It's just . . .' He hesitated. 'There's someone crying in the Ladies.'

'You leave it to me,' and she headed swiftly up the aisle.

Henry followed her and watched her disappear into the Ladies. He hovered outside.

'He didn't choose me,' he heard the girl cry. 'No one ever does. No one ever wants me.'

'Come 'ere, my love,' Henry heard Mrs Morgan say. Henry realised now that the girl was Grace. He backed away out of the auditorium, ashamed of himself for being as unfriendly to her as the others had been.

As soon as he saw her step outside he sprang to his feet.

He noticed her face was still flushed from crying.

'Oh, hello,' she said, surprised, and she gave a brave smile. 'What are you doing here?'

'Waitin' for my friend Charlie,' he lied. 'I thought he had a leave weekend but he ain't turned up. I must've got the dates mixed up. I thought you girls had already left.'

'I wanted to look at what was on next week, that sort of thing,' she said brightly.

'I didn't get in the choir,' he said.

'Me neither,' she said with a smile, 'but then you know that already.'

'It's a good job we bumped into each other, ain't it?' he said. 'Want to walk up to *Joan of Arc* together this afternoon?'

She nodded.

'Gotta go now,' he said awkwardly. 'See you later.' And he walked quickly away, annoyed with himself for not having been able to think of something he could have said to make her feel better. But what? When she sang, she did sound like a man.

'It was a bit silly taking you to see it,' said Mrs Beaumont. They grabbed the three seats at the front of the bus upstairs. 'Far too violent.'

'Don't worry, I didn't watch it when it got nasty,' said Grace reassuringly.

'Did you see any of it?' Henry asked.

'Of course,' said Grace. 'But there weren't many funny bits in it, were there?'

'Henry and I are going to see the Sherlock Holmes film at the Rex tomorrow,' said Mrs Beaumont.

'You are lucky. I shall be doing homework all day. I don't know why I bother. I've already had a detention this week.'

'What on earth did you do? Smash a window?'

'No. Usual thing.'

'Which is?'

'Mrs Beaumont, I can't read.'

'I don't like reading either,' said Henry. 'Gran says reading books is a waste of time.' And then he suddenly remembered that Mrs Beaumont wrote stories and he reddened.

'I didn't say I didn't want to. I'd love to be able to read books. It's just that I can't. I look at the page and all the letters are jumbled up and I can never make sense of them.'

'Is that why you've been expelled so many times?' asked Mrs Beaumont.

'Yes. Everyone thinks I'm doing it on purpose, that I'm rebellious, that I'm stubborn and disobedient, a wilful and ungrateful child, and so on and so on.'

'You can't read?' asked Henry, staggered.

'No. I can't write either. I don't even know how to spell my own name. I know there's an R in Grace but I can never remember where to put it.'

'But you wanted to be in the choir,' said Henry, puzzled.

'Yes.'

'But you'd need to be able to read the words of the songs.'

'I wouldn't. I'd learn them off by heart by listening.'

'Like the song you sang.'

'What song is this?' said Mrs Beaumont.

'I tried to get into the Plaza choir,' said Grace despondently. 'And I sang *It's Magic* from the Doris Day film.'

'And?'

'They didn't want me. I may like singing, but other people don't like me doing it. At my other schools I had to mouth the words instead of singing them.'

'Will you sing for me? I'd love to hear you.'

'You don't know what you'd be letting yourself in for.'

'I'm sure I can handle it.'

Grace burst out laughing. Henry was pleased to see her so happy, though not being able to read, she didn't have much to laugh about. And her so posh!

'You go upstairs and have a look in the trunks, Henry,' said Mrs Beaumont. 'I'm going to hear Grace sing her song and then I'll light the fire and we can have toast and jam.'

Henry walked up to the first landing but as soon as the sitting room door was closed he crept back down to eavesdrop. And then he heard it, that strange low voice of hers. After she had finished there was silence.

'You have a remarkable voice,' he heard Mrs Beaumont say, quietly.

'But they laughed at me,' Grace protested.

'Sometimes people laugh at what's unfamiliar.'

'But the choirmaster, why didn't he choose me?'

'Your voice doesn't belong in a cinema choir. You know who you remind me of? Sarah Vaughan.'

'Who's she?'

'A very well known singer in the jazz world.'

'What's jazz?'

'Something I'm going to introduce you to. Now let's put a match to this fire.'

Henry moved quickly up the stairs. He thought it was kind of Mrs Beaumont to pretend Grace had a nice singing voice. He turned the door handle of the room where the cameras were stored and stepped into the photographic world of Mrs Beaumont's brother.

# 7. Winding on

THE CAMERA LAY IN ITS CASE. OCCASIONALLY HENRY TOOK IT OUT to press the side button and watch the lens concertina outwards, but its beauty made him feel clumsy and stupid. The following week he finally plucked up enough courage to ask Mr Finch if he could show him how to use it.

'Bring it to the photography club I run for the first and second formers,' he said, after a tense silence.

When Henry turned up at the club, Mr Finch ignored him at first. Henry stood awkwardly by the teacher's desk, while Mr Finch talked to two girls. Eventually he walked in Henry's direction, stopped and glanced at the camera case. Nervously, Henry slid the camera out and within seconds the black bellows unfolded. There were gasps from the class. Mr Finch's eyebrows lifted.

'A Zeiss Ikon,' he remarked. 'Expensive.'

'A lady's lent it to me,' Henry began to explain.

Mr Finch gave a brief nod, showing little interest.

'Distance and light,' he said abruptly, taking it from Henry's hands. He turned the silver dial surrounding the front of the lens. 'I'll line it up to four.'

'What does that mean, sir?' asked Henry.

'Four feet. Go and stand by the door.'

Henry did so.

'Now I'm about four feet from you. If you were taking a photograph of me from there, you'd turn the silver dial till the four lay behind the dot. If I were further away you'd put it on five foot or eight or fifteen. The furthest it will go is called infinity. Come back and look at this.'

Henry returned to the desk.

'Notice the black dial behind it. That's the aperture, what's called the iris. If the area surrounding your subject is in poor light you'll need to let in as much light as possible, and less when you're in bright sunshine. If you took a photograph in here you'd probably need to put it on 6.3. That's the widest it can go.' He touched a metal square at the side of the camera. 'This is the viewfinder.' He pushed a tiny hidden lever under the edge of the square. Two miniature windows sprang up, one behind the other. The back window had a porthole in the centre surrounded by a black frame. 'When you peer through these, they magnify what you're looking at and adjust the image so that what you see through the viewfinder would be what you'd see through the camera lens if you could.'

He slid a tiny black door upwards at the back of the camera. Underneath was a window with red glass. Henry could see the number two underneath it.

'She's obviously taken one and wound it on to two. That means you can take seven photographs. When you've taken your first photograph, wind the film on till you see the number three.'

He handed the camera back, but before Henry could thank him he walked over to a small boy who was looking inside a box camera. Henry was hurt by his brusque manner, especially when he could see how friendly he was to everyone else. He closed the camera, slid it back into the camera case and made for the door.

'Get out of it,' yelled a small grubby boy, 'me first!' And he gave the boy who had pushed his way to the front of the crowd surrounding Henry an almighty shove.

It was the following Saturday morning. Henry had taken the camera out into his street to peer through the viewfinder at the children.

'I told you, no one's having a go,' Henry repeated firmly. 'This is a proper camera. And it don't belong to me. So hands off!' and he held it high above his head, out of the reach of a dozen determined hands.

'Aw, go on,' they pleaded.

'No!'

''Ere he is!' yelled a girl at the back, pointing at someone behind him.

Henry whirled round. A rag and bone man had just turned into their street with his horse and cart. The children fled towards the man, holding their empty jam jars up to him.

'Wait yer turn!' he yelled hoarsely. 'If you keep shovin' each other, you'll break 'em.'

The price the man gave for two jam jars got them into the Saturday Morning Pictures. Henry had been unable to exchange jars for money ever since his mother had started making jam.

By now the children had lost interest in him. This meant he could observe them unnoticed through the viewfinder again. He spotted young Lily Bridges in her usherette's uniform walking along the pavement, her hair tucked neatly under her pill-box hat. She glanced quickly in his direction and then looked hastily down at the pavement. Henry remembered overhearing his mum say that ever since she had returned to live with her family after her divorce she still couldn't look anyone in the face.

'Cinema Club,' yelled a woman at the door of one of the houses. 'Get yer skates on!'

Henry followed the children as they began running towards the corner of the street to queue up at the Plaza. He had just reached the steps when he saw Grace standing alone, gazing vacantly over the heads of a group of little ones. He framed her face. She must have sensed him, for she immediately turned round and broke away from the queue. As she drew nearer he moved the silver dial back from infinity to four. She was smiling.

'Is that the camera Mrs Beaumont lent you?'

'Yeah,' said Henry.

'It's beautiful,' she said. 'Are you going to the Pictures?'

'No, I want to go off somewhere and take some snaps.'

'Can I come with you?'

'It's the first time . . .' he began awkwardly.

'And you don't want someone looking over your shoulder?'

Henry shook his head.

'I'd best get back in the queue,' she said, and returned to fight her way back to where she had been standing.

After leaving the cinema, he headed towards the centre of town but he found nothing he wanted to photograph. He was nearly tempted to take one of a small elderly woman hunting for flowers among the rubble. He had watched her standing alone, clutching a straggly bunch of blue petals and green stalks among the grey, windswept, broken houses. Instead he decided to have one last try at the children. He returned to the pavement opposite the Plaza to wait. As soon as the foyer doors were flung open, they came running down the steps like a living waterfall. He clicked the shutter and wound it on to three, almost laughing with exhilaration.

'I've taken my first photograph!' he whispered.

After dinner he hung around at the top of the steps, knowing that Grace and Mrs Beaumont would be arriving for the matinee. He hid behind a queue by the wall.

'There you are,' he murmured. They were on the other side of the road, deep in conversation. He ducked down, lens and iris set. A man with a moustache in a raincoat and trilby hat was hovering nearby. *Blast!* He'd just have to risk him being in the picture.

He rose slowly and photographed them crossing the road.

'You naughty boy,' laughed Mrs Beaumont. 'But I shouldn't complain. It's nice to see you using it.'

Henry grinned, pleased with himself. He pressed the slim metal side rods and snapped the camera shut.

On Wednesday night he carried kindling in an old sack round to Mrs Beaumont's house. She was delighted to see him.

'I've got another job for you,' she said. 'In London.'

'London!' Henry exclaimed.

'I need someone sensible to travel with me. And stay overnight. You could meet my friend, Daniel. I've a feeling he could help you with your history presentation. He's quite an expert when it comes to film history.'

Henry had pushed all thoughts of the presentation to one side. Again on Friday, Jeffries and Pip had answered all Mr Finch's questions enthusiastically, and again Mr Finch had ignored him.

'Where would I sleep?'

'At my house.'

'You got a house in London?'

'Yes. I want to fill a trunk with a few things and then have it delivered here. That's where you come in. I need someone to help me carry the trunk down the stairs to a taxi. My lodgers might be there but I can't take that chance. When do you break up for half-term?'

'This Thursday,' said Henry. 'We have Friday and Monday off.'

'Splendid. We could go on Friday and come back Saturday. What do you say?'

He grinned.

'I'll take that as a yes. I'll need to speak to your parents, of course.'

'Yeah,' said Henry awkwardly.

'Ah. I take it they don't know about me?'

'No.'

'Have they seen you sawing wood?'

'Yes. I just said I was helping someone out.'

'There you are, then. I'll ask if you can help me out some more.' She stood up. 'Come on, let's take the bull by the horns. I'll ask them this evening.'

*

'Do you mind if we go round the back? If we knock on the front door we might wake Molly.'

*And have Gran calling out to me*, he thought.

'Round the back it is,' said Mrs Beaumont.

He asked her to wait in the scullery so that he could warn his mother. She was in the kitchen, draping damp clothing over the clothes horse he had made for her in woodwork.

'Mum,' he began awkwardly, 'there's this lady wants to meet you.' He beckoned Mrs Beaumont into the kitchen. Henry's mother whipped off her apron.

'Are you from the school?' she asked, flustered.

'No. I'm so sorry to pop in like this without warning, Mrs Dodge. I'm Mrs Beaumont, a friend of your son's. But please call me Hettie.'

Henry's mother looked bewildered. They stood and stared at one another, the only sound in the room coming from the wireless next door.

'Take a seat, will you,' said his mother at last. 'Will you have some tea?'

'No, thank you. We've just had some.'

'Oh,' said his mother, glancing at Henry. 'Have you?'

'Henry has been helping me.'

'With kindling,' he added.

'I live in the next road,' explained Mrs Beaumont. 'And I've come to ask you if you would allow Henry to give me some more help.'

'Well, I'm sure that's fine . . .' began his mother.

'Naturally you'll want to talk it over with his father.'

'Stepfather,' muttered Henry.

'You see, I want him to come to London with me.'

'London!'

'And he'd need to stay overnight. I'm a stranger and obviously you need to know more about me before you make a decision.'

'Why London?'

As Mrs Beaumont explained, Henry watched his mother's face closely, his fingers crossed behind his back. At the moment she looked too taken by surprise for him to guess if she would agree.

'But how on earth do you know one another?' asked Henry's mother.

'I took your son into an A film and it's got to be a habit.'

'And you want him to help you carry a trunk of clothing and books . . .'

'And stories. Mrs Beaumont is a writer,' said Henry.

'I have several of them in exercise books and I need to get them typed up,' added Mrs Beaumont. 'Which is going to take some time as I'm not much of a typist.'

'I could do that for you,' said Henry's mother simply.

'You can type?' said Mrs Beaumont.

'Yes. I have secretarial qualifications.'

'But this is wonderful!' exclaimed Mrs Beaumont.

'Haven't you forgotten someone, Mum?' said Henry. 'Molly.'

'I can type them when she takes her nap. It's Gran who's the problem. If she sees me at it, she'll want me to do something for her. She doesn't like to feel ignored.'

Henry was shocked. He had never heard her talk that way about Gran.

'Not that I mind, Henry,' she said quickly. 'There is one other problem, though. I don't have a typewriter. I had to sell mine.'

'I've my brother's one here. You can use that,' said Mrs Beaumont. 'Now about Molly. Would she take a nap in a strange place? If so, while she snoozes in the sitting room on the settee, you could tap away on my kitchen table. And of course I'll pay you.'

Henry's mother was almost laughing. 'Oh, Mrs Beaumont.' She turned hurriedly to Henry. 'Don't breathe a word of this to your grandmother.'

'Why?'

'I don't want her to know that I'm earning money.'

Henry remembered Gran saying that his father wouldn't dream of letting his wife earn any wages.

'What about Uncle Bill?'

'Uncle Bill will be fine about it.'

*Of course he will*, he thought. *Mr Miser himself.*

'Please,' she begged in a whisper.

Henry nodded. She leaned across and kissed his cheek.

'Thanks, love. You don't know what this means to me.'

Just then they heard Gran's door open. His mother looked up in alarm. Mrs Beaumont pressed a finger to her lips and bolted into the scullery. As the scullery door closed, the kitchen door was flung open to reveal Gran.

'Hello, Mrs Dodge,' said his mum brightly.

'I was wondering where my tea was,' Gran complained.

'I was just about to put the kettle on, wasn't I, Henry?'

It was all Henry could do not to laugh.

# 8. A sudden change

UNCLE BILL GAVE HIS PERMISSION FOR HENRY TO TRAVEL WITH Mrs Beaumont to London.

'Make the most of it,' he had said. 'London is like another country.'

Henry couldn't imagine him in London. He knew he worked on the Waterloo line but he assumed that he only ever saw the inside of a train cab. Gran wasn't so happy.

'Who is she?' she demanded. 'I don't think you should be going off to London with a stranger.'

'She's the lady I told you about. The one who's helping me with the History presentation. She wants me to meet this man in London. She thinks he can help me.'

'Oh,' she said, 'well, I s'pose that's all right, but it does seem an awful lot of bother.'

Henry was looking forward to telling Mr Finch in the History lesson, but when Henry raised his arm Mr Finch still ignored him, and instead listened to Jeffries and Pip talk about the Lumière brothers.

At break time, the western three stopped him on his way to see the caretaker.

'He don't want to know you, does he?' said Roberts. 'Does he know your dad's a hero?'

'Yeah.'

'And he treats you like that?' said Kemp.

'You done something wrong?' added Davis.

'No.'

'You must've done. He don't want to give you the time of day.'

'Don't matter to me,' said Henry, shrugging, and he stared at the ground. He didn't want them to see how upset he was feeling. 'I got things to do,' and he strolled away, still stinging from their remarks.

He found the caretaker in the little room, standing on a chair by the small window holding some black material over the glass.

'Good job I saved this,' he commented.

'I might be able to get some black paint over the half-term,' said Henry.

'Oh, yes? On the black market?' and he laughed at his own joke.

'You look browned off,' said his mother. 'The films weren't that bad, were they?'

Henry had just returned from the cinema. One of the

films he had seen had left him feeling a bit low.

'There was this James Mason film called *Caught* and it was supposed to have a happy ending. And it sort of did.' And he paused. 'And it didn't.'

'What do you mean?'

'It was about a woman who was married to a man who didn't love her, only she didn't find out till after she'd married him. And he treated her like he owned her. Then she found out that she was goin' to have a baby, so she was sort of trapped, 'cos he said that if she divorced him, he'd pay people to say terrible things about her so he could take the baby away from her and then she'd never see it again. And he was really nasty to her. He wouldn't let her sleep when she wanted. And he made her cook meals for him and his friends in the middle of the night. He was a bully.'

She sat down quickly and flung a hand across her face.

'What a horrible story,' she said shakily. 'Why do they want to make films like that?' and she burst into tears.

'Mum!' He was shocked. 'It was all right, Mum. She lost the baby and ended up with this nice doctor.'

'So if she hadn't lost the baby, she would have had to stay with the nasty one?'

'Yeah. He was a very powerful man. That's what I meant about the ending. It was good because she ended up with the nice doctor, but it was bad because she lost the baby.'

'What made you go and see a film like that?'

'I didn't know that's how it was going to be. I went for the western.' He stared at her, feeling helpless. 'I'm sorry, Mum.'

She gave a brief wave as if trying to shrug it off, but he could see that she was finding it difficult to speak.

'Silly me,' she said, attempting to smile, 'I get so caught up in stories. I'm just a bit tired, that's all. I'd best get to bed.'

After his mother had kissed him goodnight, Henry knocked on Gran's door.

'Come in, Henry.'

She was in bed.

'Switch off the wireless, there's a dear. Now,' she said, tapping the eiderdown with her hand, 'come and tell me all about the films.'

But Henry found it difficult to speak. He was still feeling bad at upsetting his mother.

'What's up? There's something bothering you, ain't there? I can see it in yer face. Come on, tell yer gran.'

'I was telling Mum about one of the films I saw and she burst into tears.'

'You mustn't take any notice of that, not now she's in her condition.'

'What condition?'

'She's been caught again, ain't she?'

'Caught?' repeated Henry, remembering the name of the film.

'She's in the family way, if you know what I mean.'

Henry didn't.

'She's goin' to have another little nipper, God help us!'

Henry felt as though he had been struck across the face.

'A baby?'

'All women get very tearful when they're, you know, like that.'

Shocked, Henry said nothing. He was still attempting to let this news sink in.

'I used to get tearful when I was carrying your dad. The only person who upsets your mum is that stepfather of yours.'

'He's letting me go to London, Gran.'

'Course he is. He wants to get shot of you. Once this new baby's born, he'll be eyeing up your room, mark my words. He'd like to get shot of me and all.' She sighed. 'If only we could find somewhere nice where the two of us could live together. Wouldn't that be lovely? Then you could look after me.'

For some reason Henry felt uneasy. He loved his gran, but he didn't like the thought of leaving his mum to live alone with her.

'Uncle Bill's got a job waiting for me at Hatton Station after I finish school,' he reminded her hurriedly. 'I have to stay here.'

*

'You missed the big shoot-out when he blasted his way to safety,' Henry said as he came out of *Chicago Deadline* with Grace and Mrs Beaumont.

'It was too scary to watch,' they chorused.

Outside the Apollo it was tipping down with rain.

'It's far too wet to go home yet,' said Mrs Beaumont. 'I'm taking you to the café upstairs.'

Henry and Grace had never been on this floor before. As soon as Henry saw the huge room with chandeliers, he backed away.

'Mrs Beaumont, I can't go in there. I've got my old trousers on and I'm wearing boots.'

'You're not going to eat with them, are you? All you need are good manners and you have those in abundance. In you go,' she said, nudging him through the door.

A girl in a black dress and starched white apron and cap politely showed them to a table.

'This is wonderful,' said Grace, gazing around at the paintings of gardens on the walls.

Up on a small raised platform a trio of ladies, wearing afternoon dresses and necklaces, were sitting playing classical music on a violin, viola and cello.

'I'll bring you back here on your birthday if you like,' said Mrs Beaumont.

'Too late. I had my thirteenth birthday the day after I auditioned for the choir,' said Grace.

'When are you fifteen, Henry?'

'Next month.'

'That's settled, then. We shall have an un-birthday tea today, which will be a late one for you, Grace, and an early one for you, Henry.'

The waitress wheeled a silver trolley up to their table with the most extraordinary array of cakes Henry had ever seen.

'So, Grace,' said Mrs Beaumont, sliding a tiny fork into an oozing, creamy apple strudel, 'do you have any plans for half-term?'

'No,' she said dismally. 'I've been given extra work to do so that I can catch up.'

'That's a shame.'

'When is your half-term?' Grace asked Henry.

'This Friday and Monday.'

'Is that all? We have Tuesday off as well.'

'Henry's coming up to London with me,' said Mrs Beaumont.

'Lucky thing!'

'I plan to go again in December. Would you . . .'

'Yes, please!'

'I'll try and persuade your great-aunt to let me take you.'

'Oh, thank you. I'd love that.'

'Now, eat your cake.'


'I'd like a word with you, Dodge,' said Mr Finch. 'Remain here during the morning break.'

It was the Thursday before half-term and this sudden attention surprised Henry. When everyone had left the classroom, Henry sat at his desk watching Mr Finch as he glanced out of the window above the door to check that no one was eavesdropping. He turned sharply.

'The caretaker has brought to my attention the hard work you've put into the darkroom. I'd be delighted, if I didn't suspect it was an avoidance tactic on your part.'

'But I'm doing research, sir!' Henry protested.

'With Jeffries and Morgan?'

'No, sir,' Henry murmured. 'But I've met this lady and . . .'

But he could see he wasn't interested.

Mr Finch took a brown envelope from his pocket and placed it on Henry's desk.

'When you return from half-term, I expect to see a change in your behaviour. If there is not, you will be banned from the presentation. Do I make myself clear?'

Henry nodded numbly.

'Now put that in your pocket and make use of it.' He strode over to the door and held it open for him, indicating that Henry could leave. 'It'll all be clear once you open it,' he said abruptly.

As soon as Henry hit the playground, he was pounced on by the western three.

'Why did he want to talk to you?' Kemp asked.

'I've been helping Sergeant at break times, with the darkroom,' said Henry casually. 'He just wanted to let me know that he'd noticed my hard work, that's all.'

'Teacher's pet,' said Davis.

*Whatever I do, I can't win,* he thought.

The bell rang. He was glad of an excuse not to open the envelope. Whatever was in it could wait until he was in his bedroom. He could be private there.

After school he sprinted to the grocers to tell Mr Jenkins that he would be away the next day. There was a long queue of people waiting outside the shop. He spotted his mother with Molly. She looked shattered. Molly was lying on the pavement, screaming, while his mother was struggling to hold her hand.

'I've been here for two hours,' she said. 'Can you take her home, love? I don't know how much longer I can hold her. If she dashes off, I'll have to run after her and I'll lose my place.'

Henry glanced behind her. The queue was so long it disappeared round the corner into the next street.

'Can you tell Mr Jenkins that I can't help again until Tuesday?'

She nodded. 'Thanks, love.'

Henry gazed down at his red-faced, squalling heap of a half-sister.

'Give her some bread and jam. That'll keep her going till I get back.'

She let go of her hand and Molly swiftly rolled over on to her stomach, clambered to her feet and ran across the road.

'Molly!' screamed his mother.

Henry dashed after her and grabbed her by the back of her dress. He scooped up her wriggling, fighting body and slung her under his arm. He marched to the other side of the road and turned to face his mother.

'I've got her!' he yelled.

He thrust Molly down on to the pavement and squatted down in front of her.

'Want a piggyback, Molly?'

'Piggyback, piggyback!' she chanted.

She scrambled excitedly on to his back and he stood up, gripping her firmly. She clung to his neck and began to bounce up and down. He struggled to hold her legs.

'Gallopy horse!' she cried.

Henry began galloping towards the railway station. By the time he reached the bombsite opposite their house, he was worn out. He wondered how his mother kept up with her. Five minutes with Molly and he was done in. As soon as he reached their house and shut the front door, she darted into the kitchen, slid happily on to a chair and spread her arms across the table.

'Firsty,' she stated.

'Come with me, then,' and he led her into the scullery, where he poured water into a small enamel mug. She carried it carefully into the kitchen, sat down and began gulping it noisily.

The bread was kept in a large clay pot with a lid. He put the remains of a loaf on the breadboard and cut a misshapen slice for her.

'Would you like it toasted, Molly?'

'Yes,' she breathed between loud gulps.

The fire in the range was almost out. He added a few small pieces of coal and had just finished toasting the bread on the end of the toasting fork when there was a loud banging on the wall. He whirled round.

'Auntie cross,' Molly stated matter of factly.

'Why d'you think that, Molly?' asked Henry puzzled.

'Tea!' yelled a voice. 'Where's my tea?'

The banging started again. Bang! Bang! Bang! Henry stood stunned for a moment.

And then he heard the front door opening. Within seconds his mother was hauling the shopping basket into the kitchen.

'I'm so sorry, love, I should have told you – Gran has a cup of tea when I come back from the shops. She must have heard you come in with Molly and thought it was me.'

'I expect it's difficult with her legs, not being able to do much.'

'What's wrong with her legs?' asked his mother. 'Has she hurt them?'

'No, I mean, I thought she had bad legs.'

'Oh, no, she doesn't use them, that's all.'

By now Molly was yelling, 'Bang, bang, bang!' and thumping the table with her hands.

'Can you fill the kettle, love, while I go and sort her out?'

Henry listened as his mother opened the door to the front room.

'Where's my tea?' his grandmother screamed. 'Didn't you hear me banging?'

'I've only just come in, Mother.'

'Liar! I heard you come in ages ago with that noisy girl.'

'I'm just about to put the kettle on.'

'And about time. Don't think you're getting away with it, though. I'll bang on the wall till it arrives.'

'You'll only make Molly excitable and that'll make you angry.'

'Lock 'er in 'er room, then. She needs locking away anyway.'

'I'll be as quick as I can.'

'You'd better be.'

As soon as Henry heard his mother close the door he quickly dashed into the scullery to fill the kettle. By the time he returned, not only was Gran banging the poker against the wall but the wireless was now up to full volume.

'Can you take Molly out into the yard?' asked his mother above the din.

'Has she done this before, Mum?'

His mother looked hesitantly at him for a moment. And then nodded. 'She's not the saint you think she is.'

Molly was now shouting in an effort to beat the wireless.

'Please take her outside,' his mother begged.

'Piggyback, Molly?' he asked.

She laughed and stretched up her arms.

'You're a bit quiet, Henry,' said Gran over tea.

'He's just tired,' said his mum. 'You'd best get upstairs, Henry. You've an early start tomorrow. You don't want to miss the train.'

He nodded. All during tea he couldn't look at his grandmother. He was glad of an excuse to escape.

Upstairs he lay awake, waiting until Molly was asleep. As soon as he heard her breathing become steady, he reached down to the foot of the bed where he had slung his trousers, and pulled the envelope out. To make doubly sure he wouldn't wake her, he opened it under his bedclothes and switched on his torch.

Inside the envelope was a small piece of paper. Written on it in neat handwriting were two addresses, one under R. Jeffries and one under E. Morgan. Underneath were the phone numbers of their landladies.

## 9. Another country

HENRY STARED OUT OF THE TRAIN WINDOW. SINCE LEAVING Hatton Station, he and Mrs Beaumont had had a carriage to themselves. Mrs Beaumont was buried in a huge novel called *The Good Companions* and for once Henry was glad to see a book. He didn't want to talk. He needed time to think.

Four incidents had troubled him over the last few days. First there was the threat from Mr Finch. Then there had been his mother's reaction to his account of *Caught*, followed by the unexpected news that she was going to have a baby.

He was hurt that his mother hadn't told him. He had tried to find a way of asking her if it were true, but he hadn't been able to get her on her own. He suspected that Uncle Bill had told her to keep quiet about it and had been treating his mother in the same way as the cruel husband in the film. He wondered if she would have divorced him if she hadn't been about to have a baby.

But he knew the answer to that. Divorce brought shame on a woman. His mother would rather cross a road than risk coming face to face with a divorcee like Lily Bridges or an unmarried woman like Pip's mother. So maybe she was trapped like the woman in the film.

Then there was the fourth incident and it was the most disturbing of them all – his grandmother screaming and banging the walls. How was it possible that he had never seen that side of her before?

'Penny for them?' said Mrs Beaumont. 'You look as if you're carrying the world on your shoulders. Anything worrying you?'

He shook his head.

'How are you enjoying the camera?'

'A lot,' he said, relaxing. 'Most of the time I pretend to take photos so I don't use the film up too quickly. I look through the viewfinder at people till they ignore me. I want to take them by surprise.'

She gave a wry smile.

'I seem to remember being on the receiving end of that method outside the Plaza.'

He thought about what he would really like to be able to do. He wanted to take photographs that looked like scenes in *The Third Man*, people in shafts of light by a window or under a street lamp at night in the rain, so that the wet pavement reflected the light. 'I wish I could get the light to do what I want.'

'You want to take photographs for their own sake, don't you? Not family snaps.'

'Yeah! Gran doesn't understand that.' He stopped for a moment, conscious that he was criticising his grand-mother, something he had never done before. 'I don't want ones of people putting on a smile. I want to photograph them doing things or thinking.' He wondered if he was making a fool of himself. 'Anyway,' he said, 'I like it. Even when I'm just carrying the camera, I notice things more.'

'It makes you feel more alive?'

'Yeah. Is that what it feels like when you write?'

'Yes.'

Henry smiled, relieved. Suddenly he was conscious of her gazing at him.

'Henry, about your grandmother, you haven't told her your mother will be typing for me, have you?'

'No, course not.'

'I know you're very close to her, but please don't be tempted. Your mother obviously has her reasons for not telling her.'

'I won't tell her. Promise.'

'Oh, look,' she said, glancing out of the window, 'we're coming into Woking. This is where the spacecraft landed. And where one hundred-foot-high machines walked with martians inside them.'

Henry stared at her, alarmed.

'No, I'm not going mad,' she laughed. '*War of the Worlds*. H. G. Wells. One of my son Max's favourite books.'

'*The History of Mr Polly*,' Henry said. 'That's by him too.'

'Yes. How do you know that?'

'I saw the film. It had John Mills in it.'

'Ah,' she said, 'so you obviously like *watching* stories. You just have an aversion to printed matter.'

Henry grinned.

Waterloo Station was spectacular. Rain was drumming loudly on its high vaulted glass-and-iron roof with its criss-crossing girders. It was the size of six Hatton Stations, with lines of platforms and steam and electric trains alongside one another. There was a large newsagent's shop in the centre, a chemist near two of the many gates, and a tobacconist's shop. As they walked through the gates, Henry saw restaurant and refreshment signs, and beyond the main booking office on the other side was a building with a sign saying, NEWS THEATRE.

'That small cinema is where people can watch newsreels and cartoons while waiting for their trains,' Mrs Beaumont explained.

Henry could hardly take it in. He was mesmerised by the sight of so many people milling around the station with their suitcases, some sitting on long wooden benches, others going up to a woman in a white overall and hat who was serving tea from a large urn. There were men in kilts, women in smart suits with matching hats or in long evening gowns accompanied by men in evening dress, a red carnation in their lapels. He had never seen so many men wearing bowlers and top hats. Standing near the tea urn were two brown-skinned men. They were each wearing colourful striped turbans with a jewel in the centre, above red tunics and baggy blue trousers tucked into long black boots. They looked like princes.

Behind him one of the steam trains let out a loud hiss. Henry whirled round. Black smoke was shooting upwards from one of the funnels and it was then that he spotted a familiar figure standing beside one of the newer steam trains. It was Jack Riddell from his form. He was in the railway group. One of the drivers was leaning out of the cab above him and talking to him. Henry turned back to take in the crowds again. He now understood what his stepfather had meant when he had said that London was like another country. He slipped the camera out, released the bellows and took a photograph of Mrs Beaumont.

'Caught,' she laughed.

'Here we are,' Mrs Beaumont said. 'Home Sweet Home.'

She unlocked a massive carved door and opened it into an enormous hall with high ceilings. 'The whole place needs a lick of paint,' she remarked, 'but with government regulations, that's not possible.' Three large doors led off the hall, one to the left, one to the right, from where piano music was coming, and tucked away beside the wide steps was a door leading to the back of the house.

A tall slim woman with short wavy hair and round tortoiseshell glasses peered out of the door on the left. She gave a broad smile.

'Hettie!' she cried. She took off her glasses. 'I've sorted out beds for you both.'

'I didn't expect that,' said Mrs Beaumont. 'Thank you.'

'You must be Henry,' the woman said, holding out her hand. 'I'm Violet.' They shook hands and she beckoned them in.

They trooped into a huge sitting room. In front of the window looking out on to the street was a heavy mahogany table covered with stacks of books and papers.

'I'm marking books and scribbling down ideas for the rest of the term.'

'Violet is a teacher,' Mrs Beaumont explained. 'She lives here with a fellow teacher.'

'Who's away, which is why Mrs Beaumont can sleep in her bed tonight.' She indicated the large double doors at the back of the room. 'It's our half-term too.'

'I thought the dance classes would have stopped this weekend,' said Mrs Beaumont.

'They have.'

'But there's piano music coming from the studio.'

'That's Jessica. Oh, Hettie, it's so good to see you.'

'And you,' laughed Mrs Beaumont, squeezing her hand. 'Is Daniel in?'

'Yes. And Ralph. He's on weekend leave and doing a bit of filming.'

'He's Jessica's fiancé, an actor,' Mrs Beaumont explained. 'He's the person I hope will be able to get hold of some black paint for you. Jessica lives here too. She's an Art student.'

'She's practising the piano for you,' said Violet to Henry.

'For me?' said Henry, mystified.

'Daniel will be showing you some silent films tomorrow in the studio. He's the man I told you about, the one who knows everything there is to know about film history. Jessica can play the piano really well, so Daniel asked her if she could come up with something to make the films more lively.'

Henry was staggered that strangers would go to all this trouble for someone they had never met.

'Max is coming round this evening with some friends. They're bringing reels of an Italian film, a projectionist and some film equipment. Apparently they've been extraordinarily lucky to get hold of this film. It's only just come out,' Violet added.

'Max is my younger son,' Mrs Beaumont reminded him.

'Now,' said Violet, 'about sleeping arrangements. I thought Henry could sleep in the room where all your furniture and belongings are stored.'

'Wonderful.' Mrs Beaumont turned to Henry. 'I'll have a word with Daniel first, then we can go out for a quick bite and come back here to sort through my belongings before this film starts.'

Henry followed Mrs Beaumont up two flights of stairs and into a large room at the back of the house. Its walls were stacked high with boxes, cases and furniture. A camp bed was made up in front of a high double window, which looked out on to a straggly garden. Beyond the trees and high brick wall was a graveyard and more trees. There were no curtains. Two ceiling-high shutters had been folded back, letting the late-afternoon light in.

'I thought I'd find it all covered in cobwebs, like Miss Haversham's abode. Miss Haversham was . . .'

'In *Great Expectations*,' said Henry. 'I saw the film.'

She smiled.

Henry scoured the alcoves and the boxes with his eyes. It looked as though there were a thousand or more books in the room.

'You're sure you won't have nightmares sleeping among this lot?' she said. 'The words might leap out at you in the night and torment you.'

*As long as they don't fall on top of me*, he thought, gazing up at the precariously balanced book towers.

'Now, I'd better introduce you to Daniel.'

'No need,' said a booming voice behind them.

A tall white-haired man was standing in the doorway, a pipe clamped between his teeth at the side of his mouth. The hair on that side of his face was stained yellow from the tobacco. Henry noticed he had a walking stick. The man caught his eye and tapped his right leg with it. There was a loud metallic twang.

'Lost it in a trench somewhere in France,' he said gruffly. 'I take it you're Henry, the boy who wants to know about films in 1899.'

Henry nodded.

'I've managed to find some 1895 films and a couple of 1900 ones. I hope that'll do.'

'Yes, sir! Thank you, sir!'

This was better than Henry had expected.

'Call me Daniel. Come with me.'

Henry followed. They walked into his room, which was joined to another room and spanned the width of the house. The ceiling-high dividing doors were slightly ajar. Daniel limped over to them and thrust them open. Behind the doors were stacks of flat circular metal containers.

'Films,' he said. 'I keep them all on this side and shut the door on them when I light a fire in here.'

Henry spotted a fire bucket filled with sand, and a fire extinguisher.

'Highly flammable is film,' said Daniel.

Mrs Beaumont was staring uneasily at the extinguisher.

'Why does that not make me feel wonderful?' she commented.

'Hettie, you do know you look peculiar? Are you in disguise?'

Henry was puzzled. Mrs Beaumont looked perfectly normal to him.

'Rude, isn't he?' she quipped.

'Just honest,' said Daniel. 'You know me. I call a spade a spade.'

'Most of my clothes are here,' she explained. 'The clothes I took with me eventually fell apart. These are my mother's.'

'I'll show you more tomorrow,' said Daniel. 'You'd better go and eat. You must be ravenous. And I need time to prepare for your son and his friends coming round.'

By the time Henry and Mrs Beaumont had returned to the house from a café, the afternoon sky was so dull that they had to turn the light on in Mrs Beaumont's storage room. Rain trickled down the high windows in rivulets. Mrs Beaumont drew her fingers along the sides of the window frames.

'It's not leaking. That's a relief.' She turned her back to the window and faced her possessions. 'I'm going to have to empty one of these trunks first and then repack it with what I've selected to take back to Sternsea.' She knelt down in front of one, snapped the locks to one side and flung open the lid. 'Here goes.'

'Good! That's exercise books, paperbacks and clothing,' she commented, gazing with satisfaction at a fully packed trunk, several hours later. 'Now,' she said, pulling herself up to her feet, 'I'll nip down to Violet's room and change out of these ancient tweeds into something of mine which is a little less dreary. Meanwhile you can put on this old jersey of Oscar's.' She handed Henry a thick blue woolly garment. 'Oscar's my elder son,' she added. She hurried out of the room with an armful of clothes.

It was dark outside now and chilly. Henry pulled on the jersey gratefully. From downstairs he could hear the front door opening and the sound of several male voices and laughter. Suddenly he felt painfully shy.

'Ma!' Henry heard someone yell. 'What on earth are you wearing?'

'Granny's clothes.'

*Why do people go on about what she looks like?* Henry thought, puzzled.

'You must come and listen to some records we've brought,' continued the man. 'They're a sensation!'

Henry crept out on to the landing. Footsteps were moving rapidly up the stairs. He dived back into Mrs Beaumont's room.

'You're a noisy lot of blighters aren't you?' he heard

Daniel roar. 'I could hear you nattering halfway down the street.'

'Come downstairs quickly!'

There was a loud hammering on Henry's door. Nervously he peered out. Standing there was a tall, eager man with blond hair. There was no mistaking that he was Mrs Beaumont's son. He had the same look in his eyes as if he was having a private joke.

'You're hearing this too, Henry,' he said.

Henry followed awkwardly behind them as they headed downstairs.

'This is revolutionary music,' the man said over his shoulder.

A crowd of men in sodden corduroy trousers, tweed jackets and dripping raincoats were gathered in the hall. The man swung round to Henry and said, 'I'm sorry, I haven't introduced myself. I'm Max Beaumont. Mother's told me all about you.' He turned to the other men. 'Who's got the gramophone?'

One of the men held up a wooden case and dashed into the studio.

'You will be watching the film with us, won't you, Ma? You haven't made any plans to dash off somewhere, have you?'

'No plans for this evening at all,' Mrs Beaumont said.

Henry did his best to hide his disappointment. He had hoped that they would go to one of the large London cinemas. Watching a film in the front room of someone's house would be worse than watching a film in a church hall.

Suddenly a burst of music rocketed out of the studio. A saxophone was being played so fast it made Henry feel breathless. It was the most exciting sound he had ever heard. He could hear people laughing with exhilaration.

'What is that?' said Mrs Beaumont, astounded.

'*Salt Peanut*,' answered Max. 'Charlie Parker and Dizzy Gillespie.'

'But what kind of music is it?'

'Jazz, of course.'

A young man shot his head round the studio door. 'No it's not. It's bebop!'

'It's jazz!' protested Max. 'Modern jazz.'

'It's so frenetic,' she said.

'It's so wild!' laughed Max.

'Difficult to dance to at that speed,' commented Daniel.

'Who needs to?' said Max. 'It's so mesmerising it stops you in your tracks. A friend has brought a stack of records over from America. Isn't it wonderful! Oscar will be so envious.'

Henry listened to the music transfixed.

That evening Henry sat cross-legged in the front row of the studio next to Mrs Beaumont, who was on a cushion. A white screen had been erected in front of the high windows now concealed behind closed shutters. The lights were switched off, the projector whirred and grainy black and white images appeared on the screen.

'What's the name of this film?' Mrs Beaumont whispered to Max.

'*Bicycle Thieves*,' he answered.

It was the music which seeped under Henry's skin first, pulling him into a teeming world of poverty where the possession of a bicycle meant a job and food on the table. In among the crowds of people were a man and his small son. It was they who kept Henry riveted to the screen – the pride in the boy's face when, after his parents had pawned the family sheets, his father was able to buy a bicycle and was given a job, and their determination to find it after it had been stolen.

As Henry watched, an intense pain welled up inside him. He saw the adoration in the boy's eyes for his father and the way they looked after one another and he realised he was seeing something he had never experienced. He had never known what it was like to walk beside his father, to glance up at him, to copy his mannerisms, to walk happily in his shadow.

He swallowed hard to hold back the tears, his jaw and throat aching. When the lights were switched on, there was only a stunned silence and the sound of the projector flicking the tail-end of the final reel. Henry kept his head bowed. He found himself thinking of Grace. She would have been able to follow the story in spite of not being able to read the subtitles or understand Italian, because the story was all there in the pictures.

'Wonderful,' said someone quietly from behind him. Out of the corner of his eye he saw several people nodding in agreement. A tall man with a beard was staring at Henry.

'Pretty powerful, eh?'

Henry nodded.

By now people were heading towards the door. Mrs Beaumont beckoned him to join them.

'There's a fire in Daniel's room and toast.'

He shook his head.

'I'm tired,' he mumbled. 'I think I'll go to bed.'

Upstairs, he slipped into the room, quickly shut the door and leaned against it, relieved to be alone. He couldn't even bear to switch on the light. He walked over to the window and folded back the tall shutters. Outside the rain was still streaming down the glass. He stood still for a moment, drinking in its sound. He needed it to soothe him. After a while he kicked off his boots, threw himself on the bed face down, pulled the pillow over his head and sobbed like a baby.

'I'm sorry I didn't take you to a cinema yesterday,' said Mrs Beaumont after breakfast. 'I'll take you next month when we come back with Grace.'

She was wearing slacks and a jacket. Henry was surprised to see how different she looked. He had never even seen his mother in trousers.

'I'll be leaving you with Jessica and Daniel while I shoot off to get this wretched hair cut.'

She said her goodbyes, leaving Henry hovering by the open door to the studio.

'Come in, old chap!' said Daniel, noticing him. 'I'm just setting up, which is a little tricky with a walking stick. Like to help?'

'Yes, sir.'

Daniel raised his eyebrows.

'Daniel,' said Henry.

'They're very short films, so it shouldn't take too long. Most of them are French, but there's no need to worry because they're all silent. Jessica is going to play the music.'

A young woman smiled at him from behind the piano. He gave her an awkward nod. He had spotted her briefly the previous evening. She had long red crinkly hair and freckles, and when she smiled, he noticed that her front teeth crossed one another slightly.

'Hello,' she said.

Henry could feel himself reddening. To his embarrassment he heard himself reply, 'Good morning,' as if he was in school.

'A lot of the films I'll be showing you,' Daniel said, 'are

made by the Lumière brothers and are of their friends and family. Remember, no one had seen anything like this at all. So you can imagine what a sensation it was. The first time people watched a film of a train coming into a station, they screamed. They thought it was coming in their direction. That's how real it was to them then. Right, that's the first one set up. You'll be in charge of the lights, Henry. Let's roll.'

'So,' said Daniel, after he had shown the last film, 'what do you think?'

'All those women in long dresses and straw hats coming out of the factory, they were all real people,' Henry exclaimed. 'They weren't actresses playing parts. They were people who really lived in the nineteenth century.'

'And they all looked so happy,' commented Jessica, 'as if they liked being filmed.'

'Well, it was like magic to them,' Daniel said.

'And the horse-drawn carriages. And big old cars!' said Henry.

'Which film did you like best?'

'When those men were pulling down the brick wall and the film went backwards and it looked as if they were rebuilding it again. And that bit where a big chunk of it goes up by itself.'

'I liked the one set in the garden best,' said Jessica. 'Where the old man was watering the plants with a hose and the boy sneaked up behind him and put his foot on it to stop the water coming out.'

'And he looks into it to see what's wrong and the boy takes his foot off and it squirts water in the old man's face,' added Henry, grinning.

'And he chases the boy,' said Jessica, 'and he's absolutely furious.'

'That was the beginning of using film to tell a story,' said Daniel.

'They were really good,' said Henry enthusiastically, 'but . . .' He hesitated.

'But what? Spit it out, old man.'

'Well, *talking* about films, it's a bit like . . .' He paused, struggling to find the right words. 'It's . . .'

'As odd as listening to someone dance,' interrupted Jessica.

Henry grinned.

'Yeah. Sort of. I mean, it's all in the pictures.'

'Absolutely,' said Daniel. 'In other words you'd like me to come and show these films to your form.'

'No! I mean . . .' stammered Henry.

'That's agreed, then.' He turned to Jessica. 'Like to come with me?'

'Why not?' she said.

Henry found himself laughing. He tried to imagine Mr Finch's face when he told him. He would have to be friendlier with him now, wouldn't he?

*

'You realise this is madness,' Mrs Beaumont exclaimed as Henry and Jessica carried the trunk on to the pavement. 'Once I have to sell up the Sternsea house I shall have to bring it all the way back again.'

Henry couldn't help staring at her. He felt as though she was someone else, with her newly cut bobbed hair. She looked ten years younger. And it was the first time he had seen her wearing powder and lipstick.

'But why do you want to leave Sternsea?' said Henry. 'It has twenty cinemas.'

'And the Kings Theatre and the Theatre Royal and the Coliseum. And that's wonderful, but I miss having like-minded people around me. I feel I'm atrophying.'

'Brain rot,' translated Jessica, glancing aside at him.

A black cab drew up.

'Oh, my goodness, he's here already,' cried Mrs Beaumont. 'We'd better hurry with the rest of the luggage.'

'I thought this was it,' said Henry.

'There's a gramophone, and a wooden case with records in it that I want Grace to hear.'

'And this,' added Jessica. She handed Henry a heavy cylindrical object wrapped in canvas. 'Black paint.'

He beamed. Now Mr Finch would be able to have his darkroom.

'Thanks!'

On the train journey home, Henry decided to tell Mrs

Beaumont the truth about his film group. He liked her too much to deceive her any longer. As he poured out how difficult it was for him to go anywhere near Pip and Jeffries and told her about the contents of the envelope he had been given, Mrs Beaumont listened to him in silence.

'And now Mr Finch keeps ignoring me. And he doesn't ignore anyone else.'

'Perhaps he's giving you a taste of your own medicine. Perhaps he wants you to know how it feels.'

And Henry knew she was right. It was so obvious that he felt stupid not to have realised it.

'Mrs Beaumont, I don't know what to do.'

'Oh, I think you do.'

He nodded.

'When we get back to your house,' he said, 'can I use your telephone?'

# 10. Unexpected friends

'TOP FLOOR,' WHEEZED THE STOUT LANDLADY AT THE FRONT door, a half-smoked cigarette clinging to the corner of her mouth, 'right-hand side.'

At the foot of the fourth flight of stairs, Henry could see a door on the left of a landing. A sloping skylight window looked out on to the roof. As he walked up he could see another door tucked under an alcove on the right. Under it was a single gas ring on a tiny tiled table. He knocked nervously on the door.

It was Mrs Jeffries who opened it. Instantly, Henry could see she was as nervous as he was, which was strange because he couldn't imagine anyone who sounded posh being afraid of him. In spite of her shabby clothes and gaunt face, there was something elegant about her.

'Thank you for letting me come and see Jeffries,' Henry said politely, breaking the silence.

Jeffries peered out from behind her.

'Hello,' he said shyly.

'Come in,' she said.

Henry followed them into an attic room with sloping ceilings. A window looked out at the neighbour's top window and roof. One tiny bed was pushed up against the wall underneath, and another narrower bed was placed against the wall on the left. On the opposite wall stood a black sewing machine and a towering pile of enormous stiff pink corsets. A box overflowing with coils of elastic and stocking suspenders was on the floor beside it. Henry didn't know where to look. As he turned to close the door he noticed a tiny fireplace where a fire had been laid. Jeffries and his mother were wearing thick pullovers.

'Tea?' she asked.

'Yes, please, Mrs Jeffries.'

She picked up a kettle and took it out on to the landing. He heard the voomph of the gas as she lit the ring. It didn't take long for Henry to realise that he was the one who was going to have to do the talking.

'I came about the History presentation,' he began awkwardly. 'I didn't say much before because I hadn't got much to say.'

Jeffries nodded but Henry could see that he didn't believe him.

'But I was in London yesterday.'

'London!' exclaimed Jeffries.

'Yeah. And this man, Daniel, he showed me some old films. They're not exactly 1899. They're 1895 and 1900.'

'And you actually watched them?' gasped Jeffries.

'Yeah. And he says he'll bring them down here so we can show them for our presentation.'

'But this is splendid!' exclaimed Jeffries.

Henry was a bit taken aback. *Splendid* was the sort of word posh actors used.

And then he watched Jeffries' face fall.

'But if he does that, we won't be doing anything.'

'He wants us to introduce it all. And then of course there's the piano playing.'

By the time they had finished talking about the presentation, tea was ready and Jeffries had his *Picture Goer's Annuals* and other film magazines spread out.

'One of the Lumière brothers died last year, you know,' he said. 'It's in the *Picture Goer's Annual.*'

In spite of his dislike of books, Henry found himself immediately drawn to the annuals. He told himself he wasn't being disloyal to his grandmother or his father's memory, since they were mostly pictures, photographs of the stars and interviews, and extracts from films presented like a comic strip.

'Christmas presents from Mother,' said Jeffries, indicating the annuals.

It sounded odd to Henry to hear a fourteen-year-old

boy calling his mum *Mother*. And there was something else he noticed. Jeffries spoke posher than the way he spoke at school, almost as if there were two Jeffries.

Jeffries dragged out a couple of wooden boxes from under his bed. They were filled with books. Henry spotted *War of the Worlds*.

'We went through Woking yesterday,' he said.

'See any martians?'

'No. They must have been indoors.'

And though it wasn't particularly funny, they laughed so long that it hurt. It was the strangest thing – he and Jeffries got on together.

'So did you go to a cinema in London?' Jeffries asked.

'No, but I did see a film, *Bicycle Thieves*.'

'*Bicycle Thieves*!' yelled Jeffries. 'Director, Vittorio de Sica.'

'Yeah,' said Henry, feeling like he was a millionaire from Jeffries' reaction.

'It's won awards, you know. And you saw it! What was it like?'

To his embarrassment, Henry found himself struggling for words.

'I couldn't speak when it was over.'

'That good, eh?'

'Yeah.'

'Do you have to be home for dinner?' asked Mrs Jeffries.

It was the first time Mrs Jeffries had spoken since she had begun sewing.

'Yes, Mrs Jeffries.'

'Only it's half-past twelve.'

'Is it?' said Henry, surprised. He turned to Jeffries. 'I'm seeing Pip this afternoon. To tell him about the silent films and all that.'

'Good,' said Jeffries. 'I'll see you downstairs.'

As they closed the door behind them and stood in the alcove on the landing, Jeffries said, 'We've struck gold with this room.'

'Yeah,' said Henry, not knowing quite what he meant.

'Because we're this side of the landing, Mother has her own private barre.'

Henry stared at him, still no wiser.

'Ballet barre,' he explained. 'She can do her pliés and battements, all that sort of thing, using this banister rail on the landing. Good, eh?'

'Was she a ballet dancer?' asked Henry.

'Yes. She used to tour all over the place.'

'Can't she still do ballet?'

'No. She's too old now. And she wants us to stay here so Daddy can find us. She did teach but . . .' He stopped. 'Can't say any more. Walls have ears, you know.'

Jeffries came down the four flights of stairs with him. As they stood in the hall, the awkwardness returned, neither of them knowing what to say.

'Pip will be so excited,' Jeffries said eventually.

'Pip is always excited,' said Henry.

And they both grinned.

'See you at school,' said Henry.

He was about to leave when he remembered something else.

'I've got some black paint for the darkroom. I've been helping Sergeant, you see, and I wondered . . .'

'Yes,' said Jeffries, 'I would like to help.'

Pip lived in a basement. It wasn't even a room, just a bit of a hallway with a screen for privacy at night. Being a big house, it was a large hall. As Henry came downstairs he could see a window below ground level, which looked up to a path at the side of the house. Under the window was a stone sink and beside it a wooden draining board like the one in the scullery in his house. Several buckets stood underneath. He walked over to a door and was just about to knock on it when he heard a voice say, 'We're here!' Henry swung round.

It was Pip. He and Mrs Morgan stood side by side by the stairs. Behind them, under the stairway, a camp bed was folded neatly on top of a narrow bed. Two chairs and a table were pressed up against the wall opposite.

'Hello, Henry,' said Mrs Morgan, smiling. 'I've left ginger beer and buns for you and Pip.'

'You call him Pip too?' he blurted out.

'Yes. I was that surprised when I found out people knew his second name was Philip and had shortened it. When I heard the name again in *Great Expectations*, I thought, well, why not? What's good enough for my son's friends is good enough for me.'

*So she has no idea it's short for pipsqueak,* thought Henry and if she did, she wasn't letting on.

'I'm sorry I can't stay. I have to get to work but Pip will look after you, won't you, love?'

She made no mention of the incident in the cinema when she had comforted Grace, and Henry knew instantly that Grace's secret would be safe with her. She kissed Pip, gave him a hug, and headed for the stairs.

'Sit down,' said Pip excitedly. 'You're my first visitor.'

'Thanks.'

Henry noticed a suitcase, a pile of comics and a small black paraffin stove standing beside the table with a battered saucepan on it. He put his hand near it for warmth but it was cold.

'I haven't been talking to you much,' began Henry, embarrassed.

'I know. Jeffries explained everything.'

'Did he?'

'Yes. He said you were helping get a darkroom ready and you were working really hard and that you were too busy to talk to us.'

Henry felt ashamed.

'Yeah. But I'll soon be finished. I brought some black paint back from London.'

'London!' exclaimed Pip.

He leapt up from his chair and proceeded to jump up and down, waving his arms. A thin, exhausted-looking woman carrying a bucket filled with dirty dishes was puffing down the stairs but Pip carried on with his whirling dance.

'Boy's mad,' Henry heard the woman mutter.

He returned to his chair and leaned forward eagerly.

'More,' he said, 'tell me more.'

When Henry told him about Jessica he asked, 'Do you think she'd let me see the music?'

'I suppose so. Why?'

'I might be able to play some of it.'

'Pip, it takes years to learn how to play a piano.'

'I've been learning for years,' said Pip simply. 'I practise on the one in the Plaza. Mum got permission for me to use it. She lets me in early before school. I can't play in the interval in the Cinema Club, though. That would be favouritism, see.'

It was obvious to Henry that Pip wasn't very good. If he had been, he would have been roped in to play the piano at school. He quickly changed the subject and started telling him about *Bicycle Thieves*.

'We're so lucky, me and Mum,' said Pip.

'How d'you mean?'

'Not being poor like that boy in the film.'

Henry said nothing. He remembered complaining about having to share his bedroom with Molly. At least he had a bedroom. Compared to Pip, he was rolling in it.

'Mum says if there's a storm, we're in the safest place in the house, and we've got a sink on the same floor so we don't have to carry our dishes up and down the stairs.' He paused. 'I wonder what it's like to have a dad.' He looked at Henry with such directness that it made him feel uncomfortable. 'My dad was killed in a car crash before I was born. Mum says he's in heaven and she knows that he loves me very much.'

Henry felt embarrassed. He had never heard a boy talk about love. That was sissie stuff.

'About the darkroom,' he said swiftly. 'Jeffries is going to help me out.'

'Oh. So he'll be busy. He won't want me around any more.'

'No. I mean, we thought . . . ' Henry was aware he was stretching the truth a bit, 'we thought you'd like to help.'

Pip beamed and leapt to his feet.

'You're right.'

'Shall we eat the buns?' said Henry, seeing another display of strange dancing fast approaching.

'Good idea,' said Pip, grabbing a bun and sitting down again. 'I still haven't had any luck at the Plaza. Mum asked the manager if I could go upstairs but he said, "If I let every Tom, Dick and Harry up to the projectionist's box, there'd be *mayhem*." But I'm still keeping my fingers crossed.' And he bit into the bun.

Once he left Pip's lodgings, Henry walked over to the school on the off chance that Sergeant would be about. He found him replacing a hinge on a classroom door.

'Hello, Dodge,' he said, 'you're back early!'

'I've got some black paint, sir.'

'Ah.'

'And three volunteers, me included.'

At this Sergeant gave a broad smile.

'That's music to my ears.'

'I was thinking maybe we could come in and do it tomorrow,' said Henry, 'to give Mr Finch a surprise on Tuesday.'

'I like it, boy. I like it. Now give me the names and addresses of your volunteers.'

From his trouser pocket, Henry produced the envelope Mr Finch had given him.

Back at home Henry told no one of his visits. He felt so drained he didn't even have the energy to push Molly off his knee. She must have sensed his lack of irritation because she sat quietly on his lap, sucking her thumb, and fell asleep against him. Uncle Bill lifted her up gently and carried her upstairs to bed.

'Tired?' his mother asked.

Henry nodded. As soon as Molly was settled he cleaned his teeth and went up to their room. Wide-awake, he lay back on the pillow, his mind whirling. He thought about all the things his grandmother had said over the years about Jeffries and Morgan and he mulled over what had happened that day.

'I *like* them,' he whispered. He rolled over on to his stomach and gazed at the pot of paint now standing under the window. 'And I'm going to see them both again tomorrow.'

## 11. And then there were four

HENRY AND JEFFRIES WERE ALMOST WEEPING WITH LAUGHTER. The three pairs of overalls Sergeant had brought to the school fitted them but drowned Pip. The crotch of his overalls hung so low that it reached his knees, making it impossible for him to walk, let alone paint a wall. The only part of him which was visible was his head.

'Stand on that chair,' commanded Sergeant.

Pip gathered the bottom half of the overalls up to his armpits and struggled to climb on to the seat.

'Dodge, you take the bottom of one trouser leg. Jeffries, you take the other. Now roll them up. I'll tie this piece of string round your waist, Pip.'

Eventually Pip's plimsolls came into view.

'Are you sure you're fourteen?' he asked Pip, rolling up his sleeves.

'Quite sure. Can we begin painting?'

As soon as they had begun covering the walls with the

paint, Pip started humming. Henry was used to this, because sometimes Pip got into trouble for doing it in class. Watching him closely, it was now obvious to Henry why he did it. Happiness made Pip hum.

'That's from *Words and Music*, isn't it?' asked Henry. '*Blue Moon*.'

'You're right,' stated Pip happily.

'How many times did you see it?' asked Jeffries.

'Once.'

'Once?' repeated Henry. 'How can you remember it all?'

'I just do,' he said simply. 'What kind of films do you like best, Jeffries?'

'Old films, like Alfred Hitchcock's *The Lady Vanishes*. And *The Hunchback of Notre Dame*. I'd really like to see *King Kong*. My mother was too scared to take me when it came out and I was too small to go on my own.'

'I like musicals, and films with animals in them, like *Lassie*,' said Pip.

'I know someone who likes musicals,' said Henry. 'Her name's Grace.'

'Is she your girlfriend?'

'No,' said Henry indignantly, 'she's just someone I met, that's all.'

'I'd like a girlfriend,' said Pip. 'But they don't like me.'

Henry and Jeffries glanced at one another.

'It's the same for me,' said Jeffries. 'But I don't want one.'

'Me neither,' said Henry.

'Though I do like Doris Day,' Jeffries added.

'So does Grace,' said Henry matter-of-factly.

It took them all morning to put the first coat of paint on the walls, ceiling, door, window frames and door frame. Sergeant appeared with three mugs of tea and a large portion of chips.

'Right,' he said, 'get this down you. An army marches on its stomach.'

They sat cross-legged on the floor, and after eating the chips, warmed their frozen fingers round the mugs, grinning at one another. Henry had never dreamt he could feel so happy.

'Ready for the second coat?' Sergeant enquired. 'We don't want them brushes going hard, do we? Start from where you began. It'll be drier there. And take your time. When you reach where you've just finished, it should be dry enough to paint over it.'

'What about the floor, sir?' asked Henry.

'If there's enough paint left, you can start from the far wall and work backwards towards the door.'

Later, after they had washed the paintbrushes and had scrubbed the paint from their hands, they peered into the room from outside to survey the day's work. They were all beaming at one another, pleased with what they had done. The red light bulb that had belonged to Mrs Beaumont's brother finished it off nicely.

'It's all down to Mr Finch now,' Sergeant said. 'You boys have done a good job.'

Strolling through the school gates, Henry's high spirits took a sudden nosedive when he realised that he couldn't invite them back to his house.

'Are you going to the Cinema Club tomorrow?' he asked Pip.

'Yes.'

'You don't, do you, Jeffries?'

'I go to the Odeon.'

'Why? The Plaza's much closer to you.'

Jeffries looked awkward.

'I knew you went there and wouldn't be too keen to see me.'

'You're right,' said Pip.

Henry shrugged.

'I don't mind.'

'You're sure?'

'Whoever gets there first saves a place for the others.'

'Me too?' asked Pip incredulously.

'You too.'

Henry was the first to arrive. The next person to turn up was neither Jeffries nor Pip. It was Grace.

'May I join you?' she asked.

Henry nodded. Having spoken about her to the others, he felt a little shy.

'I'm meeting some more people here,' he warned her.

'Oh. Will they mind if I tag along?'

'No, 'course not,' he added, trying to sound casual.

He spotted Jeffries walking up the steps and then falter when he caught sight of her. Henry gave him a wave.

'Jeffries, this is Grace.'

'Grace, Grace, the family disgrace,' she chanted.

'Why the family disgrace?' asked Jeffries.

'I keep being expelled from schools because I can't read.'

'You poor thing,' he said and he gave her a sympathetic smile.

To Henry's alarm, Grace's eyes suddenly filled up. Luckily Pip arrived.

'Pip,' said Henry quickly, 'this is Grace.'

'Grace, Grace, the family disgrace,' she said, hurriedly blinking.

But Pip was oblivious. He gazed stupefied at her and beamed.

'You're beautiful,' he said.

'Pip!' chorused Henry and Jeffries.

Grace laughed. Everything was going to be all right, thought Henry. They liked her and she liked them. The queue began to move slowly up the steps.

'But it was exciting when there was a fight between the saloon-keepers,' protested Grace as they left the Plaza together.

'I liked that bit too,' said Pip. 'And Hopalong Cassidy always sorts everything out.'

'But he looked like he'd just stepped out of a laundry!' said Jeffries.

'At least he didn't start singing,' added Henry.

'You're both being horrible. We liked it, didn't we, Pip?'

'Yes,' he said happily.

But it was obvious from the way he looked at her that if Grace had said she had enjoyed a film about a cow-pat, Pip would have said he had enjoyed it too.

When they left the cinema Henry wanted them to stay together.

'Let's get a pennyworth of scraps,' he suggested.

'What are they?' Grace asked.

'You've never eaten scraps?' asked Henry.

She shook her head.

'It's bits of crispy batter left over from the fish,' explained Jeffries. 'They sell them off in bags at the fish and chip shop.'

While they ate them on the railway bridge overlooking Hatton Station, the crossing bell began to ring.

'A train will be arriving soon,' said Henry.

'There's a Monty!' yelled Pip excitedly.

'Look out,' Henry warned Grace, 'it's a steam train.'

But they were enveloped in a smutty cloud before he could finish his sentence.

'I thought you liked electric trains,' said Jeffries.

'I like both,' said Pip happily. 'That's why Hatton Station is the best station in the world.'

'Why?' asked Grace, puzzled.

'Because both steam trains and electric pass through,' explained Jeffries, who was now just emerging through the cloud.

'Oh. By the way, why is your name Jeffries and not Jeffrey?'

'It's my surname.'

'I can't call you by your surname. That would be like you calling me Forbes-Ellis. What's your first name?'

'Roger.'

'I'll call you Roger, then.'

'Do you think you should be mixing with people like us?' Jeffries asked. 'You know we go to a secondary modern school?'

'Do you think you should be mixing with someone who keeps being expelled?'

When they had finished eating, Henry suggested they call in on Mrs Beaumont.

'She said we could rehearse our presentation at her house.'

He had no idea how she would take to the four of them turning up unexpectedly at her door, but he wanted her to meet his new friends. As soon as she set eyes on them she gave a broad smile and beckoned them in. Observing the others' expressions when they walked into the hall,

Henry wished he could have taken a photograph.

'Gosh,' he heard Jeffries whisper.

'Now it just so happens I have a tin of powdered lemonade in the kitchen. What do you say?'

'Good idea!' said Pip.

Although the kitchen was large, it was the warmest room in the house because of the range. Henry noticed some typed sheets and shiny blue-black pieces of paper at the end of the table.

'What are those?' asked Pip.

'Carbons,' she explained, 'for copies.'

Henry glanced at the neatly typed words on the top sheet.

'Did Mum type these?'

'Yes. She's wonderful. You didn't tell me she could do shorthand. I was going to write my stories out neatly so that she could read them but she suggested I dictate them to her instead.'

'Are you a writer?' asked Jeffries.

'Yes. But I haven't written for a very long time. These are stories I wrote three years ago.' She picked up a newspaper which was lying beside them. 'Grace, there's a film with Doris Day in it next week at the Apollo. It's an A. Do you want me to take you in?'

'Oh, yes,' she said.

'Me too,' said Jeffries.

'Is it a musical?' Pip asked.

'I'm not sure.' She glanced over at Henry. 'But if it is I doubt it will be entirely romantic. And the film with it is about racketeers so there should be plenty of crooks and wheeling and dealing for you.'

Henry smiled. He knew he was beaten.

Henry realised that sooner or later he would have to tell his grandmother he had spoken to Jeffries and Pip. He decided to wait till Sunday afternoon when Uncle Bill and his mother were out with Molly. He refilled Gran's coal bucket and then nervously sat down on the rug in her room. The wireless was playing *Family Favourites*.

'I hope that Mr Finch is pleased with what you done at half-term,' she said.

'Yeah, I expect he will be,' said Henry. He bit his lip. 'Gran,' he said slowly, 'about the History presentation, it's a bit difficult doing it on my own.'

'You're managing,' she said.

'Mr Finch wants us to work as a team, see.'

'Well, you can't and that's that.'

'And everyone else in the class is doing it together.'

'They haven't been put with the son of a deserter and a . . . you know.'

'Gran, what I'm going to tell you is going to upset you.'

His grandmother sat up straight and stared at him.

'Upset me?' she said slowly. 'I don't think anything you do would upset me.'

'This will, Gran.'

There was an awful silence. It was at this point that Henry decided to tell her only half the truth. But he'd start with the worst first and get it over with.

'I've been to see Jeffries.'

'You've what?' she said quietly.

'Mr Finch said I had to, see. He said that if I don't work with . . .' He stopped. 'He said I won't be allowed to take part in the presentation. And I'd be the only one, Gran. And I don't want to be the only one.'

'And you've spoken to him?'

'About the presentation.'

'I see.'

'I'm sorry, Gran.'

'I see,' she repeated.

'Gran, he's nice. I know what his father's done is terrible, but *he* didn't do it.'

To Henry's amazement she leaned forward and patted him on the knee.

'That's true,' she said. 'And if you think that's the right thing to do.'

'Well, I didn't, but I do now.'

'How did you know where to go?'

'Mr Finch gave me his address.'

'Well I never. I hope you didn't have to travel too far.'

'No. They live in Trafalgar Road, near the Kings Theatre.'

'Well I never. I used to walk down there quite often on the way to Disraeli Road before it was bombed.'

'Did you?' said Henry surprised.

'I sometimes do that now, so's I can sit in that little garden the council's made where the department store used to be.' She tapped her legs. 'When me pegs let me.' She gave a smile. 'Do you know, I'm sure I've passed the house where they live.'

'Was it big?'

'Oh, yes.' She looked thoughtful for a moment as though trying to remember. 'Number 63!' she exclaimed. 'Yes, that's the one.'

'No, Gran. It's Number 25. Right at the top.'

'Well I never,' said Gran. 'Fancy that.'

'So you don't mind, Gran?'

'Of course I don't mind, love. If that's what you think is best, you go ahead and do it.'

Henry laughed with relief.

She stayed looking at him, her head on one side, smiling.

'And?' she said.

Henry stared back at her.

'And,' he repeated. 'That's it.'

'You said that Mr Finch gave you Jeffries' address?'

'Yes, Gran.'

'So why didn't he give you that other boy's address? I mean, that don't seem very fair to me.'

'Well, Gran,' he struggled, 'I was going to tell you but I thought . . .'

'You didn't want me to have two shocks?'

'No.'

'You're a good boy, Henry.'

Henry smiled awkwardly.

'So,' she said, 'did you visit him too?'

'Yeah.'

Once Henry began talking, he couldn't stop. He hated keeping secrets from his gran. Describing what it was like visiting Jeffries and Pip, he could feel a massive weight on his chest dissolving. And she didn't get upset at all. She listened patiently and smiled. He was almost tempted to tell her about his mother typing for Mrs Beaumont, but then he remembered he had promised Mrs Beaumont to keep it a secret and changed his mind.

'Oh, Henry,' she said, 'I'm so glad we've had this little chat.'


'Why did you paint the room black?' asked Mr Finch.

It was the first day back after half-term and Mr Finch had alarmed Henry by taking him aside to have a quiet word. He kept his fingers crossed that Mr Finch wasn't still angry with him.

'You wanted a darkroom, sir.'

'I thought that might be the reason.' He cleared his throat. 'You don't need to have dark walls for a darkroom. You could turn a bathroom into a darkroom simply by covering the windows and putting a board over the bath to use as a table for the trays and equipment. A darkroom means not being in daylight. I suppose a better word for it would be a dim room. To avoid exposure, you just need to turn off the light.'

'Oh,' said Henry awkwardly.

'Not that I'm not grateful. In fact . . .' Mr Finch hurriedly examined his feet and Henry noticed the corner of his mouth twitching. 'You see, when Miss Dawson heard that the room had been emptied, she told the headmaster just before half-term that she had had her eye on it for some time as another laundry room for teaching the girls washing and ironing. The headmaster gave her permission to move in this morning.'

'Oh, no, sir!'

'However,' continued Mr Finch, 'unaware that your decorating team had visited it yesterday, as indeed I was . . .'

'We wanted it to be a surprise, sir,' interrupted Henry.

'Which it was, lad, which it was.' Mr Finch looked away again for a moment. 'Miss Dawson was all set to move in this morning with her mangle and ironing board . . .'

He broke off, unable to speak.

'And she walked into a black room,' finished Henry for him, imagining the look on Miss Dawson's face.

'With a red light bulb swinging from the ceiling,' added Mr Finch, his voice shaking.

For a while neither of them spoke.

'What did she say, sir?' Henry asked hesitantly.

'She didn't say anything, lad. She screamed and ran out.' Henry struggled to keep a straight face. By now neither of them dared look each other in the eye. 'So, it looks as though we'll have our darkroom after all.'

'You mean we might have lost it if we hadn't painted it black, sir?'

He nodded.

'So it's turned out to be necessary after all,' said Mr Finch.

Henry couldn't help smiling.

'This is one of those conversations which never happened, Dodge.'

'What conversation, sir?' asked Henry innocently.

## 12. Homeless

SCHOOL SEEMED LIKE A DIFFERENT PLACE. SINCE THE conversation with Mr Finch and his new friendship with Pip and Jeffries, Henry stopped pretending he didn't find the lessons easy. He jumped into French with abandon. He joined in with the mental arithmetic as though it were a game. He even stood up for the girls in Maths because he thought it unfair that Mr David never let them answer any of the questions. Eventually he was sent off to the head for his *insubordination* and a caning. Henry didn't mind, because he ended up making two new friends, Jane and Margaret. As he came out into the playground, clutching his throbbing hand, they were waiting for him.

'Thanks,' they said.

The biggest change was football. He finally admitted to himself that he didn't like it, even though he knew he would be letting Gran and his father down. Finding it boring didn't matter because Jeffries hated it, unlike Pip who was so enthusiastic about it, he almost made it interesting.

'He's good,' commented Jeffries when he and Henry were standing on the sidelines watching him.

'He's better than half the boys in the team, isn't he?' said Henry thoughtfully.

'Yes. But he'll never be picked for it.'

'I asked him the other day why he didn't get upset or angry at not being chosen.'

'What did he say?'

'He just accepts it. He thinks it's because he's not tall enough.'

'So he doesn't know the real reason?'

'No.'

And then it was the History lesson on Friday. To Henry's surprise he felt nervous again. Pip and Jeffries turned round and grinned at him. Henry gave them a casual nod.

As soon as their group was mentioned he flung his arm up.

'Yes, Dodge?' said Mr Finch.

Henry beamed.

'There's this man in London who has some old films,' he began.

'Henry tells me your mother was a ballerina, Roger. Is that right?'

They were all round at Mrs Beaumont's eating thick vegetable soup.

Jeffries nodded through a mouthful of bread.

'She was with a ballet company when she met my father and married him. The company had a season at the Kings Theatre. She gave it up to be near him. He had lots of pupils here. He was a piano teacher.'

'I wish my mother was a dancer,' sighed Grace.

'Didn't she miss it?' asked Mrs Beaumont.

'Yes. But she was tired of touring, so she didn't miss that. She used to teach at dance schools.'

'Why did she stop?'

Jeffries reddened.

'Because someone kept telling the parents of the children in her classes that she was married to a deserter and then they'd stop their children from going back. That's when she started to work at the corset factory until they found out there and she lost that job as well. That's why she had to turn down my place at the grammar school. She couldn't afford the uniform.'

Henry almost dropped his spoon.

'I didn't know you got into the grammar school,' he said.

Jeffries gave a shrug.

'I don't mind. If I'd gone there I would have had so much homework I wouldn't have had time to read books.'

'You're right,' said Pip, scraping his bowl.

'They let her back later but only so long as she worked from home. That way no one at the factory sees her.'

'Don't you have any relatives who could help you?' asked Mrs Beaumont, tipping more soup into Pip's bowl.

'They wouldn't have anything more to do with us when my mother refused to change her surname.'

'Why doesn't she move?' said Grace.

'We have to stay here so that my father has a chance of finding us if he comes back.'

Henry carried on eating, too stunned to speak. Gran always said that Mrs Jeffries had sent her son to Hatton School *out of spite*, but she was wrong. Suddenly he realised that by following his gran's advice and failing the eleven plus test for the grammar school, he and Jeffries had ended up together. The very person who had wanted to separate them had actually caused them to be in the same class.

Just then there was a knock at the front door.

'Will someone get that for me?' said Mrs Beaumont. 'Tell them I'll be there in a jiffy.'

Henry and Jeffries went up to the hall and opened the door. It took Henry a few seconds to recognise the distraught-looking woman standing in the porch.

'Mother!' cried Jeffries.

Her face was ashen.

'I'm so sorry,' she began, 'I should have waited till you got home.'

'Mrs Jeffries?' It was Mrs Beaumont. She must have followed them. She took hold of her hands. 'You're frozen.'

By now Mrs Jeffries had begun to shake.

'Mother, what is it?' Jeffries asked.

'Oh, Roger,' and her eyes welled up.

Mrs Beaumont put an arm round her and led her down to the kitchen, Henry and Jeffries behind them. 'Fill the kettle, boys. The cups are in the dresser.' She stoked the range, sat Mrs Jeffries by its warmth, poured some brandy into a small, elegant glass and pressed it into her hands. 'Drink that up,' she commanded.

Once Mrs Jeffries had taken a sip, she buried her face in her hands.

'Mother,' said Jeffries alarmed, 'are you ill?'

She raised her head slowly.

'We've got to leave,' she whispered. 'I've had the military police questioning me, asking me where your father is hiding. The landlady appeared and said she had no idea I was the wife of a deserter and she's given me a week's notice. If I don't find somewhere within a week . . .' She wrung her hands.

'Look no further,' said Mrs Beaumont, 'you can move in here. There's a room upstairs with two single beds if you want to share, and one with a double bed if you want to split up and sleep in separate rooms. Take your pick.'

Henry was astonished. Not only had Mrs Beaumont

not blinked an eyelid when Mrs Jeffries had mentioned the police, but she was inviting her into her own home, even when she knew that Private Jeffries was a deserter.

'But Mrs Beaumont,' stammered Mrs Jeffries.

'And that's another thing, you must call me Hettie.'

'But you don't know me.'

'I know enough. I suggest you move in here tomorrow. I'll order a taxi to bring your belongings.'

'Thank you, but the taxi driver will refuse to take us once the lodgers have told him . . .' Her voice trailed away.

'I've got a wheelbarrow,' said Mrs Beaumont.

'We've got one too,' Henry heard himself saying.

'But someone from the factory is coming tomorrow morning to pick up the corsets,' Mrs Jeffries said, anxiously.

'Good. We'll be there before he arrives and you can tell him your new address.'

'I don't know what to say.'

'You'll stay the night here, of course. You can wear a pair of my brother's pyjamas.'

'Oh, Mrs Beaumont,' laughed Mrs Jeffries.

'Hettie!'

'Hettie,' Mrs Jeffries repeated. 'And my name is Natasha. It's my stage name, but I've had it so long I'm used to it. Although come to think of it . . .' She broke off, almost near to tears. 'It must be ten years since anyone called me by my Christian name.'

*

Henry didn't get back home till nine o'clock. Uncle Bill was sitting at the kitchen table with another book.

'You're late for a Saturday,' he remarked.

'I was helping Mrs Beaumont. I need to borrow the wheelbarrow tomorrow. Someone's moving out of their lodgings. Is that all right?'

His stepfather closed the book and gazed at him.

'Of course it's all right.'

And then Henry realised that if his mother went round to Mrs Beaumont's house to do some typing, she was bound to meet Mrs Jeffries. He was going to have to warn her. And he knew that would upset her.

'Henry, what is it?'

'Uncle Bill,' he said slowly, 'there's something I've got to tell you.'


It was a bitter cold morning with a wind that penetrated his eardrums. Henry had arranged to go to Mrs Beaumont's house early. When he arrived, he found Jeffries and his mother in the kitchen clearing up after breakfast. Mrs Jeffries looked shattered.

Mrs Beaumont appeared at the door armed with hats and scarves.

No one spoke as they pushed the two wheelbarrows up towards the police station. They crossed the road just before they reached it and took a right turn, heading for

Number 25. Manoeuvring the wheelbarrows into a scrub of a garden, they propped them against the front wall. A group of children was playing nearby. They stared at them.

'Mrs Beaumont,' said Henry, quietly, 'I'd like to help but I don't want to leave these wheelbarrows unguarded.'

She gave the children a quick glance.

'I see what you mean,' she said. 'We'll take turns to keep an eye on them.'

She accompanied Jeffries and his mother into the house and within seconds three of the children strolled up to Henry.

'Watcha got them for?' said a boy Henry recognised from Form I.

'Putting stuff in,' said Henry casually.

'What stuff?'

'Dunno,' said Henry, shrugging.

A van from the corset factory drew up and a man in overalls walked up to the front door. Five minutes later he came out again, looking very flustered, carrying large bulging cotton bags.

'Your factory should be ashamed!' shouted the landlady after him. She waved a fist at him and stumped back inside.

Jeffries appeared looking angry.

'Go away!' he yelled at the children.

Henry had never seen this side of him before.

'The lodgers got into our room last night,' Jeffries said shakily. 'They found a photo of my father, smashed the frame and tore the photo up into little pieces.' At this he stifled a cry and looked away. 'They have no proof,' he choked out. 'A man is innocent until proved guilty. That's what they say, isn't it?'

Henry said nothing. Everyone knew Private Jeffries was a deserter. Why else wouldn't he have returned to his unit and not come home to Jeffries and his mum? Yet Henry could see how shocked and hurt Jeffries was by what had happened and he felt sorry for him.

'They ripped all the corsets my mother put together,' he croaked. 'Why did they do that? Luckily she'd put the sewing machine in its wooden case and locked it.'

Mrs Jeffries appeared, struggling with the sewing machine, a string bag with clothing in it hanging from her wrist. Mrs Beaumont followed, carrying a suitcase. Henry took the sewing machine from Mrs Jeffries and placed it in his wheelbarrow.

'Thank you, Henry.'

She walked over to her son, put her arms round him and they hung on to one another. Mrs Beaumont nudged Henry, indicating that they should be left alone. Back in the house the landlady was standing in the hallway, legs astride, her arms folded.

'I expect all that mess to be cleared up,' she stated firmly.

'I'm afraid we'll need to leave that there for evidence,' said Mrs Beaumont. 'The police might want to take fingerprints.'

'The police!' she snorted. 'What have the police got to do with it?'

'Somebody has broken into Mrs Jeffries' room. And by the way, how do you know there's a mess in there?'

The woman pursed her lips.

'I was waitin' for her to come home last night and when she didn't, I went upstairs to check up. She must have left her door unlocked. I can't watch who goes into whose rooms, can I?'

'It appears not,' said Mrs Beaumont.

She carried on up the stairs, Henry behind her.

'You ought to be ashamed of yourself mixing with the likes of her,' the landlady yelled after them.

As soon as they entered the room, Henry froze. Bits of clothing, ripped bed sheets and pages torn out of books were strewn across the floor. Photos of film stars from Jeffries' precious annuals were scattered among them.

'There's not much worth taking,' said Mrs Beaumont quietly. 'It looks like it's been destroyed by a mob.'

Painstakingly, Henry began to pick up the scraps from the two *Picture Goer's Annuals*.

'His mother gave him these as Christmas presents. He practically knows them by heart.'

'How could they be so cruel?' said Mrs Beaumont

angrily. 'Do you know they tore up all the corsets? Undid all her hard work?'

Henry nodded.

'Hopefully the factory will report it to the police. I gave my address to the man who came to collect them.'

'Do you think they'll take fingerprints?'

Mrs Beaumont shook her head.

'I just said that to worry her.'

Henry glanced at the tiny fireplace. Remains of kindling were lying on the stone square in front of the iron bars among broken glass. It looked as if they had helped themselves to coal as well.

'Private Jeffries must have known this would happen,' said Henry angrily. 'He should have given himself up.'

'Yes. A prison sentence and the slate would have been wiped clean.'

'Why does she wait for him?'

'She's convinced he hasn't deserted. She says he's not that kind of man. She thinks he's wandering round somewhere in a confused state.'

'How can she believe that?'

'Henry, she knows him. We don't. Now, let's look for anything worth keeping.'

A creak on the landing made them swing round. Standing in the doorway was Mrs Jeffries. She gazed stupefied at the room.

'They were so friendly to us here. Nothing's changed.

We're still the same people. We're not monsters.'

'But they are,' muttered Henry. To his alarm he found himself thinking of Gran. Was she a monster? And then he was ashamed of himself for even thinking of her in that way.

Mrs Jeffries gave a sad smile.

'Thank you.' She spotted the remains of the film annuals in his arms. 'Oh, that is kind,' she exclaimed and she hurriedly turned her face away.

The landlady was still waiting for them down in the hall, grim-faced.

Mrs Jeffries headed swiftly for the porch.

'Your key, I believe,' Mrs Beaumont said, holding it out to the landlady, 'or one of them.'

'And what do you mean by that?'

'Oh, I think you know,' said Mrs Beaumont, walking away. 'Mrs Jeffries told me that she is always very careful to lock her door and yesterday was no exception.'

'Good riddance!'

'My sentiments exactly,' retorted Mrs Beaumont over her shoulder as the door slammed behind her.

Henry carried the bundle of paper over to Jeffries. He looked near to tears.

'I thought we could stick some of the pages together,' said Henry.

'Or you could put them on your bedroom wall,' said Mrs Beaumont. 'They could hide the ghastly wallpaper.'

'Really?' said Jeffries, suddenly smiling. 'Can I really?'

'Of course you can. And now,' said Mrs Beaumont, smiling, 'I can go up to London more often, without worrying about squatters.'

'You mean I'll be helping you by staying in your house?' said Mrs Jeffries.

'Yes. You're my diamond in the dungheap.'

'What do you mean?'

'When life is more than somewhat rough, I call those times the dungheap and I look for the diamond in it. Sometimes it's easy to find. It just glitters among the mess and you can pick it out easily. Sometimes you have to dig deep to find it. Other times you have to wait awhile till it rises to the surface.'

Mrs Jeffries smiled. 'I've never been called a diamond before!'

Henry decided to go for a walk to clear his head after the morning's events. It seemed as if his brain was shifting. Whatever was happening inside him was making him look outwards in a different way and he needed to be alone to take it in. He headed immediately for the seafront. Striding down the streets, he was aware of wanting to move more quickly. It was as though he was carrying a volcano inside him and if he didn't physically push some of it out of his body, he would explode. He drove himself on, pushing against the bitter wind. Once he reached the stretch of common, an extraordinary sense of exhilaration swept over him. It didn't make sense. He had seen his friend treated like a common criminal. How could he feel so happy? He paused for a moment and then made for the road which led to the esplanade, with its splintered pavements and potholes.

And then he was on the beach, stumbling haphazardly and clumsily along the shingle to the grey-green expanse of sea. It bubbled towards him with a great rushing sound like an exhalation of breath. His hands planted solidly on his hips, he threw his head back and breathed it in, letting the sound of the waves soak into him. His shoulders felt lighter and he took in great gulps of air. He was letting go of something old and putrid, and in the letting go he felt a rush of pure adrenalin rising up through his throat. He now knew the cause of his happiness. All the hatred he had carried around inside him for years had been like a hard stone in the pit of his stomach, weighing down every bone in his body. Now that it had dissolved and left him, he felt light, so light, he wanted to leap into the sky.

He took out the camera. It was too dark to take a photograph, but he didn't care. Through the viewfinder he framed the lights from the island and a ferry approaching.

'Henry,' his mother said quietly, 'come into the scullery for a moment, will you?'

A week had already flown by at breakneck speed. Early that morning he had been round at Mr Jenkins' shop, cleaning the yard and running messages for him, returning home with enough money to see Humphrey Bogart in *Tokyo Joe*. And that was in addition to his pocket money, which he had planned to use to see *The Big Fight*. Knowing he would be able to see two good films put him in a good mood, so he was completely unprepared for the serious expression on his mother's face.

He noticed his stepfather giving his mother a quick glance. Henry followed her nervously, racking his brains as to what he might have done wrong. She closed the door behind them.

'What's all the secrecy?' he asked.

'That's what I should be asking you.'

And then Henry remembered the conversation he had had with his stepfather about Mrs Jeffries moving into Mrs Beaumont's house and how Uncle Bill had suggested that Henry should break the news to his mother about it. He felt his face grow hot.

'I think you have something to tell me, don't you?'

Henry looked down at his feet, mortified. How could he have forgotten to warn her?

'I knew you were working with Morgan and Jeffries on the presentation,' she said, 'because Gran let it slip. She thought I'd be shocked, but I wasn't because I didn't think you'd disobey Mr Finch. But she obviously doesn't know about Mrs Jeffries moving out of her lodgings and into Mrs Beaumont's house.'

'Did Uncle Bill tell you?'

'No. But he did tell me you were going to tell me before I went round there. Why didn't you?'

'I forgot.'

'Is that the truth?'

'Sort of. I didn't want to upset you.'

'Did you think I might not go round there to type for her if I knew?'

'Would you have?'

'I'm not sure.'

'Does that mean you won't be going there again?'

She looked embarrassed.

'Funnily enough, we got on really well, once we'd recovered from bumping into each other in the kitchen. Mrs Beaumont was in her element, of course, chatting away as if nothing was wrong and making tea. It's strange. All these years, I've dreaded meeting her again. And there was really no need.'

'I like Jeffries too, Mum.'

'It's a relief, isn't it?'

Henry nodded.

'Mum, what do you mean, *again*?'

'Since your father's funeral.'

'But they weren't there.'

She looked at him, puzzled.

'Yes, they were, love. It was her husband who didn't turn up. She and her son did.'

'I thought none of the Jeffries turned up.'

'Oh,' she said, surprised. 'I suppose you were too young to remember. But I thought Gran would have said.'

'No.'

'If I hadn't met her at Mrs Beaumont's, I would never have realised what a lovely person she is. I'm really proud of what you did for her. She told me all about it.'

'You're right about Gran, by the way,' said Henry. 'She doesn't know.'

'Oh dear, it's difficult, isn't it?'

'Yeah.'

'There's something else I wanted to mention. Mrs Beaumont asked me if she could take you up to London again next weekend, and Uncle Bill and I have agreed to let you go. She's taking someone called Grace with her too. She said she's a friend of yours.'

The day before he was due to leave for London, Henry went to see a film on his own. Mrs Beaumont had gone with the others to see a visiting ballet company at the Kings Theatre. It had been a while since he had had to ask a stranger to take him into an A film. He looked up and down the queue hoping to find a familiar face. And then he spotted a man he saw every week. He hesitated.

'Mr Finch?'

Mr Finch swung round and looked him straight in the eye.

But instead of asking him, Henry heard himself saying, 'I'm going to London tomorrow and I'm going to finish my roll of film there, and I wondered, sir, if I could use the darkroom when I come back?'

'Certainly,' said Mr Finch. 'And yes, I will take you in.' And he gave Henry a broad smile.

# 13. Liza

'*A LITTLE PRINCESS* IS A LOVELY STORY,' SAID MRS BEAUMONT, 'I'll begin reading that to you when I've finished *Five Go to Smuggler's Top*.'

'Great-Aunt Florence still thinks I should finish my homework before coming round for another chapter,' said Grace.

'But that would mean never.'

'That's what I told her.'

'And after a day of horrors at school, a generous helping of a story will give you a much-needed boost before facing the homework horrors.'

Grace laughed.

'If Pip were here he'd say, "You're right."'

'Exactly,' said Mrs Beaumont.

They were on the train journey to Waterloo. Henry couldn't remember ever not being able to read. Secretly he believed it was Grace's way of getting out of it, like he did. While she and Mrs Beaumont chatted, he took out the camera and peered through the viewfinder. Mrs Beaumont began reading a novel and Grace looked at photographs of a ballet company in a Penguin paperback.

'Could you read that bit for me?' she asked him.

She was pointing to some writing under a film still. Henry shook his head.

'I don't like reading aloud,' he explained.

'Please!' she begged.

'I'm sure if you try a bit harder, you can do it yourself.'

She gave a sharp nod.

'Yes,' she said brightly, 'I just need to try harder.' And she turned away.

Henry looked out of the window and caught sight of her reflection in the glass. She was crying. She was so silent that even Mrs Beaumont hadn't noticed. He had made a girl cry, and not any girl. He had made Grace cry.

He wanted to apologise, but he suspected she didn't want anyone to know she was upset. And there was one thing which shamed him even more. When he saw her reflection in the window, he was thinking what a good photograph it would make.

'Grace?' he heard Mrs Beaumont ask softly. 'What is it?'

'I've got some beastly smut in my eye,' she said, attempting to make light of it.

'Here,' said Mrs Beaumont, pulling a handkerchief from her bag. 'If you hold out your eyelid until your eye starts watering, that should wash it out.'

Within minutes she was blowing her nose.

'Would you like me to read to you?'

'Oh, yes, please!'

When the train drew into Waterloo, Henry leapt out of the carriage so that he could take a photograph of them stepping down on to the platform. To his annoyance Grace stepped off too quickly for him to catch her. He stood with the viewfinder level with where he thought Mrs Beaumont's face would be. And then there she was, looking down at the bag she was carrying. As soon as she turned to look at him, he snapped her.

'I should have expected that,' she laughed. 'How much film do you have left now?'

'Enough for one more photograph. Mr Finch said I can use the darkroom on Monday. He's going to show me what to do.'

'That's exciting. I'll be able to see the photograph my brother took before he died.'

After a light supper at Mrs Beaumont's London house, Henry was eager to be back in the room with the boxes. It was bitterly cold, but when he touched the camp bed it felt warm. He pulled aside the covers and found a hot brick wrapped up in a tea towel. There was a crackling sound from Daniel's room like a needle being put on a gramophone record. He slipped out on to the landing and sat at the top of the stairs. Violin music spilled out from under Daniel's door. As he listened to it he felt an intense sadness. It was as though a hand had moved into his chest and was squeezing his heart. But it was impossible to move away and so he stayed, growing colder and more miserable.

And then the music changed. The grief lifted and he felt happy, as if the joy had been lying hidden inside him and had surfaced. Once the music had ended and he rose to creep back to his room something caught his eye. Sitting huddled in a green school coat and nightdress on the next flight of stairs was someone else who had been listening. It was Grace.

After breakfast the next day they caught a 38 bus to Shaftesbury Avenue. They followed Mrs Beaumont down Charing Cross Road past a huge, ornate building, the Prince's Theatre. Pictures and posters outside advertised *King's Rhapsody*. Grace ran over to look at them. Women in long dresses and white gloves, tiaras on their heads, stood under a massive chandelier, a hundred or more lamps lit in its twisting ornate ironwork. In front of them a handsome man in a dark uniform with a sash across his chest stood next to a young woman.

'Is it a play?' asked Grace.

'A musical,' said Mrs Beaumont, 'by a man called Ivor Novello.'

'What beautiful costumes.'

They crossed the road.

'This is Charing Cross Road. It will probably give you a heart attack, Henry. It's full of bookshops, mostly second-hand.'

'But why are we here?' asked Grace, a note of anxiety creeping into her voice.

'Christmas presents,' she said. 'Also, I want you to choose some books I can read to you. I'm a bit out of touch. There are children's books in paperback now. Puffins, I think they're called.' She pointed to a tall building on a corner. 'That's where I'm taking you. There's a whole floor there which has children's books.'

As they approached it, Grace tugged at Henry's arm.

'Look!'

In the front window, displayed on white net, were twenty or more green paperback books. On the covers were two girls in tutus balanced on pointed shoes in a pale yellow cloud.

'This book has a whole window all to itself,' she said.

'It's called *Ballet Shoes*,' said Henry quietly, before she needed to ask. 'It's by some bloke called Noel Streatfeild. It's a Puffin story book and it's one and sixpence.'

'Thank you,' said Grace.

He had hated reading the information out and especially in public, but it was worth it to see her smile.

As soon as they entered the shop, Mrs Beaumont marched up to an assistant.

'Excuse me,' she said. 'I'd like to buy *Ballet Shoes* by Mr Streatfeild. Could you direct me?'

'Upstairs on the children's floor. There are lots more of her books on display there, including her latest one, *The Painted Garden.*'

'Her?'

'Yes, Madam. Noel Streatfeild is a woman.'

As they walked away from the cashier upstairs, the new book clasped in Grace's hands, she whispered, 'Are you sure I don't have to read it myself?'

'No,' said Mrs Beaumont firmly, '*I* am going to read it to *you*. I'm off to browse through the little one's section now. I want to find something for Molly. You two go off on your own.'

After a while Mrs Beaumont joined them with some paperback picture books for Molly.

'Now let's go elsewhere to find books for Pip and Jeffries,' she said. 'What do you think they'll like, Henry?'

'Pip will like anything with machinery in it and Jeffries would like something about directors and films.'

They looked in the second-hand bookshops and left Charing Cross Road with a book on cinema projectors and equipment for Pip and some second-hand film annuals for Jeffries.

They were following Mrs Beaumont down a lane off Oxford Street when Grace gave a sudden cry. On the opposite side of the road, painted on the wall, was a large picture of a ballerina in a tutu. She was balanced on the toes of one foot, her other leg folded outwards, her arms curved above her head.

'There's a shop window filled with ballet shoes,' and she pointed to a window underneath.

As if by instinct, Henry had already pulled out the camera. He watched her dash across the road and ran after her. As soon as she turned round to say something, he took her photograph. He was aware that there was a man standing nearby.

'Drat!' he muttered. 'Fingers crossed you're not in my picture.'

Someone hooted at him from a car and he realised he was standing in the middle of the road. He stepped quickly up on to the pavement.

'Henry!' Mrs Beaumont exclaimed. 'You nearly got run over.'

'That's it,' he said. 'I've used up all the film.'

He felt bereft. Once the film was removed, he would have to hand the camera back.

'Cheer up,' she said. 'You can get the film developed now.'

He nodded, overwhelmed with sadness.

'Then you'll be ready for a new roll.'

'You mean I can still use the camera?' he said, unable to stop himself grinning.

'Of course. Now come on. I need to get to the club.'

'What club?' asked Grace.

'You'll see.'

*

A man wearing a massive jumper with a colourful scarf and wide-brimmed hat opened a basement door. He looked as though he had been up all night. He nodded to Mrs Beaumont as if expecting her. They walked down a dimly lit corridor.

'Do you think this is a gangsters' dive?' whispered Grace to Henry.

Along the walls were photographs of black and white singers and musicians. In the background Henry could hear a saxophone and a piano and the faint swish of a cymbal.

'It's a jazz club,' Mrs Beaumont explained.

They entered a basement, which had tables and chairs and old sofas pushed up against the walls. Three black musicians, a tubby pianist, a tall saxophonist and a cheeky-faced drummer were sitting on a small platform. A dark-haired man greeted Mrs Beaumont with a broad smile and strode across the room towards them. He flung his arms round Mrs Beaumont and hugged her.

'This is my elder son, Oscar, and that's how he likes to be addressed. No Misters, please.'

'Hello,' he said, beaming, 'you must be Henry and Grace.'

'Yes,' said Grace and immediately added, 'Grace, Grace, the family disgrace.'

'Grace, do you have any other names?' asked Mrs Beaumont.

'My second name is Elizabeth, after one of the princesses.'

'Elizabeth,' she murmured.

The musicians on stage broke into a number. Grace moved towards them as if in a dream.

'What's that you're playing?' she asked when they had finished. 'It's beautiful.'

'*Liza,*' said the pianist. Henry noticed he had an American accent. 'Short for Elizabeth.'

'Liza!' repeated Mrs Beaumont and her son in unison.

Henry stared at them, baffled. Why were they getting so excited about a name?

'Grace, would you like to sing with them?'

'Oh, yes, I'd love to,' she said sadly and she gave a resigned sigh.

'I mean now, Grace.'

Her face reddened.

'Now?' she repeated in disbelief.

'Up you come, young lady,' said the pianist.

As soon as Grace had clambered on to the platform in her baggy woollen stockings, jumper and kilt, he beckoned her over. Grace flung back her plaits and almost danced towards him. She beamed at them and then to Henry's dismay he saw the pianist point to the music.

'Shall we try this? Tell me if you need more light to read the words.'

Grace's face fell.

'I'm afraid I can't read,' she stammered, her head down.

Henry wanted to rescue her. He wanted to grab her and take her out of the building but the pianist just nodded towards the saxophonist and said, 'Ah, you're like Joseph over there.'

'Letters all floatin' about?' Joseph remarked.

Grace stared at him in astonishment. Then she nodded.

'I got that too. So's a clarinet player I know. Can't make sense of anything that's written down.'

'Yes, that's it!' cried Grace.

'He was always gettin' beatings at school, but once he left, that's when he began to learn. Oh, yes. And he's a mean player,' he added with warmth.

'You mean there are other people like me?'

'Sure is honey. I bet you've a terrific memory.'

'She has,' said Mrs Beaumont.

'Righty,' said the pianist, 'let's try this.'

He played a few bars and sang some words in a gravelly sort of voice.

'Now you try,' he said.

Henry listened to her sing in that embarrassingly odd way of hers, keeping an eye on the musicians. If they thought she was terrible they weren't showing it.

'I think we can take that down a notch or two, don't you?'

Grace nodded happily.

'Grace, I'm taking Henry off to meet someone,' said Mrs Beaumont. 'Would you like to stay here this afternoon?'

'Oh, yes,' she breathed.

As Henry walked down the corridor with the framed photographs, he glanced aside at Mrs Beaumont.

'Are there really other people who can't read?' he asked.

'Yes. I'd come across it before but I had no idea that one of the musicians would have the same difficulties as her. That was pure luck.'

Henry hoped the luck would last. He didn't want Grace to be humiliated again.

'Where are we going?' he asked, as they headed up the steps into daylight.

'To find a Victorian camera.'

As they were waiting at a bus stop Henry suddenly remembered the conversation he had had with his mother.

'I'm sorry I didn't tell Mum about Mrs Jeffries moving in.'

'Yes. She did look rather shocked. But I'm glad you didn't. I might never have seen her again.'

'Was it terrible when they met?'

'Somewhat. The world stopped on its axis and all that.'

'Mum said you made tea.'

'Yes. It was rather like pretending not to notice there was an elephant in the kitchen.' She gave him a searching look. 'But they discovered that sometimes facing your prejudices helps them evaporate. Do you agree?'

'Yes,' said Henry happily and he laughed at what an idiot he had been.

'I'm afraid it's rather a mess,' said the elderly man who answered the door and invited them in. 'I could do with an assistant.' And he gave a tired smile.

As they stepped into a colossal hall, Henry could see, through the open doors, three massive rooms, filled with old furniture. The house seemed like a museum.

'I hire out all sorts of artefacts to film companies as properties,' the man explained.

One room was filled to the ceiling with old velvet curtains, twisting in and out of cameras on tripods and Victorian furniture.

'This is Jeffries' kind of place,' Henry murmured.

'It's very good of you to allow us to visit,' said Mrs Beaumont.

'Not at all. I'd like more people to see what's here.'

'How much did Daniel tell you?'

'Something about a presentation about life in Victorian times. I've selected three Victorian movie cameras for you to look at.'

'Daniel's taking old films down to Henry's school,' explained Mrs Beaumont.

'Ah. And he'd like to take one or two of these with him?'

'Is that possible?'

'He'll need a hand carrying them. They're quite a weight.'

'One of my sons and a young friend have offered to help.'

'Just tell me when you need to borrow them,' said the man. 'I'm sure we can work something out.'

Henry was staring at the large lenses of the cameras. They looked magnificent.

'People really used these?' he exclaimed.

'Oh, yes,' said the man, beaming.

'I wish the others could see them.'

'Hopefully they will,' Mrs Beaumont said.

When they were back on the bus again, Mrs Beaumont had another surprise for him.

'Before we pick up Grace, I'm taking you to see two more foreign films at cinemas which specialise in silent films.'

'Italian?' asked Henry.

'No. The first one is German. It's called *Metropolis*.'

'Is it a Victorian film?'

'No. It was made in 1926. Shades of things to come. Science fiction.'

Henry found himself thinking of Jeffries again.

'Mrs Beaumont, Jeffries lost one of his favourite books when those lodgers ransacked their room. It was the same book your son Max liked, *War of the Worlds*, and I was wondering . . .'

'A Christmas present?'

'Yeah.'

'A splendid idea. We should have time to nip back to Charing Cross Road later.'

After *Metropolis*, Henry sat silently upstairs in another bus, his mind filled with images of workers in their identical overalls swaying in time in underground tunnels like sleepwalking robots. He was so absorbed in thinking about the mass riots and the evil inventor in the film that he nearly didn't notice Mrs Beaumont getting off.

'So what's this other silent film called?' he asked, scrambling after her.

'*The Battleship Potemkin*,' she said. 'It's Russian.'

Like *Metropolis*, the second film was also about people rising up.

Immediately, Henry was on the side of the sailors who had refused to eat meat crawling with maggots, and he was angry when their officers began to punish them for protesting. But when the sailors fought back, took over the ship and brought it and the injured sailors into the port of Odessa, their victory seemed to be a happy one. In the port, ordinary citizens, out for a stroll in the sunshine, observed the battleship entering the harbour. But just as Henry was watching these innocent bystanders, troops of soldiers, sent to crush the mutiny, appeared at the top of the Odessa steps, their long boots marching down in perfect unison as they fired on the unarmed and terrified citizens, the smoke billowing from their guns. An old man was shot and a young mother fell senseless against her pram, causing it to judder down the steps, the abandoned baby inside screaming in terror.

A dark stain of blood suddenly spread across the smashed lens of an elderly woman's spectacles, and in the midst of all the horror, a woman carried her little boy, now lifeless, up towards the marching feet to show the soldiers what they had done.

'What do you think?' whispered Mrs Beaumont in the dark after the film had ended.

'I liked both films,' said Henry, 'but this one was . . .' he searched for the right word, 'more terrible.'

'More powerful?'

'Yeah, that's it. More powerful.'

It was late when they arrived back at the club. Young women and bearded men in duffel coats were pushing themselves eagerly into the basement, now packed with people sitting, drinking and talking in a fog of cigarette smoke, or whirling round each other in the tiny space in the middle of the floor. From the platform, four musicians were playing a swinging upbeat kind of music.

Mrs Beaumont dragged Henry quickly towards a table in the corner, half hidden by a pillar.

'You're a mite too young to be here,' she explained.

In the shadows Henry looked round nervously. He spotted a portly man in an evening jacket smoking a cigarette by the bar.

'That's the boss,' said Mrs Beaumont. 'Oscar told me he would be here tonight.'

The musicians on stage announced that they were taking a break and the couples who had been dancing returned to the tables or stood by the bar or walls, chatting and laughing.

'Mrs Beaumont, why have we come back here?' asked Henry. 'And where's Grace?'

Before she could answer, Oscar appeared at the table with lemonade for them, before returning to his place at the bar. He looked quite different from when Henry had last seen him. His suit was black and below his clean-shaven face was a brightly coloured tie.

'You'll find out,' she said. 'Be patient.'

He noticed that a new group of musicians were coming on to the platform. Among them he recognised the pianist, drummer and saxophonist.

The musicians glanced at one another, the pianist gave a nod and they began to play. It was just the sort of music he imagined Grace would have liked. It was a shame she was missing it all. Then Henry heard a piece of music he recognised. When they had finished playing, the saxophonist brought a microphone to the front.

'That was *Liza*,' he announced, 'first recorded by the

Benny Goodman sextet, and it introduces us to an up-and-coming new singer. Ladies and gentleman, would you please give a very warm welcome to Miss Liza Beaumont.'

'Liza *Beaumont*!' exclaimed Henry.

'No, I don't have a daughter. It's a sort of *nom de plume*.'

'Nom de what?'

'I wanted to keep her identity secret in case her family find out and disapprove and also the name *Beaumont* is known here. And it meant Oscar could persuade his boss to hear her.'

'Hear who?'

As the saxophonist finished lowering the microphone, Grace appeared, only she was no longer in the clothes she had been wearing when she had arrived. Instead, she wore a long red satin dress with a little brocaded jacket, and her un-plaited hair sprang out round her face like a crinkly black halo. She walked up to the microphone and glanced at the pianist with a smile.

Henry was stunned. When he turned to speak to Mrs Beaumont, he could see by the expression on her face that she had known all along.

'What the hell is going on?' Henry heard the boss at the bar whisper angrily. 'Get her off immediately! What does he think he's doing? Beaumont!'

Oscar Beaumont was now by the boss's side and there was more angry whispering. 'You didn't tell me your cousin was this age. She's far too young to be here. This is not a Butlins Holiday Camp talent show!' Henry heard the boss spitting. 'I'll be in enough trouble with the law if it gets out I have American musicians performing here, without this. Do you want me shut down? Get her off now or you'll be sacked.'

On stage, Grace looked transported. Luckily the light was in her eyes, so she was unable to see the drama in the darker part of the club. Before Oscar could reach her, she had begun to sing.

Henry sunk his face into his hands. Now everyone would hear her strange low voice, but when she had finished singing, Oscar still didn't remove her. Like the other people in the club, he remained motionless.

'And now Liza is going to sing the song Sarah Vaughan made so famous,' the pianist announced. 'Ladies and gentlemen, I give you, *Black Coffee*.'

And Grace sang so low that even the people sitting at the tables seemed frozen. *This is terrible*, thought Henry. *How could they be so cruel?* As she sang the closing notes, she smiled and turned to watch as the pianist and saxophonist quietly played the song out.

This was followed by a silence so excruciating that Henry thought he would explode. He was just about to stand up and yell, 'That's enough!' when the whole room erupted into applause and cheers and stamping. They loved her! And he could see that Grace was happy and at home up there on the platform.

'Pip's right,' he murmured. 'She is beautiful.'

When she had taken several bows and left the stage, the band went on to play the next number and the boss moved swiftly towards their table.

'Mrs Beaumont, I presume.' And he gave a grim smile. 'What do you mean by sneaking someone so young under my roof?'

'You wouldn't have heard her otherwise, would you?'

'Absolutely not.'

'And now that you have?'

'She's a jewel. Bring her back next year with a chaperone.'

'She has two with her already,' said Mrs Beaumont. 'One of them made the dress.'

'Quite a little conspiracy, eh?'

'Planned to perfection,' answered Mrs Beaumont.

Henry and Mrs Beaumont met Grace, Violet and Jessica by the cloakroom. Grace was wearing a large overcoat over her dress.

'They didn't laugh at me, did they, Mrs Beaumont?'

'Of course they didn't. But then I knew they wouldn't. You've just spent years of your young life being in the wrong place, that's all.'

## 14. In the dark

ON MONDAY, IN THE DINNER BREAK, MR FINCH AND HENRY MET in the school darkroom.

Standing under the red light, Henry gazed stupefied at the shelves on the walls, now stacked with strange equipment and bottles. Below them, two shelves, the width of tables, ran alongside the wooden draining board and the wall opposite. Under the ceiling hung what appeared to be a washing line with metal clips attached to it.

'There's a wet side and a dry side,' said Mr Finch.

'The wet side is where the sink is,' Henry said.

'That's right. That's for developing. The other side is for printing.'

There were beakers, bottles of strange chemicals, boxes of powder, packets of paper, tin trays of various sizes and depths, newspaper, tweezers, a black cylindrical container, and a large machine on the printing side that resembled an enormous black microscope with bellows and lens.

'That's the enlarger,' said Mr Finch.

There was even a thermometer and alarm clock and, standing by the socket, a one-bar electric heater.

'Is the film still in the camera?'

'Yes, sir. I didn't take it out in case I exposed it.'

Henry handed him the camera and watched him move a knob at the side under the dim red light.

'I'm turning the spool on which most of the film is now on,' he explained. 'I'll open the camera when I've reached the end of the roll.'

'How will you know that, sir?'

'There'll be no resistance. It'll move more easily. With a camera like this, you can open it in a dim light. The type of film you use in it will have paper backing, which helps protect the film from any sudden exposure.'

Henry smiled. It was hard to believe that this was the same person who had been so unfriendly towards him when he first showed him the camera at the photography club. Now Mr Finch seemed eager to explain how everything worked.

Once the back of the camera was open, Henry could see that the film was wrapped round a spool at the top. Mr Finch levered up a flat metal circle beside it, which drew the pin away from the spool and released it.

'See this sticky band here,' he said, pointing to a flap

at the end of the film, 'you need to press it down firmly to seal it. You don't want it unravelling.'

Henry handed him his new box of film.

'Watch carefully,' said Mr Finch.

Henry nodded, sweating with excitement. He had waited a long time for this moment and he was determined to learn as much as possible.

It wasn't until the next evening that they were ready to work in the dry side of the darkroom. This time Pip and Jeffries joined them. Mr Finch stood in front of two dishes filled with liquid, peering intently at a thermometer. He placed a piece of paper that had been on the printing frame into the tray of developing fluid on the left. The paper was completely blank. Mr Finch lifted the side of the tray and gently moved it up and down so that the fluid swirled around.

'You need to keep doing this,' he explained.

'Agitating it,' added Henry.

'That's right. Then the picture will develop evenly. I'll give it three minutes. The black part of the picture will be properly black by then.'

'Mr Finch found out that nine photographs had been taken,' Henry explained to his friends.

'But I thought you could only take eight,' said Jeffries.

'Ah, but if you're canny, when you wind the new film on, you can squeeze in another before the number one shows in the window,' explained Mr Finch.

'When you see a pointing finger or asterisks,' added Henry.

'And obviously the man who owned this camera knew that,' said Mr Finch.

As faces began to emerge under the fluid, Henry was conscious of a lump in his throat. The picture would either be one of the two photographs Mrs Beaumont's brother had taken, or one of his. In seconds he knew it wasn't his handiwork.

'Who are they?' whispered Pip.

A group of people were sitting round a table. He recognised it as the one he and Mrs Beaumont had carried downstairs to her kitchen. The people were raising glasses of wine and facing the camera. Hanging above them was a makeshift banner with the words HAPPY NEW 1949.

'Do you know any of them?' asked Jeffries.

'Yes. That's Max and Oscar Beaumont. They're Mrs Beaumont's sons,' he said, pointing. 'The tall man with the white hair is called Daniel. He's the man who's coming to show us the films. The woman sitting next to him is Jessica. She'll be playing the piano. Two of the other men came to see *Bicycle Thieves*.'

One had a beard. He was the man who had shouted 'bebop' round the door when *Salt Peanut* was being played at Mrs Beaumont's house.

'I don't know who he is,' he said, pointing to a stocky man with thick dark curly hair.

Mr Finch lifted the photograph out of the dish with the tweezers, holding it in the air.

'I'm letting the fluid drain off. If you hold it by the corner it helps it drain more quickly. Now we need to wash it before putting it into the fixing solution. We don't want any of the developing fluid to get into it.'

Later Mr Finch hung the photograph on the line above their heads, weighing it down with metal clips so that it didn't curl, and then placed a second piece of paper into the tray on the left. A face emerged which was instantly recognisable. It was Jessica. She was sitting on a rough brick wall, a large leafless tree bending in the wind behind her. A young man in uniform was sitting beside her, his arm around her, while she appeared to be attempting to prevent her hair from flying across her face. They were both laughing.

'That's Jessica again. The man must be her fiancé, Ralph. He's the actor who got hold of the black paint.'

The third photograph to come through the developing fluid was the first one Henry had taken. It was of the children running down the steps in front of the Plaza.

'This is a good one!' said Mr Finch enthusiastically.

'I had to wait a long time to get what I wanted,' said Henry.

'Well, your patience has been rewarded, lad.'

'It's a beauty!' Jeffries enthused.

'Ah. This one is not so good,' said Mr Finch, looking at another photograph some time later.

It was of Grace and Mrs Beaumont crossing the road to the Plaza.

'Yeah. It's too crowded to see them clearly,' commented Henry.

'You're right,' said Pip.

They waited patiently for Mr Finch to rinse and fix it and submerge the next piece of paper into the tray. This time it was Mrs Beaumont, caught off guard as she stepped out of the train at Waterloo Station.

'What do you think?' Mr Finch asked.

'Same thing. You can hardly see Mrs Beaumont.'

Disappointed, Henry hung back silently while he and his friends watched Mr Finch take it out of the tray with the tweezers.

'I'll show you how to crop and enlarge it,' said Mr Finch. 'That's where the artistry comes in.'

When the next two photographs were developed, Henry found himself trembling.

'I like this one,' said Mr Finch, pointing to the first of them. 'Who is she?'

'Molly. My half-sister.'

She looked beautiful. Her hair was tangled and there

was dirt on her face, but there was an eagerness in her eyes that was compelling. His mum had always said she was bright, but Henry had never seen it before. He had taken it by their bedroom window.

The second photograph startled him in a different way. It was supposed to be of his mother and it was a good one. She looked tired but pretty, absorbed in hanging some washing on the line in the yard. Unfortunately Gran had managed to be in it too, at the edge. Grimfaced, she was staring down at Molly, her mouth turned down, a cruel look in her eyes.

'Who's this?' asked Mr Finch, pointing to Henry's mother.

'My mum.'

'We could crop this and enlarge it so that it's all her. Would you like that? It'd make a nice Christmas present.'

'Yeah,' said Henry relieved. 'That'd be good.'

Mr Finch was still looking intently at the picture.

'And who's Shanghai Lil?' he said, indicating Gran.

'A neighbour,' said Henry hurriedly.

'M'm. A face that speaks volumes. No love lost between her and your sister.'

*That's true*, thought Henry. But she would never harm Molly. Gran was a good person. It was just a bad photograph.

Mr Finch glanced at his watch.

'Talking of mothers, I think it's well past your bedtime, lads. You'd best scarper home before I have your ones on the warpath. I can't be here tomorrow night, but I'll get permission for you to come back here after school. But you must promise to lock up afterwards.' He turned to Henry.

'I'll have some of the photographs cropped and enlarged for you to have a look at. Then you can tell me what you think.'

## 15. Alarming developments

THE NEXT EVENING, IT WAS EERILY QUIET WHEN HENRY unlocked the door of the darkroom and switched on the red light. Jeffries began to look at the photographs which were pegged up. Mr Finch had cropped and enlarged several of them. With less background, the faces now filled the bigger photographs.

'These are *good*!' said Jeffries. 'The ones of Molly and your mother are like something out of *Picture Post*!'

Henry grinned.

'Yeah, thanks to Mr Finch.'

'I wish Pip could see them,' said Jeffries. 'I've been racking my brain trying to work out why he didn't turn up after dinner.'

'Yeah. It's not like him to skip school.'

'As soon as we've finished here let's go round to his place and see if he's there,' said Jeffries, staring at one particular photograph. It was a close-up of Mrs

Beaumont stepping off the train.

'Good idea.'

'Who's the man?'

'What man?'

'This man, here, standing behind Mrs Beaumont.' He pointed to a dark-haired man with a moustache wearing a long coat and trilby.

Henry shrugged. 'I dunno. Why?'

'He's in the photographs in Sternsea and in London.'

'How d'you mean?'

'Look, here's Mrs Beaumont at the bottom step of the Plaza. There he is on the edge of the pavement.'

'Oh, yeah, I remember. There *was* a man there. So?'

'And here are two of Mrs Beaumont at Waterloo Station on different days,' said Jeffries. 'And he's standing behind her in both pictures. Look, you can see him more clearly now that Mr Finch has cropped the photographs and enlarged the sections she's in.'

Henry studied it closely.

'Coincidence,' he murmured. 'He was probably going to London the same day.'

'What about this one, then?'

It was Grace swinging round excitedly outside the ballet shop. The same man was hovering near her by the shop window.

'Blimey!' he said, startled.

'You know what I'm thinking?' said Jeffries.

'Yeah,' said Henry, alarmed. 'Mrs Beaumont is being followed.'

'You're right,' said a familiar voice behind them.

Henry and Jeffries yelped and whirled round. Pip was standing behind them.

'Pip!' they yelled.

'You made me jump,' said Jeffries. 'How did you get in without us noticing? I didn't hear the door opening.'

'I was already here. I've been hiding under a blanket behind there.' He pointed to a stack of boxes at the end of the room.

'We've been wondering where you've been,' said Jeffries. 'When you didn't turn up for Maths, Mr David reported you to the headmaster.'

'Hang on a minute,' said Henry, puzzled. 'How long have you been hiding here?'

'Since dinner time. The key was in the lock. I hid when Mr Finch came in. I was going to leave after he'd gone, but he locked the door.'

'But Mr Finch said to come after school. Why did you come here at dinner time?'

'To get a clean cardigan for Mum.'

Henry and Jeffries stared at him, baffled.

'Why did you think you'd find her cardigan here?' Jeffries asked.

In the dim red light Pip looked like a frightened rabbit.

'I don't want to go to an orphanage!'

'Why would you have to?' Henry asked, mystified.

'Because we haven't got a home any more. We had to leave last night. The landlady told us to go. She was so angry. She just kept shouting at us. And I don't know why.'

Henry had his suspicions. It sounded as if the landlady had discovered Pip was a bastard.

'But that's what happened to us!' Jeffries said.

'This cardigan,' Henry said, 'where is it?

'Behind the boxes.'

Hidden under a blanket Henry found the suitcase he had seen at Pip's lodgings. Draped over it was a pale green cardigan.

'You didn't sleep here last night, did you?' asked Jeffries.

'No. At the Plaza.'

'At the Plaza?' Henry and Jeffries exclaimed.

Pip nodded.

'Mum's got a key. We went back there after Mum finished her cleaning job at an office.' He gave a nervous smile. 'It was like being in a palace with all the chandeliers and big fancy staircases and everything. And we had the sinks all to ourselves in the toilets. Mum says she's never been so clean. This morning she let me out the back, where there's that tunnel from the exit beside the ten-penny seats.'

'Where are you going to sleep tonight?' asked Jeffries.

'Same place.'

'What if you get caught?' Henry said.

'Then I'll get taken away to an orphanage. If Mum hasn't got a home, she can't keep me. That's why I didn't want Mr Finch to find me. He'd tell the headmaster. And then he'd tell the police and I'd be taken away. And they might send me to Australia,' he added, his voice trembling.

Jeffries placed his hands on Pip's tiny shoulders.

'We won't let them, will we, Henry?'

'No, we'll look after you. You can keep your suitcase in our air-raid shelter.'

'We're like the three musketeers,' said Jeffries.

'Four, counting Grace,' added Henry.

'You're right,' said Pip bravely.

'Only seven out of the nine came out,' lied Henry.

He and Jeffries had popped in the following night to see Mrs Beaumont with six of the photographs. He didn't want her to be frightened so he only showed her one photograph with the man in it. The boys glanced at one another, wondering if she would recognise him, but she made no comment.

'Who's the man with the dark curly hair?' Henry asked quickly, and he placed one of the pictures her brother had taken in front of her. It was the photograph of the New Year's Eve party.

'Jim MacTavish. He's a stills photographer. He's very

good. He's a friend of Max's. He's had his photographs published in *Picture Post*, *Lilliput* and even the *New York Times*. Now,' she said, 'is Pip coming to see *Passport to Pimlico* with us?'

'He can't,' said Jeffries. 'He and his mother . . .'

'Are going to see another film,' interrupted Henry quickly.

At the Troxy, as Henry sat surrounded by people laughing, he felt that Pip had had a lucky escape. *Passport to Pimlico* irritated him.

'You two are rather quiet,' Mrs Beaumont remarked on the way home.

'It got on my nerves,' said Henry.

'It made me so angry!' said Jeffries. 'Why do they think people would act like children if they didn't have ration books any more?'

'Yeah,' agreed Henry.

'So you don't think the spivs and racketeers would take over if there were no rules and regulations?' said Mrs Beaumont.

'They might. But why give up if they do? If the shop-keepers had found a way round it, they could have stayed living in a happy separate country. It's as if the film is telling people the only way is the government way.'

Henry had a feeling that there was more behind Jeffries' rage than the film.

'I hate this country,' Jeffries muttered.

'Henry, what did you think?' asked Mrs Beaumont.

'I liked it at first but then it got annoying. I agree with Jeffries. But I can't think of the words to, you know, explain. He says it better.'

'That's because he reads books,' said Mrs Beaumont wryly.

When Henry slipped into the house, the only sound he could hear was light music on the wireless in Gran's room. He found his mother sitting alone at the kitchen table, reading. He hadn't seen her do that since before Molly was born. She smiled guiltily as if she had been caught out doing something naughty.

'How was the film?' she asked. It was the first time for a while Henry had been able to be alone with her without being constantly interrupted or having her only half listening while she was cooking or cleaning or running after his half-sister.

'It was funny at the beginning. These people in London found out that they weren't part of England so they didn't have to do what the government said any more. It made fun of all the restrictions that Mr Jenkins goes on about. It had some good bits in it but in the end they all went back to doing what they were told and were all happy to have their ration books back again.'

He told her how angry Jeffries had been.

'That's strange, because Mrs Jeffries told me that since she's been at Mrs Beaumont's it's the happiest they've been in ten years.'

Henry heard his gran's door open and close quietly. His mother put a finger to her lips.

'So,' she said loudly, 'are you going to the Cinema Club on Saturday morning or are you working for Mr Jenkins?'

Henry wondered why his gran stayed in the hallway and didn't come in. In the end he opened the door and peered out but there was no sign of her. And then his mother said a strange thing.

'I wonder how much she overheard this time.'

'This time? You make Gran sound like a spy.'

His mother said nothing.

'Oh,' said Henry, realising. 'You don't think she heard us talk about Mrs Jeffries?'

'I don't know. I hope not.'


On Saturday morning he met Jeffries, Pip and Grace at the Cinema Club. Pip kept dozing off.

'You can sleep on my shoulder if you like,' said Grace.

Pip immediately slumped against her. Henry glanced at him during the film, happily asleep. Because he was such a titch, he looked like a ten-year-old.

At the end of the programme, they managed to sprint out of the auditorium before the opening strains of *God*

*Save the King*, dragging a bleary-eyed Pip after them. While they stood on the steps, Henry formed his fingers into the shape of a viewfinder and peered through them, composing imaginary photographs. He was sweeping his gaze round towards Victoria Road when he spotted a familiar figure leaving Mrs Beaumont's house by the gate. It was his gran.

'What's she doing there?' he whispered.

And then the penny dropped. His mother must have decided to tell her that Jeffries and his mother had moved in with Mrs Beaumont after all, and Gran had popped in to say hello. She was befriending the Jeffries! From now on, everything was going to be fine. He and his mother had been worried over nothing.

## 16. Presentation time

'HELLO THERE!'

Uncle Bill was leaning out of the cab of the train that Henry and Mrs Beaumont and the others had just watched drawing into Hatton Station.

'Who's that?' asked Jeffries.

'My stepfather,' mumbled Henry.

'He's a *train driver*,' breathed Pip with admiration. 'That's almost as good as being a projectionist.'

'Are you Mrs Beaumont?' Uncle Bill asked.

'Yes. And you must be Maureen's husband.'

'That's right.'

'You have Molly's smile.'

He beamed.

Henry felt irritated by this intrusion, the more so since Mrs Beaumont was being friendly towards Uncle Bill.

'What brings you here?' his stepfather asked.

'Didn't Henry tell you? We're waiting for my younger

son and some friends from London. They're bringing old cameras and films for the presentation at Henry's school.'

Henry was embarrassed. He had told his Uncle Bill as little as possible.

'I expect he did and I forgot. Are these your friends, Henry?'

Henry nodded.

'Aren't you going to introduce them to me?' asked Uncle Bill.

Henry shrugged, annoyed.

'This is Roger Jeffries.'

Jeffries gave a wave.

'This is Pip Morgan. And this is . . .'

'Grace,' Grace blurted out. The boys stared at her expectantly, waiting for her to add *the family disgrace*.

'That's all,' she said happily. 'Grace.'

'It's a pity they're only inviting grandparents and great-grandparents to the presentation,' Uncle Bill said. 'Maureen and I would have liked to have seen it.'

'Really?' asked Mrs Beaumont, turning to Henry.

'Yeah.'

'So your grandmother will be there?'

'No, she can't, because of her legs.' He had been disappointed when she had told him she couldn't come. He knew she wasn't upset by him doing the presentation with Jeffries and Pip any more. She was over all that. But it did puzzle him that she had decided to stay at home.

'Hello there!' boomed a voice from behind them. 'Am I glad to see you. We're carrying a ton weight between us.'

It was Daniel. Behind him were Jessica and Max with two wooden boxes on wheels and heavy leather satchels dangling from their shoulders. The boys ran to their aid.

'Are you an actor?' Pip asked Daniel.

'No.'

'You sound like one,' said Pip. 'You look like one.'

Daniel beamed. 'I shall take that as a compliment.'

The guard was on the platform with his whistle.

'Time for me to go!' yelled Henry's stepfather, waving. He disappeared from the window and the train pulled out.


'Leave all the equipment here in the hall for the moment,' said Mrs Beaumont. 'After we've pushed back the settee and armchairs in the sitting room, you can rehearse in there. Jessica, the piano's in the room opposite the hall door. I'll go and make you and the others something to eat. You must be starving.'

'And parched,' added her son over the tripod he was assembling.

'Can I listen to you play, Jessica?' asked Pip.

'Of course,' she said.

'I'll come with you,' said Grace.

Daniel and Max followed Mrs Beaumont down to the kitchen, leaving Henry and Jeffries to push the furniture aside in the sitting room. Henry decided it was a good moment to find out if Jeffries knew anything about his gran's visit to the house. It had been five days since he had seen her leaving it but neither he nor Mrs Beaumont had mentioned it. It was all a bit odd. He was about to ask Jeffries if there had been any visitors when Mrs Beaumont called up to them.

'Tea and toast everyone!' she said.

'Toast!' exclaimed Jeffries, and shot out of the room.

'Blast!' Henry muttered. He would have to ask him another time. But being left alone with the cameras more than made up for his frustration. He had been eager to have a closer look at them. Staring at them, it was extraordinary to think that someone fifty years ago had actually handled them and had taken the earliest moving films. What sort of camera, he wondered, would a fourteen-year-old boy be holding in 1999? He touched them and then headed for the hallway to join the others. As he ran down the steps towards the kitchen he could hear Jessica playing one of Grace's favourite songs, *It's Magic*.

He found Daniel, Max and Jeffries sitting round the table poring over the film page in the *Sternsea Evening News*. Mrs Jeffries was putting plates on the table when Jessica appeared. Henry suddenly realised he could still hear the piano. Jeffries looked up, shot Henry a glance and immediately leapt from the table.

'What's going on?' asked Mrs Beaumont, but they

had already dashed out of the room.

Up in the hall, Henry flung the study door open.

'And the next bit goes like this,' said Grace, who was standing beside Pip. She hummed a melody and Pip played it back.

'That sounds splendid,' said Jeffries.

'Yes, it's a lovely piano isn't it?'

It was obvious to Henry that Pip was completely unaware of how good he was and it gave him an idea.

'Jeffries, how about if Pip plays some of the music for the silent films?'

'That's just what I was thinking,' said Jeffries. 'Do you think you could, Pip?'

'Of course he could,' said Grace.

'You're right,' said Pip, 'but I'm not allowed to play the school piano.'

'So where do you practise?' asked Grace.

'At the Plaza, early in the morning when no one's about.'

'But why haven't you played on this piano before now?' asked Jeffries.

'Because I thought I wouldn't be allowed to.'

There was a moment of silence.

'How do you know you can't play the piano at school?' said Henry.

'Mum asked Mr Barratt a long time ago and he said "*No*". I told you about it when you came to see me. Remember?'

Henry nodded. That was when he had thought Pip had been refused permission because he was no good. It now dawned on him that the reason Pip wasn't allowed to play during the interval at the Saturday Morning Pictures was for the same reason he wasn't in the football team at school.

'Mr Barratt said I might damage the keys,' Pip added.

'But that's silly!' Grace protested.

Henry had to control his anger for Pip's sake.

'It'll be dark when people are watching the films,' he said slowly.

'You're right,' said Pip.

'So dark Jessica said she would need to ask your Mr Finch for a light above the music,' said Grace.

'She and Pip could swap places in the dark after the lights have been turned off! Is that what you're thinking?' said Jeffries.

'Yeah,' said Henry, and he grinned.

Just then Mrs Beaumont arrived at the door with toast and jam and four cups of tea.

'The gang's all here I see,' she commented. 'And staying for the duration by the look of it. I guessed you'd prefer your tea and toast up here. I have a feeling you have a lot to talk about.' And she gave them a mischievous smile and left them to it.

They were eating their way through the toast when Jessica and Daniel appeared.

'Daniel,' began Henry, 'we've had a change of plan.'

'Oh, yes?' he said.

'But we need Jessica's help,' added Jeffries.

'That's why I'm here,' she said.

'Let's get started,' said Daniel. 'Then you can tell me what you've got up your sleeves.'

Daniel placed a small machine on a table in the study.

'You'll be pleased to see I've managed to get hold of the latest kind of projector,' he said. 'A friend has joined up all the little films so that they're all on one reel. Much less cumbersome.'

Jessica and Max showed Henry and Jeffries how to set up the screen. Pip stood by Daniel's side watching.

'I have a feeling you're the one who's interested in projectors,' said Daniel.

'You're right!' said Pip.

'I'm afraid this is not as exciting as a cinema projector, but if you want to ask me anything, fire away.'

As they rehearsed, Jeffries and Henry took turns to read out information about the films while Pip sat next to Jessica with a torch aimed at the music.

Grace watched, entranced.

'I know I've got homework,' Henry heard her whisper to Mrs Beaumont, 'but I wouldn't miss this for anything.'

Later, Jessica played *Blue Moon* in a low key and Grace sang. It was strange to think he had once thought her voice had sounded horrible.

'Wonderful,' murmured Mrs Beaumont. 'But I think that's enough for tonight. Your great-aunt will be on the warpath if you're not back soon.'

'You're right,' said Grace.

Jeffries and Henry laughed.

'What's so funny?' said Grace, puzzled.

'You sounded just like Pip,' said Mrs Beaumont.


The following morning Jessica and Daniel arrived in a taxi early in the morning and the boys and Mr Finch helped carry the Victorian cameras, film and projector into the school hall. The film group were going to be the last to perform in the History presentation. Everything seemed to be going well until Mr Finch took Henry aside for a private word. He looked serious.

'The headmaster has informed me,' said Mr Finch, lowering his voice, 'that Morgan is forbidden to go anywhere near the piano.'

Henry was shocked.

'But, sir . . .' he protested.

Mr Finch held up his hand.

'However, I have persuaded Mr Barratt to continue to allow him to turn the music pages for Miss Jessica. But why didn't you lads tell me? Apparently Mr Barratt's worried about damage to the keys. What's that all about? Has Morgan ever . . .?'

Henry could no longer contain his anger.

'It's nothing to do with that!' he exploded. 'Pip would never damage anything!'

He wanted to tell him more but was afraid Mr Finch would guess what they were up to and stop them. And then he remembered the words Mr Finch had said to him at the beginning of the term – *Morgan is a pupil in my class and he will be treated equally.* He decided to take a risk.

'Mr Barratt doesn't want him near it because he doesn't want him to *play* it, sir.'

Mr Finch's eyebrows shot up.

'Dodge, are you telling me Morgan can play the piano?'

'Yes, sir.'

'I see.' He looked thoughtful for a moment. 'Right,' he said firmly. 'I have expressly told the headmaster that turning pages is all that Morgan will be doing today.'

'Yes, Mr Finch,' said Henry despondently.

'And as you know, the head will be sitting in the front row with some of our visitors, watching the films in the pitch dark.'

'Yes, sir.'

'While I will be in charge of the lights at the back of the hall.'

'Oh,' said Henry, feeling even worse. 'I'd forgotten about that, sir.'

'Making sure that said lights don't come up too soon,' he added meaningfully.

Henry grinned.

'Is this another of those conversations which never happened, sir?'

'You're learning, lad. You're learning.'

'Are you chaps ready to roll?' Daniel whispered to them.

'Yeah,' answered Henry and Jeffries, but their voices came out in a croak.

'Nerves of steel, men,' Daniel commanded and he gave them a wink.

Pip, however, was beaming.

'He can't wait to get his hands on that piano,' muttered Jeffries to Henry.

The hall had been decorated with drawings of Victorian times. Bits of old velvet were draped everywhere. Two of the girls were taking it in turns to wind up a gramophone and play old music-hall records while everyone was seated. The lights were dimmed, there was the sound of organ music, and the curtains opened to reveal a girl dressed in a Victorian bridal gown. There was a gasp from the audience. So much material after years of rationing was seldom seen outside the cinema. Another girl stepped forward.

'A rich woman's wedding dress in 1899.' The third girl in the group appeared in an ordinary dress with a tiny bunch of artificial flowers. 'A poor woman's wedding dress in 1899.'

*

The confectionery group walked out in front of the audience.

'Only this group to go,' whispered Henry to Daniel. 'And then it's us.'

They watched the group arrange a selection of colourful old tins on a table as though it were a sweet shop.

'Oh, my goodness!' cried a woman in the second row, 'I remember them,' and she laughed.

A tiny woman in her nineties stood up and very slowly read an account of her memories about selling sweets in 1899.

'That's our cue,' said Jeffries to Pip, and they gave Jessica a nod. She and Pip slipped out of their seats with sheets of music and headed for the piano at the back of the hall. The little light above the keys was already on and Jessica began to play the stirring and melancholy music of a Victorian melodrama.

Mr Finch and Daniel had taken their places at the back of the hall. Henry and Jeffries walked swiftly backstage and stood behind the curtains. Henry became aware that his hands were shaking. He shoved them hastily into his pockets. In the semi-darkness, he glanced nervously at Jeffries. He smiled and gave Henry a thumbs-up sign and Henry returned it.

The music ended. They pushed the curtains aside, stepped forward into the light and stood either side of the screen which had been erected for the film. Henry stared out at the audience but all he could see was darkness. *What if he forgot what he was supposed to say?* If he'd had a piece of paper with the words written on it, he would have had something to do with his hands. His heart pumping, he listened to Jeffries talking about the Lumière brothers and how, in time, other film-makers had hit on the idea of filming a story. And then it was his turn to speak. He swallowed and concentrated on a small spot at the back of the blacked-out hall. As soon as he opened his mouth he was sucked into the dream world of films Daniel had shown him, and his excitement about the magic of the cameras which had captured and created those images seemed to spill out effortlessly.

He spoke eagerly about early photography and he and Jeffries showed the audience a Victorian stills camera and one of the first movie cameras. Henry was certain that the sight of the large wooden and bronze boxes would be a revelation to those in his form who had only handled a small black box camera.

'We've shown you the cameras,' said Henry.

'And now we're going to show you the films,' said Jeffries.

And they grinned at one another with the knowledge that Pip was about to break a school rule.

The audience clapped loudly at the end of the films, the

lights were turned back on and Mr Barratt made a thank you speech to the elderly guests for coming.

'We did it!' whispered Henry.

'And he never suspected a thing,' added Jeffries, stifling a laugh.

As the guests were escorted from the hall by a group of girls in makeshift Victorian costumes to the cookery room for tea and biscuits, a photographer from the *Sternsea Evening News* popped his head round the door. It was the same man who had photographed Uncle Bill in August.

'Let's have you hold your sweet tins in the middle,' he said to the confectionery trio, 'nice and close. Now where's the group with the old cameras?' He glanced at Henry for an instant and gave him a quick nod of recognition. 'All look at me. Nice big smiles!'

After the photographer had left they returned to the classroom, where Mr Finch praised everyone and handed each group a bag of broken toffee. With sweets so difficult to buy, Henry guessed it must have taken Mr Finch months to find.

The bell rang, he bade them good afternoon and Henry watched his classmates bolt out of the door.

'Are you coming?' said Jeffries. He was standing next to Pip, who looked as though he were about to explode with excitement.

'In a minute. You go on. I'll catch you up.'

He hovered awkwardly by the door watching Mr Finch tidying up.

'Yes, Dodge?' said Mr Finch, glancing in his direction.

And Henry couldn't think of a single thing to say. He stared back at him, struggling to find the right words. And then he knew. He took a deep breath.

'Thank you, sir.'

# PART TWO

*Caught*

# 1. The informer

'SO? DID IT GO WELL?' ASKED GRAN.

'Yeah, it did,' said Henry. 'We were a *grand* team. That's what Mr Finch said, which is good because we nearly weren't a team at all.'

'Really? Why was that, then?'

'Jeffries and his mother had to leave their lodgings.' He stared at her intently but she remained silent. 'If Mrs Beaumont hadn't let them stay with her, they would have been homeless.'

'Well, that was lucky, wasn't it?'

Henry was puzzled. *Why didn't she say anything about her visit to Mrs Beaumont's house?*

'Yeah. And Pip had to leave his lodgings too. If it weren't for the Plaza, we would have lost him as well. If you haven't got anywhere to live and you have children, they get taken away.'

'What do you mean about the Plaza?'

'That's where him and his mum are sleeping.'

'Well I never.'

'Yeah. But we did it, Gran. We did it.'

'Well done, Henry. I'm really proud of you.'

'And tomorrow afternoon we're all going to see *Kidnapped* and a Walt Disney film. Me, Jeffries, Pip, his mum, everybody.'

'Lovely,' said his gran. 'That'll give you something to look forward to.'

Henry waited. But still she said nothing.

'And where's that showing, then?' she said after an awkward silence.

'The Plaza.'

'So it'll be very convenient, won't it?'

'Yeah, well, Pip's mum sometimes sees films for free with Pip because she works there.'

'That'll be nice for her, then, having the company.'

'Yes. It'll be the first time her and Pip will have seen films with other people.'

His gran went quiet and Henry had a feeling he had said too much.

Outside it was pitch black and a thick mist was creeping along the street. It had already obliterated the bombsite opposite. Hastily Henry made for Victoria Road.

When he arrived he was disappointed to find that Jeffries and his mother had left for the Kings Theatre, but

Mrs Beaumont insisted he come in. She looked serious.

'I'm glad we have some time alone,' she said. 'I need to talk to you.'

They sat at the kitchen table. Henry glanced at some freshly typed sheets.

'Not mine,' she said. 'Jeffries. Did you know he was writing a novel?'

Henry shook his head. He had no idea.

'The mob ripped it apart. I'm dictating it to your mother and she's taking it down in shorthand and typing it up. It's a Christmas surprise for him.'

'Why didn't he tell me?'

'You don't read books. He probably didn't think you'd be interested.'

Henry felt uncomfortable.

'Is this what you wanted to tell me? About him writing a book?'

'No. Something rather unpleasant has happened. I haven't told Jeffries and his mother yet. They're so happy at the moment, I didn't want to upset them.'

'What is it? Has Private Jeffries been found?'

'No. I've had a surprise visitor. An informer.'

Immediately Henry remembered the man in the photographs.

'She must have spotted them entering the house,' Mrs Beaumont said.

'She?' Henry exclaimed.

'Yes. She came to say that the woman who had moved in here was the wife of a deserter and she felt duty bound, as a good citizen, to tell me. The awful thing was she was so nice about it, as if she was doing me a great favour by giving me the information.'

'What did you say?'

'Nothing. That sort don't give up. If I'd said anything, I might have inadvertently provided her with ammunition for later. In fact I wouldn't be surprised if we have a visit from the military police.'

'Do you think she's the person who told Mrs Jeffries' landlady?'

'I'm sure of it.'

'What will you do if they come?'

'Stay calm. Forewarned is forearmed. I need to start looking for a diamond in this dungheap because, believe me, this woman has created one. Let's hope I'm jumping the gun and they don't visit us.'

'But you think they will, don't you?'

'If my suspicions about this woman are correct, yes. It beats me how she found out.'

'When did she visit you?' Henry asked.

'Last Saturday morning, when Jeffries was at the pictures and his mother was out shopping. She must have been waiting outside. She left minutes before he arrived back here.'

Henry looked away. He felt sick.

'What did she look like?' he asked, aware of not wanting to know the answer.

'Dumpy. A bit breathless. On the old side. Oh, and she wore an awful pink hat with a squashed artificial flower stuck on the side.'

*Like the one on top of the wardrobe in the front room at home,* Henry thought.

'Don't be downhearted, Henry. I'll let Mrs Jeffries know and reassure her that if we do get a visit, it won't make a jot of difference. I'm determined to have a full house for Christmas this year.'

Henry knew he couldn't go home. He struggled through the yellowing mist towards the railway bridge. Once there, he clung to the wall and tried to catch his breath. He felt winded. The fog enveloped him and he was glad of it. He didn't want to be seen.

'Gran's an informer,' he muttered, shaking. 'She must have overheard me and Mum talking!'

Suddenly he remembered the clever way she had prised the number of Jeffries' address out of him and realised why Pip and his mother had been thrown out of their lodgings. He had given her their address too. He could almost hear his grandmother telling the landlady how Mrs Morgan was an unmarried mother, which would explain why the landlady had been so angry.

He shivered. There was something else his

grandmother knew now. She knew where Mrs Morgan and Pip were sleeping every night. He had to warn Pip. But how? He wouldn't be able to get into the Plaza after it had closed because it would be locked, and it would be too risky to stand outside and shout to them. He remembered the look of terror in Pip's eyes at the thought of being taken away from his mother.

'Mrs Beaumont!' he murmured. He'd go back and ask her what to do. But then he remembered she was seeing a film that night. He would have to leave it till the morning.

Turning to go home, he found himself facing a fog so thick that he couldn't even see his feet. He clung to the wall and gingerly manoeuvred himself alongside it.

Not wanting to waste any time getting dressed in the morning, Henry lay fully clothed under the blankets, wishing for the daylight to come. When he woke he was alarmed to find Molly's bed empty. He leapt out of bed and grabbed his boots. His mother was in the kitchen hoisting a clothes rack above the range. Molly was at the table drawing squiggly circles on a newspaper.

'What time is it?' he asked anxiously.

'Gone ten. You were in such a deep sleep I didn't have the heart to wake you.'

There was no sound coming from the front room.

'Gran's not listening to the wireless.'

'She's gone to the shops, I suspect,' his mother said irritably.

'With her legs?'

'Your gran's fitter than she makes out.'

Henry was quite certain she was nowhere near a shop. He ran out of the house and sprinted round to Mrs Beaumont's house. Mrs Jeffries answered the door. Mrs Beaumont, he was told, was out.

'You'll see her this afternoon at the Plaza,' she said. 'Can't it wait?'

*No*, thought Henry, *it can't*.

He couldn't think straight. He paced up and down on the pavement in the hope that he would catch sight of Mrs Beaumont coming down the road, but there was no sign of her. In desperation he waited at the foot of the Plaza's steps. Eventually the huge foyer doors opened, spilling out children. He searched through the thousand or more faces pouring down towards him. But what was he going to say to his friends when he met them? What could he say? *My gran is an informer?* Tell Pip he was going to be homeless again?

He spotted Grace waving to him, and her cheerful smile raised his spirits. Jeffries and Pip were jumping down the steps beside her.

'Where were you?' Grace asked.

'I over-slept.'

'Are you coming back to Mrs Beaumont's?' asked Jeffries.

'Yeah. That's why I thought I'd wait for you out here.'

But by early afternoon Mrs Beaumont still hadn't returned and Henry headed back home for dinner. He was dreading seeing his grandmother again. When he entered the kitchen everyone was sitting round the table in silence.

'Sorry I'm late, Mum,' he mumbled.

It was shepherd's pie and he was starving, but as soon as the food hit the back of his throat he seemed incapable of swallowing it.

'If you'd got back in time,' said Uncle Bill, 'it wouldn't be cold.'

'I'm not hungry,' Henry muttered. 'Sorry.'

'You're not leaving the table till you've finished every mouthful.'

'Bill,' said his mother nervously.

'I won't have any more money wasted in this house.'

'Daddy cross,' stated Molly, slamming her spoon down on the table.

Henry hadn't seen Uncle Bill so angry in a long time. Out of the corner of his eye he noticed his grandmother looking very pleased with herself.

'I said I was sorry,' he said quietly.

'And I accept that, Henry,' said Uncle Bill, 'but I won't have good food thrown away. You finish it and that's that. Come on, Molly, we'll take a walk.'

Molly scrambled eagerly off her chair and grabbed

hold of her father's thumb. Henry could see that his mother was distressed. As soon as Uncle Bill and Molly had stepped outside into the yard, his grandmother said, 'Take no notice of him. You give your dinner to me and I'll get rid of it.' And she gave him a conspiratorial smile. Henry stared at her. It was still the same old Gran, the Gran he loved, smiling and friendly. Could he possibly be wrong about her?

'I'm sorry,' said Henry's mother softly, 'but if Bill says he has to eat it, then he has to eat it.'

'He's not his father.'

'More's the pity.'

There was an awkward silence.

'What do you mean by that?' said Gran.

Henry noticed his mother looking flustered.

'I mean,' she stammered, 'that he could have had the same surname as Molly if you hadn't have interfered.'

'Good job I did, eh, Henry?'

Henry didn't reply. He hated being between them when they were arguing. He gazed down at the fast-congealing food on his plate, feeling sick, knowing that if he didn't eat it, he wouldn't be meeting Mrs Beaumont at the Plaza.

The queues were already weaving their way down Victoria Road and round the corner to the nearest side street. He spotted Mrs Beaumont at the bottom of the steps, waving frantically. Jeffries, Grace and Pip were with her. And Mrs Morgan. He would have to wait till after the film before he could speak to Mrs Beaumont in private.

'We thought you weren't going to make it!' said Grace.

'What kept you?' asked Mrs Beaumont.

'Dinner,' answered Henry ruefully. 'I wasn't hungry but Uncle Bill said I had to eat everything on my plate.'

'Poor thing,' said Grace. 'My parents are always doing that to me. When they're home from abroad, they order the maid to heap a mountain of food on my plate so that I have to sit on my own with it in front of me all day till I've eaten every little scrap.'

Just then a stout man came lumbering down the steps towards them.

'Mrs Morgan!' he shouted.

It was the manager of the cinema.

'Good afternoon, sir,' said Pip's mother, surprised.

'I'd like a word, Mrs Morgan,' he said curtly. 'Now!'

Henry felt his stomach turn.

'Did you want me earlier tomorrow morning?' Mrs Morgan asked.

'I may not want you at all, *Mrs* Morgan, if what I've been told is correct.' He threw back his shoulders. 'It has been brought to my attention that you are sleeping in this cinema at nights like a common squatter,' he declared loudly. 'Is this correct?'

Henry noticed the people above them whispering to

one another. Mrs Morgan stared at him, her mouth open, unable to speak. Henry was angry. He could see the manager was trying to embarrass her in front of everyone.

'This is quite absurd,' Mrs Beaumont snapped, 'and the most vindictive nonsense I have ever had the misfortune to hear.'

'I'll thank you not to interfere, Madam,' said the manager.

'And I'm surprised that a man in your position should believe it,' Mrs Beaumont continued. 'As it happens, Mrs Morgan and her son are residents in my property, where I'm sure she would have preferred you to visit, at an arranged time, when you could have discussed this malicious gossip in private.'

By now the manager's face had turned a bright red.

'I had no idea,' he stammered.

'I think an apology is due, don't you?'

'Mrs Morgan, what can I say?'

Henry fought down a smile, at the same time crossing his fingers. He was hoping Pip wouldn't say anything.

'The person who informed me seemed so respectable,' he said. 'I'm afraid I've been duped.'

'Indeed you have, sir.' Mrs Beaumont turned to Mrs Morgan. 'You haven't snubbed some admiring gentleman lately, have you?'

Mrs Morgan, who was still speechless, shook her head.

'It was a woman,' said the manager, 'an elderly woman.'

*Clever Mrs Beaumont. She had managed to get more information out of him.*

'And her name?'

Henry held his breath.

'Oh, I couldn't divulge that even if I knew.'

'Pity. We could have taken her to court. Defamation of character and all that.'

'Oh, dear,' said the manager. He turned to Mrs Morgan and almost bowed. 'Please accept my sincere apologies. If there is anything I can do to make it up to you?'

He left the question dangling in the air. Mrs Morgan was still staring at him in shock.

'As a matter of fact there is,' broke in Mrs Beaumont. 'Mrs Morgan, didn't you tell me that your son wanted to meet the projectionist?'

## 2. The Morgans are rescued

HENRY EASED OPEN THE BACK DOOR INTO THE YARD AND dragged Mrs Morgan's suitcase out of the air-raid shelter where he had hidden it for Pip. He shoved it lopsidedly into the wheelbarrow and piled sawn floorboards and blocks of wood on top to conceal it. He gave a jump at the sound of the scullery door being opened.

'Henry?'

It was his mother.

'Yeah.'

'Gran wants to see you about something. She didn't say what,' she added wearily.

Henry kept piling on the wood.

'Sorry, Mum, but I'm taking this wood round to Mrs Beaumont.'

'I'll explain that to her.'

'Thanks, Mum.'

To his alarm she stepped out into the yard and walked

towards him. A corner of the suitcase was still visible. He placed a piece of wood over it and prayed it wouldn't slide off.

'I'm sorry I was a bit short with you earlier,' she said. 'Uncle Bill had some bad news just before you came in. He's a bit worried about money, see.'

'Does he know about your typing money?'

'Yes, but you haven't told Gran, have you?'

'No, course not.'

'We're in a bit of . . .' She stopped. 'Anyway, we'll sort it out.'

They gazed at each other in the dusk.

'You're a good boy, Henry,' she said.

'That's not what Uncle Bill thinks,' he muttered.

'You're wrong. He thinks the world of you.'

'He doesn't let you go to the Pictures.'

'That's not true. He'd go too if . . .' She hesitated.

'He wasn't so mean,' Henry finished for her.

'If only you knew,' she murmured. 'Look, let's not argue. I really want us to have a lovely Christmas and it's only a week away. Please try to get on with him.' She leaned over and kissed him on the cheek. 'You're growing up,' she said softly.

He watched her return to the scullery. He waited until she had shut the door before heading towards the back of the yard. As soon as he turned the corner of the alley into the street, he spotted Gran hovering in the doorway.

'Here goes,' he whispered. 'I'll be back soon,' he said cheerily as he drew closer.

'Can't that wait till morning? I want to hear all about the films. Did you see Pip?'

'Yeah. He was laughing,' he lied.

'Really? Why's that?'

'He'd been pulling my leg and I fell for it.'

'Oh? What about?'

'Him living in the Plaza. He just made it up.'

His grandmother's expression never wavered. She smiled and put her head to one side.

'Well, I never,' she said.

He pushed the wheelbarrow with such ferocity that it tipped over to one side, sending wood sprawling all over the pavement. He grabbed the wood and righted it again.

'She shouldn't ask you to do that,' his gran said. 'Not with it being so late.'

'It's not late, Gran. It's just that it gets dark earlier now.' He quickly wheeled the wood past her. 'I'll be back soon,' he yelled over his shoulder. He didn't look back. He knew she would be watching him, willing him to change his mind.

Jeffries and Pip met him outside Mrs Beaumont's.

'We've been asked to take you round the back.'

When Henry reached her back garden he saw what appeared to be a miniature house.

'What's that?' he asked.

'Haven't you been round here before?' asked Jeffries, surprised. 'It used to be a tailor's. Now it's empty.'

The conservatory door at the back of the house was open. They carried the wheelbarrow up the step, wheeled it towards two heavy wooden doors with stained glass windows and into the study and past the piano. Mrs Beaumont walked in.

'Wood?' she commented. 'A little large for the fire, don't you think, Henry?'

He pushed the planks aside and lifted out the suitcase.

'Ah, the MI5 touch.'

'I didn't want my mum to know. I thought it would be too complicated to explain.'

'Quite right. Good thinking.' And she took the suitcase from him. 'Mrs Jeffries has cooked a batch of scones and we're having them in the kitchen.'

Downstairs Mrs Morgan was sitting at the kitchen table, a small empty glass by her hand. It looked as if she had been given the brandy treatment. In spite of the flush in her cheeks, the rest of her face looked yellow and there were mauve shadows under her eyes. She still looked shocked.

'Now,' Mrs Beaumont said to her, 'I suggest a hot bath and some sleep.'

'But I've got an office to clean tonight,' she protested, 'and then I've got to go straight to the Plaza early tomorrow morning and clean there, ready for the matinee.'

'You look exhausted,' said Mrs Beaumont.

When Pip told Henry that his mother cleaned at night, Henry hadn't realised that he meant *all* night. No wonder Pip was so tired when they were thrown out of their lodgings. He thought back to his visit there. Night after night, Pip must have been on his own in that damp basement hallway while his mother had been out working. Henry would have hated that. He liked knowing that his mum was in the house. It made him feel safe.

'I suppose I could go to the office tomorrow afternoon,' she said hesitantly. 'As long as it's ready by Monday morning . . .'

'That's settled, then. I'll make you up a bed on the settee. Henry, while I do that, can you bring me an armful of wood from the log basket in the study?'

Henry nodded, eager to help.

When he returned with the wood, he found the sitting room door closed. He could hear that Mrs Morgan was still upset and, from the tone of her voice, he didn't think it was a good moment to walk in.

'But I want to tell you because you might not want us to stay after I do, and I have to know so's I can make other plans.'

Henry couldn't move. He knew he should go downstairs but something made him want to stay.

'Pip's father and I were courtin' soon after we left

school,' he heard Mrs Morgan say. 'We were about fifteen then. When we were nineteen we wanted to get married, but my father wouldn't hear of it. He wanted me to stay at home and help in his shop so's he wouldn't have to pay anyone. We waited till we were twenty-one when we wouldn't need his permission.

'We tried to book a weekend honeymoon but the only time we could get was the weekend before the wedding. So we took it. Two days before the wedding he was killed in a car accident. I was in such a state, it wasn't till a few months later that I realised I was expectin'.'

Henry heard her crying.

'Anyway, when my dad found out I were going to have a baby, he said I had to have the baby adopted. He dumped me in this awful place where I was locked up. Some old school pals of mine got wind of it and helped me escape. So now you know.' There was a pause. 'Mrs Beaumont, Pip is illegitimate.'

'It's not the end of the world being illegitimate.'

'Try telling other people that. Even my father cut me off. He said as far as he was concerned, I was dead.'

'Judging by the sound of him, wasn't that a blessing?'

'Yes, it was!' She laughed. 'He's a horrible man.'

'Ah. That's your diamond in the dungheap.'

On Monday, Pip visited the projection box at the Plaza. Henry and Jeffries waited for him outside so that they could walk together to the Apollo, where they were meeting Mrs Beaumont and Grace.

'I hope he gets treated all right,' said Henry.

But it was obvious from Pip's face as he ran down the steps that he had.

'There are two enormous projectors up there,' he told them excitedly, 'and when the films arrive at the cinema they come in bits.'

'Bits?' said Jeffries.

'Ten-minute reels.' They began walking towards the Apollo. 'And the projectionists have to join them up into pairs with this special glue and the rewind boy has to . . .'

He was unstoppable. Everything he had seen came bubbling out in a great rush. As he began to go over the technicalities of the workings of the projectors, Henry noticed Jeffries' eyes glaze over. They grinned at one another over Pip's head.

'And the Chief said I can go back tomorrow,' continued Pip. 'And Mr Hart, he's the third projectionist, he said to come with Mum on Friday when it's the Chief's day off. And he was really nice to Mum. He made her smile. And he said I was a quick learner.'

'Why can't you go on your own?' Jeffries asked.

'Mr Hart said that film catches fire very easily. That's why the usherettes stand by the exit doors so they can lead people quickly out of the auditorium if there is one, and he said that just in case that happens I might want to be near her.'

As they passed Princes Road police station, Henry caught sight of the queue outside the Apollo. They ran to join it. Huddling close to one another, the cold piercing their jerseys, they talked about the man they had spotted in the photographs in the darkroom.

'What if it's just a coincidence?' said Henry.

'How could it be?' said Jeffries.

'We should go to the police,' said Pip. And then he looked frightened. 'No,' he added hurriedly. 'That's not a good idea.'

'There must be someone we could speak to about it,' Jeffries said. 'Not my mother. She gets jumpy at the idea of anyone being followed.'

'And mine would just think I'd been watching too many films,' said Henry. 'Let's tell Mrs Beaumont after Boxing Day.'

'Yes. We don't want to spoil her Christmas,' Jeffries said.

'Good idea,' added Pip.

'Where is she?' said Henry to himself. 'We'll have to buy the tickets soon.'

'Do you think Grace would like to see *Pink String and Sealing Wax* next week?' said Jeffries thoughtfully.

'I dunno. If she doesn't come soon, she won't see this programme – let alone one next week.'

The queue continued to move forward. They stopped talking, all eyes on the road.

'They've got to come soon,' said Henry. 'We're almost at the box office.'

'There's Mrs Beaumont!' yelled Pip, pointing to a figure walking past the theatre.

'But where's Grace?' asked Jeffries.

As Mrs Beaumont approached, Henry could see she was not happy.

'Where's Grace?' Henry called out. 'Is she ill?'

'It's worse than that I'm afraid,' said Mrs Beaumont. 'Grace has been expelled.'

# 3. Grace

THEY DIDN'T FEEL LIKE SEEING THE FILM WITHOUT GRACE. Silently the four of them trudged back to Mrs Beaumont's house. Eventually Henry could no longer keep his feelings to himself.

'Mrs Beaumont, if Grace has to leave school, will she go to another one here?'

'No. It'll probably be another boarding school or another aunt.'

'But if Grace has to leave here, no one will hear her sing again. No one will know how good she is.'

'I know,' said Mrs Beaumont quietly.

'We've got to do something!'

'I agree.'

When they reached her front door, she announced that she wanted to have a private word with Pip's and Jeffries' mothers.

Downstairs in the kitchen Pip half-heartedly drew

projectors from every angle on a scrap of paper while Jeffries fiddled miserably with the broken pieces of his crystal set.

Henry heard the sitting room door open and the click of the phone receiver being lifted. Immediately they all looked at one another, headed for the door and eased it open.

'Miss Forbes-Ellis?' they heard her say. 'Oh. It's Mrs Beaumont speaking. May I speak to Miss Forbes-Ellis? . . . Thank you.'

'What's happening now?' asked Pip anxiously.

'Shush!' urged Jeffries.

'She must be waiting for Grace's great-aunt to come to the phone,' murmured Henry.

They heard Mrs Beaumont nervously clearing her throat.

'Miss Forbes-Ellis! . . . I'm ringing about Grace. I believe her parents are somewhere in the Middle-East. Could you tell me how I might contact them? . . . Oh, thank you . . . Yes, I've written that down . . . Through an operator? Yes . . . Do they know about her expulsion?'

There was now a long pause.

'I see . . . Of course it's not your fault. It's not anyone's fault . . . Miss Forbes-Ellis, I think I might be able to help . . . Yes, of course . . . I quite understand. Thank you for your help, Miss Forbes-Ellis. Goodbye.'

They heard her take a deep breath and murmur, 'Well, here goes.'

The sound of dialling began again. Henry crossed his fingers.

'Hello. Could you put me through to . . .'

'She's going to ring her parents,' said Pip excitedly.

Henry and Jeffries beckoned him to keep his voice down.

'The operator must be connecting her to a number,' Jeffries whispered.

'Good afternoon. Is that the residence of Mr and Mrs Forbes-Ellis? . . . Oh, good. I wonder if I might speak to Mrs Forbes-Ellis. My name is Mrs Beaumont and I'm ringing from England . . . Thank you.'

This was followed by another interminable silence.

'Why is she taking so long to come to the phone?' said Jeffries.

'I expect she's got to walk down one of those huge stairways,' Henry said. 'Like in *Gone with the Wind*.'

'Mrs Forbes-Ellis,' they heard Mrs Beaumont say.

By now they were all crossing their fingers.

'My name is Mrs Beaumont. It's about your daughter Grace.'

There was a pause.

'The reason I'm phoning you is that I live in the same road as her great-aunt . . . Yes, she did tell me . . . I do understand your concerns but I think she's a very intelligent girl and I'd like to help. I realise you don't know me but her great-aunt can vouch for me. When are you planning to return to England? I see. What I'm suggesting is that instead of sending her to another school, have you thought of home-tutoring? . . . No, not with you. With me. I taught my sons at home. They're both grown up now and doing well. And I happen to know some teachers who are more than willing to help me, a dance and needlework teacher, and someone who could show her how to cook, knit, do arithmetic and type. I could take care of English, Music Appreciation and History. She would receive a good all-round education.'

Henry stared at Pip and Jeffries, who were almost bursting with suppressed frustration.

'That's why she wanted to talk to your mothers!'

'Ssssh!' they responded in unison.

'Because I see great ability,' said Mrs Beaumont, 'and I know from what her great-aunt has told me that you are both busy people. Living in the same road would make coming to my house for lessons extremely convenient . . . Yes, of course you must discuss it with Mr Forbes-Ellis . . . Yes, of course . . . Thank you so much. And I do apologise for waking you up. I'd forgotten the difference in time . . . Yes. Good after– Goodbye, Mrs Forbes-Ellis.'

Henry heard the clunk of the receiver being replaced, followed by approaching footsteps. They just had time to sit nonchalantly on the kitchen chairs as Mrs Beaumont opened the door.

'You were eavesdropping, weren't you?' she said.

'You're right,' said Pip.

*

As Henry drew closer to his street, the sinking feeling in his stomach returned. Why would Gran do what she did? The moment he stepped into the hall, he heard her call out to him. He took a deep breath and opened her door.

'Now, sit down,' she said. 'I know you must be starvin', but I've hardly seen you this week. You've been keeping yerself to yerself.'

'Course I have, Gran.'

'What do you mean?' she said, looking alert.

'Christmas, Gran. On Sunday. Only four days to go.'

'Silly me!' She laughed. 'So have you just come from Mr Jenkins?'

'Yeah. He's very busy now. Is Molly in bed yet?'

'I'm not sure.'

'I can't risk wrapping anything up, then.'

'You can wrap in here.'

'Then you'll have no surprises.'

'I'm too old for surprises.'

'No, you're not,' said Henry.

'You go and get something to eat. But give yer old gran a kiss first.'

He leaned down and kissed her on the cheek. Maybe she had meant it for the best, he thought. Maybe she didn't realise that what she had done was wrong.

The kitchen was empty. He cut himself a slice of bread and spread some jam on it. He was on his way out when his mum came down the stairs.

'Now you come straight home after the film, won't you?'

He nodded.

She took him by the arm and drew him in front of an old mirror on the wall.

'You've grown some more,' she said. 'I can rest my head on your shoulder now. Look.'

Henry smiled at his reflection. With any luck he would be taller than Uncle Bill and then he could look down on him.

'See you later, Mum.'

She yawned.

'I don't think so, love. I've some sleep to catch up on. This little one has started to kick and is keeping me awake nights.'

Henry turned away quickly. He didn't want to hear about the baby.

When Mrs Beaumont's front door swung open, Grace was standing there.

'Grace!' he yelled. He suddenly had the urge to fling his arms around her but, overwhelmed with shyness, he just stood and grinned. 'Are you staying?'

'Yes, yes, yes,' she cried, and she took hold of his jersey and dragged him in.

Jeffries and Pip were hovering behind her in the hallway, both beaming.

'And I'm going to school here in this house,' she said. 'My parents have agreed. And I won't see them till the spring.'

'And Mrs Beaumont is going to teach you?'

'Yes and no. She will, but she's told me she won't be like the teachers in school. Mrs Jeffries is going to teach me ballet and dressmaking, and Mrs Morgan is going to do arithmetic with me, which will be mostly about money. Mrs Beaumont says she's an expert at how to make every penny go a long way. And your mother is going to teach me how to knit and type. I hope she's patient.'

Remembering how his mother was with Molly, he nodded.

'Very patient.'

'Oh, good. And Mrs Beaumont is going to see if the lady who gives Pip piano lessons can teach me some new songs. But the best thing of all is that I am going to do no reading, no writing and no homework. She has forbidden it. She's going to read to me and choose programmes on the wireless for me. Isn't it wonderful? I don't have to go to school and be hated by teachers. And Mrs Beaumont doesn't believe I'm a lost cause.'

'Good, isn't it?' said Pip.

'And I'm joining in,' said Jeffries.

'You're leaving school?'

'No, but when I come home I'm doing ballet with Grace.'

'Ballet!' yelled Henry. 'Ballet's for girls.'

'No, it isn't, you chump. There were men in my mother's company.'

'I'm doing it too,' said Pip.

'You're not!' said Henry.

'I think it's a good idea.'

'Why?'

'So I can be with Grace.'

'Pip!' chorused Jeffries and Henry.

Henry then found them staring at him.

'Oh, no,' he protested, 'I am not doing ballet.' And then he grinned. 'But I can take photographs.'

'I have a little surprise for you,' said Mrs Beaumont as they walked to the Apollo. 'I'm taking you to see *Holiday Inn* on Boxing Day. Henry, your stepfather is going to look after Molly so that your mother can come with us. I thought of asking your grandmother, but your mother didn't think she'd be interested.'

Henry swallowed.

'No,' he said, but his voice came out in a croak.

'You lucky things,' said Grace dismally.

'Won't you be here for Christmas?' asked Jeffries.

'No. My great-aunt has to go away so I'll be with two of my other aunts.'

'Which brings me to my next piece of news,' said Mrs Beaumont. 'I've had a word with your great-aunt and she has agreed to let you stay here and spend Christmas with me, if you want.'

'Oh, Mrs Beaumont! Yes, yes, yes!' Grace cried, and she flung her arms round her.

Pip proceeded to do a strange whirling dance in the road, much to the amusement of people heading for the queue.

'And I'm treating you to ice creams today. I think it's a time to celebrate, don't you?'

The air of Christmas was infectious. By the time their part of the queue had reached the doors, they could hardly hear themselves speak above the chattering crowd of excited people in the decorated foyer. Henry took the camera out. With any luck there would be enough light to take a photograph.

'Why do you like taking photographs of people you don't know?' asked Jeffries.

'Dunno,' said Henry. 'I just do.'

'You're a people-watcher,' said Mrs Beaumont.

'Is there such a thing?' asked Grace.

'Oh, yes. On the Continent people sit outside cafés and watch people for hours.'

Henry looked through his viewfinder, swinging it slowly round the foyer, past a placard announcing that the cinema was changing its name to the Essoldo, and then on to the front of the queue. And that's when he spotted him – the man from the photographs. He was at one of the box offices handing over money. Henry snapped him and then quickly turned away. Could it just be another coincidence that he was here at the same time as Mrs Beaumont?

'There aren't any bulbs powerful enough, you see,' he heard Pip telling Jeffries, 'so to make light, you need two sticks of carbon.'

'Pip!' interrupted Jeffries.

'And Mr Hart said that one was negative and one was positive. And he touched them with this handle.'

'Can you tell me about it later?' pleaded Jeffries.

'Good idea,' said Pip happily. 'Then I can tell you about the lamp house. You have to look at the flame through this window of dark blue glass. That stops you hurting your eyes, see?'

'Pip!' protested Jeffries.

'I watched Stan, the second projectionist, adjust the carbons,' he said, turning to Henry. 'He had to work out exactly how far apart they had to be and then suddenly voomph, they gave light!'

Jeffries gave a groan and Henry smiled at him. An usherette took their tickets and another one swung a torch down towards the cheapest seats.

'The carbons slowly burned away during the twenty minutes the first reel was being shown on the screen,' Pip whispered, following Jeffries between a row of seats, 'and then Stan re-adjusted them in the lamp glass so that there was enough carbon left to do the next twenty minutes, for the next reel.'

Pip only stopped talking when the B film began, and Henry returned to thinking about the man he had seen in the foyer. Suppose the man just liked going to the cinema? After all, the first photograph had been outside the Plaza, but then why would he be outside a ballet shoe shop in London? Maybe he was Christmas shopping. He wouldn't have been able to find a shop like that in Sternsea. Henry looked back up at the screen and began to relax.

Immediately the film ended, a spotlight from the projectionist's window swung down on the usherette selling ice creams. Grace leapt up to bag a place in the fast-forming queue.

*She's going to need another pair of hands*, thought Henry, heading up the aisle. Within seconds Pip had joined them, money from Mrs Beaumont in his hand.

'So when it had finished burning,' Henry heard Pip say to Grace, 'he had to release the clamp and wind right back here,' he added, spreading his arms, 'so he still had all that amount of carbon to use.'

'Gosh,' she said, handing Pip two of the ice creams to hold.

'Then he clamped it up again so there'd be enough carbon left for the next twenty-minute reel.'

'Pip,' said Henry.

'It's all right,' said Grace, 'I don't mind listening.'

'But do you know what he's talking about?'

'Not really,' she said, smiling.

'And then he had to do the same thing with the negative carbon. Oh, I forgot to tell you how big the carbon is. It's about the size of a pencil.'

'The ice creams are melting,' said Henry.

'You're right,' said Pip, and he moved quickly back to their seats.

Henry and Grace came down the aisle with the rest of the ice creams. Henry noticed the man again in one of the rows. He had removed his hat and was staring up at the screen. Henry quickly looked away. This was no coincidence.

The man was sitting in the row behind them.

# 4. Present hunting

HENRY COULDN'T SLEEP. EVERY TIME HE CLOSED HIS EYES, HE would see the man sitting there in the crowded cinema. Being cold didn't help. He tucked his pyjama trousers into his socks and flung his old raincoat over the bed, but he was so tense that even rubbing his feet together to warm them made no difference. He envied Molly, sleeping peacefully.

He kept thinking back to the previous evening over and over again. Throughout the second film he had kept an eye on Mrs Beaumont, ready to protect her should the man make a move towards her seat. But nothing happened. As soon as the closing music filled the auditorium, people stood up and blocked his view. By the time he had reached the aisle, the man had disappeared.

Henry wanted to tell Jeffries as soon as they were back at Mrs Beaumont's house, but once there, a paraffin heater was lit in the study and Grace and Pip began to mess around with tunes, Grace singing, Pip finding the notes. One look at Jeffries' smiling face and Henry knew that wild horses wouldn't have dragged him away. He would have to wait.

That night he had hardly drifted off to sleep when his mother was calling him to get up. Being the day before Christmas Eve, suddenly everyone was beginning to do their Christmas shopping and Mr Jenkins needed the extra help. When he arrived at the shop, piles of neatly wrapped packages were already stacked on the left-hand counter and a long queue of women were shivering outside in the crisp half-light.

Henry had brought the camera with him. As more light began to seep into the sky, he looked into the viewfinder. At first the women smiled and waved at him or turned away protesting, but after a while they grew uninterested in the protruding lens and returned to chatting or staring vacantly into the distance or battling to hang on to their small children, and that's when Henry took a photograph.

His mother was out when he returned home. Only his gran was in the house.

'Yer mum's taken that girl to some Christmas party,' she said. 'And I'm hungry. Why don't you make me a nice cuppa and keep me company. That man has been driving me round the bend. You'll never guess what he's gone and done now.'

Henry dreaded the thought of listening to hours of complaints about Uncle Bill, and he was desperate to tell Jeffries about the man who was following Mrs Beaumont.

'I'm going to the Pictures,' he lied, stoking up Gran's fire and adding a few lumps of fresh coal. 'Mum'll be home soon.'

Grace dragged him excitedly into Mrs Beaumont's hallway.

'Max and Oscar are here,' she said. 'They're in the sitting room putting up the Christmas tree.'

Suddenly Henry heard a high-pitched squeal coming from downstairs.

'Is Molly here?' he asked, surprised.

'Yes. She's helping make decorations.'

'I thought she was at a party.'

'Did you?' Grace shrugged. 'Well, I suppose it is a bit like a party downstairs. Come and see.'

He found his mother and Molly sitting at the table with Mrs Jeffries and Pip, surrounded by coloured paper chains and lanterns, a bowl of glue standing in the centre. Sweet smells were coming from the range and Mrs Morgan was pulling out a tray of ginger biscuits from the oven. Molly was engrossed in cutting a strip of coloured paper, her tongue curled round her upper lip.

'Hello!' exclaimed his mother. 'Does Gran know you're here?'

'I told her I was going to the Pictures,' he admitted guiltily.

'Oh, dear,' she said, 'and I'm no better. I lied too. Have you seen the tree?'

'Not yet.'

Mrs Morgan removed her jacket from the back of the door and slung it on. 'See you all tomorrow,' she said gaily.

Pip followed her into the hall.

'Where's she going?' asked Henry, puzzled. 'The shops will be closed.'

'She still cleans offices at night,' said his mother. 'But at least she knows Pip has company now.' She dangled a paper chain in front of him. 'We need all the help we can get. Paper chains or lanterns?'

Already Grace was sitting beside Molly, chatting to her and making encouraging noises, and Molly was beaming up at her.

'Lanterns,' Henry said, 'but you'll have to show me what to do.'

Mrs Beaumont appeared with the gramophone and put it on the dresser.

'Grace, why don't you choose something upbeat and cheerful, like the music at the jazz club.'

'Molly, you're putting glue all over the table,' said Henry.

Molly presented the end of her paper chain and as he

helped her put glue on it, he glanced aside at his mother. She was happier than he had seen her for years. He guessed it was because she was away from Uncle Bill, and he wished he could be out of their lives for ever, but there was no hope of that ever happening. Molly worshipped him and he worshipped Molly. The knowledge that his mother was stuck with him caused Henry to feel so angry that he had to get out of the room.

'I'll go and help with the tree,' he said suddenly.

'Good idea,' said Pip.

'Me too,' said Jeffries, following them.

Leaving the warmth of the kitchen made the rest of the house seem freezing. In the sitting room, they found Max and Oscar wearing scarves and gloves, hopping up and down in the middle of the room.

'Hello, there,' said Max. 'What do you think?'

Standing solidly in half a wooden barrel filled with earth was the tallest fir tree Henry had ever seen. On a nearby table Henry noticed boxes of tiny glass ornaments.

'Stupendous!' Jeffries exclaimed.

'We're leaving the fragile decorations to Ma. But we can shift some of the furniture out of the bay window to make room for the tree.'

'Want any help?' said Henry, eager to do anything that would take his mind off Uncle Bill.

Strains of jazz could be heard coming from the kitchen.

'Yes, please, but let's nip downstairs and thaw out first.'

As Max and Oscar darted out of the room, Henry hung back. Pip was already by the door. This was his chance to tell Jeffries about the man.

'Jeffries!' he whispered urgently.

'Yes?'

Pip turned and smiled at them. A wave of laughter came from the kitchen. It was the wrong moment.

'It's good that Grace can stay here for Christmas, isn't it?' Henry blurted out.

'It's good for us too,' said Jeffries. 'Mother says she's going to have to learn how to cook again. She's so used to using one gas ring, she's forgotten what to do with an oven.'

'I've never had Christmas dinner in a house,' said Pip.

Jeffries looked puzzled.

'But you lived in a house.'

'Yes, I know. But we never had Christmas dinner there. We had it in a British Restaurant. Mum saved up for it.'

'We had tinned ham,' said Jeffries.

'Us too,' said Henry. 'Do you know what you're having this year?'

'Chicken!' they chorused and they headed for the hall.


'Done your Christmas shopping, then?' asked Mr Jenkins on Christmas Eve.

'No, Mr Jenkins.'

'Good job I only need you this morning, then. You can do it this afternoon, eh? And those chocolates you want for your mother you can have at half price.'

'Thank you, Mr Jenkins.'

'And I've found a box which I think will be right for your sister.'

Henry's mother had told him that she and Uncle Bill were giving Molly a doll for Christmas. Observing how everyone enjoyed Molly's company at Mrs Beaumont's house had made Henry think differently about her. She seemed less annoying there. He had always thought of her as a nuisance, but not any more. For the first time, Henry wanted to give her a present, but had decided to keep it a secret from Gran. A doll, he had told Mr Jenkins, would need a bed. Mr Jenkins produced a heavy slatted wooden box that had previously been filled with precious oranges and it was in good nick. It already almost looked like a cot. Henry was so pleased with it he couldn't speak.

'Now go on with you,' said Mr Jenkins brusquely. 'And you can make room in that raincoat pocket for this tin of pineapples,' he added when they were in the yard. He placed a finger on his lips. 'Keep mum, and give it to Mum. And there's a little something for you towards the Pictures.'

Henry saw at a glance that he had given him enough to get into the cheap seats for two programmes.

'Thank you, Mr Jenkins!'

'Keep that to yourself. I don't want Frank upset. He's a good lad. And I doubt he'll finish deliveries today much before midnight.'

'Yes, Mr Jenkins. Merry Christmas, sir.'

Henry shoved the tinned pineapples into his tight-fitting raincoat and made his way past the queue of shoppers. As he walked out on to the pavement, Frank was hopping off his delivery bike, his basket empty. He glared angrily at Henry.

'Are you still 'ere? There's no gettin' rid of you, is there? You keep turning up like a bad penny, you do. If you think you're havin' this bike, you've got another think comin'. I've worked hard all year for Christmas tips and I'm not havin' you takin' . . .'

'I've finished,' Henry interrupted. 'I'm off.'

'Oh,' he said scowling. 'That's all right, then.'

'Happy Christmas.'

'Don't push yer luck!'

As Henry stepped into Mrs Beaumont's hall, he noticed a small suitcase propped by the wall.

'It's mine,' said Grace. 'Great-Aunt Florence left this morning. Why are you carrying that box?'

'It's going to be a cot for Molly's doll. I can't leave it at home and I have to go shopping.'

'Hello, there!'

Mrs Beaumont poked her head out of the sitting room.

'I heard,' she said. 'And yes, you can leave it here. It's a beauty. Need any paint?'

'Yeah! Got any?'

'White or pink is what we need,' she said thoughtfully. 'Whitewash. We must have some left over somewhere. And you'll need a pillow and a mattress.'

'That's what I was going to buy at the shops.'

'Get her something else. I have all sorts of scraps here. I'm sure we can make them. Mrs Jeffries is the person to talk to. She's a genius on the sewing machine. Would you like me to ask her advice?'

'Yeah. Thanks.'

'Hand it over. And now you'd better dash. You don't have much time left.'

Although Henry was excited about buying a present for his half-sister, his excitement diminished rapidly once he had visited one tiny store after another. The noise of small yelling children around him was deafening, and it was torture standing among girls' toys. There were dolls' dresses but not only were they too expensive but he had no idea if Molly's doll was going to be big or small. Then to his horror he heard someone calling out his name. He swung round ready to bite their head off if they made fun of him. It was a girl from his class called Jane Taylor.

'You look a bit lost,' she remarked. 'Are you trying to find a Christmas present for a girl?'

'Yeah,' Henry mumbled.

'How old is she?'

'Two. Nearly three.' Embarrassed, Henry wished that she would go away.

'Is it a doll you're looking for?'

'No. Something to go with a doll. I've got a box for a cot.'

'That's good. Follow me. The stuff here is too expensive.'

Henry stared at her.

'Come on,' she said, turning.

Disgruntled, he shambled after her, keeping his distance in case anyone spotted them together and teased him in school for 'going out' with a girl in his form. She led him down an alley to a tiny ramshackle building filled with old and new toys, grabbed him by the hand and dragged him through the door.

'Dolls,' she said, pointing to an untidy pile of boxes in the corner.

'I don't want . . .' But it was pointless saying anything. Jane was already heading for the pile.

Behind a dusty glass counter filled with puppets and second-hand Hornby trains stood an ancient couple. They beamed at him. Henry gave them an awkward nod and hurried to join Jane.

'There!' Jane squealed, pointing at some satin material. It was hanging from underneath one of the crumpled boxes. As she tugged at it, the boxes began to topple. By now her enthusiasm had started to filter through to him. He grabbed them and shifted them to one side.

'Gently,' said Jane to herself, pulling it out.

It was a tiny eiderdown, covered in dust and cobwebs, pale blue on one side, pale pink on the other.

'One side for a boy, one side for a girl,' she exclaimed.

'It looks just the right size,' he said, grinning.

'It'll need a good brushing down,' said the shopkeeper, smiling. 'I take it you want it.'

It cost Henry a visit to a cinema.

As they left the shop, Jane said, 'We're quits now.'

Henry stared at her, puzzled.

'You stuck up for me and Margaret in Maths and got caned for it, remember? When Mr David kept ignoring us. The teachers think us girls are only good for getting married and having babies. Well, we're not.'

Henry had never heard a girl speak so vehemently before. He gazed at her, silenced by this sudden outburst of anger.

'Well, anyway, that's what I think,' she said, 'so do you need any more help? I know boys hate to be anywhere near a shop.'

Henry smiled.

'There's my gran,' he said.

She looked thoughtful for a moment.

'An embroidery set. How about that? I know where you can get some really cheap ones.'

In a run-down haberdasher's shop she found a small tablecloth with outlines of flowers in the corners and centre. It came with two packs of pale coloured silk thread, sewing needles and instructions.

'I have to go now,' she said. 'I haven't bought my sister's presents yet.'

Before he could thank her, she was halfway down the road, weaving her way in and out of the Christmas shoppers. And then he remembered one other person he had yet to buy a present for.

'Uncle Bill!' he moaned.

He didn't want to give him anything but he knew his mother would be upset if he didn't. He walked miserably along the streets, racking his brains for an idea. He was just crossing a road when he remembered that the second-hand bookshop Jeffries and Pip visited was in the street which ran alongside it.

'Of course,' he said. 'A second-hand book! Perfect!'

His stepfather would be pleased to receive any book and his gran would be pleased because it wasn't new. But would he get there in time? He started running. As he drew nearer he could see a single light bulb swinging at the back of the shop. Relieved, he pushed open the jangling door.

'Can I help you?' said a voice in the semi-darkness.

A thin pale man with a tangle of grey hair was peering with interest at him over his spectacles. Henry caught sight of the ceiling-high corridors of bookcases. It looked like a maze. Without a map, he reckoned his skeleton would be discovered in the shop the following Christmas.

'Yeah. Please.'

'Are you looking for a book for a girl or a boy?'

'A man,' said Henry.

'What does he like to read?'

Henry's mind went blank. He could feel himself reddening and then he remembered.

'Short stories. Penguin New Writing. Graham Greene.'

'Graham Greene,' said the man thoughtfully. 'I think you'll find a hardback copy of *Brighton Rock* over there. It's almost new.' He pointed to a pile of books in a dingy corner. 'I did have an anglepoise lamp you could have plugged in over there, but the other day a woman bought it as a Christmas present for her husband, so I'm afraid you'll have to squint, but you have young eyes,' he added with humour.

Henry nodded his thanks politely and headed towards his doom. The books in the corner were stacked up so high they reached his knees. He wondered how on earth the man ever found anything. And then he saw the word *Rock* staring out at him, almost as though the book was waiting for him to collect it. He eased it out and was about to take it to the counter by the front window when he spotted what looked like a schoolboy annual. Above a large picture of a boy in a helmet sitting in a racing car was the title, *So You Want To Be* . . .

He opened it and began to look through the Contents page.

'Chapter Three,' he murmured. '*So you want to be a train driver.*'

*Not really,* thought Henry, *but that's what Uncle Bill wants me to do.* Uncle Bill had told him that if he worked in an area where railwaymen stayed in the same job year after year, it could take as long as twenty years. The thought of spending twenty years working on the railways made Henry feel desperate, unlike Jack Riddell, one of the boys in the Victorian railway group. Jack was down by the railways every moment he could find. He would have given his right arm to have Henry's job waiting for him, but he didn't come from a railway family. It had been easy for Henry. Uncle Bill was a third generation railwayman.

'Found what you were looking for?' asked the bookshop man. Henry dropped the book, startled. 'Ah, still looking,' he said, and left Henry to it.

As Henry went to pick it up, his eye fell on another of the chapter headings, the title of which shook him. Trembling, he flicked over the pages until he found himself reading a step-by-step description of all the different jobs one had to do before becoming a camera operator in a film studio. It was much like the road to being a train driver, in that it took years. He already knew that to make a film you needed a film crew, but what he hadn't known was that within each film crew there were smaller crews. His finger stopped at one sentence. *The job of everyone who has a hand in helping make a film is to tell a story.*

'That's what I want to do,' he whispered.

Like Jeffries, he wanted to tell stories, but with pictures, not words. Reading that sentence made him realise that not only were there people who thought like him but there were people who made a living out of it. He now understood Grace when she had said in the jazz club, 'You mean there are other people like me?'

He returned to the book, hungry to learn more. He discovered that the director of photography concentrated on lighting the scenes for the camera operator, and it was the artistry of the camera operator which helped tell the story.

'But how do I start?' whispered Henry impatiently.

He traced a finger down the page until he found what he was looking for.

*'Boys can join a camera crew straight from school to start their training. Their first job is only a tiny link in the film-making process but it is a job that is vital.'* Henry closed the book.

'Clapper boy!' And he was thrown back to the day

when Mr Finch had asked them what they would want if they could wave a magic wand. And Henry had seen himself closing a clapperboard. It was like a premonition.

Suddenly he felt so excited that he wanted to yell at the top of his voice, because at long last he now knew what he really wanted to do when he left school. He also knew that Uncle Bill would do everything in his power to stop him. As he sat among the dust and debris of hundreds of books, it dawned on him that he was about to begin the most important fight of his life.

# 5. Christmas

'COME IN QUICKLY OUT OF THE COLD,' MRS BEAUMONT SAID, 'and see what we've done.'

She thrust open the door into the kitchen with a flourish. Immediately Henry spotted the box with its slatted sides on the table. It had been painted white.

'I put it in here so it would dry quickly near the range,' she said.

'It's like a real cot,' he exclaimed. Beside the box were a small pillow, sheets and a cream-coloured woollen blanket. 'Where did you find the little bedclothes?'

'Mrs Jeffries made them.'

'Thanks, Mrs Jeffries!' he said.

'I enjoyed it,' she said, glancing up from rolling pastry. 'It made a nice change from corsets and Molly is such a lovely little girl.'

'I'll make up the rest of the bed,' said Mrs Beaumont.

'I've bought something to go in it,' he said, putting the

bags on the table. 'It's a bit dusty though.' He pulled out the tiny eiderdown.

'Oh, Henry, that will finish it off beautifully.'

Within seconds the door burst open.

'I told you he was here,' said Grace triumphantly. Pip and Jeffries were behind her.

'Come upstairs,' said Pip.

'Hurry up,' added Jeffries.

In the sitting room, the enormous tree was now festooned with glass animals. Small candles in metal candleholders were clipped to the branches. The walls of the room were hung with greenery and paper chains, and freshly chopped wood was banked up beside a fire. A shovel filled with chestnuts was propped on top of the glowing coals.

'Isn't it wonderful?' said Grace.

Henry nodded enviously. He imagined them round the tree opening presents together, and later sitting around the table he and Mrs Beaumont had carried down the stairs. He remembered her remark that night: *'I wonder which seven people will join me round it?'* Now with her two sons, Mrs Jeffries and Jeffries, Pip and Mrs Morgan, Grace and her, eight people would be sitting round it for Christmas dinner.

'Wrapping paper,' said a voice behind him.

Mrs Beaumont was holding sheets of red and green paper. 'You'd better wrap up your presents here. You'll never be able to do it in secret in your house while Molly's around.'

Downstairs she gave the tiny eiderdown a good beating and placed it over the sheet and blanket inside the box. It fitted perfectly.

'It's so sweet!' cried Grace. 'Molly will love it.'

Henry sat at the table listening to their chatter. He still hadn't been able to find a moment to talk to Jeffries about the man in the cinema. It would have to wait till after Christmas.

His mother was standing outside the front door with Molly. Guiltily Henry remembered her having asked him to help with the decorations.

'Don't go in,' she said excitedly.

'Are you waiting for Uncle Bill?'

'No. It said in the *Sternsea Evening News* that the cathedral bells would be rung this Christmas Eve. I thought we might be able to hear them from here. Shush!' she said suddenly. And faintly in the distance Henry could hear them slowly chiming. 'They're wishing us a very merry Christmas and a happy new year, Molly. In eight days time it will be 1950. Come on, let's get into the warm.'

Henry followed them in with his parcels. As they passed Gran's room, he noticed the wireless was on again. It didn't sound like the kind of programme Gran would be interested in at all. He wondered if she just put it on out of habit. He suddenly remembered seeing his mother carrying the wireless accumulator into the scullery – she was worn out and soaked from the rain after her walk back from having it recharged. His gran must realise it was a waste of power, surely?

'Mum, when you take Gran's accumulators to be recharged, how long does it take you to get there and back?'

'With Molly, anything from half an hour to an hour there, and half an hour or more back. I have to concentrate on not spilling any acid on my clothes, which can be a bit tricky if Molly is in one of her excitable moods. And then of course I often have to queue as well.' She looked puzzled. 'Why this sudden interest?'

'Gran has it on a lot, doesn't she?'

'Yes. But it keeps her happy.'

His mother had placed a silver Christmas tree on a box in the corner of the kitchen. It was the same one they had used the year before. After having seen Mrs Beaumont's tree, it suddenly seemed very small.

'By the way,' she added quietly, 'Mrs Beaumont has invited us round to her place after *Holiday Inn*.'

Suddenly Molly stiffened. The front door had been opened and Henry heard footsteps rapidly moving up the stairs. 'Daddy! Daddy!' Molly yelled. Henry's mother held her arm.

'Daddy will be down in a minute.'

Henry guessed Uncle Bill was on his way to the bedroom to hide presents.

'Want Daddy!' she shouted.

Through the wall they heard the wireless being turned up.

'That's all I need,' muttered his mother.

'Auntie, cross,' said Molly.

The footsteps were now thundering down towards the kitchen. The door was flung open and Uncle Bill strode into the kitchen in his grimy overalls and cap. From the state of him, Henry knew he must have been on one of the goods trains that day. Molly charged at him and flung her arms around his legs. He laughed and picked her up.

'Mission accomplished,' he said, giving Henry's mother a wink.

'Bill, you never went to the shops looking like that?'

'No time to change. Quick wash of the hands and I hared out of the station. I was quite a conversation stopper, I can tell you. Are those mince pies I can see?' He leaned over the table and grabbed one. 'And then I must start decorating the tree.'

'Not till you've got out of those filthy overalls and had a cup of tea and a bite to eat.'

He sat down on a chair with Molly on his knee.

'Did you hear the cathedral bells?' asked Henry's mother.

'Yes. Just as I'd made a decision.'

His mother held the teapot, not moving.

'And?'

'I agree with you.'

'Oh, Bill.'

Henry looked from one to the other, not knowing what was going on. His mother glanced at him.

'I think we should tell Henry.'

Henry could feel his fists clenching. He was still upset that they had left it to Gran to tell him about the baby.

'It's not that we've been keeping secrets from you, Henry,' said Uncle Bill, 'it's just that there was no point in saying anything before I'd made up my mind.'

'Uncle Bill's teacher, Mr Cuthbertson, has persuaded Uncle Bill to apply for an interview next month,' said Henry's mother.

'An interview for what?' asked Henry.

'Teacher training,' answered Uncle Bill. 'If I'm successful, I'll start training in September. But don't worry about your job at Hatton Station. It'll still be waiting for you after you finish school. And anyway I might not be accepted, so there's no point mentioning it to anyone.'

'Why do you want to be a teacher?' Henry asked.

'To give children the chances I missed out on and a taste of what I've discovered late in my life. We'll have to tighten our belts, though.'

'Does Gran know?'

'We'll tell her next week,' said his mother. 'She might

take it badly and we don't want to spoil her Christmas.'

*As if he cares*, thought Henry. *He'll use the teacher-training thing as another excuse to be even meaner.*

Just then Uncle Bill spotted the paper chains and lanterns.

'Did you make all those today?' he said.

'No. Yesterday. At Hettie Beaumont's. We wanted it to be a surprise.'

'They look cracking. You too?' he asked Henry.

'A few,' he muttered. He shoved his hands awkwardly into his raincoat pocket and came across the tin. 'I've got something from Mr Jenkins for you,' he said, struggling to prise it out.

'You really need a bigger raincoat now,' said his mother.

'You're nearly as tall as me,' said his stepfather. 'Tall enough for a man's raincoat, eh, Maureen?'

'As soon as Christmas is over, we'll pop round to the WVS clothing exchange and get one.'

Henry spread the raincoat out on the table, held it down firmly and yanked the tin out.

'Pineapples!' his mother exclaimed. 'Oh, how lovely. I got some grapes too in the market. They've not been selling so well this year so they cut the price down. And I managed to get a chicken. It's only four pounds but I've got a bit of ham to go with it.'

Henry felt like an outsider again as his mother and Uncle Bill chatted to one another. Molly didn't look too happy about it either. She tried to stop her father speaking by placing her hand across his mouth while he repeatedly removed it.

'You might want to open my Christmas present to you early, before you start cooking the Christmas dinner,' said his stepfather, significantly.

'No, I'll wait.'

'But it'll save you time when you . . .'

'Don't tell me. I can guess what it is, but I can use it next year when I've got used to it.'

*Is she really happy?* Henry wondered, staring at his mother's glowing face, *or is it an act to make everything nice for everyone?* If so, she was putting on a very good show.

'Want to decorate,' Molly interrupted.

'She's been dying to start on the tree all day but I told her she had to wait till you came home.'

'Which reminds me,' said Uncle Bill. He took a little package from his pocket wrapped in waxy yellowy-white paper. 'You must unwrap it very carefully,' he said to Molly.

'For me?' she asked.

'For the tree.'

It was a fairy. Henry couldn't believe that a grown man would buy a fairy and then he remembered he had bought a doll's eiderdown. The dress on the fairy was spread out in a circle so that it could be placed on the top of the tree. It had semi-transparent cream wings, curly blonde hair and a tiny silver and gold crown and wand.

'You can put her on,' Uncle Bill said, and he lifted her up. She plonked it on top and it slumped to one side. 'Looks like she's had one too many,' Uncle Bill said.

'Bill,' cried Henry's mother, laughing, 'you are awful!'

He placed Molly on the floor and straightened the drunken-looking fairy. Molly stared up at it, slapped her cheeks, and began dancing around the floor, shrieking with excitement, at which point the volume from the wireless from the next room rose to a crescendo. Henry noticed his mother give Uncle Bill a glance. Quickly she picked up the bag of paper chains.

'Come on, Molly,' she said hastily. 'Let's put these up, shall we?' There was a loud hammering at the front door.

'I'll get it,' said Henry, glad of a chance to escape.

He had hardly opened the door when Mrs Henson from next door pushed him aside, stormed into his grandmother's room and turned the volume down.

'And keep the ruddy thing down!' she yelled. 'We can't hear ourselves think. I got my daughter and her children stayin' with us and you've woken the baby!'

'It's that girl,' he heard his gran say, 'she makes such a noise I can't hear it.'

'Get yourself a hearing aid, then. You can get one for free now. Then we can all have a bit of peace.' She had hardly stormed out of the room when she whirled back round again, a finger raised. 'And if you turn it up one more time, I'll send Mr Henson round to nab your accumulator!' She marched past Henry in a fury. He was about to close the door after her when she stopped and gave him a stern look.

'I know I'm speaking out of turn,' she said quietly, 'but your mum ought to do something about her. She don't because you're so fond of her. But you're getting older now. Time for you to have a word with her.'

Bewildered, Henry watched her stump off.

'What's she talking about?' he muttered.

Something bulky and heavy was lying on top of his feet. He peered sleepily down at the foot of his bed in the half-light. It was one of Uncle Bill's long woolly socks. A slim parcel was sticking out of it. He fumbled around under the covers for his jersey and pulled it over his pyjama top. Molly was still asleep. He had promised his mother that as soon as she stirred he would wake her. But she hadn't said anything about him opening his stocking at the same time. He hesitated, but only for a moment. He switched on his torch and went immediately for the thin parcel. It was a large black umbrella with a cane handle. Perfect for standing in cinema queues in the rain. What followed was fudge, a Christmas copy of *The Dandy*, a new roll of film, a hand-knitted scarf, an orange, an apple, nuts and chocolate coins. He wrapped the scarf round his neck and read the comic, eating the chocolate coins. He wondered if Grace, Pip and Jeffries were awake yet. It was good knowing they were just around the corner, yet he felt envious that they would have each other's company. He switched off the torch, slipped under the covers and closed his eyes again.

He was woken by small fingers tugging at his face.

'Ow!' he yelled.

'Farver Christmas!' said an excited voice.

Henry looked blearily over the covers. The door was flung open and his mother raced into the room in an old dressing gown while Uncle Bill shivered behind her in his pyjamas.

'Presents!' declared Molly, and she hugged her bulging sock.

They sat at the end of his bed and watched transfixed as Molly impatiently pulled out a small parcel and ripped the paper off. Inside was a box of wax crayons. His mother smiled at Henry.

'You've been up early I see,' she said, glancing at the wrapping paper strewn across his blanket. 'Do you like the presents Father Christmas brought you this year?'

'Yeah!'

'And from the chocolate on your face you didn't waste any time enjoying one of them.'

Molly meanwhile was frantically tearing paper off a colouring book.

'I'll take a photo of her,' he whispered, slipping out of bed to get the camera.

'Lovely!' said his mother.

After breakfast, Henry dressed in his bedroom while his mum laid the fire in the front room. He could hear Gran grumbling. He opened the door to eavesdrop.

'It's freezin' in 'ere,' she complained.

'You can dress in front of the range. I can keep the others out of the kitchen while you do. It's nice and warm in there.'

'But you've already laid the fire in 'ere so why not light it?'

'Because it's a waste of coal having it burning while we're at church.'

'Not if you bank it up. Then it'll be nice and warm for when I get back.'

'But we're all going to be in the kitchen to open the presents under the tree.'

Henry closed the door.

He hoped they weren't going to squabble all day.

As soon as they returned from church they made for the warmth of the kitchen, except for Gran.

'I'll put the presents round the tree,' said Uncle Bill.

'Lovely,' said Henry's mother. 'That'll give me time to see if everything's cooking nicely in the oven.'

When various saucepans were simmering on the range, she sat down.

'You can call Gran now, Henry.'

'It's bitter in my room,' Gran complained as she entered the steamy kitchen. 'When are you going to get my fire going?'

'I told you, after we've opened the presents,' said Henry's mother, putting on a brave smile. 'You should have sat in here. It's lovely and warm.'

'Not with that noisy girl.'

Henry noticed that Gran was only carrying three small presents. He wondered which person she had left out. She handed them to Uncle Bill to be put by the tree and sat down.

'Ready?' said Uncle Bill cheerily. He lifted up a large rectangular box. 'To Molly,' he read, 'love from Mummy and Daddy.'

'Mummy and Daddy,' he heard his gran mutter under her breath. 'Nothin' wrong with Mum and Dad.'

Molly tore off the wrapping paper. As soon as she saw the picture on the box she gave an excited scream. Her father helped her open it. Inside was a doll which looked like a baby. She grabbed it and cuddled it. Henry noticed his mother smile at Uncle Bill.

'To Auntie, best wishes from Maureen, Bill and Molly,' he read next.

It was a large knitted shawl in pink and blue wool.

'Very nice,' said Gran, stiffly.

'To Gran, love Henry,' said Uncle Bill, passing the parcel of embroidery to her.

'Oh my!' sighed his grandmother. 'You thoughtful boy. This is so pretty and it's something I can do when I can't get out.'

'I thought it'd look nice in your room.'

'Oh, it will, dear. Give us a kiss.'

'To Henry, lots of love from Uncle Bill and Mum.'

He passed Henry a bulky package. Inside was an ex-RAF rucksack in thick grey-blue canvas.

'It's waterproof,' said his mum. 'We thought it would be useful for when you travel up to London again. Your old one's got so many holes in it.'

'Thanks, Mum.'

'It's from Uncle Bill too,' said his mother.

Henry muttered a 'thanks' in his direction.

His stepfather lifted up a heavy box and put it on the table where his mother was sitting.

'To Maureen, love Bill,' he said, grinning.

Painstakingly his mother unwrapped it. Henry guessed it was so she could use the paper again.

'Oh, Bill,' she exclaimed. It was a pressure cooker. 'This will save hours of cooking and save on coal too. Thank you, love. Do mine next.'

He lifted up a strangely shaped parcel which appeared to have a long neck.

'Giraffe!' said Molly, pointing.

'To Bill, love from Maureen,' he announced.

It was an anglepoise lamp with a dark green lampshade.

'It's second-hand,' she said, 'but it works. You can read more easily at night now.'

Henry remembered the man in the second-hand bookshop telling him about the woman who had bought the lamp. It must have been his mother.

Uncle Bill was beaming. For a moment, the two of them smiled at one another as if there was no one else in the room. His mother really did love Uncle Bill, thought Henry, observing them. He could see it was no act. But he still couldn't understand why.

'Don't forget my presents,' said Gran.

She had given his mother, Uncle Bill and Molly a handkerchief each.

'To Mum, love from Henry,' Uncle Bill read out.

'Oh, Henry, it's like something out of a magazine,' his mother cried, looking at the photograph Henry had taken of her in the yard. 'And chocolates! I haven't seen a box as nice as this in ages. Thanks, Henry. I'll put these well out of the way of you know who.'

'What's this?' said his stepfather, eagerly opening Henry's parcel. '*Brighton Rock*!'

'Isn't that by that Graham Greene you like?' asked Henry's mother.

'Yes. And a hardback too. I am spoilt. Thank you, Henry.'

Henry noticed his grandmother was scowling. It was strange that she hadn't given him a present. He wondered if he had upset her.

'Now there's a funny thing,' she said, catching his eye, 'I could have sworn I'd brought your present in here. I must have left it in my room. Henry, could you go and get it for me, there's a love. I'm a bit squashed here with this table up so close against the wall.' And she gave a little laugh.

He spotted the parcel as soon as he walked into her room, large and bulky at the end of her bed. It felt soft. He carried it back to the kitchen.

'Big parcel,' said Molly.

'Oh, Mrs Dodge, you shouldn't have,' said Henry's mother, looking concerned.

'Open it, then,' said his gran, smiling.

'What is it?' he said, unwrapping it. As he pulled out the contents, his mother gasped. It was a man's stone gabardine raincoat, not knee length but long, the sort of raincoat Humphrey Bogart might wear.

'Blimey!' he gasped.

'Put it on,' said his grandmother.

As he slipped it on, it seemed to flow over him. It fell down to his shins. He buttoned it up and did up the belt.

'All you need now is a hat,' said his gran proudly. 'A trilby, of course.'

'Yeah,' he said laughing. 'Thanks, Gran.'

It was only when he looked at his mother that he was aware of a tension in the room. She seemed frozen in shock. Uncle Bill appeared to be motionless too.

'That looks like a very good raincoat,' his mother said dully.

'Nothing is too good for my grandson,' said Gran, determination in her voice.

There was an embarrassing silence.

'I've got a present for Molly,' Henry said, suddenly finding it awkward being the centre of attention.

Uncle Bill seemed to wake from a trance.

'Oh, yes?'

'It's under the table.' He dragged it out from under the table.

'Goodness!' said Gran in a clipped voice. 'That's a big present for a little girl.'

As Molly tore away at the wrapping paper, revealing the box, Henry was aware of a look of surprise from Uncle Bill.

'Bed!' yelled Molly. 'For the baby.'

Immediately she pulled down the covers and placed the doll's head on the pillows.

'Mr Jenkins gave me the box and I found the quilt in an old toy shop near Disraeli Road.'

'And I helped make the rest,' his mother added hurriedly.

Henry realised she didn't want Gran to know Mrs Jeffries had made them. He noticed she was twisting a tea towel nervously in her hands.

'I'll go and light the fire in the front room now,' and she dashed out of the room.

She seemed upset, thought Henry.

'You'd best take that raincoat off,' said Uncle Bill, 'and hang it in the wardrobe. You'll need to take care of that.'

'Oh, let him sit in it for a while,' said Gran. 'I like to see him in it.'

For the rest of the day there was a taut atmosphere in the house. Henry observed everyone going through the ritual of pulling crackers, putting on hats and looking for money in the pudding. It wasn't until he was alone with Gran in her room that he realised what it was all about.

'Did you see your stepfather's face when you unwrapped your raincoat?'

'No,' said Henry.

'He was so angry.'

'Why should he be?'

'Jealousy. He'd never give you anything like a new raincoat. He's so choked that I've spoilt you.'

The next morning he found his mother in the kitchen attempting to settle Molly with the wax crayons and some paper. *Brighton Rock* was on the table. A bookmark was sticking out of it. Uncle Bill must have been reading it after they had gone to bed while waiting to leave for the night shift. *He must really like it, then*, thought Henry. He didn't know whether to be pleased or annoyed.

'Oh, Henry,' Mum exclaimed, her face flushed, 'could you keep her occupied? I want to get the washing finished before dinner and get it on the line.'

Steam was wafting into the kitchen from the scullery.

He sighed.

'Thanks, love.'

As he drew up a chair beside Molly, he noticed that on the other side of her feet her doll was tucked up in the cot.

'Dolly sleep,' she said, her finger on her lips. She thrust a blue crayon at him. 'Sky,' she demanded.

Henry took the crayon, drew three large clouds and started to colour in the areas around them.

'Maureen!' yelled Gran, from the next room.

'Just coming.'

Henry watched his mother go through to the hall.

'What's going on?' he heard his gran say. 'Some Christmas this is.'

'I've got to get the washing done now because we're going to have an early cold dinner. Me and Henry are meeting Mrs Beaumont at the cinema. You know that, Mrs Dodge. She's gone up there early to save us a place in the queue. Now I must go and wake Bill up.'

'My fire's nearly out,' she said plaintively.

'I'll ask Henry to sort that out for you.'

Henry carried a shovel full of hot coals from underneath the copper in the scullery to the fireplace in Gran's room.

'I shall be left all alone,' she said, her mouth quivering.

'You can come to the cinema with us,' said Henry, hoping she wouldn't.

'You don't want to see *Holiday Inn*,' she said. 'It's not your sort of film, is it?'

'There's a western with it. And Mum's looking forward to it.'

'It's a wonder she has the time.'

'And Uncle Bill will be with Molly at the Kings Theatre so you'll have the place all to yourself. You're always saying you want a bit of peace and quiet.'

'Dinner's ready!' he heard his mother call out.

The silence round the table was unbearable. Molly tugged at her father's arm while he yawned and ate, having only had a few hours sleep after coming off his shift at six a.m. Gran picked at her food and his mother hardly sat at all, popping up and down to check the washing and hang it on the line in the yard. By the time the meal was over, Henry decided to make his escape. As soon as Gran had returned to her room and his mother was carrying crockery into the scullery, he said, 'I'm going out to start queuing. See you there!'

'Henry!' began his mother. 'Wait!'

'Had a accident,' he heard Molly state matter-of-factly.

Henry raced upstairs. He grabbed his new raincoat from the wardrobe, ran down the stairs and slipped out of the front door.

Walking briskly towards the railway station, he felt inches taller. He could imagine people looking at him with admiring glances. It was a good half-hour's walk to the cinema and the biting wind was bringing with it a flurry of light snow. He glanced at his reflection in the shop windows. The raincoat made him look mysterious, like a secret agent or an undercover reporter for a Chicago newspaper.

But when he reached the cinema queue half an hour later, he began to feel self-conscious. He approached it casually, looking for Mrs Beaumont, but to his alarm there was no sign of her.

Someone called out his name from behind. He whirled round. Max and Oscar were waving to him near the top of the queue. He ran up the steps to join them.

'We didn't recognise you at first in that raincoat,' said Oscar.

'Very Scotland Yard,' said Max.

'A Christmas present?' added Oscar.

Henry nodded.

'Lucky you.'

'You were expecting to see our mother,' said Max.

'Yeah. She's not ill, is she?'

'No. Just tired. We suggested the others catch up on sleep. We can have a nap on the train.'

'Aren't you staying, then?'

'No, we have to get back to London.'

'So you were all up very late?' asked Henry, feeling a little jealous.

'Not exactly,' said Oscar slowly. 'Up a little early, I'm afraid.'

'You mean you got up early and they went back to bed?'

'In a nutshell. Yes.'

Henry noticed they were giving each other strange looks.

'We'd better tell him,' said Max. 'He'll find out soon enough.'

'Find out what?' asked Henry, puzzled.

'We didn't exactly choose to get up,' Oscar said. 'We were woken up well before dawn.'

'By what?'

'The military police.'

Henry suddenly felt cold.

Oscar laughed.

'They tried to arrest me. They thought I was Private Jeffries. When they realised I wasn't, they searched every room.'

'Once they'd gone and we'd got over the shock,' said Max, 'the others had hot drinks and went back to bed.

What gave them the idea Mother was harbouring a deserter, I don't know.'

'Apparently,' said Oscar, 'she has her suspicions.'

Henry nodded, not daring to speak. He had his suspicions too.

## 6. Spilling the beans

'YOU'D THINK THEY'D HAVE ENOUGH TO DO WITHOUT TAKING notice of an old lady,' said Oscar.

'She must have seen one of us going into the house and assumed he was Private Jeffries,' Max added.

'You don't think Ma's slept through all those alarm clocks, do you?' Oscar remarked.

'Well, if she has, she's sleepwalking,' said Max, over his shoulder.

Henry turned to see Mrs Beaumont coming up the steps with Grace and the others. He felt his face growing hot. Grace ran up to him, gaping at the raincoat.

'You look like somebody in a film,' she said admiringly. 'Have you heard? We were all woken up in the dark.'

Mrs Beaumont had now almost reached him.

'Yeah,' he said, reddening.

'Where's your mother?' asked Mrs Beaumont. 'Isn't she coming?'

'Yes. I came early to keep you company.'

'You've heard about our dawn raid I expect.'

Henry nodded. He scrutinised her face to see if she had guessed the identity of the informer.

'I don't think they'll be back. Our informer may have attempted to spoil our Christmas but she didn't succeed.'

'Is Mrs Jeffries . . .?' he began.

'She's fine. Pip is the one who's taken it badly. He thought they were coming to take him away from his mother.'

She looked over her shoulder. Henry followed her gaze. He could see Jeffries chatting quite happily with his mother but the normally cheerful Pip was clinging nervously to Mrs Morgan's arm, like a drowning man hangs on to the wreckage of a ship.

'That's some raincoat,' said Jeffries, as he and Pip drew nearer.

'You're right,' added Pip quietly.

Henry could see he was forcing himself to smile and he had a strong desire to hug him fiercely.

'Henry!' It was his mother. She was running breathlessly up the steps to join them and was staring, horrified, at the raincoat. 'Oh, no! Why did you wear it? What if you get marks on it? Gran won't be able to take it back.'

'Why would she want to take it back?'

'In case it doesn't fit you properly,' she said hurriedly.

'But it does,' he said, puzzled.

Just then the doors were opened and the queue began to move.

Pip sat between Grace and Mrs Morgan. Henry saw Grace take hold of Pip's hand and squeeze it. Mrs Morgan spread her jacket on the seat next to her by the aisle and whenever anyone tried to sit there she told them it was taken, which was strange because there was no one there. Soon the cinema was plunged into a swelling musical score and *Holiday Inn*.

Henry had hoped that the film would blot out the pain gnawing away inside him, but it was so jolly it seemed to jar every bone in his body. He glanced at Jeffries and Mrs Jeffries. They were smiling up at the screen, as was Mrs Beaumont, while his mother sat next to him, clasping his raincoat on her lap, frowning and biting her lip. She was still upset because he had worn his new raincoat. A whispering from his right caused him to swing round. Mrs Morgan was removing her jacket from the seat and a tall, smartly dressed man sat down beside her. Grace turned to Henry and touched his arm.

'It's Mr Hart, one of the projectionists from the Plaza,' she whispered.

Henry returned to the film. But he couldn't enjoy it, not even when half the audience sang *I'm Dreaming of a White Christmas* with Bing Crosby.

As he gazed up at Fred Astaire, dancing on New Year's Eve, he remembered the last time he had seen Pip look so terrified. It was in the darkroom after he and his mother had been thrown out of their lodgings. Sitting there thinking about the way people like Pip were treated, he was suddenly filled with rage. And yet before Mr Finch came to the school he had been no better. Now he despised his grandmother's attitude, and for the first time he didn't feel an ounce of guilt for disagreeing with her.

The exuberance from the screen finally pulled him in, and as Fred Astaire danced around exploding firecrackers, his mother reached out and squeezed his hand.

'Happy Christmas, love,' she whispered.

'But you mustn't tell anyone,' said Pip.

'We won't,' said Grace impatiently. 'Go on.'

They had gathered on the bombsite to listen to Pip's secret away from prying ears.

'Mr Hart is going to sneak me and Mum into the projectionist's room this week while the Chief's away and he's going to let us watch a whole programme.'

'You do remember what's on at the Plaza, don't you?' Jeffries said.

'*The Romantic Age* and *The Story of Molly X.*'

'And you still want to see them?' Henry exclaimed.

Pip nodded excitedly.

'She was willing to kill for love,' quoted Jeffries

dramatically, 'and ready to give ten years of her life to hide it.'

'I don't mind,' said Pip, 'I just want to see what he does.'

'When will this be happening?' asked Henry.

'Tomorrow.'

Henry immediately saw a chance for him to be alone with Jeffries and tell him about the man who was following Mrs Beaumont.

'Jeffries, do you want to see *Fighter Squadron* at the Troxy with me?'

'Can I come?' said Grace.

'I don't think you'd like it,' said Henry swiftly.

'I like a bit of excitement too. Unless of course you're trying to get rid of me.'

'Of course not,' said Jeffries, 'are we?'

Henry was so frustrated, he couldn't speak. He gave a shrug.

The Troxy was only a five-minute walk from Mrs Beaumont's house. Henry met them opposite the Plaza.

'You're very quiet,' commented Jeffries as they passed the railway station road. 'What's up?'

'Are you cross because I've come with you?' said Grace.

'Not really,' he grunted.

'Oh,' said Grace, sounding hurt.

'It's just that I wanted to tell Jeffries something in private.'

'And you think I can't keep a secret?'

'I don't know.'

'My great-aunt doesn't know I'm with you. Is that proof enough for you?'

Henry glanced at Jeffries. He nodded.

'The railway bridge,' said Jeffries.

They turned back. The bridge was deserted. They leaned over the wall and gazed down at the track.

'There's Jack Riddell,' Jeffries exclaimed. 'On the platform.'

'Who's he?' Grace asked.

'A boy in our form who's mad about trains.'

He was sitting on a bench with a sketch-pad, drawing.

'So then, what is it?' asked Jeffries.

Henry told him about seeing the man at the Apollo.

'And you haven't said anything for a week?' stormed Jeffries. 'Why?'

'I didn't want Pip to know. He'd have given the game away. You know how excited he gets. And I couldn't get you on your own.'

'I don't understand,' said Grace. 'What's going on?'

'I think we ought to tell her,' said Jeffries.

'*The Lady Vanishes*,' said Grace quietly when they had finished.

'What do you mean?' asked Henry.

'Don't you remember? We saw it together. An

ordinary-looking woman vanishes because she's a spy or secret agent or something. I'm not saying that's what Mrs Beaumont is but . . .'

'No. You're right,' interrupted Henry excitedly. 'When we first met her she looked like an old lady in tweeds. Now she looks completely different.'

'Even her hair,' added Grace.

'And when I first went up to London with her, one of the first things Daniel said to her was, "Are you in disguise?"'

'Really?' Jeffries exclaimed.

'Yeah. And Max laughed at her when he saw what she looked like.'

'This is serious,' said Grace. 'I think we should tell her as soon as possible.'

'What about the film?' Jeffries asked.

'Blow the film. She could be in danger. The woman in *The Lady Vanishes* was kidnapped and drugged. We have to warn her.'

'I'll go back home and get the other photographs,' said Henry.

Mrs Jeffries was in the study busy making up corsets. They could hear the whirr of her sewing machine as they crept into the hall and down into the kitchen. Mrs Beaumont was sitting at the table, a pile of exercise books beside her.

'Hello,' she said, surprised. 'Come in. I could do with a breather. So could your mother, I expect. I'll put the kettle on and give her a call.'

'Can we talk to you alone first?' Henry said quickly.

She gazed at them for a moment.

'I take it this is about Pip, since he's not here.'

'No,' said Henry, 'it's just we were afraid he might spill the beans.'

'Is it about the informer?'

'No,' interrupted Henry hurriedly.

'Well, what is it?'

'It's about the photographs I took.' He pulled out the ones from his rucksack and spread them out on the table. 'I didn't show you these.'

She looked at them and smiled.

'Why not? They're very good, Henry.'

'Look more closely,' said Jeffries.

Mrs Beaumont frowned and peered at them again.

'Oh, my goodness!' she exclaimed. 'It's the man, isn't it?'

'Yes,' said Henry. 'I thought it was a coincidence at first, but last Thursday he sat in the row behind you at the cinema.'

She nodded thoughtfully.

'I suppose it had to happen one day,' she murmured. She gave a tense smile. 'I've been found out, it seems.'

'Are you a spy?' asked Grace.

'Nothing so exciting, I'm afraid. I think this is all about tax. Though I have paid my dues. Even though I haven't been quite honest about my identity.'

Henry glanced quickly at Mrs Beaumont.

'Are you really Mrs Beaumont?' Jeffries asked.

'Oh, yes. But I've been writing under my late brother's name. He was badly gassed during the First World War and suffered a nervous breakdown. He couldn't cope with going out to work, but as I told you, Henry, he could type. The money for my stories was sent to him and we split it in half after putting a bit aside for tax. I suspect this man has something to do with the Inland Revenue. All very boring really. Unless of course I have to pay a fine. That would not be boring.'

'What are you going to do?' asked Grace.

'What I should have done when my brother died. Tell the publishers that it was I who wrote the stories, not my brother. I'll write to them this weekend.'

'Why didn't you tell them before?' asked Jeffries, puzzled.

'Because most of my stories are set in boys' boarding schools. I thought they might not accept them if they saw a woman's name.'

'But how did you know what to write?' asked Grace. 'You haven't been to a boys' boarding school.'

'The same way Pip, Roger and Henry wrote their talk for their presentation.'

'Research,' said Jeffries.

'That's right, and my brother was sent to one so I used to badger him for information. It was a nicer subject for him to think about than memories of his time in the trenches.'

'Does my mother know?' asked Henry.

'She had to. She's been typing his name at the end of the stories. But she was sworn to secrecy.' She glanced at the photographs again. 'Do you mind if I hold on to these for a while?'

'No,' said Henry.

'Oh, dear,' she sighed. 'What a start to the new year.'

'Remember what you keep telling me,' said Grace, 'you have to look for the diamond in the dungheap.'

'Quite right.' Mrs Beaumont smiled. 'And now that you've got that off your chests, I suggest you sprint back to the Troxy.'

## 7. Selecting the worthy

'THE FIRST GROUP OF BOYS ARE TO GO INTO THE HALL AND THE girls to the needlework room. The second group of boys are coming with me to the darkroom,' said Mr Finch.

Henry, Pip and Jeffries were in the second group. They grinned at one another. Being in the darkroom with Mr Finch would seem more like a holiday than a lesson.

Nine of them squeezed into the tiny room and stood under the red light.

'I've developed a roll of film and it's ready for printing,' Mr Finch said. 'The two trays you can see on the dry side are filled with developing fluid and hypo. If you can learn to develop your own photos, you can save quite a bit of money.'

'But once we leave school, where will we find a darkroom?' asked a voice from the back.

'Look out for evening classes,' Mr Finch began. He was interrupted by a groan. 'I'll pretend I didn't hear that. It's not like school. You can choose what you want to learn.'

They left the darkroom at break time. Jeffries and Pip ran off to join the queue for the boys' toilets and Henry caught sight of Jane Taylor, the girl who had helped him to find Molly's Christmas present. She was with her friend Margaret. She looked upset and angry. Before he had time to think he found himself strolling in her direction. She whirled round. At first he thought she was going to shout at him, but then she caught his eye and relaxed.

'What's the matter?' he asked.

'It's Miss Plimsoll! All us girls had to go and speak to her separately in the needlework room about what shops we'd like to work in when we leave school and who'd like to work in the corset factory. That sort of thing. And I told her I wanted to be a nurse and do you know what she said?'

Henry shook his head.

'"Girls from secondary modern schools don't become nurses." She just brushed it aside as if I was stupid or something. So I said, "That's what I want to do." And she said in that hoity-toity voice of hers, "Don't talk foolishness, my girl. Only grammar-school girls become nurses. You be grateful if you can find a nice shop to work in before you get married and have children."'

'My mother got her school certificate,' Henry said. 'And she left school at fourteen.'

'Did she?'

'How did she do that?' said Margaret.

'Evening classes.'

'We could do that, Jane.'

'Of course we could,' said Jane vehemently. 'That'll show her.'

'I want to be a teacher,' said Margaret. 'But not like Miss Plimsoll. Like Mr Finch. His lessons are interesting.'

Henry was about to add, *And I want to be a camera operator*, but changed his mind. He didn't want them to laugh at him or think he was being cocky. There was an awkward silence.

'Molly liked the quilt,' he said eventually.

At that Jane smiled. 'Did she? Did she really?'

As they gazed at him Henry felt tongue-tied again.

'I've gotta go,' he said, and ran off to find his friends.

On the way to the boys' toilets, he was stopped by Jack Riddell. He was looking secretive.

'I want to ask you something on the quiet,' he said.

'All right,' said Henry, puzzled.

'In private,' he added.

They headed in the direction of the prefab.

'What is it?' asked Henry.

'When you start your job, can you sneak me in sometimes and let me help?'

'I dunno,' said Henry, feeling that this was not the time to tell him that he was never going to work on the railways.

'Oh.' He looked devastated. 'You're lucky. My dad wrote to Hatton Station and Sternsea Station and the Harbour Station askin' if there were any vacancies in the Foot Plate Grade as a boy cleaner. But they all said no. See, I don't have anyone workin' in the railways like you do. And this man we just seen in the hall . . .'

'What man?'

'He's got some funny name. Careers something or other. He had all this information about joining the Navy and getting apprenticeships at the aircraft factory, and taking exams for the dockyard, that sort of thing.'

Henry wondered why the boys Mr Finch had taken to the darkroom hadn't been sent to see him.

During the afternoon break, when he had returned to the darkroom to watch Mr Finch pegging up wet photographs on the line, he asked him.

'You already have apprenticeships or jobs waiting for you,' he said.

'Sir, Morgan and Jeffries don't.'

Mr Finch was visibly ruffled.

'If you have any complaints, Dodge, I suggest you speak to the headmaster, but I wouldn't recommend it.'

Henry could see that he was angry. He didn't need to ask what he meant. 'I understand, sir,' said Henry quietly.

'Which is more than I do,' muttered Mr Finch. 'This is another of those conversations which never happened, Dodge. Understand?'

'Yes, sir.'

Outside, Henry looked for Jane and Margaret in the playground. As soon as he spotted them he headed briskly towards them. 'What I'm telling you is a secret,' he said hurriedly as he reached them. 'While you were having your chats with Miss Plimsoll, the boys were seeing a Careers Officer.'

'A Careers Officer! What on earth is that?' said Jane.

Henry urged her to keep her voice down. He then repeated what Riddell had told him but left out the conversation he had just had with Mr Finch.

'So that's how it is,' said Jane. 'Miss Plimsoll for the girls and the Careers Officer for the boys.'

'Don't say anything.'

The girls shook their heads.

'The other girls aren't bothered anyway,' said Jane. 'They think we're making a lot of fuss over nothing. But thanks for telling us, Henry. And don't worry, we'll keep mum, won't we, Margaret?'

It was during woodwork the next day that Henry found himself glancing at Riddell. He felt guilty at having a job lined up that he didn't want but which was like gold dust to Riddell. Was that what growing up was all about? Having to do work you didn't want to do?

The headmaster, Mr Barratt, ushered Henry into his study. Henry stood in front of his desk, his hands behind his back, ready to take what was coming to him. He was still mystified as to why he had been asked to report to Mr Barratt. He had enjoyed his first week back at school. He was sure he had done nothing wrong. Out of the corner of his eye he took in the selection of canes fanned out against the wall. The headmaster sat behind his desk and surveyed him.

'I've summoned you here, Dodge, because it was brought to my attention at the end of last term that you were put in a group with Roger Jeffries and Edward Morgan.'

Henry had to fight down a smile. It sounded strange hearing Pip's Christian name.

'Yes, sir.'

'Mr Finch has informed me that you will be continuing this History presentation business and finding out how things were between 1925 and 1935, and that you have been put in the same groups. Naturally you must obey your form master. Nevertheless, you may join one of the other groups and your present team members can work as a pair.'

'Please, sir, I don't want to join another group.'

'I beg your pardon! Since when do you make decisions in this school?'

'I'd like to stay with Jeffries and Morgan, sir. We're a good team.'

'It would not be in your best interests if you

remained in their company. I'm thinking of the future. Fraternising with them would make you seem tarred with the same brush.'

'What brush would that be, sir?'

'You will not be in their group. There is no discussion, Dodge.'

'Jeffries and Morgan are my friends, sir.'

The headmaster took a quick intake of breath.

'Then I will have to break some very unpleasant news. I thought, boys being boys, you would have picked it up.' He indicated a chair. 'I think you'd better sit down.'

As Henry sat, Mr Barratt stood up, turned towards the window and gazed awkwardly out on to the playground. He cleared his throat.

'Morgan is illegitimate. That means he was born out of wedlock. To be more precise . . .'

'He's a bastard, sir.'

The headmaster whirled round.

'I will not have that language used in this school. Is that understood?'

'Yes, sir.'

There was a moment's silence.

'However, it appears that you know already.'

'Yes, sir. Everyone does. I used to believe people like him being treated badly was how things were, but now I don't. I think it's wrong.'

'I'm not interested in your opinion, Master Dodge.

Morgan is extremely lucky to be in a school at all.'

'I think the school is lucky to have him, sir.'

'What did you say?' he roared.

'He's friendly. He's got brains and he's a good piano player.'

'I have never heard anything so ridiculous. Aside from which I am not in the least bit interested in your opinion.'

'And no one is interested in him, sir. Even the Careers Officer.'

'What do you know about that?'

'I know that he and Jeffries weren't asked to see him.'

'People like them are not going to be offered apprenticeships. They must make their own way in the world.'

Henry said nothing. He was determined not to be separated from his friends. He watched the headmaster eyeing him up and down.

'I suppose you know about Jeffries as well?'

'Yes, sir. He reads more books than anyone in the school and he's written a novel. He got into the grammar school but his mother couldn't afford the uniform.'

'He's the son of a deserter,' Mr Barratt said, as if there was a nasty taste in his mouth. 'Do you know what that means?'

'Yes, sir. He's taking the rap for his father.'

'I won't have that American gangster talk here.'

'The blame, sir. He's taking the blame for something he didn't do.'

'Your father was a hero, Dodge.'

'Yes, sir. He died saving Private Jeffries' life.'

There was a stunned silence.

'Are you telling me that Roger Jeffries' father was the man whose life was saved by your father?'

'Yes, sir.'

The headmaster looked embarrassed.

'I had no idea. For goodness sake, why wasn't I told?'

'I thought you knew, sir.'

'If I had known, I would have had him removed post-haste, which I will do now.'

'If he leaves, I go with him, sir.'

'This isn't making sense, Dodge.'

'Sir, we fought against bullies in the war. Now we're bullying innocent people, like Jeffries and his mother, for something they never did.'

'You know Mrs Jeffries?' he asked, astounded.

'Yes, sir. She's a friend of my mum's.'

The headmaster shook his head in disbelief.

'Go back to your form,' he ordered. 'I wash my hands of you.'

'Yes, Mr Barratt. Thank you, Mr Barratt.'

As soon as Henry was outside and had closed the door behind him, he grinned. At long last he was no longer letting his father down. He was beginning to follow in his footsteps. He felt like a hero.

*

That evening Henry went to the Plaza with Grace, Pip and Jeffries to see *Abbott and Costello Meet the Killer* and a comedy-western called *The Gal Who Took the West*. After it was over and they had started to walk up the aisle, Pip suddenly dashed back to the ice cream girl's spotlight and waved up at the projectionist's box.

'I was waving to Mum and Mr Hart,' he explained when he rejoined them. 'It's the Chief's day off.'

'I thought it was supposed to be a secret,' said Jeffries.

'It is.'

'It won't be for much longer if you wave up at them in a spotlight,' said Henry.

Pip slapped his forehead with his hands.

'You're right,' he said.

'Why is your mother with Mr Hart?' Henry asked when they reached the crowded foyer.

'They like to chat. She's taken him a thermos of tea.'

'You'd better keep quiet about that too,' said Jeffries. 'If the Chief or the manager found out about that, she might lose her job.'

While they were talking, Henry spotted Frank from Mr Jenkins' shop. He was standing motionless, staring at them while the cinemagoers milled around him. Henry waved at him but he didn't wave back. Instead he smiled to himself and walked off, as though he were pretending he didn't know him. Henry had never understood why Frank was always so unfriendly towards him. He couldn't really believe he was after his job, could he?

Outside, it was freezing. Henry had given his old raincoat to Pip and had left his new one in the wardrobe. He had grown tired of people pointing at him when he wore it in the queues. And twice he had been stopped by a policeman who had been convinced he had nicked it. Instead, he wore the thickest jersey his mother had knitted for him and wound his Christmas scarf round his neck.

They said their goodbyes and Henry turned into his road, his head lowered to counteract the bitter wind. As he approached his house he noticed that Gran's curtains had not been drawn. He suspected she would call out to him as soon as she heard the front door open and bombard him with questions about Pip and Jeffries, and he was wise to the fact now that any information she got out of him she would use. He lowered himself on to his hands and knees, crawled under her window and sprinted towards the alley further down the road.

Uncle Bill was in the kitchen hanging a small damp cardigan on the wooden clothes horse in front of the range.

'Where's Mum?' Henry asked.

'Upstairs, getting Molly settled.'

The sound of the wireless was coming through from Gran's room and it annoyed him. It wasn't her who had to keep getting the accumulator recharged. He heard the door in the yard open and close.

'Mrs Henson, I expect,' said his stepfather, catching his eye, and he stepped into the scullery to open the back door.

'Oh, hello!' Henry heard him exclaim.

To his surprise, Mrs Beaumont walked into the kitchen. She pressed a finger to her lips, glancing at the wall. Henry gave a nod to show that he understood that she wanted to keep her visit a secret from Gran. Behind her stood a short stocky man in a long tweedy-looking overcoat. He had thick white hair and as he beamed, the lines surrounding his eyes seemed to shoot upwards.

'This is my publisher,' she whispered, 'Mr Hale.'

'Sit down,' said Uncle Bill.

'We can't stay long,' she said, taking the chair Mr Hale had pulled out for her. 'Mr Hale is catching the next train back to London.' Mr Hale sat opposite her, never taking his eyes off her, still smiling. 'I felt I had to tell Henry as soon as possible.'

To Henry's annoyance, Uncle Bill sat down with them.

'The man you thought is following me is not a private detective hired by the publishers or the Inland Revenue,' she said. 'However, we're still no wiser as to his identity. But it's a good job I had the appointment with Mr Hale, because the publishing company have been sending mail to my brother's address and the letters have been returned to them with *address unknown* on them. Consequently there is not only a pile of unanswered letters but also some uncashed cheques.'

'But what about . . .' began Henry impatiently and then he hesitated.

'Mrs Beaumont has told me about her male pseudonym,' said Mr Hale. 'And we're more than happy to live with it.'

'What's all this about a man following you?' asked Uncle Bill.

*Mind your own business*, thought Henry.

'Hasn't Henry told you?' asked Mrs Beaumont.

Henry shook his head.

'Ah.'

Henry gave her a pleading look in an effort to stop her from telling Uncle Bill, but she didn't seem to notice and she divulged the whole story about the man in the photographs.

'But I've found my diamond in the dungheap,' she said, beaming at Mr Hale.

'Do you mean me?' he said, looking delighted.

'I mean,' she said, smothering a laugh, 'a commission.' She turned to Henry. 'I've been asked to write stories set in *girls'* schools under my own name as well as ones for boys. Now all I have to do is find out about them. I was home tutored, you see.'

'You won't have to look very far, then, will you?' said Henry.

Mrs Beaumont looked at him, puzzled.

'Grace,' said Henry.

'Of course!' She turned to Mr Hale. 'I have a young

friend who has been to thirteen girls' schools, boarding and day. She will be a mine of information.'

'Can I see the photographs?' asked Uncle Bill.

'Why?' Henry muttered. *Why couldn't he keep his nose out of it?*

'Certainly,' said Mrs Beaumont, ignoring Henry, and she spread them out on the table.

'I see what you mean.' Henry's stepfather looked thoughtful. 'Do you know, I'm sure I've seen him somewhere.' He shook his head. 'No, I can't place him.'

Mrs Beaumont slid them back in the envelope. She and Mr Hale said their goodbyes and crept out to the scullery. There was a creak on the stairs and the door handle moved slowly. His mother peered round the door. She was smiling.

'Molly's fast asleep,' she whispered with relief, 'I'll put the kettle on.'

'No, you won't. You sit down, love,' said Uncle Bill.

She eased herself into a chair. *She looks done in*, thought Henry.

'Was that Mrs Henson popping in for sugar again?' she asked.

'No. Mrs Beaumont with a man from the publishers.'

'Oh, that'll be Mr Hale. But why were they here? Does she want me to do some more typing?'

'No.' Uncle Bill glanced at Henry. 'Does your mother know?'

'Oh, yes,' she interrupted. 'Is she in trouble for using her brother's name?'

'No, it's all turned out for the best,' said Uncle Bill. 'But the man in the photographs is still a mystery.'

'What man?'

'Mum doesn't know that bit,' said Henry.

'Henry thinks a man has been following Mrs Beaumont. She thought the publishers had hired a private detective, but they don't know anything about him.'

'Really? Why do you think he's following her, Henry?'

'He kept turning up all over the place. Here and in London and at the cinema.'

'Perhaps he likes going to the pictures. Lots of people do.'

'But he turned up in this small road in London when she was visiting there.'

'I expect it was just a coincidence. You've seen too many gangster films.'

'Funnily enough, he looked familiar,' said Uncle Bill.

'You've seen the photos?'

'They're in that envelope.' He pointed to it on the other side of the table.

'Can I see them?'

'Henry?' asked his stepfather.

Henry shrugged, pulled the photographs out and spread them in front of her.

She rested her hands on the table and examined

them. Suddenly, she gave a sharp intake of breath as though someone had punched her violently in the stomach. With a look of terror she let out a frightened scream and collapsed to the floor, the photographs tumbling over her like dead leaves.

# 8. The stranger is identified

'FANCY MAKING SUCH A FUSS OVER SEEING A RAT!' SCOFFED GRAN.

It was nearly midnight. Henry's mother was upstairs in bed and Mrs Henson was still with her. Henry was sitting at the kitchen table with his grandmother and Uncle Bill.

'It was the suddenness of it,' said Uncle Bill, and he gave Henry a warning glance.

After his mother had fainted, Henry had been sent upstairs to see to Molly, who had been woken by the scream. He had hurried out of the kitchen, aware of Uncle Bill swiftly picking up the photographs and slipping them back into the envelope. His mother had sat slumped in a chair, speechless, the expression on her face vacant and dazed, as though she had been slapped, and from Gran's room the wireless had boomed even more loudly.

When he reached his bedroom, he had found Molly sitting bolt upright and sobbing. All he could think of saying was, 'Mummy fell over.' He knelt down beside her and she shot out of bed and flung her arms round him. He wrapped himself round her small shuddering frame and held her tightly, glad to be comforting her. Like her, he needed to hug someone. The scream had shaken him too, like a forgotten terror.

Gradually he prised Molly's tiny fingers from the nape of his neck and placed her doll in her arms. She was shivering. He pulled off his jersey and draped it round her. It gathered in a heap on the floor. He picked her up and tucked her into bed. From downstairs he could hear his grandmother shouting.

'Auntie cross,' Molly hiccupped. And a look of alarm crossed her face. 'Auntie hit Mummy again?'

Henry stared at her, frozen. He must have misheard her.

'Molly, has Auntie ever hit Mum?'

She nodded.

'Molly frighted. Molly hide.'

She began to sob again.

'You stay here and look after Dolly.'

Hurtling on to the landing and down the stairs, he could still hear yells. It was then that he noticed that the wireless was unusually silent. He dashed into the kitchen. His mother and Uncle Bill were sitting at the table holding hands, both ashen.

'Is everyone deaf?' Gran shrieked from her room.

Henry's mother was trembling violently, her eyes blank.

'Don't go in there,' Uncle Bill said urgently to Henry. 'I'll do the talking. Ask Mrs Henson to come round. When you've done that, run to the telephone box and call the district nurse. Don't mention the photographs. I'll explain why later.' He pulled some coins out of his pocket. 'Take my coat. And hurry!'

When Henry had returned, Uncle Bill told him to stay with Gran. Reluctantly he obeyed. But he hated sitting in her room listening to her complaints. Still shocked, he only had to glance at her and Molly's words came back to him, *Auntie hit Mummy again?* Once the district nurse had been and gone, he heard Mrs Henson taking his mother upstairs and he dashed into the kitchen to find out what the district nurse had said. He found Uncle Bill standing by the range wrapping a piece of flannel round a stone hot-water bottle. Molly was standing beside him, still cocooned in Henry's jersey.

'Molly's going to sleep with your mother tonight,' Uncle Bill said abruptly. 'I'll sleep in the camp bed in your room. You'll have to stay here tomorrow morning while Mrs Henson does the shopping for your mother. She's going to look after Molly till I get back in the afternoon.'

'Gran was shouting because the power on the second accumulator ran out,' Henry explained.

'I know. Your mother hasn't had time to get the other one recharged. When Mrs Henson returns from shopping, you can deal with that. Now, we'd better get to bed.'

*

It was awkward lying in the dark with his stepfather in the same room and he still hadn't told Henry why his mother had been so upset by the photographs.

'What's wrong with Mum?' he asked eventually. 'Is it bad?'

It was so quiet he thought Uncle Bill must have fallen asleep. Then he heard a sigh.

'You could say that. Look, I can't talk now. I'll tell you tomorrow night after work. The district nurse says the baby's all right but your mum's not to get out of bed tomorrow. Don't leave her on her own, will you?'

'No.'

'You might find your gran a bit –' he paused – 'a bit more demanding with the wireless out of action. Whatever you do, don't let her go upstairs to our bedroom to disturb your mum.'

Henry was woken by a crash and the sound of his mother screaming but as he listened to the house there was only silence and darkness. He checked that Uncle Bill was asleep, slipped out of bed, padded out on to the small landing and peered into the other bedroom. His mother and Molly were wrapped round one another, sleeping.

The next time he woke, Uncle Bill was standing by his bed in his blue overalls.

'The kettle's just boiled. Mrs Henson's popping round

in a couple of hours. I've taken your mum a cup of tea but I've left it to you to make her and Molly some toast. I've changed Molly's nappy and her clothes are warming in front of the range. You'll have to clear the grate in Gran's room and lay her fire. And don't forget to have breakfast yourself.'

Daylight was beginning to filter into the room.

'What time is it?' yawned Henry.

'Half past five. You won't be able to go to the Pictures this afternoon but maybe you could go tonight.'

'Yeah,' said Henry sleepily.

He swung his legs to the floor and quickly pulled on his clothes. He heard the front door being closed and Uncle Bill's boots hitting the pavement. Shivering, he looked around for his jersey and then remembered that Molly had it.

He spotted it as soon as he entered the kitchen. Uncle Bill had hung it next to Molly's clothes in front of the range. As he slipped into it he could feel it warming his bones. Around seven he stepped into the freezing hall and knocked on Gran's door.

'Come in,' she commanded crossly.

Henry peered in.

'Oh,' she said, surprised, 'I thought it was yer mum.'

She was sitting in bed with a hairnet on.

'Would you like a cup of tea, Gran?'

'Lovely,' she said, smiling.

By the time Henry had taken her a cup and Molly had slid backwards down the stairs on her stomach, Mrs Henson had arrived. She dressed Molly and packed a change of nappies and clothes into a basket.

'I'll take your mum the toast,' she said. 'I need to have a word with her anyway.'

Within minutes of Mrs Henson leaving the house with Molly, there was a thumping noise on the wall. Henry knocked on his gran's door again.

'And about time!' she screamed.

He opened it.

'Oh,' she said, 'I thought you were out. Where's yer mum?'

'In bed.'

'What's she doing there?'

'The district nurse told her to stay there, remember?'

'You don't want to take any notice of her. Get her down. I need a fire. It's freezing. You could hang meat in 'ere and it would stay fresh.'

'It's warm in the kitchen.'

'I ain't goin' in there with that girl running around.'

'Mrs Henson has gone to the shops with her.'

'Who's goin' to do my fire, then?'

'I am.'

At that she beamed.

'You? Oh, that is kind.'

It was a laborious job. First he made a mess of

shovelling all the ash out into a newspaper, and when he tried to carry it out, the paper burst and it went everywhere. After brushing most of it into a dustpan, he began to lay the fire, screwing paper into balls and laying them on the grate, lining wood on top in a pyramid, thinner wood first, then thicker. Then he gingerly placed the old coal on the wood and placed new coal on top. He wondered how his mum managed to do this every day with Molly around. Suddenly it occurred to him that it was daft lighting a fire in Gran's room when the range was lit in the kitchen, and he remembered conversations he had overheard between his mother and Uncle Bill about the amount of fuel they were getting through.

'We're lucky I work for the railway,' Uncle Bill had said once. 'At least we get wood delivered from them.'

'Ain't you goin' to light it, then?' Gran said when he stood up to leave.

'Why don't you go in the kitchen?'

'It's comfy in 'ere and when I'm dressed you can come and sit in 'ere and we can have a nice chat.'

Henry didn't want a chat. He wanted to see how his mum was feeling but he suspected that if he didn't get the fire going, there would be no peace. It took ages and it didn't help having Gran suggest that it would be much easier if he called his mother down to do it. For a fleeting moment he wondered why she didn't do it herself.

'After that your mother can go and get the accumulators recharged,' Gran added.

'I'm doing that,' said Henry firmly, 'when Mrs Henson comes back. I don't want to leave Mum on her own.'

'But she won't be on her own, will she? I'll be here.' And she smiled. 'And don't worry about the mess on the floor. Yer mum can clear that up later.'

Henry gazed at the bits of charred newspaper scattered round his feet.

'No, I'll do it.'

'Don't be daft. That's woman's work.'

Henry finished sweeping up the mess, ignoring her protests. As soon as he had emptied the dustpan for the last time he crept quietly up to his mother's room and gave a light tap on her door.

'Come in, love,' she said.

He poked his head round it.

'I knew it was you,' she said and she smiled. 'Shut the door.'

Tears began to roll down her face. Quickly she brushed them aside with her fingers. She looked exhausted. If Henry hadn't seen her sleeping, he would have sworn she hadn't slept at all.

'What's the matter, Mum?'

'The district nurse thinks I've been overdoing things. Your hands!' she exclaimed hurriedly.

'I've been making Gran's fire.'

'Thanks for staying and helping, love. I know you're missing the Pictures.'

He shrugged.

'I can go tomorrow,' he said.

'Give us a hug.'

He sat on the bed and she put her arms round him.

'I love you, no matter what, you know that, don't you?' she whispered.

She was shaking. When she let go of him she looked frightened.

'I'd best get some sleep,' she said hoarsely.


'You look after Molly while I put the shopping away,' said Mrs Henson. 'You can get the potatoes and the peeler out. It'll take me no time to cook dinner. Spam, cabbage and mashed potatoes with a nice bit of gravy should do.'

Once dinner was on the table she nipped next door to cook for her own family. Henry took a plate of food up to his mother, leaving Gran to watch Molly. He was only gone a few minutes when there was a yell. He ran down the stairs back to the kitchen. Molly was crying.

'I gave her a good slap,' said Gran shortly.

On the side of Molly's face was a red mark.

'Mum doesn't allow slapping,' Henry blurted out.

'Want Mummy,' whimpered Molly.

'Well, she's not 'ere, is she?' Gran snapped. 'I wish

we could get rid of her, eh?' she said to Henry, indicating Molly.

Henry stared at her. For two years he had heard his gran complain about Molly, and they had both laughed about how awful she was. Now he wanted to smash his gran's face with his fist.

'Gran, why don't you go in your room and I'll bring your dinner in to you.'

She smiled.

'Lovely. Then I won't have to look at her ugly mug, will I?' And she gave a laugh.

As soon as he had got rid of her he held Molly tightly.

'Molly bad girl?' she asked, trembling.

'No,' whispered Henry. 'Molly good girl. Molly clever. Auntie bad. Shake finger at Auntie.' And with that he shook a finger at the wall.

Molly shook a finger sternly at it too and then Henry grinned and she giggled.

'Time to eat your dinner now.' He could still feel her shaking. 'Come on,' he said, and he lifted her on to his knee.

After washing the dishes, keeping Molly occupied so that she wouldn't disturb his mother, and answering his gran's requests to put more coal on the fire, Henry had to use all his willpower not to lose his temper so that by the time Mrs Henson returned to look after Molly, he was exhausted. It was then time for him to take the accumulators to be recharged. Gingerly he picked them up by their handles and stepped out into the yard. It was bitterly cold. The wireless shop was a good mile away and Henry had to admit he was grateful that Uncle Bill had insisted that he borrow his jacket.

'Two accumulators!' remarked the man from behind the counter. 'Have you been sleeping with the wireless on? More money than sense,' Henry heard him mutter as he disappeared into the back room. Within seconds he returned with two recharged ones.

'Your dad ought to get himself an electric one,' he said. 'I've plenty of nice ones here.'

The whole trip together with the time in the queue had taken Henry one and a half hours. He carried the accumulators carefully, so that the acid didn't spill on his clothes. He was surprised that Uncle Bill paid for the accumulators to be recharged so often. And then the penny dropped. It was his mother who paid for it with her typing money. That's why she didn't want Gran to know about it. She didn't want her to find out how mean Uncle Bill was.

Once he was home he put one accumulator on a shelf in the scullery and the other one behind the wireless in Gran's room.

'I'll get the range going and make you a cuppa,' he said hurriedly and she gave him one of her broad smiles.

On the kitchen table Henry spotted a note from Mrs Henson explaining that she had taken Molly to Number 12 to play with the children there. Henry felt uneasy that his mother had been left alone. He heard the back door open.

'Mum!'

She was dressed and carrying a bucket of coal.

'What are you doing out of bed?'

He removed the bucket from her hands.

'She started her banging,' she said wearily. 'If I'd made time to take the accumulator back to Mr Morris when they needed recharging, she could have had the wireless on and I could have had some peace. I never dreamt she'd get through the second accumulator so fast.' She sat down. 'Oh dear, what shall I do?' she said, shaking her head.

'Go to bed, Mum.'

By the time Uncle Bill had returned from his shift, Henry had laid the table and put potatoes in a saucepan on the range to reheat them. He saw him glance at Mrs Henson's note.

'I'll just nip up and see your mum,' was all he said.

Henry had a mug of tea waiting for him when he came back down.

'Thank you,' he said, surprised. 'I got a thirst so strong I could drink a river.'

'I'm sorry I left Mum on her own. I didn't know Mrs Henson was going to take Molly out.'

'I'm sure you did your best. Wait till I've had a wash. Then you go and get Molly and I'll watch the potatoes and connect the accumulator to the wireless. Do you want to go to the Pictures tonight?'

'No. But I'd like to see Pip and Jeffries.'

'You do that. But no mention of what happened last night. Not yet. If you want to see a matinee tomorrow, I'll be here till half past one and then Mrs Henson's going to take Molly next door. She'll bring her back and put Molly to bed.'

'Mum's scared,' said Henry quietly.

Uncle Bill looked away.

'I'll tell you tonight. In your room. Away from prying ears.'

'But what about Molly?'

'She's sleeping with your mother again.'

'Hello, stranger!' said Mrs Beaumont. 'The others were expecting you hours ago. Grace has already gone home. Did you go to the Pictures on your own?'

Henry shook his head, breathless from running.

'I had to help out at home. Mum's ill.'

'Oh, my goodness,' she said, ushering him in, 'is it the baby?'

'No. She had a shock and it made her ill.'

'What was it?'

Henry thought quickly.

'She saw a rat.'

Downstairs Pip was drawing and Jeffries was reading a book. Henry spotted the open newspaper between them. They both looked up.

'Where have you been?' Jeffries asked.

'Why didn't you come earlier?' added Pip.

'His mother's been taken ill,' explained Mrs Beaumont, sitting by an overflowing waste-paper basket. A pile of papers was heaped on the table.

'Oh,' said Jeffries, looking concerned.

'Uncle Bill is with her now,' said Henry, pulling out a chair. 'Mrs Henson is going to look after Molly tomorrow, so I can go to a matinee.'

Jeffries grabbed the newspaper.

'You must listen to this,' he said excitedly. '*Hamlet* and *The Red Shoes* have second and third place in a poll for best films conducted by *Mein Film*, a Viennese film fan paper,' he read.

'British films,' commented Henry.

'So the British are good at something?' said Mrs Beaumont, eying them sardonically. 'It's not only the Americans who can make award-winning films, then?'

'Tell him about tomorrow,' urged Pip.

'*William Comes to Town* is on at the Gaiety, Shaftesbury and Palace. And it's Pip's turn to have first choice. The film with it is called *Strange Gamble*. Could be a gangster film. It's a U as well. Are you coming?'

Henry nodded. It would be good to sit in the dark with his friends and let some nonsense roll over his head.

'It's a good week,' said Jeffries and he slid the newspaper towards him.

As they talked, Henry drank in the warmth and laughter in the kitchen, but it was as though he was in a fog, observing them from a distance.

Bath night was usually on a Sunday but Uncle Bill decided to have it a night earlier so that Henry's mum could have a good soak. Then it was Molly's turn. Henry was impatient for everyone's turn to be over, for Molly to go to sleep and for the house to be silent, but the baths seemed to take hours. And his mother was still feeling no better. From his bedroom he overheard Uncle Bill on the landing saying, 'Don't worry. I'm nearby. Call out if you need me.'

Uncle Bill went back downstairs to switch off the lights and, after a while, Henry heard his slow step on the stairs. The door opened and he walked in, his overcoat over his pyjamas. He closed the door gently behind him, his head bowed. Henry was sitting bolt upright, the blankets up to his chin. Behind him the wind rattled the window frame, sending a cold draught down his neck. His stepfather sat at the end of the bed, his hands clasped. He was staring at the floor.

'I'm not sure how to begin,' he said quietly.

'Mum knows who the man is, doesn't she?' said Henry.

He nodded.

'Before I tell you, I have to ask you to keep it a secret, to give us time to think. And you mustn't tell your gran. She'll have to know soon enough. But not yet.'

As he turned to face Henry, he could see that he was shocked too.

'Henry, this is terrible for your mother and it's terrible for me.' He paused. 'You already know he's not following Mrs Beaumont.'

'Yes.'

'Henry, he's been following someone else.'

'Mum?' he said, alarmed.

'No.'

'Who, then?'

'You.'

'Me?' said Henry, astounded. 'Why would he follow me?'

'I don't know.'

Henry was now completely baffled.

'You think he's following me but you don't know why?'

Uncle Bill nodded.

'How can you be sure he's following *me*, then?'

'Because he's your dad.'

# PART THREE

## Dodge

# 1. In shock

'HE'S DEAD,' HENRY SAID SLOWLY, AS IF SPEAKING TO A MAD man. 'We went to his funeral.'

'It's him,' said Uncle Bill. 'Your mother's absolutely sure. No doubt.'

'But it can't be.'

'It is.'

'I don't understand,' said Henry, bewildered.

'Neither do I. I've heard of people coming back from prison camps after the war, years after they've been reported missing, but your father was never taken prisoner. When he died . . .' He stopped. 'When he disappeared, he was in this country.'

Henry couldn't take it in.

'Uncle Bill,' he said slowly, 'if he's alive, then Mum's married to both of you.'

'Not exactly. It means she went through a marriage ceremony twice.'

'That's the same thing,' he said, trying not to show his irritation. Why did he have to make things so complicated?

'It's not. The second marriage doesn't count. If you go through a second marriage while you're still married to another person, it's a criminal offence. It's called bigamy.'

Henry suddenly felt sick.

'Could Mum be arrested?'

'Yes.'

He hardly dared ask the next question.

'Could she go to prison?'

'Yes.'

'But she didn't know!'

'That'll go in her favour.'

'So you and Mum aren't married, then?'

'No.' He looked down at the floor and clasped his hands together. 'So you see,' he said hoarsely, 'I'll have to sleep separately from your mother until we can sort this all out.'

Henry turned away. It was a miracle. Uncle Bill was no longer his stepfather. He would have to leave the house and his real father could move back in. They would be a family again.

'And there's Molly and the baby,' Uncle Bill continued. 'In the eyes of the law your mother has been unfaithful to her husband and has had a child by another man.'

Henry was shocked. No wonder his mother had looked so terrible. Even now he could imagine people in the street avoiding her and talking about her behind her back the way they did about the divorcee Lily Bridges and Pip and Mrs Morgan.

'What are we going to do?' he whispered.

'Keep quiet for the moment. One of the photographs was by the Plaza. I imagine he's found out where we live. We also have no idea of his state of mind. Have you seen him since that visit to the cinema before Christmas?'

'No. P'raps he's gone away,' said Henry anxiously.

'I doubt it,' said his stepfather in a tone that sounded almost bitter.

He stood up and turned off the light.

'We'll keep those photographs to ourselves for the moment,' he said in the dark. 'It's a good job you've only shown them to Mrs Beaumont.'

As Henry listened to him getting into the camp bed, he thought of Private Jeffries. It couldn't have been his father who had saved his life. It must have been the man who had been buried. His father hadn't been a hero after all.

'*Isn't* a hero,' he whispered.

He stayed awake till he could hear the sound of steady breathing, slipped out of bed and crept over to the window. People were coming out of the Plaza, talking in low voices. He thought back to the previous summer when he used to get out of bed on a Saturday night to watch the usherettes leaving the cinema after the last film, glamorous in their pretty dresses and heeled shoes, picking their way through the rubble on their way to a dance hall at the end of Hatton Road.

He stared down at the pavement, expecting to see a lone figure gazing up at his window, but the street was deserted.

This time when he woke, the screaming continued. He flung the covers back and ran towards the landing. It was coming from downstairs. He stood paralysed, feeling small and helpless. There was a crash like furniture being broken and he could hear his mother crying out, begging for whatever was happening to stop. To his horror something warm and wet flooded into his pyjama trousers.

He woke up with a violent jolt and was relieved to find that his pyjamas were dry. It had only been another bad dream. Some instinct made him roll over and glance down at the camp bed to make sure Molly was safe, only to find Uncle Bill sleeping there. It was still dark and the house was silent. Exhausted, he closed his eyes and was flung back into the nightmare. This time he could hear a repetitive thudding sound. And still his mother screamed. He decided to stay awake. Listening to the silence was better than listening to his mother screaming in his dreams.

The next time he opened his eyes, the room was empty. He dressed quickly, grabbed his boots and ran barefoot along the floorboards, shivering with the cold. There was no one in the kitchen but the range had been lit. He sat in front of it, savouring its warmth, pulling on a pair of well-darned socks. As he tied his laces he heard the wireless. Irritated, he headed for the hall and knocked on his gran's door.

'Yes,' said a martyred voice. 'Come in.'

She was still in bed.

'Are you ill, Gran?' he asked.

'I soon will be if that fire isn't lit. I'm too cold to get up.'

*But not too cold to get out of bed and turn the wireless on*, he thought.

'What are you listening to?'

'Dunno. I just have it on for company.'

'Well, I'm up now so you don't need it on,' and he leaned over and switched it off. 'I'll bring you a cup of tea and make up your fire.'

Some time later he was finally sitting down to some toast and a mug of tea when he heard the yard door open and Molly's high-pitched chatter. Through the window he spotted her sitting on her father's shoulders. She was holding his upraised hands oblivious to the sadness in his eyes. Without thinking, Henry put the kettle back on the range.

It was the first thing Uncle Bill spotted when he lowered himself under the doorway.

'I saw you coming,' said Henry gruffly. 'I've done Gran's fire.'

He gave a nod of thanks.

'I had to get little'un out,' he said. 'When did you wake up?'

'About an hour ago. I don't even know what time it is.'

'Midday.'

Henry was annoyed.

'Why didn't you wake me?'

'Looked like you needed the sleep. It'll soon be time for queuing for the matinee. You'd best take your umbrella. Looks like rain. What are you going to see, or don't you want to tell me?' he added wearily.

Out of habit Henry was about to snap at him, but for some reason he stopped himself.

'It's Pip's choice really,' he said.

'Can you nip upstairs and get your mum's stone bottle? It probably needs reheating.'

Henry nodded.

Upstairs, his mother still looked exhausted. He lifted the covers and glanced at her feet, now encased in bed socks.

'Uncle Bill told me about the talk you had last

night,' she said quietly. She looked as though she was struggling not to cry. 'You know it means I'm still Mrs Dodge?'

'Yeah,' he murmured. 'Is Molly called Molly Dodge?'

'I'm not sure. Mrs Beaumont has a solicitor. I'm going to ask her if she can get some information from him for me. I'll pretend I'm asking for a friend.'

'What are we going to do?' Henry asked.

'I don't know. Your father might not want to stay married to me.'

'You mean he might want to divorce you?'

'If he can afford it. Yes.'

Henry knew that his mother would never be able to look anyone in the eye if she ended up being a divorced woman.

'I'm sure he won't,' he said reassuringly.

His mother looked alarmed.

'Is Uncle Bill looking after Molly?' she asked quickly.

'Yes.'

'I'm glad you're going out with your friends this afternoon. It'll be good for you to get away from here.' And with that her face began to crumple.

He couldn't bear to see her cry.

'I'll make you a cup of tea,' he said.

'That would be lovely,' she said, tears running down her face.

*

Henry didn't notice much of the journey to the Gaiety. He walked beside his friends in a fog, half listening to them, half remembering the revelation from the previous night. Luckily they didn't seem to notice. Pip spent most of the time chatting to Grace, recounting the plots of the two films he and his mother had watched from the projectionist's box at the Plaza.

'How did you manage to get up there without being seen by the usherettes?' Grace asked.

'They never go up there,' Pip explained. 'It's like another world.'

'A *forbidden* world,' added Jeffries melodramatically.

As they queued outside the cinema, Henry kept looking around.

'There's no need to look for the man who's following Mrs Beaumont because she isn't here,' said Grace, noticing.

'And anyway,' said Jeffries, 'he isn't following her, is he?'

'Who is he following, then?' asked Pip.

Grace and Jeffries laughed.

'No one,' they chorused.

Henry felt his shoulders drop. *So far so good*, he thought. They didn't have a clue he was following him.

The film was a comic romp for children. Grace and Pip lapped it up while Henry and Jeffries exchanged weary glances over their heads, but it meant they were surrounded by a thousand or more children and it made Henry feel strangely protected.

When they stepped out of the cinema into the dark, they were greeted by rain. As they huddled under his umbrella, Henry felt as though someone was tugging at his guts. It made him feel so lonely that it hurt. To his surprise he felt Grace's arm slip into his.

'Is your mother very ill?' she asked quietly. 'Is that why you're so quiet?'

He nodded. It was easier than inventing an explanation.

He ran with them to Mrs Beaumont's house, where they had bread and jam and tea. When he dragged himself from the table to go home, Mrs Beaumont followed him into the porch.

'Try and persuade your mother to come here tomorrow. If she's ill, we can look after her. She'd have more rest. And I can look after Molly. Will you do that for me?'

'Yeah, 'course,' he muttered.

When Henry arrived home, he found Gran in a very bad mood. Her fire had gone out. Molly was with Mrs Henson next door and Uncle Bill was at work. She had tried to force his mother to get out of bed but for once she had refused. Henry slipped upstairs to pass on Mrs Beaumont's message.

'She's right,' his mother said. 'And I must think of Molly. She's playing up because she knows I'm upset.'

'But you're pleased that Dad's alive, aren't you, Mum?'

'It's a little more complicated than that,' she said slowly.

## 2. Becoming an outcast

'I WON'T BE NEEDING YOU TODAY, DODGE,' SAID MR JENKINS firmly, when Henry pushed open the shop door, 'or the rest of the week.'

'I'll come in next Monday afternoon shall I, Mr Jenkins?'

'I shouldn't bother if I were you.'

Henry caught sight of Frank out of the corner of his eye. He was grinning.

'Frank here has been telling me about the company you keep.'

Henry stared at him, uncomprehending.

'Master Jeffries?' Mr Jenkins added.

'Yes?' Henry answered, still no wiser.

'No need to play the innocent with me, young sir. Frank saw you with him at the cinema the other day.'

Frank, by now, was looking triumphant.

'Jeffries?' repeated Henry.

'That is correct. The son of a deserter.'

'Jeffries isn't a deserter,' he began.

'Like father, like son.'

'Who says?' said Henry.

'It's a fact of life. And I'll thank you not to answer me back, young man. At least you're not denying it. Does your mother approve of you mixing with this boy?'

'Mum's ill,' he said, avoiding answering the question.

'Oh, yes?'

'The district nurse had to be called on Friday night. You can check if you like.'

'There's no need for that. Your mother will continue to be welcome here, but while you keep company with that scum, I'll thank you to stay away from here.'

As Henry left the shop he overheard Mr Jenkins say, 'His father must be turning over in his grave.'

'Oh, good, I'm glad you've come,' said Grace, beaming. 'We're discussing Mrs Beaumont's birthday,' and she dragged him downstairs.

Henry willingly let her boss him. He was still feeling too stunned to think, let alone protest. From downstairs he could hear laughter. To be somewhere where he felt welcome after the scene at the shop already began to make him feel less wounded.

'I think Grace's idea is the best one,' said Mrs Beaumont, 'and what about Jeffries coming with us to London? I'll pay his fare.'

'No,' protested his mother.

'Please!' begged Jeffries.

'You can make something for me in exchange,' Mrs Beaumont suggested.

'Like what?' Mrs Jeffries asked suspiciously.

'I don't know. An overcoat from a blanket?' She turned to Henry. 'I'd like you to come too, but I suppose that depends on how well your mother is.'

Up until that moment Henry had sat silently listening to her. Now everyone was staring at him.

'What is it, Henry? You look shattered. Is it your mother?' interrupted Grace. 'Has she got worse?'

'I dunno. I haven't been home yet. I went straight from school to Mr Jenkins' shop but he didn't have any jobs going. He doesn't think he'll have any more for me now.'

'Oh, that's a shame,' said Mrs Beaumont.

Grace gave him a penetrating look.

'How old will you be, Mrs Beaumont?' she asked suddenly.

Henry could see she was trying to change the subject to take the attention away from him. She must have guessed how upset he was feeling.

'Grace!' exclaimed Mrs Jeffries. 'That's not very polite.'

'I'll be sixty,' said Mrs Beaumont. 'Now how about me having a word with Daniel about British films between 1925 and 1935? That's the next period Mr Finch wants you to look at, isn't it? There's Grierson, of course. But that's documentary. And Hitchcock.'

'And cinemas. Does he know anyone who built cinemas then?' asked Jeffries.

'Mr Hart might,' said Mrs Morgan and she blushed.

'He knows everything,' said Pip happily.

It was when he was hauling a bucket of coal into Gran's room that Henry decided to ask the same question Grace had asked Mrs Beaumont, but he wanted to find out about Gran's age in a more roundabout way. He glanced at the photo of his young grandfather in his Army uniform on the mantelpiece. It was next to the one of his father. Now that he looked more closely, he could see that his mother was right. The man following him was his dad.

'It was 1917 when Grandad was killed, wasn't it?' he said casually, kneeling in front of the fire.

'That's right, dear.'

'How old were you?'

'Only twenty,' she sighed. 'No more than a girl really.'

As Henry thrust the poker among the glowing coals he made a quick calculation. His grandmother was only fifty-three. He had always assumed that she was in her seventies. It was a shock to discover that she was seven years younger than Mrs Beaumont, who looked and behaved like someone twenty years younger.

He grabbed the tongs and lifted coal from the bucket to the fire, taking a good look at Gran's legs in their thick brown stockings. *There's nothing wrong with her legs*, he heard his mother's voice say inside his head.

Leaving her room, he met his mother coming down the stairs. She put a finger to her lips and beckoned him into the kitchen. It was good to see her up and dressed again, though her face still seemed colourless.

'I don't want Gran to know I'm out of bed,' she whispered.

In the kitchen she made him a spam sandwich and a mug of tea.

'Been helping Mr Jenkins?' she asked.

He wanted to tell her everything but he knew she had enough on her plate without having to worry about Mr Jenkins. He just hoped she would keep her friendship with Mrs Jeffries to herself.

'Yeah. But he didn't have any work for me today. I went round to Mrs Beaumont's instead to talk about old films.'

'Oh, yes?'

'Would you help me?'

She drew up a chair and sat opposite him.

'I'll try.'

'Mr Finch wants us to look at films from 1925 to 1935.'

'Let me see,' she said. 'I started going to the Pictures when I first started working.'

'Was that when you were a maid?'

'That's right. I worked for this lovely lady who had all these children's books on her shelves. She let me borrow them and I used to read them in bed. She even had me read ones for little 'uns, those Beatrix Potter books. I read them to you when you were little . . .'

'But I didn't like them,' finished Henry for her.

'Why do you say that? You loved them.'

'Gran said.'

'Oh. Anyway,' she said hurriedly, 'every now and then, me and the cook would go to the Pictures. I must have been about your age then.'

'So what date would that have been?'

'About 1928. They were all silent films of course. But about a year after that came the talkies. They were building lots of new picture houses then.'

She looked happier now, Henry thought, reminiscing about her days in service. Her father had been killed in the Great War when she was Molly's age. After the war, both she and her mother went down with Spanish flu. Her mother didn't survive and she was put in an orphanage.

'That's when I learned how to mend, cook and clean,' she had told him one day, 'but I learned little about love.'

'I carried on going to the Pictures till I married your father and we moved down here. I didn't go again till you were six, a year after he died. We went every week from then. Do you remember?'

'Yeah. And we stopped when Uncle Bill moved in,' he muttered.

'No, love. We stopped when your gran moved in.'

'But she said . . .'

'She says a lot of things. She gets a bit muddled.'

'So why did we stop?'

His mother looked away for a moment.

'I thought she might be a bit lonely on her own and, anyway, you were ten by then. I thought you'd want to be with your friends.'

Henry had a feeling it was only half the truth.

They heard the click of the yard door. His mother's face lit up and she whirled round to look out of the window.

'It's your stepdad!' And then she turned back to face him. 'Uncle Bill, I mean.' And the tiny flicker of happiness Henry had seen in her eyes was now extinguished.

The darkroom became Henry's sanctuary at school, although it reminded him that he hadn't used the camera for some time. It took him a while to realise why. He was frightened. It was as if it was the camera's fault for discovering the truth about his father and his mother's bigamy. What else might it discover? Instead he volunteered to help Mr Finch develop other people's negatives.

'Anything troubling you, Dodge?' Mr Finch asked one break time as Henry quietly watched images emerging in the tray.

'My mother's ill,' he muttered.

Once he was on his own again, he found himself asking the same questions over and over again. What had his father been doing for nine years? Why had he appeared now? When were they going to tell Gran? And what was his mum going to do now that she loved two men?

'Every time I see that film,' said Mrs Beaumont, as Henry and his friends left the cinema after seeing *Whisky Galore*, 'I feel as though I've taken a brief holiday.'

It was the second time Henry had seen it. And he had to agree with her. Sadly he knew he wouldn't be able to have many more of those 'brief holidays'. He only had enough saved for two more visits to the Pictures and then it would be down to once a week using his pocket money. But Mrs Beaumont came to his rescue.

'I need a word with you, Henry,' she said. 'You three go on ahead and get the kettle on.'

She waited till they were out of earshot.

'Is it about Mum?' Henry asked quickly.

'No, I need chopped wood for my fire, which naturally I will pay for. Can you help me?'

He nodded, grinning.

Over the weekend and after school the following week, he scoured the bombsites and the seafront for driftwood, carrying the wood to his backyard in an old sack. The damp wood he put in the air-raid shelter to dry, the rest he sawed and chopped. As he toiled he realised that this was his diamond in the dungheap. Working in the grocery shop would have been terrible. He couldn't have faced being near so many people. Through helping Mrs Beaumont, he could be on his own and have time to think.

The following Saturday she offered him more work.

'I need help to prepare a studio,' she said and she took him into her back garden to the strange building that looked like a miniature house with its two windows. Even the door was like an ordinary front door with two frosted windows at the top and a letterbox.

She unlocked the door and switched on the light. It was an enormous room with a wooden floor. Heavy dark Victorian furniture was piled up to the ceiling: trunks, boxes and stacks of old framed paintings. At one end was a huge chest-high cupboard.

'A tailor used to store all his materials in this cupboard,' she said, resting her hand on it, 'and this room was filled with rows of sewing machines and tables.' She pointed to the end of the room. 'Beyond that door is a tiny cloakroom, lavatory and basin. As you can see, after the tailor left, my parents used it for storing other people's unwanted furniture. I want this to be a dance studio for Mrs Jeffries by the spring. But don't tell her. It's to be a surprise. I need the furniture here to be taken into the house.'

'Just for Grace, Jeffries and Pip to have lessons?' he said, astonished.

'Not exactly. You see I have a feeling that once we begin a class here, word will get out, Mrs Jeffries will have more pupils, and she will never ever have to make corsets again. Jeffries will be helping so you won't be on your own.'

Henry couldn't stop smiling. He would be away from the horrible atmosphere at home and he would be able to go to the cinema more than once a week *and* he could buy film for the camera.

'You look like the cat that's got the cream,' she remarked, 'so I take it you're willing.'

When they returned to her kitchen, his friends were waiting impatiently for him round the table, the newspaper open.

At the Troxy there were two U films, the major feature was *Fire Over England* and starred an actor called Laurence Olivier. Henry remembered him playing Hamlet.

'Flora Robson, Raymond Massey and Vivien Leigh!' exclaimed Mrs Beaumont. 'I know you don't need me to get you in but if you don't mind I'll come too. I love them.'

Pip meanwhile looked as if he was about to burst.

'Are you feeling all right?' asked Henry.

Pip nodded, beaming.

'He's been like this for hours,' said Jeffries. 'You're going to have to tell us.'

'It's about Mr Hart,' he blurted out.

'He's going to let you draw the entire innards of his projectors?' guessed Jeffries.

Pip shook his head wildly.

'He's going to take Mum to a dance on his night off. And Mrs Jeffries is making her a dress!'

'Oh, how romantic,' sighed Grace.

'That's very interesting,' said Jeffries, 'but could we get back to business. A very important film is showing at all three Odeons. But it's an A,' he said, glancing at Mrs Beaumont. 'It's called *The Rocking Horse Winner*. And Valerie Hobson, who stars in it, will be making personal appearances at each Odeon on Monday.'

'Oh, can't we go and see her, Mrs Beaumont?' pleaded Grace.

'John Mills is in it too,' continued Jeffries, 'he's the actor who played Pip in *Great Expectations* and Scott in *Scott of the Antarctic*, last year. You like him, don't you?'

'Yes. Can I have a look?' Mrs Beaumont gazed thoughtfully at the newspaper.

'Sternsea Odeon, seven o'clock. Grace, if you come here after tea, we could see the supporting film and *The Rocking Horse Winner* afterwards. Then I can take you back to your great-aunt's flat after we've seen Valerie Hobson, and you boys can then do what you like,' she added, winking at them. 'Now I've been meaning to talk to you about an American film I'd like you to see, *Little Women*.'

Henry shuddered.

'Little *Women*!' he muttered. It was bound to be a sickly romance.

'And I'll pay for the tickets,' she said. 'It's based on a lovely book and I've heard good things about the film.' She smiled at Henry. 'Henry, you look as though I've tied you to a torturer's rack!'

When Henry walked home he mulled over the three trips to the cinema he would make over the following week. He could pay for *The Rocking Horse Winner* and *Fire Over England* out of his pocket money and savings, and on Saturday afternoon he would be seeing *Little Women* for nothing. That would leave him with enough money for one film programme plus the film his pocket money would cover, for the week after next. By then he would be clearing out the strange little building at the back of Mrs Beaumont's house.

He broke into a joyful run. It wasn't till he entered

the kitchen at home and caught sight of his distraught mother battling with Molly that he remembered that his family were sitting on an unexploded bomb.

## 3. First contact

'SHE'LL BE HERE ANY MINUTE!' WHISPERED TWO WOMEN IN THE row behind Henry.

The closing credits for *The Rocking Horse Winner* were rolling down the screen. Grace was half standing, peering over the heads of the row in front of her. The lights came on and the manager strode on stage in bow tie and black jacket.

'Here she comes!' squealed one of the women so loudly that Henry had a strong urge to laugh. He was about to give Jeffries a dig in the ribs when he noticed that he was looking as stage-struck as Grace and Pip.

'Miss Valerie Hobson!' announced the manager.

Coming up the steps at the side was a young woman in a long flared red skirt, little matching jacket, hat and gloves.

'Oh, isn't she lovely!' chorused the duo behind Henry.

'Oh, yes,' Henry heard Jeffries whisper in agreement. 'Isn't she?'

As Valerie Hobson stepped on to the stage there was a gasp, followed by thunderous applause. A little girl in a frilly pink party frock appeared on the opposite side, half hidden behind a large bouquet. She walked up to the actress, curtsied and presented it to her. The actress clasped it and waved to the audience, smiling. Lights popped from two newspaper photographers standing at the front. A large microphone was placed in the centre of the stage, and as she walked up to it Henry slid the camera out of its case.

'It'll never work in this light,' said Jeffries.

'I know,' said Henry, 'but it's worth trying.'

What Henry didn't mention was that he was more interested in the audience. He noticed a group of people standing on the far side of the stalls. And that's when he saw the man he had been told was his dad, leaning against one of the pillars.

He gave an involuntary start. With shaking fingers, he peered into the viewfinder and aimed the lens at Valerie Hobson. Slowly he swung it round towards the pillar but there was no sign of him now. And it was time to leave.

'Aren't you staying to watch it again?' asked Jeffries, when Henry stood up with Mrs Beaumont and Grace. 'Pip's staying.'

'No, I've got to help back home.'

Outside, he and Mrs Beaumont and Grace struggled down the steps through the excited crowd. Henry said his goodbyes and headed towards his street. He walked past the Plaza and turned the corner, looking uneasily over his shoulder.

He decided to go to bed early so that his mother wouldn't suspect he was keeping something from her. Later he heard Uncle Bill returning from work, and after what seemed like hours, while he washed and had something to eat, Henry heard his footsteps on the stairs.

As soon as he had closed the door Henry said, 'I've seen him again.'

Uncle Bill looked alarmed.

'Did he notice you looking at him?'

'I don't think so, although he disappeared soon after I tried to take a photograph.'

'That's interesting. Perhaps he knows he's been caught before.'

The word *caught* startled Henry.

'Is there something else you want to tell me?' asked Uncle Bill, picking it up.

Henry shook his head.

Later, lying in the dark, he mulled over the word, *caught*. Why should it unsettle him?

On Friday night the district nurse called again.

'Your wife,' she said to Uncle Bill, 'is losing too much weight. Is she eating properly? And are you doing anything to alleviate the rat problem?'

Uncle Bill nodded but Henry noticed he looked worried.

'I have concerns for the baby if she continues to lose weight this rapidly. I've ordered her to stay in bed. I noticed your daughter was already asleep there. I presume that's to make life easier for her should Molly need her in the night.'

Uncle Bill nodded awkwardly.

'Now about your wife's first mother-in-law, she needs to roll up her sleeves . . .'

'There's a neighbour helping,' interrupted Henry quickly.

'That would be Mrs Henson, I presume.' The nurse gave Uncle Bill a piercing look. 'Is there anything else worrying her?'

'I don't think so,' said Uncle Bill quietly.

'I suggest that from now on someone else takes the accumulator to be recharged. Mrs Henson told me that she spotted her taking it to the wireless shop today.'

'I'll do that,' said Uncle Bill.

'Me too,' added Henry.

'I'll pop in again next week and if I don't see an improvement she'll have to go into a nursing home where people can keep an eye on her.'

After she had left, Henry and Uncle Bill sat quietly at the table. If his mother couldn't have the baby at home, Molly would play up even more.

The following morning, Henry rose early. He laid

Gran's fire while she slept, made Molly some toast and looked at some picture books with her. She was exhausting. She knew something was up and it made her want to get at everything and take it apart, including the books. When Mrs Henson popped round he was happy to hand her over. He left Uncle Bill to look after his mother and fled to Mrs Beaumont's house. He felt ashamed of himself for wanting to escape, but the neighbours were going to help out after Uncle Bill had gone to work, and they would be able to do a much better job of keeping an eye on his mother than he could.

'Mrs Beaumont's gone shopping,' said Grace, 'but she's left a note with instructions. She says it'll explain where to put it all.'

It was the day Mrs Beaumont was taking them to see *Little Women* and Henry had agreed to help Jeffries carry furniture from the building in her garden into the house.

'In a spare bedroom upstairs,' added Jeffries.

'Grace and me will be your door openers,' said Pip.

It took an hour for Henry and Jeffries to manoeuvre a wardrobe up three flights of stairs to a large room, which was now going to be Mrs Beaumont's alternative storeroom.

'At this rate, it's going to take us weeks,' puffed Henry.

'More like years,' Jeffries gasped.

By the time Mrs Beaumont returned from shopping,

the 'storeroom' upstairs was full and there was still more furniture to move from the building in the garden.

'This isn't going to work,' Mrs Beaumont said gloomily. 'I really need to get rid of it, but my hands are tied. I shall just have to come up with another idea.' She smiled. 'Never mind. Let's forget about it, have something to eat and head for the Apollo.'

As the Technicolor swept across the Apollo screen, Henry watched the opening of *Little Women* with its snow, tinkling music, church bells ringing and candles being put on a Christmas tree.

'Too bright,' he muttered. 'It's like a Christmas card.'

It wasn't that he didn't like the actresses who played the four little women, but it was difficult to take the girls' talk about how poor they were seriously.

'Their sitting room is bigger than our house,' he whispered to Jeffries in the dark, '*and* they have a servant.'

'But it's an old servant,' Jeffries pointed out.

'They're beautiful,' said Pip, ignoring them.

And they were, thought Henry, if you liked that sort of thing.

*I like the tomboy one, Jo*, he thought.

Unfortunately the Jo character had to go and spoil it all by going all dreamy-eyed too.

'Oh, no!' he moaned as she walked into her home with the man who had asked her to marry him and the music rose to a crescendo, as did the camera, to a rainbow above the rooftop.

'Treacle,' he murmured.

Grace sat wiping her eyes.

'Well, I thought it was lovely,' said Mrs Beaumont. 'And you must admit there were some funny moments.'

'I liked *those* bits,' said Henry slowly.

'It was so *sad*!' said Grace.

It was when they were outside walking past the queues for the next showing that Henry spotted the man again, darting into a café opposite. They stopped outside the Kings Theatre. The others were so busy talking they hadn't noticed him.

'*Goldilocks and the Three Bears* is still being performed twice daily and *Peter Pan* is coming shortly,' read Pip to Grace.

'Are you interested?' said Mrs Beaumont.

'I've never seen *Peter Pan*,' said Grace. 'I could ask Great-Aunt Florence . . .'

Henry knew he had to do something quickly.

'Blast,' he said, pushing his hand in his trouser pockets, 'I must have dropped my handkerchief in the cinema. I'll just run back and tell someone, in case one of the cleaning ladies picks it up. I'll catch you up.'

He sprinted back until he was standing on the pavement opposite the café. As he crossed the road his throat seemed to constrict and he found himself struggling to swallow. Once outside the café window, he forced himself to look inside. The man was sitting, his hat placed to one side on his table. His black hair, which was longer than someone in the Army would have had, was sleeked backwards. He was staring into his cup, completely unaware that for once he was the one being observed. And then he lifted his head. It took all of Henry's nerve to stay there. The man gazed down at his cup again. A moment later he appeared to freeze.

'He knows,' Henry murmured to himself.

Slowly the man turned his head and looked towards the window. Henry willed himself to look him in the eye. He wanted him to know that he knew he was being followed. What was odd was that the man didn't appear to be surprised. It was as though he had been waiting for this moment. Henry gave him a brief nod and then broke away to join the others.

And collided with Grace. Quickly he began striding ahead of her.

'You didn't go back for your handkerchief, did you?' she asked, running alongside him. 'It's him, isn't it? The man in the photograph?'

'You mustn't tell the others.'

'Henry!' she gasped. 'You know who he is, don't you?'

'So he knows you've spotted him?' said Uncle Bill.

It was later that night in the bedroom that Henry told

him about the incident at the café. He decided not to mention that Grace was with him and that she now knew everything.

'Yes.'

'There must be some way round this,' Uncle Bill whispered.

'Shall I tell Mum?'

'No, I don't want her going downhill again. She's started typing a new story for Mrs Beaumont and it's like a tonic. She dreads coming home, though, and that's sad.'

It was all so simple, thought Henry. All Uncle Bill had to do was to move out. His real father could then move in. After all, it must be terrible for him to know that another man was living in his house. Molly could then go and visit her father somewhere else, couldn't she?

When Henry next woke, he discovered that the camp bed was empty. It was still pitch dark. He slipped out of bed and crossed the landing. Molly was fast asleep but there was no sign of his mother. He crept downstairs. Light was spilling out from under the kitchen door.

'But what about the police?' he heard his mother say.

'There's no point rushing into things. We must think about you and the baby first.'

'Oh, Bill!' and she gave a muffled cry. 'I don't want to have this baby in prison.'

# 4. Waiting and watching

UNCLE BILL TOOK MOLLY TO THE SEAFRONT IN THE MORNING SO that Henry's mother could prepare the Sunday dinner without Molly getting under her feet. Henry noticed that she still wasn't using the new pressure cooker.

'I'm saving it for a special occasion,' she stammered, and walked hurriedly into the scullery.

He did his best to avoid Gran. Even when he was in her room, he concentrated on tending the fire rather than looking her in the eye. She had a way of wheedling information out of him without him realising, and he couldn't forget the conversation he had overheard on the stairs. He had to keep his mouth shut to protect his mother. He prayed that Grace was keeping her mouth shut too.

After dinner, Mrs Henson took Molly out, and his mother went upstairs to put her feet up. While Henry and his stepfather washed and dried the dishes, Henry brought up the subject of Gran.

'Have you told her what the district nurse said about her helping Mum?' he asked.

'No.'

'Has Mum?'

'No.'

'Why?'

There was a pause.

'Best leave well alone.'

'She's not old, you know. Not very, anyway.'

'What makes you say that?'

'I worked it out. She's younger than Mrs Beaumont.'

'Yes, I know.'

'You know?' said Henry, surprised.

'She's happy in her room and well,' he hesitated, 'she might be a bit in the way. Two women in the kitchen and all that.'

Henry said nothing. Three women shared Mrs Beaumont's kitchen and they got on all right. He was just being weak. And Henry couldn't tell Gran to help. He wasn't a grown-up. It was up to Uncle Bill.

It wasn't until Wednesday that Henry returned with Jeffries and Pip to the second-hand bookshop. Pip asked the bookseller if he had any music scores while Henry made his way back to the stack of unsorted books to reread the details of *So you want to be a camera operator* in the schoolboy annual. He hadn't been there long when the bookseller appeared with an anglepoise lamp and plugged it in. It was identical to the one his mother had given Uncle Bill at Christmas.

'The husband of the woman who bought it sold it back to me,' explained the bookseller and he switched it on.

Henry sat in the small pool of light, gaping at it. He knew Uncle Bill was mean, but to sell a present his mother had worked hard for and chosen for him, shook him. He bowed his head in an effort to conceal his rage.

'I can't find anything useful yet,' said Jeffries, peering round a bookcase. 'Cheer up!' he said, taking in Henry's face. 'We can come back when we've got more time.' And he began calling out for Pip.

'No luck,' said Jeffries. 'I couldn't find anything about films twenty years ago.'

'Never mind,' said Mrs Beaumont. 'Plug in the electric fire up in your bedroom and you can look through my brother's film magazines.'

They trooped up the stairs. When Henry stepped into Pip and Jeffries' room, he was surprised to see the walls covered in photographs of film stars.

'They're from my *Picture Goer's Annuals*,' said Jeffries. 'You rescued them, remember?'

Henry nodded. That day when he had stood guarding a wheelbarrow outside Jeffries' old lodgings seemed a lifetime away. He stood in front of an actor in chain mail.

'That's Laurence Olivier addressing his soldiers in *Henry V*,' said Jeffries. A bedraggled Humphrey Bogart was looking over the barrel of a rifle in *Treasure of the Sierra Madre* in another picture. 'What do you think of this one?' He pointed to a sepia photograph of a tanned Jean Simmons, her dark wavy hair brushed away from her face, leaning back with her eyes closed against the trunk of a palm tree, in a sarong. Underneath it said, *Jean lazily enjoys the hot sun of the South Seas after a hard day's location work on* The Blue Lagoon. 'Do you remember seeing her before?'

'Ophelia in *Hamlet*,' said Henry.

But the biggest surprise was two enormous film posters, the kind one would only see in a cinema foyer. The one above Pip's bed was in black and red, DICK BARTON STRIKES BACK.

Pip stood beside it, beaming.

'That's the crowd fleeing from the sound rays,' explained Pip, pointing at the rays spreading out from a picture of Blackpool Tower.

A woman was clasping her hands to her ears, her body bent backwards as though in agony. Above her were the words, THE BBC'S SENSATION! – LISTENED TO BY 10,000,000 NIGHTLY! At the bottom was a line of small pictures of the cast and dog.

'The picture that puts showmanship back in show

business!' read Pip with a flourish. 'You know the scary bit at the end of the film, well, Mr Hart told me that the chief projectionist told him and Stan, the second projectionist, to use *full application of sound* to blast the audience out of their seats! That's why people screamed when they saw it.'

He pointed to the poster between the two windows, a vividly coloured one of *The Adventures of Robin Hood.*

'Mr Hart asked one of his friends to get me that. He gives us all sorts of things. And sometimes he takes my mum to tea in the Plaza café.'

'You should have seen the dress my mother made for her,' said Jeffries. 'She made it from old curtains.'

'It looked like something out of a magazine,' said Pip. 'And Mrs Jeffries dyed a pair of Mrs Beaumont's gloves to match the shoes we dyed.'

Jeffries laughed.

'Your face,' he choked, pointing at Henry.

'You're talking about *fashion*!' Henry said.

'When Mr Hart came here to collect her,' continued Pip, undeterred, 'he went all red. So did she.'

The bar on the heater began to glow. Henry moved closer to be near its warmth.

'Let's look in the cupboard,' he said hurriedly.

Jeffries threw open the doors and Henry's eye fell on the large magazines piled horizontally on the bottom shelf – the *Picture Posts*. As he looked up at the shelves with the novels on them he immediately spotted one called *Caught* by Henry Green. Instinctively he reached for it.

'Why are you taking that book down?' asked Pip.

'Wasn't that made into a film, with James Mason in it?' said Jeffries.

And then Henry remembered. It was the film he had told his mother about, the one that had upset her so badly, about a woman who was married to a bully.

He had a quick look inside but it seemed to be about a man who was a voluntary fireman in the war. He returned it to the shelf.

'These look good,' said Jeffries, spotting some smaller magazines.

He selected a handful and laid them out on his bed. As he opened them Henry could see pages of closely typed essays.

'You know I think everyone will be bored if we do the same old presentation again,' said Jeffries thoughtfully. 'I think we ought to show a proper full-length film.'

'And introduce it,' said Henry.

'Briefly,' added Pip.

Henry and Jeffries glanced at each other and grinned.

'Good idea,' they chorused.


'It's got Bud Abbott and Lou Costello in it,' said Jeffries over the newspaper.

'What has?' asked Pip.

'*Lost in a Harem*.'

'Oh, they're really funny,' said Grace. 'They're so silly.'

'And Jimmy Dorsey and his Band is in it too. My mother loves them. And there's a police film, *The Blue Lamp*, showing at the three Odeons. A bit more lively than *Little Women*, eh?' he said, grinning at Henry.

Henry pretended to collapse with relief.

'And it says James Cagney is RED HOT in *White Heat* at the Savoy. The unending battle of city streets,' he added dramatically.

It was a good week, thought Henry. With any luck he wouldn't have to spend much time at home at all.

On Saturday, Mrs Beaumont came with them to see *The Blue Lamp*. The film followed the day to day life of PC Dixon, a friendly London copper patrolling his beat. Henry was so absorbed in the film that he forgot all the trouble at home, until they came to a scene at the police station where PC Dixon noticed a tiny boy waiting in front of the desk, 'Hello, son', he said cheerily. 'Come to give yerself up for bigamy?'

As the people in the auditorium laughed, Henry shrank into himself. Could his mother really go to prison? The policeman's words haunted him throughout the film.

The following afternoon, Henry couldn't get away from home fast enough. He, Pip and Jeffries ran to the Troxy to see a double bill of A films. Mrs Beaumont couldn't come, so as soon as they reached the picture house they began looking for a likely person to take them in.

'Shame on you!' yelled a voice from behind.

Henry whirled round. It was Frank. He lifted his chin and began sniffing.

'Something smells awful bad round 'ere.'

'Come on,' said Henry to his friends and moved to another part of the queue.

'What was all that about?' asked Jeffries.

'He doesn't like me.' Suddenly he spotted someone he hadn't seen for months and his spirits lifted. 'Charlie!' he yelled.

He ran up to him.

'Hello, Henry,' he said cheerfully.

'Will you take us in?'

'The three of you?' He stared at Pip and Jeffries. Henry's stomach tightened. After a brief silence Charlie gave a grin. 'No skin off my nose,' he said. 'Hand yer money over.'

Once they entered the barn-like cinema, they separated. Balanced precariously on the broken seats in the front row they watched an action-packed *The Rats of Tobruk* and a gun-toting drama called *The Man from Texas*. It was just what Henry needed. As cowboys were flung off their horses and rolled in the dust and their enemies fired volley after volley of bullets from behind high rocks above narrow canyons, the tight feeling in his stomach disappeared along with his worries.

It was when they left the cinema that Henry spotted the man again. He was standing on the pavement opposite. Henry looked away quickly.

'It'll be good to see Daniel again when we go up to London at half-term, won't it?' he said, making conversation.

'Yes. I wonder if he'll have a film to show us,' said Jeffries.

'Don't you wish you were coming, Pip?'

'No. It's the Chief's day off and Mr Hart's going to teach me how to lace a projector.'

They reached the Plaza.

'See you tomorrow,' said Henry, waving casually.

He watched them till they were halfway up the road before running back towards the Troxy.

The man was standing under a street lamp near the railway station, his head bowed, the shadow from his hat hiding half his face. As Henry stood on the kerb he glanced up at him. Again he showed no surprise. Henry's chest felt tight. He tried to catch his breath and attempted to walk casually across the road. A car appeared from nowhere and hooted at him. He jumped backwards and watched it pass. He moved forward again, as if in a dream, his body seeming to be one step behind him. Once he reached the kerb on the other side, he ambled slowly up to the man, his hands clenched tightly in his pockets.

'I'm Henry Dodge,' he said. 'Are you...?' He hesitated, almost afraid to say the word. 'Are you my *dad*?'

'YEAH, THAT'S RIGHT.'

Henry was taken aback. He had always imagined that his father would sound posh and commanding, like John Mills in *Scott of the Antarctic* or one of the films where he was in charge of a submarine, saving hundreds of lives. Within seconds he realised that he had been stupid. He and his gran were Londoners. His father had only moved down south after he had married his mother.

They decided to talk on the railway bridge, where Henry thought they would be less likely to be spotted. For a while they stood side by side in silence, their elbows on the iron wall.

'Where have you been?' Henry asked, eventually.

'That's the problem,' his father answered roughly. 'I dunno. Only bits are coming back to me, see. I've had to go and visit doctors.'

'You lost your memory?'

'Yeah. But not the memory I thought I lost.' He paused as if not knowing quite where to begin. 'I wakes up in this hospital bed, see, and they tells me who I am, but it ain't Alfred Dodge. They says, "You're Walter Briggs." I says, "I can't be Walter Briggs or I'd remember," and they says, "Well, what do you remember?" And I says, "Nothin'." And they says, "Yer papers say you're Walter Briggs so that's who you are." And they treats me for concussion and sends me packin'. Anyway, there's this envelope with Walter's address on it, in London. They tells me they think I'd come down on a day trip to the coast. So I goes up to London hoping someone in his street will recognise me, tell me the story of me life and that. But when I gets there, the street's rubble. So I gets in touch with the Services to see if this Walter has been called up. And he was, but he failed the medical. Asthma.'

'So you lost your memory but you still thought you were Walter Briggs?'

'Yeah.'

'So when did you think you were someone else?'

'Last year. I'm a driver, see. Up to then I was workin' between London and the Midlands. Then I gets this job pickin' up lorries from the dockyard down 'ere and driving them to London. I travels down in the train. Sometimes it's the other way round.

'Anyway, I'm sitting in this train carriage and there's this newspaper on the seat what someone's left behind.

So I picks it up and there's this photo in it.'

'End of last August?'

'That's right. And there's this woman standin' next to a man with a little girl. And it just hit me out the blue. That's my Maureen. Just like that. Well it give me a bit of a turn, I can tell you.'

'But didn't you recognise the streets when you first came down?'

'Not at first. The place has taken a bit of a poundin', ain't it? Lots of the streets I knows ain't here any more. Once I recognised yer mum in the photo, other stuff began to come back. The door in the photo had a number on it so I knew where she lived. I didn't even know if you or your gran were alive cos you weren't in the photo. Then I thought, I can't just turn up out of the blue in case I give someone a heart attack, so I hung around for a bit, watchin', whenever I come down on a job.'

'And that's when you saw me?'

'Yeah. I thought, that boy could be me. And then I remembered being in the Army, so I contacted them and they sent me to see some medical bloke. He tells me I'm dead, that I'd been killed on leave while I was down 'ere.'

'Private Jeffries said you saved his life.'

'Who's Private Jeffries?'

'This other soldier. He wrote a letter to the *Sternsea Evening News*. He said you threw him aside and took the blast.'

'Well, I never.'

'We went to your funeral,' Henry said quietly.

'Well, it weren't me you buried.'

'It must have been the man who saved Private Jeffries' life. Maybe he saved your life too.'

'Mebbe he did.'

'Private Jeffries didn't turn up for the funeral, though. He went AWOL. You know, Absent Without Leave.'

'Yeah, I do know what it means,' said his father and he smiled.

'Sorry. Anyway, his wife doesn't believe it. She thinks he's wandering around somewhere in a daze.'

'Like what I was?'

Henry nodded.

They stared silently at the railway line.

'Mum knows,' said Henry quietly. 'She recognised you from the photos I took.'

'Yeah. I saw you snapping away. That's some camera you got.'

'It's not mine.'

'Oh?'

'It's on loan.'

There was another silence.

'I expect she was a bit shocked,' said his father at last.

Henry nodded.

'When I saw her in the newspaper and I saw she'd married again and had another nipper, I thought, this is a bit of a mess. I'll have to tread carefully. A lot of people could get hurt.'

'Uncle Bill says his marriage to Mum don't count.'

'No,' said his father quickly, 'but I don't suppose, now she's met someone else, I mean, I shouldn't think . . .' his voice trailed away.

'You mean she might want a divorce?'

'That's right, son.'

Henry almost jumped at the word *son*.

'She'd never want a divorce. You know Mum. She'd rather die.'

'Does yer gran know?'

'No.'

'It took me a while to find out where she was.'

'She moved in. And then Uncle Bill did.'

'You don't sound too happy about that.'

'I'm not. Gran can't stand him. But he can move out now and you can move back in, can't you?'

'We can't rush things. I got a place of me own in London. And work.'

'You can live in two places.'

He smiled.

'I've told you quite a lot about meself. How about you? You'll soon be leaving school now, won't you?'

Henry nodded.

'Got any work lined up?'

'I want to be a camera operator.'

There, it was out. Easy. And it was such a relief to say it.

'Camera operator? Like in a photograph shop?'

'No. What people call a cameraman. A film cameraman.'

His father smiled.

'You and me, we've met at the right time. London's the place for you. And I got contacts.'

'Really?'

'I sometimes work for film people as a driver. I'll keep me eyes open.'

'Thanks!' He was about to add *Dad*, but it felt too awkward.

'So,' he said, 'd'you remember much about me?'

'Gran's always talking about you. She tells me what sort of things we did together when I was little. She keeps photographs of you on the mantelpiece. She didn't want Mum to marry Uncle Bill. She thinks he's stuck-up.'

'Yeah. I saw he got that Higher Certificate.'

'He wants to be a teacher.'

'Does he now? How does yer mum feel about that?'

'She's all for it.'

'And you?'

'I don't care. He tried to make me go to the grammar school but I didn't answer any of the exam questions. He was so angry with me. Gran was pleased, though.'

There was another silence.

'I have to catch a train back to London tonight,' said

the man. 'I'll be back again next Sunday. It might be wise if we keep my sudden appearance *in the family*. Know what I mean?'

'Because Mum might end up having the baby in prison.'

'Baby?'

'Oh,' said Henry awkwardly. 'Of course, you don't know about the baby.' And then Henry had a terrible thought. 'If the Army know, won't they tell the police?'

'Not yet. They know her as Mrs Dodge, not Mrs Carpenter. That'll give us a bit of time, won't it?'

He gave a broad smile and Henry felt in an instant that somehow his father would make everything work out fine.

'Best we say goodbye 'ere, son.'

Henry nodded, suddenly feeling very shy.

'See you next Sunday. On this bridge. About this time.'

'Yeah.'

His father walked away. Henry stayed on the bridge and waited so that he could see him step on to one of the platforms. It was strange to think that his father might have been on a train that was being driven by Uncle Bill. He watched his train pull in and then he lost sight of him.

That night he didn't dream about his mother screaming. He dreamt he was standing in a graveyard in Vienna, surrounded by police, and then suddenly he was running, looking for his father down dark alleyways, past shadowy porches and doors, aware that he was in some kind of danger.

'What's asthma? What does it do to you?'

Mrs Beaumont was going through a pile of old papers at the kitchen table, Pip and Jeffries were messing around with a new crystal set that Pip had been given as a birthday present from Mr Hart, and Grace was leaning against the dresser listening to an American jazz record on the gramophone.

'Difficulty in breathing. These awful pea-souper fogs we sometimes get can kill people suffering from asthma. That's how badly it affects them.'

'So if someone with it was called up, they'd fail the medical test.'

'Probably. Asthma can also be brought on by stress and there's nothing more stressful than being in battle. Why?'

'Oh, something I heard,' Henry said casually, and he flicked over the page of the *Picture Post* he was browsing through.

When he stood up to go home, Grace insisted on seeing him to the door.

'You've seen your father again, haven't you?' she whispered to him in the porch.

He nodded and tried to walk down the steps but she tugged at his sleeve.

'You've spoken to him too.'

Henry said nothing.

'I knew it,' she said.

'I haven't said I have.'

'You haven't said you haven't.'

'All right, I have.'

'What's he like?'

At that Henry couldn't help smiling.

'Nice. He really wants to get to know me. He listens to me. Not like Uncle Bill.'

'I like your Uncle Bill.'

'You don't know him.'

'So where's he been all these years?'

'Walking around with amnesia, like John Mills in *The October Man*. He's only been remembering things over the last year. He thought he was someone else.'

Henry told her his story.

'What about the third man?' asked Grace puzzled.

'How did you know I was dreaming about that film last night?'

'Not the film. I meant the man who was buried as your father. Oh. Perhaps that's why you're dreaming about *The Third Man*, because the man who was buried was the third man, wasn't he?'

'No. The third man in the film was alive. But you're right about there being a third man. His name was Walter Briggs. He wasn't missed by the Army because he wasn't in it. He suffered from asthma and he doesn't have a family.'

'There must have been someone who missed him.'

'His street was blitzed.'

'But couldn't you find out if any of his friends survived and were evacuated somewhere?'

'Why should I do that?'

'They'd want to know, wouldn't they?'

'I'll ask my dad when I next see him.' It sounded good saying *my dad*.

'So is your father still in the Army, then?'

'No. But he's seeing some Army doctor because of all these bits of memory coming back. He wants me to go to London. He's going to help me get a job.'

'When?'

'He didn't say. When I finish school I s'pose.'

'I wonder where I'll go,' she said quietly.

'It'd be good if you could stay with Mrs Beaumont.'

'You don't know my parents. If they suspect I'm happy, they'll stop me.'

'Why?'

'I have to be punished.'

'For what?'

'For deliberately not reading and writing.'

'But you can't help it.'

'They don't believe that.'

'Then they should.'

'You didn't.'

They fell silent for a moment.

'Have you told Jeffries?' she asked.

'No!'

'You should.'

'I can't.'

'Why not?'

'Because my mother could go to prison. No one must find out.'

'They're going to find out some time, aren't they?'

'I know, but I think my mother wants to wait until after she's had the baby.'

'But what if the baby's taken away from her when she goes to prison?'

'Uncle Bill can look after it till she gets out.'

Even as he said the words, the horror of his mother going to prison made him feel sick.

'But if she's not really married to your Uncle Bill . . .'

She was right. He wouldn't be able to look after the baby. It would be his gran. And his gran would have to look after Molly as well. And she hated Molly.

'You promised not to say anything, Grace.'

'I won't.'


'I'd like to see *Boys in Brown* at the Plaza,' said Mrs Beaumont. 'On Sunday. Jeffries?'

'No, thanks. I'm saving up for London.'

'And I'll be watching it with Mr Hart upstairs,' said Pip.

'Henry?'

'Yeah, I'd like to see it too.' And the Plaza, like the Troxy, was near the station, where he would be meeting his father.

'Me too,' said Grace.

'Are you sure?' asked Henry, surprised. It wasn't really the sort of film she usually liked. It was set in a Borstal institution.

'What kind of school is this?' Grace whispered to him on Sunday night in the darkened cinema.

'It's a boarding school you go to when you're too young to go to prison.'

As *Boys in Brown* began, Henry was conscious that he would be meeting his father again in a couple of hours, and he felt a tightening in his throat.

Once the programme ended, Henry stood up, pulling his sodden umbrella out of the way so Mrs Beaumont and Grace could pass.

'Ah,' said Mrs Beaumont quietly, 'you're staying to watch both films through again, then?'

Henry nodded. Grace didn't move.

'I'd like to do that too,' she said. 'Just for the one they're showing now. It was so romantic.'

Henry was puzzled and alarmed. He wouldn't be able to see his father if she stayed.

'Soppy more like,' said Henry, hoping to put her off.

'I'd best get you back home,' said Mrs Beaumont.

He waited a good fifteen minutes after they had left before leaving the auditorium. A strong wind had blown up. It tugged at his umbrella as he tried to push it open in the rain on the steps outside. He held it high above his head as he manoeuvred his way between the two queues. Stepping quickly on to the road, he thought he heard footsteps behind him, but he put it down to the wind. It wasn't until he caught sight of his father standing by the steps to the bridge and noticed him glancing to one side that he discovered that Grace had been following him. Her flat woollen tartan hat lay sodden on her head and her plaits were dripping. He held the umbrella over her head.

'Who's the girl?' his father asked.

'A friend,' said Henry, 'she won't say anything.'

'Why did you bring her?'

'I didn't. She must have been waiting outside the cinema and followed me.'

His father glanced at her.

'Why?' he said abruptly.

'I'm nosy,' she said.

He stared at her for a moment.

'I won't blab or anything,' she said, 'because I wouldn't want to upset Mrs Carpenter.'

'Posh, ain't she?' he commented.

'I promise,' she added.

At that moment, the sky gave a loud rumble and the

rain turned into hail. Henry watched the tiny white balls bouncing off the pavement.

'And I've no umbrella.'

His father gave a nod and they headed for the steps to the bridge, Henry and Grace following. The three of them stood by the wall.

'Thought any more about what we were talking about?' his father said at last.

'About moving to London?'

'Yeah.'

His father took out a packet of cigarettes and lit one under the shelter of Henry's umbrella while the rain dribbled off his black trilby.

'Have you spoken to anyone who's in a film unit yet?' Henry asked awkwardly, aware that Grace didn't know that he wanted to be a cameraman and was listening.

To his relief, she kept silent.

'I been askin' around. But it takes time. I'll sort something out. I always do.'

'There's Mum, I'm a bit worried about people finding out what she's done.'

'If we moved up to London, no one would know, would they?'

'How d'you mean?'

'Here everyone knows her as Mrs Carpenter. A new neighbourhood and we could be Mr and Mrs Dodge. And you wouldn't be at school any more, so no one would find out there. No one would know anything about us.'

'What about Molly and the baby?'

'I'd see them right,' and he smiled. 'Course it would be better if she joined us later, after she'd had the baby, while we look for a bigger place. And that might take a bit of time.'

Henry felt torn. He couldn't have wished for anything better than to work for a film unit and be with his real father, but he hated the idea of leaving his mother.

'Couldn't we wait till we could all move together?'

'If a job comes up for you, you can't say you've got to wait till there's a place big enough for yer mum, can you?' he said gently. 'They'd give the job to someone else who'd jump at the chance.'

'But I can't work for five months anyway. Couldn't you find a place by then?'

'Five months? I was thinking sooner than that. I've heard of a job coming up in April.'

'We break up in March. I can do it in the holidays.'

'Why go back?' he said, smiling. 'You're fifteen.'

For some reason Henry felt a sense of panic. Everything seemed to be happening too quickly. He glanced at Grace. She was staring intently at his father and frowning.

'Uncle Bill wouldn't let me,' he remembered.

'Uncle Bill ain't yer father. He has no rights. I have.'

'But the school doesn't know you're alive and if I don't turn up for the summer term, they'll go to him and ask him what's going on. Mum won't want me to leave earlier either.' Henry avoided saying that since Mr Finch had come to the school, he liked the lessons and he wanted to finish the term with the rest of his form. And then he realised that all his excuses made him sound feeble. Some hero he was. 'I'll ask them,' he said quietly.

'That's my boy. It'll give us more time to get to know one another, won't it?'

Henry nodded.

'Dad,' he began slowly, glancing at Grace, 'when you thought you were Walter Briggs, and you found his street bombed, did you try and find his family?'

'First thing I did,' he said, gazing down at the railway track. 'They was all killed. Direct hit. I tried to trace other relatives but there was no one. I was alone in the world. Or so I thought.'

He gave another drag on his cigarette.

'And you really don't mind about Molly and the baby?'

'I'll have a ready-made family, won't I? I'm not saying it'll be easy, but after what I've been through, it's worth a try.' He gave Henry a pat on the shoulder. 'In April you could start a new life. Think about it.' He looked at his watch. 'I'd better get a move on. I got a train to catch.'

'We could meet earlier next time,' Henry suggested.

'It's better by night. Less chance of being spotted. We have to think of yer mum.' He indicated Grace. 'And your lady friend will keep quiet, won't she?'

Grace pressed a finger to her closed lips. Henry realised that for a chatterbox, it must have taken a lot of effort to stay silent.

His father drew up the collar of his soaked raincoat and pulled down his hat. It was a wonder his cigarette was still alight, thought Henry. As he watched him walk away he felt an intense sadness. He didn't want him to go.

'Same time next week,' said his father over his shoulder. 'On yer own.' He gave a friendly wave and turned the corner to go down the steps. Henry listened to his footsteps fade and then leaned over the wall.

'What a liar!' Grace burst out.

Henry swung round. For a moment, he was too stunned to speak. They stared at each other under the umbrella, the rain pouring off it like a waterfall.

'What do you mean?' he asked, outraged.

'Didn't you see how he kept turning away when you asked him questions?'

'What's wrong with that?'

'And rubbing his nose?'

'So.'

'And fiddling with his cigarette?'

'It's raining. He was trying to keep it alight.'

'And when you asked him a question about that Walter man, he couldn't even look you in the eye.'

'You don't have to look at people's eyes all the time, you know.'

'I may be no good at reading books but I can read faces, and he's a liar.'

'Don't you call my father a liar! You're just jealous.'

'Why should I be?'

'Because he's searched for me and followed me and wants me to join him and live with him as soon as possible, and your father doesn't want you at all.'

'At least my father's honest about it. At least he tells me to my face that the sooner I'm married and off his hands the better. But your father is a liar.'

'You're the one that's a liar!'

'Wait and see.'

'I was going to walk you back to your great-aunt's flat under my umbrella, but you can go on your own.'

'Good. I like the rain.'

'I'm never going to speak to you again.'

'I don't care.'

'I suppose you're going to break your word now and tell everyone about him after you've promised not to.'

'Why should I?' she said angrily. 'If I make a promise, I keep it. *I'm* not a liar!'

And with that she stomped off, the pavement splashing under her feet, her wet plaits swinging angrily from side to side. Henry felt like smashing his umbrella against the wall. He felt betrayed.

He ran home with his head bowed. The rain was hammering down now. As he stumbled into the yard, he saw his mother in the kitchen. She was standing motionless, staring into space, looking so small and lost that it alarmed him. He could see that she had become thinner. It wasn't right. It wasn't her fault that everything was such a mess. She hadn't known she was doing anything wrong. She glanced down to where her hands were resting on her stomach. Her fingers twitched and he realised that the baby was kicking. He had heard her talk about it but he had never seen it happening. He wished he had the camera. He wanted this image of his mother framed in the window with her unborn baby. And then it dawned on him. That baby was his half-brother or half-sister.

He decided there and then that he must earn some money. He would take the job in London and send her as much as he could. But he wouldn't tell her yet.

Battling with his umbrella in the darkness, he suddenly realised that he was leaving his friends behind already. Pip was at the Plaza every moment he could find and Henry had started finding it difficult to speak to Jeffries in case he accidentally blurted out something about the sudden appearance of his father. And now there was Grace. As he struggled with the soaked laces on his ankle boots, he could still hear her words ringing in his ears, *Your father is a liar.*

## 6. London and a dream in sight

SITTING ON THE TRAIN TO LONDON, HENRY WAS RELIEVED TO SEE that Jeffries and Mrs Beaumont had no idea that he and Grace weren't speaking to one another. While she and Mrs Beaumont chatted, Jeffries had his nose in *Great Expectations* and Henry stared out of the carriage window.

Once they arrived at her house, it was soup and bread offered by Violet, the schoolmistress who lived downstairs, after which Henry and Jeffries went upstairs to join Daniel for a chat by his fire. They had hardly sat down when Jeffries immediately began to talk about the presentations.

'Mr Finch wants us to take them out of the classroom,' he said. 'The confectionery group will be presenting their talk in a chocolate factory and the boys who are mad about fishing will speak at the fish market, which means we'll be doing ours in a cinema!'

'It's going to be for a whole week,' added Henry. 'Ours will be on the Friday morning.'

Daniel frowned. 'I'm afraid I haven't had much experience with a cinema projector.'

'That's all right,' said Jeffries, 'Pip knows the projectionists at the Plaza. He can ask them.'

'What you need is a short film to begin with made in the 1920s, followed by an interval where you can take your audience from then to 1935, before showing them a film from that year.'

'That boys *and* girls are going to like,' added Jeffries.

'Ah. A bit of romance.'

'A tiny bit,' said Henry, 'not too much.'

'Mrs Beaumont mentioned Alfred Hitchcock,' said Jeffries.

'Of course!' cried Daniel, banging his artificial leg, '*The 39 Steps*! It's a thriller. That'll cover the thirties. It came out in 1935.' He looked thoughtful. 'Twenties films,' he murmured. 'Most of the British ones I'm familiar with are about doomed romances and would be too long. But don't worry. I'll think of something.'

Jeffries was glancing at a pile of tiny bound newspapers. Daniel noticed his interest.

'They're full of film reviews. Help yourself. You might also like to take a look at these,' and he opened the partition doors.

'Cans of films!' Jeffries exclaimed.

Daniel laughed. 'You look like Aladdin in the cave of treasures.'

'How do you find what you want?' Jeffries asked.

'I don't know, but I usually do.'

Henry envied the easy way they chatted with one another. Daniel was so posh and clever. Even Jeffries sounded like him sometimes, always finding the words he wanted to say so easily. When Henry tried to talk, it was as though there was a wall between his brain and his tongue.

'I'd like to work in an archive like that,' he heard Jeffries say when Daniel was talking about the National Film Library.

Lying in their camp beds later that night, Jeffries was still exhilarated.

'London's the place to be and I'll get here somehow,' he said in the semi-darkness. '*And* I can be anonymous here.'

'London is like another country,' said Henry without thinking, and then he remembered it was Uncle Bill who had told him that.

When he woke, it was bitterly cold. He and Jeffries opened the high wooden shutters to find snow falling. They were hurriedly getting dressed when Mrs Beaumont called up to them.

'Breakfast in a café,' she yelled.

They were waiting for her in the hall when they heard voices coming from the dance studio. They peered in.

Daniel poked his head round the screen he was erecting and Jessica looked up over a wad of music on the piano.

'Hello!' she said, giving them a brief wave.

'It'll all be ready by the time you come back,' said Daniel. 'Max and some of his friends might pop in later to watch the films too.'

At the café, Henry sat by the window so that he could look out at the street and avoid looking at Grace. No one seemed to notice. After they had finished eating, she and Mrs Beaumont walked as far as the door of her house and said their goodbyes.

'Where are you two off to?' asked Jeffries.

'We're off to do girl's business,' Mrs Beaumont said. 'It would bore you senseless if I told you. See you later,' and they walked briskly away.

'Shops, I expect,' said Henry, when they were out of earshot.

Stepping into the hall, they could hear chatter and laughter coming from the studio. They stood in the doorway and peered in.

Max Beaumont was talking earnestly to two young women and Daniel was in the middle of a conversation with three men. As soon as Daniel spotted Henry and Jeffries he limped over towards them.

'Come in. Don't be shy. I've found a short Sherlock Holmes film. 1921. I know it's earlier than you want but I think it'll do, don't you?'

'And I have a suggestion for your interval,' said Jessica excitedly. 'Instead of talking about what happened between 1925 and 1935, why don't you have Pip play some music from the films?'

Jeffries and Henry looked at each other and grinned.

'Perfect!' said Jeffries.

'Take your seats, everyone,' Max called out.

'Floorboards you mean,' chipped in one of the young women.

'We do have an interesting selection of cushions,' said Daniel, pointing to a pile behind the door.

The rest of the morning was magical. They watched reel after reel of old films, silent melodramas, music-hall capers and seering romances, while Jessica played the piano. Soon after Max and his film friends had left, Mrs Beaumont and Grace arrived back, cradling fish and chips wrapped in newspaper. They ate them in Daniel's room, crowded round a one-bar heater.

'So, did you watch *The 39 Steps*?' asked Mrs Beaumont.

'This afternoon,' said Jeffries through a mouthful of chips.

'And?'

'It's the right choice isn't it, Henry?'

'Yeah, and it's got some funny bits in it too.'

As their train drew out of Waterloo it reminded Henry that he would not only be meeting his father the next day but that he had to give him an answer. But what should he tell him? If he agreed to go to London, he would only miss the last term. But then he would have to give an explanation to his friends and the only explanation was the truth. By the time they arrived at Hatton Station he felt lost. He didn't want to go home or to Mrs Beaumont's house or to a cinema. With limbs like lead he dragged himself across the road, waving goodbye to the others.

Immediately he stepped into the hall he noticed Gran's door was open. Within seconds she appeared, dragged him into her room and hurriedly closed the door.

'What's up?' said Henry.

'That bloke who taught your stepfather, that Mr Cuthbertson, he's been round again, all excited. Your stepfather's got another of them letters. He's been offered teacher training! Teacher training! Can you believe it? Who does he think he is? Anyway, I was waiting for it all to go to his head but he never said a word. And neither did yer mum. One minute it's newspapermen at the door, the next minute there's not a peep out of them. It don't add up. There's something else too, something you've kept very quiet about. I found out your mum's got that girl sleeping with her and your stepfather's been kipping in your room. Why didn't you tell me?'

Henry shrugged.

She gave a wicked smile.

'Looks like they've fallen out over somethin', don't it?'

'It's Molly,' Henry began. 'She's been getting nightmares.'

'Don't you believe it. Something's up and I mean to get to the bottom of it.'

The next morning after church, Henry asked his mother about the letter.

'What's Uncle Bill going to do?' he asked.

'I don't know,' she said quietly.

'How did Gran find out about him sleeping in my room?'

'I overslept. So did Molly. She came up and found me and Molly together.' She gave a tight smile. 'You get out of here. Go round to Mrs Beaumont's. The atmosphere's a lot more cheerful there, especially now that . . .' She stopped.

'Especially now that what?'

'Let Pip tell you. Here, take this,' and she handed him his pocket money plus a little extra, 'that's for him to go to the Troxy with you.'

'Thanks, Mum.'

Her kindness made him feel guilty about meeting his father in secret.

'What's the film again?' she asked.

*The Undercover Man*. It's about the U.S. Secret Service and a criminal investigation. There's this man who's a secret agent and he's trying to uncover evidence which will convict a master criminal.'

'Oh. Not very cheerful,' she said sadly, 'but exciting, I suppose.'

Henry nodded. He hated seeing his mother looking so lifeless.

'I'm going to make everything all right for you, Mum.'

'I wish you could, love. Right now I feel I'm standing in one of Mrs Beaumont's dungheaps and I can't find a diamond anywhere.'

'What about Dad? Isn't he a diamond?'

And then he remembered that because he was still alive she had committed bigamy.

She smiled but it looked as though it took an enormous effort.

'Don't mind me,' she said, 'I'm just a bit tired. You get on out.'


'Has your mother told you?' Jeffries asked as he opened the door.

'Told me what?'

There was laughter coming from the kitchen. Henry followed him down the steps. Pip and his mother were sitting side by side at the table, beaming. Grace was standing by the range. As soon as she spotted him, she turned away.

'Pip,' said Mrs Beaumont. 'He's here now.'

Pip sprang to his feet.

'Last night, Mr Hart asked Mum to marry him and Mum said "yes". And he wants to adopt me so we all have the same name. I'm going to have a dad who's a *projectionist*!'

'That's not the reason I want to marry him, Pip,' protested his mother. She smiled at Henry. 'And Mr Hart has said that as long as the manager is willing, he'd be happy to be the projectionist for your films.'

'And Grace and me have been looking at the music Jessica gave you,' added Pip.

They could all get along without him, thought Henry, gazing at them. Pip was more interested in being with Mr Hart now or playing the piano for Grace. And he and Jeffries were more of a pair than ever now that they shared a bedroom. They wouldn't miss him if he went to London.

'Good news, isn't it?' said Pip.

Henry nodded and forced himself to smile.

'I got a bit of news too,' he said slowly. 'My stepfather's been told he can go to this place that trains teachers.'

To Henry's surprise everyone began leaping around the kitchen and cheering. Even Grace, he noticed, was smiling, though she still avoided looking at him.

'You don't look too happy about it,' commented Mrs Beaumont.

'I'll be out working, won't I?'

She said nothing but stared at him with such intensity that he had to look away.

'Pip,' he said hurriedly, 'Mum gave me some extra money for you to come and see *The Undercover Man* with us.'

'Mum?' said Pip. 'Can I?'

'Of course you can. What a lovely thought. You thank your mum from me,' she said.

*The Undercover Man* was so gripping that Henry forgot his worries for a while. Later, stepping out of the cinema into the bitter wind, he walked silently with his friends as far as his street. When he was sure they were far enough away, he sprinted over the road, his eyes glued to Hatton Station.

But there was no figure watching for him from under the street light. For a horrible moment he wondered if he had missed him. He waited under the lamp, hugging himself for warmth. A sound from behind him caused him to swing round. He was just in time to see his father's shadowy figure slipping up the steps to the bridge. He wanted to run after him but he knew he mustn't draw attention to himself. To his annoyance, he noticed that he was beginning to shake.

His father was leaning over the wall, staring down at the railway lines. Henry walked slowly in his direction, pretending he didn't know him. He felt a little like the undercover man. He stopped a couple of feet away.

'Good to see you, son,' said his father, staring into the distance.

'I would have come sooner but I was . . .'

'I saw them,' he interrupted. 'Friends, are they?'

'Yeah. But I haven't told them about you.'

'That's good.' He paused. 'You remember what we talked about last week? About you workin' in films? I've been doing a lot of askin' around. Anyway, there's this bloke what owes me a favour and he says there's a job waitin' for you in a film unit.'

Henry slapped his hands down on the wall.

'You mean I'm going to be a clapper boy?'

'I thought you said you wanted to be a cameraman.'

'That takes years. You have to do lots of other jobs first. Being a clapper boy is the first rung on the ladder. He's the one who numbers the scenes and helps to synchronise the sound. Him shutting the clapperboard is a signal for the sound people, see.'

'How do you know all that, then?'

He was about to say, *I read about it in this bookshop*, when he remembered his father didn't read books.

He shrugged.

'I just picked it up.'

'Then a clapper boy is what this bloke must have meant.'

'Do you know what kind of film it is?'

'I'll ask,' he said.

Henry was so excited he wanted to leap up and down and yell at the top of his voice. 'First week in April,' added his father, inhaling on his cigarette.

A slow stream of smoke drifted out of his father's nostrils, intermingling with a cloud of warm breath.

'That soon,' Henry murmured.

'You know what these film people are like. They hang around for months, then suddenly the money comes through and they have to move.'

Henry nodded. He remembered Mrs Beaumont explaining how difficult film jobs were to come by, which was why even big stars were touring in the theatre.

'Until September,' his father added.

'September! I'd have to miss my last term at school.'

'You won't be missing much,' his father remarked.

'I'll ask Mum.'

And then Henry realised he would be leaving her and he felt sick.

'Does she know we've been meeting?'

'I'm telling her tonight. And Gran.'

For a while neither of them spoke.

'I been wanting to see yer gran,' said his father, 'but I didn't want to scare her, know what I mean?'

Henry nodded. He was aware of people crossing over the bridge on their way to the Troxy and the Plaza. He stared out at the railway tracks with a mixture of anticipation and nervousness, realising that soon he would be travelling to London not for a visit but to start work.

'Let me know all about it next week?' he heard his father say quietly. 'Then I can work out when I come round, yeah?'

Henry was startled. Surely he couldn't be leaving yet?

They had hardly spoken. He had to keep him with him a bit longer.

'Do your friends call you Briggs or Dodge?' he asked quickly.

'Briggs. No point telling them I'm Dodge till I got all me documentation sorted out. That's what this military doctor says. He gives me advice and I do what he says.'

'When you meet him again, could you ask him if the same thing could have happened to Private Jeffries?'

'I already done that and he said yes.'

'I could ask Mrs Jeffries if she's got a photograph of him.'

'You know her?' he asked, surprised.

'She came to your funeral, I mean, the funeral we went to. She thought you saved her husband's life.'

'Yeah, of course. But a photograph wouldn't be no good. I wouldn't recognise him, would I?'

'But he must have known you because of the letter he wrote to the newspaper.'

'He must have been writing about the other man.'

'The third man?'

'Yeah. He must have seen my identity card and got us mixed up.' He put his hand on Henry's shoulder and smiled. He had the same infectious smile as Gran. 'You tell yer mum how lucky you are to get a job like this and she'll see sense. And while she's looking after the baby down 'ere we can get to know each other better.

She'll be so busy, she won't notice you're gone.'

Henry suspected he was right and he couldn't help but smile back. His dad might not be a war hero but he was as good as one now.

'Same time next week?' his father said.

Henry still didn't want him to go.

'I don't have to go to the Pictures next Sunday. I could meet you earlier,' he said.

'I can't get here any sooner. We'll have plenty of time to have a chinwag after April, when we can be by ourselves.' He stubbed out his cigarette on the wall. 'I'll leave first.' And with that he moved swiftly towards the steps. Within seconds he was out of sight.

Henry had to wait until Molly was settled in bed and his mother had returned to the kitchen before he could tell her. It nearly drove him to screaming point, what with everyone taking turns to have a bath in the tub and the hanging of towels in front of the range and him making more excuses to stay downstairs in his pyjamas waiting for the right moment.

'I *have* to stay down here,' he said firmly at one point, looking directly at Uncle Bill.

Uncle Bill gave a small nod to indicate that he guessed Henry needed to say something important. His mother returned from the scullery and put a kettle on the range. Uncle Bill told her to sit down. She looked at him in alarm.

'Henry needs to tell us something. Am I right?'

Henry nodded. His mother drew up a chair and he told her about the meetings and the offer of a job in London, but not what kind of job. That was Henry and his dad's secret. His mother shook her head vigorously. 'No!' she whispered. 'I won't allow it.'

She stumbled from her chair making gagging noises and ran towards the scullery. Uncle Bill sprang after her. From the scullery Henry could hear sounds of vomiting.

Numb and angry, he listened to the swishing of water from the tap in the sink. Uncle Bill reappeared, took one of the towels from the clothes horse and disappeared again into the scullery. Eventually his mother returned, looking ashen. She lowered herself slowly into a chair and gazed steadily at him.

'I'm sorry, love, but that's my final word.'

'But I can look for somewhere for us to live. I can earn some money for you.'

'I'm looking after your mother,' Uncle Bill said firmly. '*And* you. You finish your schooling.'

'You can't tell me what to do,' Henry said bitterly. 'Or where to live.'

'But I can,' said his mother.

'So can Dad,' said Henry.

'And what am I supposed to say to your headmaster?'

'You can tell him I've been offered a job.'

'You already have a good job waiting for you.'

'But I've got this chance in London.'

'To do what?'

'It's private.'

'I bet it is,' muttered his stepfather.

'Don't you say anything about my father. He's a hero. He saved . . .' And then he stopped as he realised what he was about to say.

'We don't even know where he lives. And what about your friends? Are you just going to turn your back on them?'

'Pip's busy. Jeffries is always reading. Grace doesn't speak to me any more.'

'Oh? Why is that?'

He shrugged.

His mother and Uncle Bill exchanged glances.

'She doesn't know, does she?' asked his mother.

Henry didn't answer.

'This is not good,' said his mother, 'this is not good at all.'

'She won't squeal.'

'I'm not thinking about that. Has he seen her?'

'He was very polite and friendly,' said Henry.

To his surprise, Uncle Bill sank his head into the palms of his hands.

There was a tense silence.

'We've got to tell Gran,' said Henry quietly. 'Tonight.'

Uncle Bill gave a sigh. 'He's right, Maureen. I'll nip upstairs and keep an eye on Molly. Henry, you'd best ask your gran to come out to the kitchen.'

Henry waited till Uncle Bill was on the landing before he knocked on Gran's door. As soon as she opened it her face fell.

'What is it? I can see something's wrong from your face.'

'Can you come into the kitchen, Gran? Mum wants to talk to you.'

## 7. A few home truths

GRAN STARTED TO SCREAM SO LOUDLY THAT HENRY WAS convinced she could have been heard at the Plaza. Through the window he spotted Mrs Henson striding into the yard and the next thing he knew she was in the kitchen, standing legs astride in front of her.

'It's the rat!' Henry said quickly. 'She's seen the rat.'

Before he or his mother could stop her, Mrs Henson gave his grandmother one almighty slap across the face. Henry's mother looked shocked but it stopped Gran screaming.

'Sorry, Maureen,' said Mrs Henson, 'but that's what they do in films when someone's hysterical.'

'Henry, get the brandy,' said his mother.

Henry glanced at Mrs Henson as he crossed over to a small bottle on a high shelf in the alcove by the range. There was a slight twitch at the corner of her mouth as though she was suppressing a smile. He suspected Mrs

Henson had been dying for an excuse to slap his grandmother for months.

'We'll be fine now, Vera,' said Henry's mother, 'won't we, Mrs Dodge?'

Gran nodded, stunned.

'I should get on to the Plaza if I were you,' said Mrs Henson, 'they're probably leaving their rubbish out somewhere and that's what's attracting the rats.'

As soon as Mrs Henson had left, his mother poured the brandy into a chipped cup and pressed it into his grandmother's hands.

'Drink that,' she said gently.

As Gran drew the cup shakily to her mouth a trickle of brandy ran down her chin.

'Why didn't he come 'ere? Why didn't he come and see me first?'

'He was afraid of scaring you,' Henry explained.

'Is he in trouble? Is that what it is?'

'No. But Mum is.'

And then Henry saw his gran's expression change from shock to horror.

'Bigamy!' she gasped. 'Adultery!'

His mother let out a sob.

'He wants us to go to London,' said Henry. 'No one knows us there.'

'He's right. The neighbours must never find out,' Gran said vehemently, 'especially her next door. You should never have married that man, Maureen. I told you Alfred wouldn't have wanted you to marry again. But would you listen?'

'Not in front of Henry,' begged his mother.

'Now I know why. I must have guessed something was wrong inside me head.' She swung round and looked at Henry. 'But how come you didn't know it was him when you saw the photographs? You've seen his pictures on my mantelpiece hundreds of times.'

'He's got a moustache now and his hair's longer.'

'You should have told me.'

'He said I had to keep it a secret.'

'From me?'

'From everyone. Till he gets everything sorted out. He's got a job for me in London. He says I could help him find a place for us and then we could all move up there.' He looked at his mother. 'He didn't know about the baby.'

'It'll have to be adopted,' said Gran. 'And Molly.'

'No!' cried his mother.

'It's all right. Dad says he doesn't mind. He'll take care of them, Gran.'

'Then he's a ruddy saint. You go, Henry. Get away from that Mr Finch and his funny ideas. If your dad says you're to leave, then you do as he says. He always wore the trousers when he were alive.' She stopped. 'When he were . . .' She faltered. 'Anyway, what he says, you do.'

'Not if Mum says I can't,' Henry grumbled. 'No one

knows Dad's alive so Mum's still in charge.'

'We're staying together as a family till he's eighteen,' his mother said, her voice trembling. 'He's got his National Service to do after that. Come July he'll start his job at the railway and there's an end to it.'

'We'll see about that, my girl,' said his grandmother. 'My life has been a living hell since that man moved in.'

'*He* moved in? *You* moved in.'

'Mum!' cried Henry. 'That's not true!'

'Oh, yes it is.'

'I don't think a woman like you can afford to be so high and mighty.'

'What do you mean, a woman like me?'

'I'm not going to say the words in front of my grandson.'

'You've said them already.'

Gran turned and grabbed Henry's hand.

'When are you next seeing him?'

'Next week.'

'You tell him. You tell him, *yes*.'

'I can't, Gran.'

'Tell him I want to see him. You will, won't you?' she begged.

He nodded.

That night the screaming nightmares returned. He must have cried out in his sleep because when he woke, he heard Uncle Bill whisper, 'Are you all right, lad?'

When he drifted back to sleep he had the strangest

sensation that his mother was in the room, kissing him on the cheek.

Henry didn't know how he would get through a week of school, but once he was there he was swept up into the comforting routine of lessons, and because no one knew of the dramas at home, there was no one who could ask him awkward questions except Mr Finch.

'Anything bothering you, Dodge?' he asked Henry one break time when they were in the darkroom.

'My mum's still ill,' he said.

'Sorry to hear that. But you're still working with Morgan and Jeffries on the presentation, aren't you? Only you seem to be hiding in the darkroom rather a lot this week.'

'Me and Jeffries saw Daniel again at half-term.' He told Mr Finch about the visit and how Mr Hart had agreed to be the projectionist and had got permission to have the films shown at the Plaza.

'That's excellent. How old is the Plaza, by the way?'

'I don't know, sir. I'll find out.'

'Good lad.'

But he didn't bother. Once he walked out of the school gates, an overwhelming lethargy left him feeling exhausted.

On Sunday afternoon, after he and his friends had seen a couple of films at the Troxy, Henry made his usual walk with them up to the Plaza before nipping back across the road towards the station. His father was in his usual place, leaning on the wall, cigarette in his hand. Henry strode towards him and then stopped, hovering behind him.

'She won't let me,' he said bitterly.

'Don't you worry, son,' he said, giving his ash a forceful flick. 'You leave it to me.'

For the next five nights the nightmares continued, and the bouts of interrupted sleep left Henry feeling irritable and short-tempered. He felt helpless and angry, and guilty for hating his mother.

On Saturday afternoon the house was empty, but to avoid being home when Gran and his mother returned from the shops, he hurled himself out of the front door only to collide with a soldier on the pavement.

''Ere, where's the fire?' cried the private.

It was Charlie.

'Sorry,' said Henry, flustered. To his dismay he could see that Charlie wanted a chat.

'I didn't get to be a driver,' Charlie began.

'Oh,' said Henry politely. 'That's a shame.'

'Yeah. They got me sittin' behind a desk messin' around with hundreds of frigging forms. It's so boring it makes covering lumps of coal with whitewash look like an assault course.' He gave him a slap round the shoulders and to Henry's relief strode on towards his house at the end of the road. 'Be seeing you,' he yelled over his shoulder.

'Yeah,' Henry yelled back, and he broke into a sprint in the opposite direction and headed for Mrs Beaumont's house.

'The others told me you were off taking photographs,' said Mrs Beaumont in the porch.

'I am. I was just wondering if you'd like to come with me down to the harbour.'

Suddenly he didn't want to be on his own.

'Oh, Henry, I'm about to leave for *The Forsyte Saga* at the Apollo. Otherwise I'd love to. But you're going to need the camera.'

Henry looked at his chest. There was no camera case hanging there. He had bolted out of the house in such a rush he had left it behind.

Gran's door was open, which meant she had either got back already or was in the toilet in the yard. He leapt up the stairs to his room and grabbed the camera case from the shelf in the wardrobe. He had just stepped out on to the landing when he heard raised voices coming from the kitchen. He quickly retreated and hovered by the doorway. He recognised Uncle Bill's voice, but not the owner of the second one. Puzzled, he crept towards the banisters. And then he knew. It was his dad. He had come to fight for him to go to London.

'He doesn't know you,' Uncle Bill was saying. 'You're a stranger. He hasn't seen you for ten years.'

'Think I don't know that? This is my chance to pick up where I left off.'

'He doesn't have to leave home and live with you.'

Henry was incensed. How dare Uncle Bill speak to his father like that!

'Looks like I come back 'ere in the nick of time. He needs a firm hand to get his feet back on the ground. He lives with his head in the clouds. Always off to the Pictures.'

Henry froze. His father had never said anything about him seeing too many films.

'He's earned money to pay for most of the tickets,' he heard Uncle Bill say, 'and it's better for him to be there than hanging around the streets getting up to mischief.'

'I'm not talking about that. I'm talking about all this airy-fairy nonsense you've been shovelling into his brain.'

'I've never forced him to read books. I gave that up a long time ago.'

'Not books. I'm talking about this daft business of him wanting to be a cameraman.'

Henry gasped. It was as if he had been punched in the stomach. He gripped the banister, fighting for breath.

'Cameraman?' said Uncle Bill.

'Yeah.'

'First I've heard about it.'

'Don't give me that.'

Henry cringed. He sank on to one of the steps, his forehead in his hands.

'How stupid of me. It's been staring me in the face,' he heard Uncle Bill exclaim. 'The way he is when he holds that camera . . .'

'Cut the flowery lingo,' snapped his father impatiently.

'But I can't understood why he never told me.'

'Because I'm his father, that's why. Of course I let him have his say.'

'Wait a minute, does Henry think you've gone along with it?'

'Course he does.'

'Is that why he wants to go to London?' There was a silence. Henry raised his head. 'Are you telling me you've lied to him?'

'Once in London, he'll come round to my way of thinking. I'll introduce him to the real world.'

'And what might that be? As some useful face that the police don't know?'

'What do you mean by that?'

Henry sprang to his feet, his fists clenched.

'Oh, I think you do. You had it all planned. You *wanted* him to spot you following him, didn't you?'

'Don't be daft.'

'Maureen doesn't want him to go to London.'

'Maureen doesn't have a choice, does she?'

'Meaning?'

'She's committed bigamy.'

Henry heard a match being struck.

'No one smokes in this house. If you light that cigarette she'll smell it as soon as she walks in the door and know someone's been here.'

'All right, all right.'

Henry took another step down the stairs.

'If he comes to London with me, no one need ever know. I won't tell anyone. You don't need to tell anyone.'

'Henry is family.'

'You're not his dad.'

'I've been his dad for the last four years.'

'He doesn't like you.'

Henry began to shake.

'I know, and I'm sad about that. It doesn't help having your mother spoiling everything good that happens in this house.'

'Problem solved. I can take her as well. Then you and Maureen and your kiddies can play happy families.'

'Maureen couldn't live with me as my wife knowing that she's still married to you.'

'She won't divorce me. She'd rather die than appear in a court and say she's been living with another man.'

'What about desertion?'

'What are you accusing me of?' his father snapped. 'You'd better watch what you say.'

'I mean, you've been living separately from Maureen for ten years.'

'So? Why would I agree to a divorce because of that?'

'You don't love her.'

Henry waited for his father to deny it, but all he heard was a short staccato laugh which chilled him.

'Maybe I'm not explaining myself clearly enough,' he said. 'If I don't have Henry, then I will move in 'ere and be her husband again and I'll put your daughter and your other little bastard up for adoption.' Henry shook his head in disbelief. 'You'd hardly expect me to feed and clothe another man's nippers, would you?'

'You evil . . .! What about your mother? I've fed and clothed her for years! Maureen and I have been getting her out of debt regularly. Maureen had to hand over a typewriter and a gramophone that had taken her two years to save up for, to bailiffs demanding money for your mother's debts – mostly spent on hats. After Christmas, we had to return the Christmas presents we gave each other to pay for a raincoat your mother bought Henry on tick. We're still paying for it now.'

Henry was stunned. How could he not have seen what was going on?

'Maureen hates going into the front room because of

all the photographs of you on your mother's mantelpiece. They remind her of what life was like living with you. She's told me everything.'

'Have you been saying things about me to Henry?'

'No. We don't talk about you at all. We leave it all to your mother. She paints a very rosy picture of you. Henry thought you were a hero.'

'That's not my fault. I didn't know where I was for a long time.'

'It's convenient you got your memory back now, isn't it?'

'I ain't following you.'

'When Henry's reached school-leaving age and can earn some money for you.'

Henry steadied himself on the banister and took another step down.

'I heard you're going to train to be a teacher,' his father said. His voice was cold. 'I don't think they'd want to train someone who's married to a bigamist, do you? I expect your morals have to be as white as the driven snow. Know what I mean? Can't have you corrupting the pupils, eh?'

'You filthy little blackmailer!'

'Don't waste your fancy words on me,' his father interrupted. 'If you don't want to lose them nippers of yours, you'll persuade Maureen to let me take Henry. If she don't, I'm sure the courts will be on my side once they read the doctor's reports. They'd understand why I'd put the kids up for adoption. And I don't think you need me to remind you that since you ain't married to Maureen, you ain't got any legal rights over what happens to them.'

Henry didn't want to hear any more. He moved down the last few steps and made for the front door. To his alarm the outline of his gran appeared behind the frosted window. He ran into her room and hid behind the door, listening to her footsteps in the hall getting closer. The door handle turned. He could hear her breathing. She was obviously eavesdropping.

'He's my flesh and blood. And he's moving to London to live with me!'

He heard the kitchen door being flung open.

'You tell him, son. You tell him,' cried Gran.

'Mum!' he heard his dad yell.

'At last!' Gran cried. 'You've come to rescue me. I told you what I was up against!'

Henry waited till the kitchen door was closed before slipping into the hall. Once he had bolted out of the front door and into the street, he began running. His legs felt like jelly. *I told you what I was up against*, his gran had said. She and his father must have already met one another during the week. But when and where? And how could she have been able to hide it so well? Resisting the urge to vomit, he drove himself forward with ferocity. His eyes were hurting from the strain of suppressing his tears, and his jaw was so clamped it ached. He stumbled on past Mrs Beaumont's house, ignoring the pain in his side. It was only when he found himself staggering past the Princes Road Police Station that he realised he was on his way to the Apollo.

Mrs Beaumont was only yards away from the box office. Sweating and shaking, Henry blundered up to her, thrust a hand into his trouser pocket and prayed that the handful of coins he held out to her would be enough.

'Henry,' she said, 'you'd rather die than see this film.'

'I wouldn't,' he lied.

'It's full of romance.'

'I can take it.'

She closed his fingers around the money.

'Put it away.'

'But I need you to get me in.'

'No, you don't. It's a U.'

'Is it?'

She took hold of his arm and marched him firmly out of the queue.

'You'll lose your place,' he stammered weakly.

'I'll see it later. Come with me.'

She walked briskly with him back towards the Kings Theatre and into a small café. She dragged him towards a table in the corner where it was most private. Henry watched her in a daze as she ordered buns he would be unable to eat and a pot of tea. They waited silently for the waitress to bring the tray to their table. Once she had left them alone, Mrs Beaumont poured Henry a cup of tea and dunked two large spoonfuls of sugar into it.

'I don't have sugar,' he began.

'You do this afternoon. You look as if you've seen a ghost.'

Henry stared at her. He could feel his lower lip trembling from the sheer strain of holding everything in.

She pushed the cup across the table towards him.

'Talk,' she said.

## 8. Undercover work

'THAT'S QUITE A DUNGHEAP,' SAID MRS BEAUMONT QUIETLY.

Henry nodded miserably. 'You won't find a diamond in there,' he muttered.

'On the contrary. There's one staring you in the face.'

'I can't see it.'

'The diamond is that you know, and no one else knows that you know except me. That puts you in a very strong position as long as you keep quiet about it and play innocent.'

'Like him,' he muttered.

'He's obviously a good actor. Perhaps he's had a lot of practice at deceiving people.'

'Grace told me he was a liar.'

'Grace has met him?'

Henry nodded.

'Oh.'

'She won't say anything.'

'I know that and you know that but will your father? I'd keep her well and truly out of the picture if I were you. For her sake.'

'Do you think he might hurt her?' Henry asked, alarmed.

'I don't know. He sounds a nasty piece of work to me. And your stepfather obviously suspects he's up to something criminal. You're needed urgently for some kind of job and it's not in a film unit. If it's because the police don't know your face, it implies that the police in London know your father's face. Unfortunately Grace knows his face too.'

'So do you,' said Henry, remembering the photographs, 'and Jeffries. And Pip.'

'But your father doesn't know that, does he? He might think she'll tell someone about him and try to stop her.'

'What can I do?'

'Find out the truth. The more information we can find out the better. Your mother and Uncle Bill have been deceiving you too, probably to protect you. We now know that she hates seeing your father's photographs. But we don't know why. What else has she and your stepfather been keeping from you? Meanwhile, I need to find an excuse to visit my solicitor again because you've solved another mystery for me.'

'Have I?'

'Yes. Your mother told me about a neighbour who's

just discovered she's committed bigamy and who's too nervous to go to a solicitor, and she asked me if I could ask my solicitor various questions. Thanks to you, I now know that no such neighbour exists. *She's* the one who needs help.' Mrs Beaumont frowned for a moment and then gave an enormous smile. 'Got it! Oh, I do love killing two birds with one stone. The furniture!'

'The furniture?'

'The wretched furniture you and Jeffries have been carrying out of the building at the back. I'll suggest to the solicitors that while they continue to look for the deeds they've lost,' and she winked, 'that'll make them feel nice and guilty, could they also give me permission to dispose of that furniture? Then I'll casually ask them questions about bigamy and divorce over the tea and biscuits.'

'Do you think it'll work?'

'It's worth trying. Your mother should really go to the police, but since I'm not supposed to know anything, *I'm* not the one to persuade her.'

'Me?'

'You.'

'How?'

'You'll find a way.'

'I hate my father. I'd like to tell him what I think of him.'

'Don't. That's your diamond. Spin him a yarn. If he

knows you know, he could turn nasty. When are you next meeting him?'

'Tomorrow night.'

'That doesn't leave us much time. What we need is someone he doesn't know to follow him. Someone who travels on a Sunday night and wouldn't look out of place, Like your friend Charlie returning to his unit after a weekend pass.'

'He's here. I saw him this afternoon.'

'Splendid! Do you have any film left in the camera?'

'Yeah. Why?'

'He could follow him and take photographs of who he's mixing with, that sort of thing.'

'But it's a posh camera and my dad's seen me with it. Most people have got box cameras round here. He might recognise it and get suspicious.'

'Not if he's carrying it in an Army rucksack. I've got one here you can borrow.'

'But he won't have time.'

'You're right. How about if I arrange for one of Max's photographer friends to be waiting for him by the platform exit at Waterloo. Charlie could walk behind your father and give Max's friend the nod so he knows who to follow.'

'But there'll be loads of servicemen all arriving at the same time. How will he know which one is him?'

She looked thoughtful for a moment and then smiled.

'He could carry a parcel! If Max's friend manages to follow your father and take any snaps, he can then catch the next train down here. After that it's down to you.'

'How do you mean?'

'Think you can develop them in your school darkroom?'

'Yeah!'

'Of course we might get nothing at all. But it's worth trying.'

'Wait a minute,' said Henry, suddenly remembering a conversation he had had with Charlie, 'Charlie thinks my dad's a hero.'

'You don't have to tell him who the man is.'

'What do I say, then?'

'I always think it's best to steer near the truth. Tell him this man has offered you a job in London but your mum and stepfather think there's something fishy about him. Explain that you need some photographs of him working to put their minds at rest or to find out if he's up to no good.' She looked intently at him. 'We've very little time. You need to find Charlie and I need to get hold of Max, and for all I know he could be filming in the middle of nowhere. This is one of those rare occasions when I hope he's out of work.'

Henry knocked at Number 18. A large cheery woman answered the door, her hair hidden under a red and white spotty turban.

'Hello, Henry!' she exclaimed, beaming.

'Is Charlie in?'

'Is he ever? He'll be at the Plaza. He's soft on that usherette, ain't he? If you wait outside, you might catch him. That's if he don't stay and watch everything all over again.'

Luckily, Charlie didn't stay. Henry spotted him in the crowd coming down the steps and hurried towards him. They strolled over to the bombsite away from listening ears. As soon as they were alone he took a deep breath.

'Charlie,' he began, 'I need you to do me a favour. But you have to keep it a secret.'

'So you want me to help you find out if this bloke is for real?' said Charlie.

'Yes,' said Henry.

'Okeydoke. Anything for a bit of excitement. But you'll have to do me a favour in return. Can you take a photograph of me and Lily?'

Henry felt embarrassed. How on earth was he going to do that? Lily Bridges was so ashamed of being divorced she couldn't look anyone in the eye. She'd never let anyone with a camera near her.

'She's a bit shy,' he said hesitantly.

Charlie grinned.

'You don't half go around with your eyes shut. She's wearing an engagement ring now.'

'You're going to marry her!' Henry said, shocked.

'Yeah, yeah, yeah, so she's a divorcee. So what? We make each other happy.'

'Good,' said Henry, awkwardly, not knowing what else to say.

'Fire away, then, what do I have to do?'

'I meet this man after the Sunday matinee at the Troxy or the Plaza. After the film I need you to wait at the foot of Hatton railway bridge so you know what he looks like. When he leaves the bridge, follow him on to the platform.'

'Okeydoke. Me and Lily can say our goodbyes there. So it looks normal.'

'Could she give you a present wrapped up in coloured paper?'

'I s'pose so. Why?'

'A photographer is going to be looking out for you at Waterloo Station. You need to be walking behind the man who's offered me this job so that the photographer knows he's the one to follow. The only way he'll be able to spot you in the crowd of uniforms is from the parcel you're carrying. Then you hand the rucksack with the camera in it over to him.'

When Henry arrived at Mrs Beaumont's house, Grace answered the door. She took one look at him and turned away. Henry grabbed her arm. She swung round crossly but he could see that he had hurt her.

'Sorry,' he blurted out.

She gave a nonchalant shrug and stared at the floor.

'Grace,' he said miserably. 'He *is* a liar.'

She looked up. For a moment neither of them spoke.

'I'm sorry too,' she said.

'For what?'

'For being right.'

They walked silently down the steps to the kitchen. When he opened the door he spotted his mother sitting next to Molly with paper and crayons. Jeffries was waving a newspaper frantically at him from the table.

'The Rex is going to be showing foreign films. Listen! First Sternsea Screening,' he read, 'London Film Productions present the international prize-winning drama *Open City*. Directed by Roberto Rossellini with English subtitles. Here! Right on our own doorstep.' He lowered the paper. 'There's only one snag. It's an A.'

'There's no problem there,' said Mrs Beaumont. 'I'd love to see it.'

'I know someone else who'd like to go,' said Henry's mother, 'but you wouldn't want to be seen with him.'

Henry was embarrassed that his mother had revealed his hatred for Uncle Bill in front of the others. And then he suddenly realised that he didn't hate him any more.

He gave a shrug.

'I don't mind,' he said slowly.

Uncle Bill's shift finished at ten o'clock that week. Henry heard him let himself into the house and sat up and listened to the kitchen door open. After a while there was the slow familiar creak on the stairs, footsteps crossing the landing and his mother murmuring, 'Goodnight, love.' Quickly, he lay down as his stepfather padded about in the dark. He waited till he had climbed into the camp bed.

'Uncle Bill?'

'Did I wake you?' he whispered.

'No, I couldn't sleep.'

'Yes, there's a lot to think about, isn't there?' he said after a brief silence.

Henry had rehearsed what he was going to say but it all felt so stilted now. He knew he had to be careful not to let him know he had overheard the quarrel between him and his father.

'Anything you want to get off your chest?'

'Yeah,' Henry said eventually.

'You'd best tell me, then.'

He tried to speak but the words wouldn't come out.

'Is it about your mum?'

'No.'

'School?'

'No.'

'Leaving school?'

Henry couldn't answer.

'The railway job?' Uncle Bill added.

There was a long silence.

'You don't want it, do you?' he said at last. Henry remained silent. 'You've avoided talking about it, so I put two and two together. I didn't say anything because you didn't seem to know what else you wanted to do.'

'I do now,' Henry said slowly.

'Are you going to tell me what it is?'

'Yes.'

And still Henry didn't speak.

'Try me.'

'I want to be a camera operator,' Henry said, aware of a catch in his throat.

'Then that's what you must be.'

'You mean it?' he whispered.

'Course I do.'

'But the ones I've met all speak posh, like they do on the wireless.'

'Things are changing, Henry. Look at me. Five years ago I'd never have dreamt that someone with my background would get a Higher School Certificate, let alone be offered teacher training, so there's no reason why you can't be a camera operator. But you'll have to take it a step at a time.'

'I know,' said Henry. 'I'd have to start as a clapper boy. That job in London, the one I wouldn't tell you about, it's for a clapper boy in a film unit.'

Henry waited to see if Uncle Bill would let on that he knew his father had lied.

'Do you know the name of this unit?'

'No.'

'Why don't you ask your father?'

'I've already asked and he said he didn't know.'

'Perhaps you could explain that your mother might be happy for you to take up that job when you find out more about it. The name of the person who's employing you, for a start.'

*He wants me to find out my father's a liar for myself,* Henry thought.

'There's something else,' said Henry. 'There's this boy in my class, Jack Riddell, he wants to be a train driver but no one in his family has ever worked for the railways.'

'And you'd like me to put in a good word for him? See if he can have your job?'

'Yes.'

'He'll have to have a medical.'

'He's very fit. He's in the school's gymnastic team.'

'I'll talk to someone about it on Monday.'

'Thanks, Uncle Bill.'

'Now tell me, what happens after you've been a clapper boy?'

'You get to be a focus puller . . .'

His dad was waiting for him in the usual spot. Henry was

relieved they weren't supposed to look at one another. If they had have done, he was convinced he would have given everything away. Charlie and Lily had already followed him as far as the bridge. They were waiting by the foot of the steps near the street light. Once his father left for the station, Henry had arranged that he would stand behind him at the top of the steps so that Charlie would know which man to follow.

He stared down at the railway line.

'I told Gran,' he said.

'Oh, yeah? How did she take it?' he asked.

'She was very shocked,' Henry said slowly.

'Yeah, I thought she might be. But has she got used to the idea now?'

*As if you didn't know,* thought Henry.

'Yes.'

'Does she want to see me?'

Henry glanced quickly at his face. There was nothing to show from his father's expression that he and Gran had already met. He had even more proof now that however friendly his father appeared and acted, it was all show, and it pleased him to know that his father had no idea he had given himself away.

Henry nodded.

'That's good. I'm looking forward to seeing her. It's been a long time.'

*Yeah, all of thirty hours*, thought Henry.

'Did you tell her I'd got a job lined up for you?' his father asked.

'Yes.'

'And?'

'She's all for it.'

'But you still want to do what yer mum says?'

'Yeah, but I think she's coming round to the idea. She just wants to know where I'd be living and the name and address of the man who's giving me the job.'

'I'll sort that out.'

*Oh, yeah?* thought Henry.

'Do you want me to tell Gran where we meet?' Henry asked carefully.

'Not a good idea, son. She might throw her arms about me and anyone passing might see. I'll sort something out, don't you worry. Seeing as I'll be telling your mum where I live, you'd better tell me where you live.'

He lied so easily. He had even forgotten that he had already told Henry he had seen the number of the house in the newspaper photograph.

'Number 6. It's the street round the corner from the Plaza.'

'Number 6,' he murmured to himself. 'That shouldn't be hard to remember. P'raps I could pop round when your Mr Carpenter is out. We don't want to upset him, do we? After all, it ain't his fault that he ain't married to yer mum. I'm sure once me and your mum have a nice little talk we can sort it all out.'

'Thanks, Dad,' he managed to mutter.

There was an awkward silence.

'Once we're on our own in London we can have a proper chat. Eh?'

'Yeah.'

'Chin up, son,' and he turned and looked at him out of the corner of his eye, giving one of those convincingly friendly smiles. 'I'm like the Mounties. I always get my man.'

Henry forced himself to return the smile.

'We'll meet same time next week,' said his father, stubbing out his cigarette on the wall.

'A bit later,' said Henry. 'I'm going to the Rex to see an Italian film.'

'An Italian film?'

'It's got subtitles.'

'That's handy.'

'So I'll be here about an hour later.'

'I've a train to catch.'

'I'll try and get out earlier.'

'You do that, son.'

But Henry could see that he was rattled. And he was so pleased, so very pleased.

'March nineteenth, then, Dad.'

'Getting close to April,' his father pointed out tersely.

Henry felt he had gone too far and he kicked himself.

'I'm really looking forward to that, Dad,' he said with all the strength he could muster and he forced himself to smile again. 'I can't wait to be a clapper boy.'

His father gave a nod and moved past him towards the steps. Henry watched his back and quickly followed him. He stayed at the top. His father's head was lowered. He could see Charlie looking over Lily's shoulder. Henry indicated his father and he and Charlie gave each other a nod. Swiftly Henry returned to the bridge.

Lily was carrying the rucksack and a box-shaped parcel covered in colourful wrapping. As the train approached she handed them to Charlie and gave him a kiss. They waited while his father got into one of the carriages. Charlie got into the one next to it and sat by the window. As soon as the train pulled out Henry ran down the steps. He needed to see Mrs Beaumont as soon as possible.

It was Jeffries who opened the door.

'Hello!' he said, surprised.

Immediately Mrs Beaumont appeared behind him.

'Oh, I'm sorry, Henry,' she said, winking over his friend's shoulder, 'your mother and Molly left some time ago. Have you just come from the Troxy?' she asked casually.

'No. The railway bridge. I saw an old friend of mine, Charlie.'

'Oh, yes?'

'And I thought I'd wave him off. He's engaged now to one of the usherettes at the Plaza. She was with him and I thought they'd want to be alone so I waved to him from up there. She gave him a present,' he added.

'How lovely,' she exclaimed.

'Yeah. He's going to have to carry it all the way back to his unit and it sticks out a bit.'

'Oh?' she said curiously. 'Why is that?'

'Because of the wrapping paper. She must have saved it from Christmas. It's red, green and gold.'

'That *will* stick out,' she said, winking.

'Roger!' called a voice from upstairs. 'Your turn.'

'Bath,' explained Jeffries.

'Oh, yes, me too. I'd better get back,' Henry said quickly.

Mrs Beaumont was already dialling a number on the telephone. They caught one another's eye and Henry let himself out.

It was difficult to concentrate on lessons. At midday he could only swallow a forkful of the school dinner and had to sit at the table for the remainder of the break until he had finished. After school he walked to Mrs Beaumont's house with Pip and Jeffries. She was waiting for him.

'I'm so glad you popped round, Henry,' she said. 'You left your rucksack here,' and she handed it over to him. 'And the camera's in it. You must have been wondering where you'd put it. I hope you don't mind, but I had a look and you've nearly finished the film. Only one more snap left. I'm really looking forward to seeing what you've taken,' she added meaningfully. 'When do you think you'll be able to develop it?'

'Soon,' said Henry. 'I'll go and take the last photograph now. See you tomorrow,' he said to Pip and Jeffries.

He caught a bus to the church where he had attended his father's funeral, walked through the graveyard and took a photograph of the gravestone with *Alfred Dodge* written on it.

It wasn't until Wednesday evening that Henry watched the first images emerging in the developing tray. Immediately, he could see that the photographs had been taken by an expert. Whoever Max's friend was, he must have taken a lot of risks. The first picture was of open suitcases filled with coupons. The second photograph had been taken through ceiling rafters. It showed his father in a brightly lit warehouse watching a young boy, not much older than Henry, pouring petrol through a gas mask into a metal container.

The third photograph was of his father standing next to a man with a craggy face, wearing a light-coloured coat with a dark collar. They were both smiling. In the background were a row of petrol cans and some dark machinery.

By half past six he had six prints pegged out to dry on the line. He planned to come into school early to remove the London photos before Mr Finch spotted them. He would leave the two other photographs he had developed so that there would be something hanging there for him to see.

'Mr Finch has given me permission to come in early before school,' he told Sergeant when he handed back the key.

It was only when he reached home that he realised he had left the negatives behind.

The following morning when he entered the darkroom to retrieve them, the smell of the developing fluid was still strong and he was alarmed to find the room still warm.

'Oh, no!' he cried. 'I must have left the heater on all night.'

But it was still unplugged, just as he had left it. He checked the prints. To his relief they were dry. He took down the three taken by the professional photographer and the one of his father's gravestone. The latter had come out quite well. In the photograph a shaft of late afternoon sun appeared like a spotlight on the gravestone. Mrs Beaumont had given him an envelope with some stiff card in it to protect them. Carefully, he slid them inside it and put it in his rucksack. He was about to leave when he noticed that the positioning of the aperture on the enlarger was set at maximum, as though he had been cropping and framing. He stared at it, puzzled. He could have sworn he had left it halfway down. It was almost as if someone had been in the darkroom after he had left. But that was impossible. He had handed the key to the caretaker. Henry stared at the enlarger, completely perplexed. Eventually he shrugged it off. He must have accidentally moved it when he was clearing up. He slipped out, locked the door behind him and swung the KEEP OUT notice hanging from the doorknob to the blank side.

When he returned to the darkroom in the dinner break, Mr Finch was waiting for him.

'I thought I'd take a look at your prints,' he said, gazing up at the two Henry had left pegged on the line.

'I've got three more to print, sir. Four of the negatives didn't come out so I threw them away. I must have got the light all wrong, or over-exposed them. Anyway, sir, I've got a new roll of film,' he added hurriedly.

'Who's this couple?' Mr Finch asked.

'That's my friend Charlie. The girl is his fiancé.'

'They look very happy. You could crop this one and enlarge their faces.'

To his relief, Mr Finch asked no questions about the missing negatives. He suggested he bring the camera in the following day.

'I'd like you to put the film in yourself,' he said. 'I'll stand by in case you have any problems.'

*

As soon as he arrived at Mrs Beaumont's house, she suggested they go up to the room where he and Jeffries had stored the furniture so that she could look at the photographs in private. Once the door was closed, Henry whipped them out.

'There's no doubt he's involved in some kind of criminal activity, is there?' she murmured. 'See that boy pouring petrol through a gas mask? Any idea what he's up to?'

'No.'

'I do. He's removing the pink dye in the petrol. I've heard about this sort of thing from Oscar. Clear petrol is much easier to sell on the black market. Your father is obviously mixed up in all this. I would do everything you can to steer clear of him.'

'But he could have Molly and the baby taken away!'

'Not if your mother divorces him.'

'He won't let her. He'll use the doctor's reports to say he'd lost his memory and that it wasn't his fault he didn't come back.'

'I think these photographs might persuade him. Do you still have the negatives?'

'Yes.'

'Give them to me. I'll keep them in a safe place.'

'But what about Mum? She'll never divorce him.'

'She might. If you can persuade her.'

Suddenly Henry felt so sad that it hurt.

'You don't want her to, do you?' Mrs Beaumont said quietly.

'I do,' he whispered, swallowing back the tears.

'But I can see it's upsetting you.'

'He's not my dad, see,' he said, struggling to explain. 'I mean he is, but . . .'

'He's not the imaginary father you've been living with for years.'

Henry nodded.

'I don't like this one. I feel . . .' But he couldn't find the words.

'You feel that the imaginary dad has died all over again and you're missing him?'

'Yeah. I used to think about him a lot and now I can't. Does that sound stupid?'

'Of course not.'

'Anyway,' he said briskly. 'He's gone now and I don't want this one to be around Mum. But how can I get her to divorce him?'

'I don't know. But I can remove one obstacle. She'll need money. I've been to see my solicitor and he says that I can sell the furniture as long as I hand the money from the sale over to him. That money can go towards paying his firm's legal costs should a friend of mine, your mother, choose to divorce her husband. It can be my wedding present to her when she remarries your stepfather.' She looked at Henry intently. 'Which she will probably do if she divorces your father, you do realise that, don't you?'

Henry shrugged.

'I can take it.'

She smiled.

'We've a long way to go yet. I can work behind the scenes. The rest is up to you.'

# 9. Breaking it to Mum

'HELLO, LOVE!' SAID HIS MOTHER. 'I THOUGHT YOU WERE AT THE Cinema Club.'

Molly was sitting on her lap sucking a piece of toast. Henry stared at her nervously. Mrs Beaumont had planned that he should have a chat with his mum on Saturday morning while Mrs Jeffries and Mrs Morgan were out shopping and his friends were at the Pictures.

'Come on, Molly,' said Mrs Beaumont, stretching her arms out. 'Let's go and play on the piano.'

'That sounds nice,' said Henry's mother, rising.

'Henry wants to have a private word with you.'

'Does he now?' commented his mother suspiciously.

They sat in silence until they heard the study door close.

'Henry, if it's about you going up to London, don't waste your time. My word is final.'

Henry gazed back at her speechless. Suddenly he didn't have a clue how to begin.

'Oh,' she said suddenly and her face softened. 'I think I know what this is all about. It's those bad dreams you've been having, isn't it?'

Henry was taken aback.

'You know about them?' he said.

'I've sometimes heard you yell out in the night and looked into your room to make sure you're all right, and Uncle Bill told me you were having nightmares.'

'Did you come in and kiss me when I was asleep?'

She nodded.

'I wondered when you were going to tell me. I suppose you didn't want to worry me. Is that it?'

'Yeah.'

'Uncle Bill told me they started the night I saw those photos.'

'Yeah, but that's not what I want to talk to you about.'

'I think you should while Molly's out of the way. Get it off your chest.'

'But I don't get them so often now.'

'But you still have them?'

'Sometimes.'

'What sort of nightmares are they?'

He hesitated.

'*You* screaming, Mum, from downstairs. Sometimes it don't feel like a dream at all. But then I wake up and it's all quiet again. So I close my eyes and the screaming starts again, only in the next dream, there's crashing and banging and shouting.'

His mother looked frozen.

'I don't want to upset you, Mum.'

'I'm fine, you go on.'

'And I'm at the top of the stairs and there are these loud footsteps and I know they're coming for me. And I hide. And they get closer and closer. And there's a strange smell coming from the mouth of this enormous shadow and the shadow grips me so hard it hurts and my face is pushed into a mattress. And the mattress is wet. And I can't breathe. And I think I'm going to die.' It was then that he noticed that his mother was shaking. 'Mum, what's the matter?'

Her eyes were brimming.

'I thought you'd forgotten,' she whispered. 'You were so little.'

'Forgotten what?' Suddenly Henry had a horrible suspicion. 'Mum, this isn't a dream, it's a memory, isn't it?'

She nodded.

'And you screaming?' And then it dawned on him. 'Mum, did my dad ever hit you?'

'I'm so sorry, love . . .' and she stifled a sob.

'Did he, Mum?'

'Yes,' she whispered. 'He was a brute. Especially when he came home late from the pubs.'

'Why didn't you tell me?' he asked angrily. 'Why

did you let me believe he was a hero?'

'Because I thought he was. Because I thought for once in his life he'd done something worthwhile. And you were so happy. And you didn't talk about it so I thought you'd forgotten it all and we could start fresh. Then when your gran moved in . . .' She hesitated. 'How could I tell you then, after all the wonderful things she said about him?'

'Mum, don't let him frighten Molly the way he frightened me.'

'Of course I won't. I won't let him near her.'

'But how will you stop him if you're still married to him?'

'What are you saying, Henry?'

'Mum, you've got to get rid of him.'

'That's easier to say than do.'

Henry stared at her,

'There is one way,' he said slowly.

'What do you mean?' And then she gasped. 'You want me to divorce him, don't you?'

Henry nodded.

'Do you know what I'd have to do? I'd have to stand up in court and say that I'd been living with another man while I was still married, that I'd committed . . .'

He could see she couldn't bring herself to say the word.

'And go to the police,' he added firmly.

'You don't know what you're saying!'

'I've taken a photograph of the gravestone with his name on it, to show them that you and everyone else believed he was dead. And I've developed it so we can take it to the police station with us.'

'Us?'

'I'm coming with you.'

'I can't, Henry.'

'Mum, if you don't tell the police, he can still blackmail you, can't he? And anyway it might go in your favour if you tell the police first, before they find out.'

She took a sharp intake of breath.

'But I can't afford to get divorced.'

'You could do extra typing. Mrs Beaumont could ask that Mr Hale if the publishers need more people to type for them.'

'Maybe. But you've forgotten your father. He's used to getting his own way. He'll hoodwink the judges and refuse to let the divorce go through.'

'Not when he sees these,' said Henry, and he spread the photographs out in front of her.

'Oh, my goodness!' she gasped, 'So Bill was right. Did you take these? Oh, Henry, you're not mixed up in this, are you?'

'No. I'm not that good a photographer. I got someone to follow him with the camera. So, will you do it now?'

She nodded, almost crying with relief.

'I'll be a divorcee, you realise that, don't you?'

'Only until you get married to Uncle Bill again.'

'Give us a hug,' she said, laughing.

They sat nervously by a wall opposite what looked like a counter. Henry's mother had left Molly with Mrs Beaumont but had decided not to tell Uncle Bill until after the visit to the police station was over. If she were put in a cell, Mrs Beaumont would let Molly stay overnight at her house.

'Next,' said the police sergeant, glancing at Henry's mother.

She rose shakily. Henry noticed him glance at his mother's swollen abdomen. He gave her a warm smile. Henry stood by her side. She whispered something but Henry couldn't hear what she was saying.

'Speak up, my dear,' said the sergeant. 'Let's have your name, shall we?'

'My name?' she stammered. She turned to Henry. 'Oh, my goodness, what shall I say?'

Henry pushed a piece of paper across the desk. Written on it were the words *I have committed bigamy*. The police sergeant picked it up and read it. Henry watched his face change. He stared at her, the smile gone.

'Her name is Mrs Carpenter,' Henry blurted out. 'Can she see one of your women police?'

'Women police?' repeated the sergeant, frowning.

'In *The Blue Lamp* there was this woman policeman

with three stripes on her arm.'

'This is Princes Road Police Station, sonny,' yelled a woman in the queue, 'not a ruddy Ealing film! They don't have women 'ere. Only us,' and she gave a hoarse laugh which disintegrated into a coughing fit.

'That'll do, Edie,' said the desk sergeant. 'If you'd like to wait,' he added quietly.

Henry's mother nodded and he led her back to the chair. The sergeant handed a young constable the piece of paper, indicating Henry's mother and returned to the desk.

'Next,' he said.

After a while the constable opened a door off the waiting area.

'Mrs Carpenter?' he said.

Henry's mother nodded. By now she looked so pale Henry was afraid she would faint. Towering behind the young PC was a stocky policeman with greying hair. Henry and his mother rose. He felt her overbalancing as though her legs were giving way. He gripped her arm firmly as they walked together through the door. They were shown into a small room where there was a table and four chairs.

'And you are?' asked the policeman, looking at Henry.

'Her son.'

'By my first husband,' explained his mother.

'But I'm called Dodge. Henry Dodge.'

'Dodge?' repeated the policeman, startled. He glanced

quickly at the young constable. 'Have you got that, PC Kemp?'

'Yes, sir.'

'Henry knows all about it,' said Henry's mother. 'You see, Mr Dodge got in touch with him before I knew anything about it. Up to then we thought he'd been killed in the war.'

Hurriedly she took out a handkerchief from her handbag and blew her nose.

'PC Kemp, I think Mrs Carpenter could do with a cup of tea. And give CID their names, will you?'

'Yes, sir,' said the young constable and he left the room.

They all sat down.

'How long have you known he was still alive?' asked the policeman.

'A month. I was too frightened to come sooner because of the baby. I have a two-year-old daughter as well.'

Henry pulled the envelope out of his rucksack, took the photograph out and slid it across the table.

'Your father's gravestone,' remarked the policeman.

'Yes,' said Henry's mother. 'The funeral was in 1940.'

'Dodge,' said the policeman, reading it slowly. 'Alfred Dodge.'

He looked up at Henry.

'Nice photograph. Did you take this?'

'Yes, sir. And developed it. We have a darkroom at my school.'

'Oh? And where would that be?'

'Hatton Road Secondary Modern.'

'Will you be putting me in a cell?' interrupted his mother.

'No. Naturally we need to go through certain procedures. Now when was the marriage ceremony between you and Mr Carpenter?'

The young constable returned with two cups of hot sweet tea, accompanied by a plainclothes detective, an ordinary-looking man in a tweed jacket, who sat in front of Henry and proceeded to play around with his pipe.

To Henry's surprise, the detective turned his attention to him and not his mother, as if he was keeping him company. They chatted casually for a while, talking about Henry's interests, including going to the Pictures and taking photographs.

'So,' said the man, smiling. 'You took this photograph of the gravestone with your father's name on it.'

'Yeah,' he paused. 'I thought he was a hero.'

And then it all poured out. How Jeffries and his mother were treated so badly because Private Jeffries was a deserter, how Henry was followed by a strange man who turned out to be his father, how his father had suffered from amnesia, how he thought he was Walter Briggs. Everything spilled out effortlessly except the content of the latest photographs from London. Mrs Beaumont had warned him to keep silent about those, pointing out that if the police knew of his father's criminal activities, he would be arrested there and then and sent to prison. Once there, he would probably refuse to divorce his mother out of revenge, since he would have nothing to lose. Henry mentioned that his father had offered him work but that was all.

'Must be exciting for you,' said the detective, puffing leisurely on his pipe.

Henry shook his head.

'I don't really know him.'

'Bit of a shock for your mother, though, him appearing out of the blue like that.'

He nodded. And then more seemed to tumble out till he wasn't quite sure what he had said and what he had left out, but afterwards he felt a tremendous sense of relief.

The man rose.

'You look after your mum,' he said, pointing the stem of his pipe at Henry, 'and keep out of trouble.'

'Will she go to prison?' Henry blurted out.

'No. But we'd like to see your first marriage certificate, if you still have it,' he added, turning to Henry's mother. 'And we'd prefer it if you kept this visit to yourself for the moment. Don't mention it to your Mr Dodge yet.'

'Oh,' said Henry's mother, looking puzzled.

'We'll be tracing any relatives of this Walter Briggs so that we can break the news of his death ourselves, to put their minds at rest. They must still wonder why he didn't return. At least we can tell them what's happened to him now and where he's buried.'

Henry and his mother had tea and buns in the Plaza café. It was like the old days when he was little and they used to go out for tea and to the Pictures on a Friday night after she had been given her factory pay. Sitting opposite her, he couldn't take his eyes off her. She looked transformed, pretty, and the colour in her face had come back.

'There are so many questions I want to ask you, Mum.'

'I think it's about time you asked them, then,' she said.

The most surprising revelation was the house. He had always believed his father had lived in it originally, but it turned out that Uncle Bill had lived in the house long before he and his mother had met. It was one of the houses owned by the railway.

'Then Gran turned up on the doorstep and moved into the sitting room. It was only for a couple of weeks till she could find somewhere else to rent but you and her got on so well that Uncle Bill agreed to let her stay. You'd just had your tenth birthday and were top of the class at school. I thought she was proud of you.'

'But she was, wasn't she?'

'Yes, but it seems she was more proud of you if you pretended to be someone else.'

Listening to his mother, it dawned on Henry that he had been living in a make-believe world invented by his grandmother. He decided to start from the beginning.

'How did you meet Uncle Bill?'

She smiled.

'I was working in the office part of the factory, and I was picking things up really quickly so I thought I'd take a shorthand and typing course. This other girl and me came top in the examinations and we decided to get a bit more education and went to the WEA. That's the Worker's Education Association. It's for working people who still want to keep learning and that's where we met Mr Cuthbertson. He persuaded us to study for the School Certificate even though you had to learn Latin for it. He was on this crusade to give those who'd missed out on an education a chance. He still is,' she said, smiling.

Henry nodded. He remembered the day Mr Cuthbertson had burst into their house bringing the newspapermen with him.

'I know it seems daft, but working towards it gave me courage. It made me feel as if I was going to have a future. Mr Cuthbertson wanted there to be a different society after the war. More equality. I wanted those chances for you. So did Uncle Bill, which is why we were so upset when you failed the eleven plus examination.'

'And why Gran was so pleased,' added Henry bitterly. 'I failed it on purpose, Mum.'

'We knew that, Henry.'

'You still haven't told me how you met Uncle Bill.'

'He sometimes turned up for the Latin classes when he was on leave. He was in the Royal Engineers, as you know, doing the same kind of work on the railways. I often overheard Mr Cuthbertson giving him homework and arranging to give him lessons at other times. The railways between here and London took a real hammering. But when there was a lull in the bombing, he'd read those books Mr Cuthbertson gave him, those Penguin New Writing books and paperbacks that are on our shelves.'

'But Gran says Uncle Bill wasted money buying those books!'

'Gran says a lot of things, love.'

*So that was another of her lies*, thought Henry.

'You still haven't told me, Mum . . .'

'How we met? It was simple really. Mr Cuthbertson always gave an annual party for his students. Uncle Bill turned up at one. We got talking and hit it off straight away. We both knew within an hour of us meeting we were made for each other.'

'How?'

'We had the same dreams.'

She looked so happy that he felt bad about wanting to bring up Gran's Christmas present. Even though he knew about it already, he wanted her to tell him herself. He wanted no more secrets between them.

'Tell me about my new raincoat, Mum.'

'How do you mean?' she said, reddening.

'I didn't see the pressure cooker and the lamp afterwards.'

'Oh.' She fell silent. 'Looks like you've put two and two together.'

'Tell me, Mum.'

'Your gran got it on tick. Uncle Bill and me have been paying it off.'

'She knew you'd have to do that, didn't she?'

'You needed a raincoat anyway,' said his mother evasively.

'But not such an expensive one.'

'No. I was hoping to be able to take it back to the shop.'

'But I wore it to the cinema the next day and it was snowing.'

She nodded.

'Why didn't you tell me?'

'Because you're fond of your gran and I didn't want to spoil your Christmas. It's your turn to talk now,' she added slowly. 'I think there's something you've been keeping from me too. About Gran. Am I right?'

'Yes. And it was all my fault. I told her where Jeffries and Pip lived.'

'She's the informer.'

'Yes.'

'Vindictive old bat.'

'She was smiling when I told her. I thought she was

being kind. She *looked* kind. How can someone look kind when they're planning to do something nasty?' And then he remembered his father behaved in just the same way.

'When you divorce my father, she'll have to move out, won't she?'

'Yes.' She took hold of his hand across the table. 'Henry, it's not going to be easy. I know you have the photographs, but when your father wants something he doesn't let anything stand in his way.'

'Mr Carpenter,' asked Jeffries, 'have you ever seen an Italian film before?'

They were outside the Rex with Mrs Beaumont and Uncle Bill.

'Never.'

'I hope they show *Bicycle Thieves* here,' Jeffries said.

Henry looked over his shoulder at the queue. People had travelled by train and ferry from miles away to see *Open City*. Suddenly he spotted Mr Finch.

'That's our form teacher,' he said, pointing.

'I'd like to have a word with him some time,' murmured Uncle Bill.

'What about?'

'Teacher training.'

There was no supporting film at the Rex, only trailers, news and documentaries, followed by the inevitable queue for ice creams. All around him people were chatting to one another excitedly. Henry could almost touch their anticipation.

When the film began Henry felt let down. It looked like an amateur film. It had none of the colour and gloss of an American film. It was in black and white and it was jerky, and some of the slums seemed very badly lit. But bit by bit his feelings changed. It was as though he were watching a documentary about real people caught up in the war, so that when he saw German soldiers hauling men into a truck and a distraught Italian widow running after it, her arm flung upwards in an attempt to reach the man she was to marry, it shocked him.

It was as though someone was actually there with a hidden camera.

They didn't speak when they left the cinema. It was Jeffries who broke the silence.

'That's real heroism,' he said quietly. 'That priest.'

'I agree,' said Uncle Bill, 'and I know it didn't have a happy ending, but it showed that the people in the Italian Resistance who sacrificed their lives helped liberate their country from Mussolini and Hitler.'

'And yet there were so many funny moments, weren't there?' said Mrs Beaumont. 'I suppose it was the priest's sense of humour which made those people's lives bearable.'

'You mean like when he and the little boy hid the bomb and the old rifle under the blankets of that sick old man,' said Henry, 'and they hit him over the head with a frying pan to stop him giving the game away to the German search party?'

'Yes. And knelt by the bed pretending to give him the last rites.'

And it was this priest who made such an impression on Henry. He wasn't the tall handsome kind of priest you might see in a Hollywood film. He was a short tubby man in a cassock who wore spectacles, one moment refereeing a football game for a group of small boys, the next moment delivering much needed money hidden in old books to a member of the Italian Resistance – calm, unhurried and down to earth.

'What about when he got angry,' said Jeffries, 'and told the Gestapo officer that although his men had killed that resistance fighter, they had only managed to kill his body but not his soul.'

'I thought he'd live when the Italian firing squad fired over his head,' said Henry.

'As did the gang of small boys peering through the wire,' added Mrs Beaumont.

'I never expected the German officer to do the job for them and shoot him,' Henry added.

'Neither did I,' said Jeffries.

Passing the railway bridge, Henry was aware that his

father was waiting there to meet him. Mrs Beaumont and Jeffries said their goodnights and Henry and Uncle Bill turned into their street.

'I'll wait for you behind the yard,' said Uncle Bill. 'It'll look suspicious if we don't come in together.'

'Thanks,' said Henry and he headed back towards the railway.

His father was waiting impatiently for him by the wall.

'I don't have much time,' he said curtly.

'I came as soon as I could,' said Henry.

'I saw you with the man your mum married, or rather didn't marry.'

'I didn't know you knew what he looked like,' Henry said carefully.

'His picture was in the newspaper, remember? And I saw the old woman you go to the pictures with and a boy.'

'That's Roger Jeffries. The son of the man I told you about.'

'Oh, yeah?' There was a pause as his father took a drag from his cigarette. 'A bit lah di dah going to a foreign film, ain't it?'

'It was about the Italian Resistance,' Henry murmured.

'Lots of shooting, eh?'

'A bit. But it was more about the people struggling to stay alive. There was this priest . . .' and then he suddenly felt he couldn't speak. He didn't want his father's remarks to contaminate his experience of seeing the film.

'How could you tell what was going on?'

'Subtitles.'

'Oh, yeah, you told me. Lots of work having to read them all the time, eh?'

'I didn't notice it after a bit. It was good.'

'The wops were the enemy, you know.'

'Not after 1943.'

Suddenly Henry realised he had answered his father back! He waited for the cuff round the ear but to his surprise there was silence. And then he heard the question he had been dreading.

'Has your mum come round, then?'

'She wants to know your address.'

He pulled out a scrap of paper from his raincoat pocket and handed it to him. Henry could see that an address had been written on it. A false one, Henry suspected.

'Thanks, Dad,' he said, gritting his teeth in a forced smile.

'I'll bring more information about the film unit next week. When do you break up?'

'March twenty-ninth.'

'Not long now. The job starts the first week in April. Fits in nicely,' he added, smiling. 'You and me, son. We'll make a good team.'

'Yeah,' said Henry nonchalantly. And then he couldn't

resist adding, 'I hope we have enough time to see each other. People who make films work long hours.'

His father nodded sagely.

'Once you're in London, we'll think about all that sort of thing, don't you worry.'

And then he was gone, only this time Henry didn't watch him wait on the platform for his train. He walked down the steps, his head bowed, the image of the Italian priest in his head before he was about to face a firing squad. 'It's easy to die decently,' he had said to a fellow priest, 'It's not so easy to live decently.'

He was so absorbed in his thoughts that he didn't notice a man on the other side of the road watching him.

## 10. The 39 Steps and blackmail

ON MONDAY MORNING HENRY'S FORM WERE TAKEN TO A chocolate factory and in the afternoon they visited a greyhound stadium. On Tuesday it was the fish market and a visit to a church where a wedding ceremony was acted out with the vicar and an organist present.

On Wednesday and Thursday it was a riding stable, an aircraft factory and a dressmaker's shop.

In the evenings, Henry and Jeffries rehearsed their talk, trying to make it as short and as simple as possible. Pip spent every spare moment at the piano while Mrs Jeffries sat at her machine and sewed an old black suit she had cut up into a smaller version of itself for Pip. Her head bowed in concentration, a dozen pins wedged between her lips, she guided the material under the juddering needle and listened to Pip playing. On Thursday evening, Henry raced round to Mrs Beaumont's house for their final rehearsal.

He was immediately bustled down to the kitchen where Grace was standing in front of the range, beaming.

'Grace and I have an announcement to make,' said Mrs Beaumont. 'We kept a little secret from you boys when we were in London. While you were watching films, I accompanied her to an audition at a highly regarded stage school. Afterwards they told me that Grace has a natural and original voice.'

'Oh, Grace,' Mrs Jeffries breathed, looking up from sewing a button on Pip's jacket.

'I received a letter from the school this morning. Grace has not only been offered a place at the school but they have also awarded her a scholarship.'

Pip leapt up and down and did one of his strange twirling dances round the kitchen and Grace began laughing.

'This is *magnificent*!' yelled Jeffries.

Henry grinned.

'When do you start?' asked Mrs Jeffries.

'September,' she said.

'Grace will stay with me in London,' said Mrs Beaumont, 'if her parents will allow it. We haven't told them yet. But they're coming to England in the spring so it's fingers crossed. There'll be more room in the London house in the autumn. Violet and her friend are moving to Cornwall in July. And Daniel has found a home for his film reels and will be moving to Oxford with an old Army pal.'

'And I'll be singing and dancing and having acting lessons,' said Grace happily.

'Everyone seems to be going to London,' said Jeffries quietly. 'I wish we could go.'

Mrs Jeffries looked quickly down at Pip's jacket. As long as Private Jeffries didn't return, Jeffries would be stuck in Sternsea.

She bit off the thread and shook out the jacket.

'Pip, you'd best try this on,' she said brightly.


'Are you nervous?' asked Jeffries.

Henry nodded.

'Pip?'

'Excited,' he said.

They were standing on the steps of the Plaza with their form, waiting for the other fourth form to join them. A crisp blustery wind was blowing and those without coats were shivering. In the distance they could see the teachers leading a line of pupils. It was to be a big event. All in all there were to be over eighty pupils with teachers attending the film.

'There's the headmaster,' muttered Henry, spotting Mr Barratt.

As soon as everyone was assembled they moved up the steps, with Mr Finch leading.

'Look!' yelled Pip.

In the foyer Twenties' music was coming from a

gramophone with a large horn.

'This way, please, Ladies and Gentlemen,' said the usherettes dressed in 1920s' cinema uniform, and they escorted them along the tiled flooring.

'Mum washed this floor this morning,' announced Pip.

In the auditorium they were shown to their seats. Mr Finch's form sat on the left side of the central aisle and the other fourth formers were shown to the right.

'Not the cheap ones,' said Jeffries, impressed.

The head was now striding up and down, glaring at anyone who was even thinking of being rowdy.

'I'm glad we've made the talk short,' whispered Henry, glancing at the other form. They were already looking restless. Henry didn't think they would have the patience to sit through anything that was too long.

'Good luck, lads,' whispered Mr Finch.

Henry and Jeffries made for the centre of the stage where a large microphone had been placed. As they stared out at the darkened auditorium Henry suddenly realised that he couldn't breathe.

'This cinema opened in 1928,' began Jeffries. 'The man who designed it wanted the audience to feel as though they were going outside when they entered the auditorium. Through the column of pillars on your right you would have seen a huge painting filling the entire wall. It was of the Grand Canal in Venice. On the left wall there was an Italian garden.

'The tiled floors as you enter the foyer were carpeted, and outside there was a special ornate building for the audience to queue in. When the audience entered the Plaza they were walking into a world of luxury. Lots of the cinemas built around that time and in the Thirties made people feel they were entering a palace, and that's how they came to be called Picture Palaces.'

Henry's mouth was now dry as dust.

'Here in the Plaza, the audiences could also listen to the Plaza's very own orchestra between the films,' concluded Jeffries.

He stepped to one side for Henry to take over. Henry took a deep breath.

'In 1929 a fire broke out in the projectionist's room just as the Plaza was about to show the first talking film ever to be seen in this town. The fire brigade and the staff at the theatre not only stopped the fire from spreading but also found the equipment they needed to go ahead with the opening of *Singing Fool*.

'Since then, people have continued to queue at the Plaza and the ones that are queuing for balcony seats even have their own place to wait, away from the wind and rain inside a beautifully decorated area.' *So far so good*, thought Henry. 'The first film we will be presenting to you this morning was made in 1921, so it's a little earlier than 1925, but it will give you an idea of what silent films were like then. It's a Sherlock Holmes' adventure and it's called *The Solitary Cyclist*.'

As they walked off the stage, a piano was pushed on and an elderly gentleman who had been invited by the Plaza to play the piano, as he had done for the cinema in the Twenties, sat down in front of it. Above him the screen was filled with silent flickering black-and-white images and the auditorium was filled with tinkling music. While the film was being shown, Pip slipped away to get changed. Henry and Jeffries sat with their fingers crossed.

At the end of the film, the pianist disappeared but the piano remained. Henry heard Jeffries murmur, 'This is it!'

They walked briskly back on to the stage.

'We are now going to give you a musical history of films from 1925 to 1935,' announced Jeffries formally, 'after which *The 39 Steps*, directed by Alfred Hitchcock and made in 1935, will be shown.'

At this the pupils began talking excitedly.

'To perform this *musical interlude*,' added Henry, with as much authority as he could muster, 'we present the third member of our team, Pip Morgan.'

As he and Jeffries returned to their seats, Henry could hear a rumble of disbelief from the auditorium. In the darkness he could make out the angry figure of the head-master striding down the left aisle towards Mr Finch.

'This must be stopped immediately!' Henry heard Mr Barratt whisper furiously. 'And then later you will come to my study.'

'Too late,' muttered Henry.

A tiny figure appeared on the stage dressed like a concert pianist in black tails, patent shoes, black trousers and a bow tie, his hair greased back. There was an undercurrent of jeers.

'I won't be a party to this!' Henry heard the headmaster mutter angrily, and out of the corner of his eye he saw him march back towards the foyer. He and Jeffries exchanged a worried glance.

Pip walked into the pool of light encircling the piano. He flicked back his tails and sat on the stool.

By now the other fourth formers were throwing paper darts and toffee papers at him and had started booing. One skidded along the top of the piano, another stayed lodged in his hair. Pip appeared to be unaware of it. His fingers touched the keys and he was off. It took less than a minute for there to be silence. Henry smiled. It was a silence that was magical. Surrounded by paper debris, Pip sat looking totally at ease. He was nothing like the grammar school boys who played in the interval at the Cinema Club. They played with refinement and precision. Pip, however, played as if the keys were his home, his tiny fingers moving effortlessly across them.

Henry felt Jeffries nudge him. He was pointing to the other side of the auditorium. Near the right Exit sign, standing behind one of the pillars, was the headmaster and the corpulent manager of the Plaza. The two men were staring at Pip, riveted. It was all Henry could do not to laugh. Recognising the closing chords, Henry and Jeffries quickly headed down the aisle. Pip bowed to his audience and walked off to a stunned silence, while the piano was pushed into the wings and out of sight.

'And now without further ado,' announced Jeffries into the microphone.

'*The 39 Steps*,' added Henry.

'I was keeping my fingers crossed that Mr Barratt wouldn't stop everything when that foreign woman in the film invited herself to the Canadian's flat,' whispered Henry as they stepped into the aisle.

'What, in case he thought she was *a woman of the night* or *a woman of ill repute*?' added Jeffries dramatically. 'And it was a bit too saucy?'

'Yeah. I knew that as long as he heard her say she was involved in counter-espionage and we got to that bit where she staggers in with a knife in her back, we'd be safe.'

'Do you think he was so shocked by Pip that he missed that bit?'

Henry shrugged.

'Who knows?'

'Who cares?' added Jeffries, smiling. 'We got away with it.'

'But did Pip? Where is he?' said Henry, suddenly noticing he had disappeared.

'You don't think he's been whisked off to see Mr Barratt, do you?'

They found Pip in the foyer, surrounded by girls.

'Why have you kept it such a secret?' they heard one of them say.

Henry looked around for the headmaster. He spotted him at the foot of the wide central stairway with Mr Finch and the manager. Before Henry could slip past the other pupils to listen in on their conversation, Mrs Morgan and Mr Hart appeared. Pip immediately broke away from his circle of admirers.

'Mum!' he yelled.

'You were wonderful,' she said, her voice shaking. 'And Mr Hart gave you a lovely spotlight.'

'Well done, son,' said Mr Hart, placing a hand on Pip's bony shoulder. 'You showed 'em.'

'Preparing a steam engine in the Twenties and Thirties is not much different from now,' Jack Riddell began, facing the crowd of fourth formers, as bemused passengers walked past him on the platform.

Henry could see that he was in his element. He stood with the camera prepared. Mr Finch had given him permission to return home for it, as he wanted Henry to take some pictures.

'Before setting off, the driver and fireman have to prepare the engine and that can take as long as an hour,' Jack continued. 'The driver has to oil every part . . .'

An electric train drew in behind him. A crowd of naval ratings hauled their kitbags through the door and peered at them from the corridor over Jack's shoulder, waving to everyone. Henry took a photograph. 'You will notice, as you look around Hatton Station, all the different sheds,' Jack went on, unaware of the audience behind him, 'the coal shed, the water pipe . . .'

The train drew out of the station.

It was when Jack and his friends had finished their talk that Henry suspected Mr Finch had something up his sleeve.

'Before we go back to school I have a special announcement to make,' Mr Finch said, facing them. 'Jack Riddell, will you please come forward.'

Jack took a step, a look of uncertainty on his face.

'On Tuesday, Riddell took a medical which he passed with flying colours and on Wednesday he had an interview with the depot master here at Hatton Station. At dinnertime his father telephoned me at the school because he knew we would be here today.' He turned to face Jack. 'He wanted me to tell you the news this afternoon.'

Henry noticed one of the railwaymen stop to listen.

'Riddell, from July you will be in a gang of four boys

and you will be the boy cleaner. Your job will be to go under the steam engine and clean all the rods and pistons. When you arrive you'll be given two pairs of overalls and . . .' He stopped and glanced at the railwayman. 'May I borrow your cap, sir?'

The man grinned, swept it from his head and strolled towards Jack, who was smiling so broadly it looked as if he was about to cry.

'You'll be given one of these,' said the railwayman. 'There'll be no badge on the front. A badge is something you have to earn. Only when you become a fireman will you be given one to wear on your cap. If you work hard, one day you'll be a steam engine driver.'

'Put it on, lad,' said Mr Finch.

Henry looked at Jack through the viewfinder. Jack lifted the cap to his head. As his hand slowly came down he appeared to grow an extra inch and, as though it was planned, a steam engine goods train passed behind him and Henry snapped. Lowering the camera and listening to the cheering, he suddenly realised that it was all over, that a life on the railways was no longer mapped out for him. Jack had taken his place. There was no turning back.

'You could have heard a pin drop,' said Jeffries, 'apart from Pip playing, I mean.'

'But you say no one clapped?' said Mrs Jeffries.

'I think they were too surprised,' said Henry.

They were in Mrs Beaumont's kitchen. Mrs Jeffries had Molly in her arms so that Henry's mother could type undisturbed. Mrs Morgan sat at the table, her arm around Pip's shoulders. Just then the telephone rang. Mrs Beaumont left the kitchen to answer it and reappeared soon afterwards.

'Rosie, it's for you. It's the manager at the Plaza.'

Mrs Morgan looked as if she was about to be sick. As soon as she closed the door behind her, Mrs Beaumont said, 'No eavesdropping, you boys.'

When she returned she looked flushed.

'Rosie, you haven't lost your job, have you?' asked Mrs Jeffries.

She shook her head and gazed at Pip. Mrs Beaumont drew out a chair for her.

'What is it?' she asked.

'It's about you, Pip. The manager wants you to play the piano tomorrow night during the interval between the two films – in your tails and everything. He's heard how I'm going to marry Mr Hart and how he's going to adopt you, so he's suggesting you should be introduced as Hart to get used to it. He wanted to call you Edward as well but since all your friends know you as Pip, I said, "I'd rather have him called that, if you don't mind." And he said, "I don't like shortening names. I'll introduce him as Philip Hart."'

Pandemonium followed. There were whoops and

cheers and patting of Pip's back but Pip stayed seated not speaking a word. Eventually everyone quietened down and stared at him.

'So what about it, love?' said his mother. 'What do you think?'

He smiled.

'Wonderful,' he said simply.

As soon as they opened the front door Henry heard the wireless from Gran's room. Henry and his mother glanced at one another.

'I'll get supper,' she said, ushering Molly into the kitchen.

Within seconds his name was being called.

'Where have you been?' Gran asked crossly when he walked into her room.

'At Mrs Beaumont's.'

'Again?'

'We finished our presentations today. And we had a bit of a celebration'.

'Celebration?' she interrupted. 'What were you celebrating?'

Henry hesitated.

'Pip played the piano on the stage at the Plaza.'

'Did the manager know?'

'He was there. And he wants him to play there again.'

'What! Does he know what he is?'

'A very good piano player.'

'You know what I mean.'

'Mr Hart is adopting him.'

'Who's Mr Hart? And why should he want to adopt the likes of him?'

'He's the projectionist.'

'Does he know what his mother is?'

'Yes. The woman he's going to marry next month.' Gran gasped. Henry looked away quickly. 'I'll put some more coal on the fire for you.'

He knelt on the hearth and picked up the tongs. He had been aware, at odd moments of the day, that Sunday was drawing closer and he was dreading having to tell his father that he wouldn't be taking the job in April. And then he hit on an idea. If he could give Gran little bits of information, chances were she would relay them back to his dad.

'Still, you won't be seeing much of those boys now, will you?' said his gran. 'Once you're working with your dad up in London.'

'But I won't be working with him, will I?' he said carefully. 'He's got a job for me in a film unit.'

'Oh, yes,' she said quickly, 'he told me all about that. I forgot.'

*Liar*, thought Henry.

'I'm glad you brought that up, Gran.'

'About the film business?'

'No. About me working up in London. You see, I've got a better idea.'

'Oh, yes?'

'Dad says he wants to find us a bigger place to live in. It'd be much better if you went to London next month instead of me and helped him. That's a woman's job, isn't it?'

'There's me legs,' she reminded him. 'You've forgotten me legs.'

'But he could take you to have a look at the places to give them the once over.'

'Don't you want to be with your dad?'

'Course I do,' Henry lied, 'but I want to be around for when the baby's born.'

She gave a wide smile. A few weeks ago that smile would have melted him. Now, it was just a broadening of her mouth.

'I don't suppose yer mum'll be keeping the baby,' she said. 'After all, it's not yer father's child. It wouldn't be right for him to bring it up, now would it?'

Henry felt a rush of anger. It took him all his concentration to speak in a soft voice the way she did.

'Dad told me he would look after the baby, don't you remember? And Molly too. He said it would be like having a ready-made family.'

'Well I never,' she said. 'He's a kind man. Too kind for his own good, perhaps?' And she tipped her head to one side. 'You don't want a baby around, do you?'

'I'll be the baby's half-brother,' said Henry gently.

His gran's face changed dramatically and for a fraction of a second he spotted the cruel expression he had seen in one of the photographs he had taken.

'Of course,' she said, the smile quickly returning, 'but you'll have to think about what's best for the baby, won't you? And Molly.'

'Molly's looking forward to the baby coming.'

'She'll forget. She's young. She can start new too.'

'What do you mean?'

'Adoption. That's the best thing for the little horror, don't you think?'

There, it was out in the open. Henry shook his head.

'No,' he said firmly. 'She's not going away,'

There was an awkward silence and then she smiled again.

'Your dad told me about that girl you were with,' she said brightly. 'What was her name?' She looked away for a moment as though she was thinking and then clapped her hands. 'Grace! That was it.'

Henry looked away from her eyes.

'Very nicely spoken,' he said. 'Do her parents know she's walking out with a boy? Your father said she only looked about twelve.'

'She's thirteen,' Henry said quietly.

'Very young, dear.'

'And we're not walking out together.'

'Just a friend, eh? Still, I don't think her parents would be too happy to know she goes out on her own with a boy, a boy from a secondary modern school. I sometimes see her aunt about. Elderly woman. Refined. Number 52, that's where she lives, ain't it?'

Henry stared at her. So that was it. Lose Molly and the baby, or lose Grace.

'And she's always popping into that house. Do her parents know that the woman what lives there is sheltering the wife and son of a deserter and that an unmarried woman lives there with her . . .'

He began to count to ten inside his head and picked up the bucket.

'I'll go and get some more coal,' he muttered.

# 11. Surprises among the china

'HIGH TEA?' REPEATED HENRY, MYSTIFIED. 'IS THIS A DIAMOND?'

They were sitting in Mrs Beaumont's sitting room with the door firmly closed.

'This is a case of digging one up,' she said, leaning forward conspiratorially. 'Your grandmother is threatening to tell Grace's great-aunt about the terrible company she's keeping. Let's pip her at the post and invite her great-aunt here for tea before she can get to her. I'll unpack my parent's silver and china, hunt through some recipes and we'll treat her like royalty. But whatever you do, don't tell your grandmother, otherwise she'll be over there like a shot. And thank you for having the guts to tell me it's she who's our informer. Though I have a small confession to make.'

'Mum told you?'

She nodded. 'Soon after you told her.'

She sprang to her feet and walked briskly out of the

room into the hall. Henry stood in the doorway and watched her pick up the phone and begin dialling. She caught his eye and winked at him.

'Hello, Miss Forbes-Ellis,' she said. 'It's Mrs Beaumont speaking . . . It's about Grace . . . No. She's not being any trouble at all . . . On the contrary I'm delighted with her work, which is partly why I'm calling you. I and the other ladies who are teaching her would like you to come to tea tomorrow afternoon and look at her work. I also thought you'd like to meet their sons. They occasionally chaperone Grace.' She glanced at Henry and smiled. 'I know it's rather late notice but . . . Oh, good! . . . That would be delightful . . . About five o'clock? . . . We'll look forward to seeing you then. Yes. Goodbye, Miss Forbes-Ellis.'

She replaced the receiver and then dashed into the study where Jeffries was measuring and cutting up pieces of elastic for his mother, who was half hidden behind a wall of half-made peach and pink corsets. Henry wondered nervously if Mrs Beaumont was going to tell them about his gran, but to his relief she explained that the tea was a way of breaking the scholarship news.

'We need all the help we can get,' she finished. 'And then after she's had a lovely time I'll tell her.'

Mrs Jeffries was beaming.

'Black treacle!' she exclaimed. 'You've a tin in your cupboard. I could make some dark gingerbread.'

'It's been there for some time.'

'It'll still be better than adding gravy browning. We'll need to buy bread, of course, rather than baking it ourselves. We must use any flour and eggs we have to make cakes.'

'Cakes!' said Jeffries over a box of suspender clips.

'We'll need your help too, boys,' said Mrs Beaumont.

'We've only done a term of cookery,' said Henry.

'Not cooking. Cleaning the silver. And I've just remembered there's a damask tablecloth upstairs. It's wrapped up inside a suitcase.'

Between the four of them they brought down the suitcase, one box of tarnished silverware and two boxes containing glasses and crockery wrapped in newspaper.

They carried the drop table into the centre of the study, lifted the sides and slid them all together, making a long table. Mrs Jeffries unwrapped the packaging around the tablecloth and lifted it tenderly out of the suitcase.

'Oh, it's beautiful!' she whispered. She struggled to unfold the starched material but it stood in the centre of the table like a stiff, lopsided, white pyramid. 'Let's leave it overnight. If it hasn't softened up by the morning, I'll iron it. Now,' she said eagerly, 'let's take the boxes down to the kitchen and find out how much we have left in the way of flour, sugar and colouring.'

'You're enjoying this, aren't you?' said Mrs Beaumont.

'Absolutely. It's far more exciting than making corsets.'

They carried the boxes down to the kitchen and placed them carefully on the table.

'Henry, will you explain to your mother what it is we're planning to do and ask her if she's willing to give any of her rations for this week,' said Mrs Jeffries, 'and I'll ask Pip's mother. Now let's see what's in these boxes.'

Gingerly they unwrapped each small object. After half an hour the kitchen table was littered with elegant bone china, cups and saucers, a silver sugar bowl, tiny silver teaspoons and the smallest forks Henry had ever seen.

'They're for eating cakes with,' Mrs Beaumont explained.

'I've never seen my mother eat a cake with a fork before,' said Henry.

'She can copy me. And talking of your mother, you'd best get home.'

'We must make sure Gran doesn't leave the house tomorrow,' said his mother in the scullery.

'I'll make up her fire in the morning,' Henry offered, 'and give her breakfast.'

'Would you, love? Then I can go earlier to the shops and get to the head of the queues. Once I'm back I can keep an eye on her. Whatever happens we must stop her going out before five o'clock.'

The following morning Henry's mother woke him early. Downstairs he discovered that she had already been sorting out some ingredients. A pot of homemade blackberry jam, several other tiny parcels and an egg were on the table.

'Dried fruit,' she whispered. 'Not much but I'll bring back this week's ration of flour once I've been to the shops.'

Henry packed the food into his rucksack, crept up the stairs with the egg and wedged it between an old jersey and some socks on the shelf in the wardrobe. He was just taking the camera down when a small voice from behind made him jump.

'Molly clever,' she said proudly, holding a tin chamber pot with a chipped green rim. It was not empty.

Henry took the pot from her and held her hand. He walked quietly downstairs to the kitchen.

'Henry look after Molly,' he said. 'Give Molly breakfast. Mum gone out.'

And then he realised that he was speaking like her.

'Molly clever,' she repeated, smiling up at him.

'Molly very clever,' said Henry, realising that if he didn't praise her she would repeat it again.

'Henry wipe Molly's bottom,' she demanded.

Henry nodded and led her out into the yard to the toilet.

After he had washed his hands and dressed her, he cut her a slice of bread. He had just handed it to her when there was a loud knock on the wall.

'Auntie hungry,' stated Molly. 'Auntie wants tea.'

By the time Uncle Bill had returned from the night shift

and gone to bed, Henry had lit Gran's fire and given her breakfast. Unfortunately her fire kept spitting, and what with her knocking on the wall for him to put on more coal and move the fire guard, and Molly demanding his attention, he had to use every ounce of energy to control his temper. He longed for his mother to return from the shops but when she did, hours later, she looked shattered. Henry quickly took the shopping bags from her and she sank gratefully into a chair. Immediately Molly tried to climb on to her lap, getting cross because there was less space now that his mother's pregnancy was more advanced.

'I'll make some tea for you,' he said, worried.

'Thanks, love, but don't use the new tea leaves. Use the damp ones in the vacuum flask. I'm going to give some of our tea ration to Mrs Beaumont for this afternoon.'

She was interrupted by a loud banging on the wall.

'I've got to cook lunch,' she said wearily.

'I'll go and see what she wants.'

They smiled at one another like conspirators but Henry was still worried about her. She looked so pale.

'Would you like me to take Molly with me when I go round to Mrs Beaumont's?'

'Oh, yes!' she murmured. 'Would you, love?'

He remembered that the district nurse had told his mother to take an afternoon nap. He couldn't see Gran allowing her to do that.

'Why don't you come too?'

'I wouldn't be much help. I'm done in.'

'You can have a sleep on her settee. We'll all be down in the kitchen.'

'But don't we need someone here to keep an eye on Gran?'

At that moment there was another bang on the wall.

'I'll come with you,' she said quickly.

The table was laid with scones, slim wheatmeal tinned-salmon sandwiches, mock banana sandwiches, jam sandwiches, gingerbread, carrot cookies and chocolate buns made from cocoa powder. What remained of the sugar ration was now in the silver sugar bowl with its ornate handles. Draped over the silver jug filled with milk was a tiny lace cover. Blackberry jam was in the blue glass dish in the silver container and strawberry jam was in a small cut-glass bowl next to a bowl of artificial cream. Three silver spoons lay beside them.

'The bowls are downstairs ready for another little treat. Mrs Jeffries and Mrs Morgan have made ice cream and a little lemon sorbet,' said Mrs Beaumont.

'But you don't have a refrigerator,' Henry's mother said, puzzled.

'The Plaza has. Mrs Morgan has taken it over there and she's going to whip back and pick it up during the tea.'

'The table looks beautiful!'

'Henry, take that wonderful egg downstairs before the heat of your hand causes it to hatch.'

'There are more bits and pieces in his rucksack,' said his mother.

'Any flour?'

'Yes. And jam.'

'Splendid.' Mrs Jeffries took Molly into the hall. 'I have some very important stirring for you to do.' She looked at Henry's mother and pointed firmly in the direction of the sitting room. 'Go and lie down. You can join us when you've had a sleep.'

Down in the kitchen Pip was flattening out pastry using a bottle as a rolling pin, and Jeffries was stirring a cocoa mixture. Pip's mother was removing another tray of scones from the oven.

'Hello, love,' she said, smiling. 'Oh, my word!' she cried. 'An egg! Just in time. Our ration of eggs is all used up. Lovely!'

There was a loud knock at the front door.

'That'll be Grace,' said Pip excitedly and he presented the milk bottle to Henry to take over and fled from the room.

'They'll be doing their rehearsing,' said Mrs Morgan.

'They're going to give Miss Forbes-Ellis a little concert,' Mrs Beaumont explained.

By a quarter to five, Henry and Jeffries were wearing flannel trousers, jackets, shirts and ties, their hair slicked back. Pip was wearing his concert outfit minus the tails.

'Now remember to tuck your napkin in your collar and sit with your stomach touching the table,' said Mrs Morgan, 'so that if any ice cream or jam falls, it won't touch your trousers. You've got to keep your clothes clean for the Plaza.'

Henry was standing with his friends in the hall when there was a knock on the heavy outer storm door, which had been left open. A shadow appeared in the porch and across the stained glass window of the hall door.

'She's here!' whispered Mrs Beaumont and she frantically beckoned them to take Molly downstairs. 'Not you, Grace!' she said, grabbing her arm. 'You need to stay with me in case she asks any questions about your work.' Once out of sight, Henry hovered by the kitchen door eavesdropping, while Pip and Jeffries kept Molly amused.

'Good afternoon, Miss Forbes-Ellis,' Henry heard Mrs Beaumont say. 'Do come in. Would you like a glass of sherry?' and then there was the sound of the sitting room door closing.

After a while there were footsteps on the steps and Mrs Jeffries and Mrs Morgan appeared. They closed the kitchen door behind them.

'What's she like?' whispered Jeffries.

'Grim,' said his mother.

'Let's just say she's not giving anything away,' added Mrs Morgan.

'When we go into the dining room, remember not to sit down until she sits down,' said Mrs Jeffries, 'and don't start eating until she starts eating.'

The door swung open. It was Mrs Beaumont.

'Up to the sitting room, you boys. Time for introductions.'

An elderly white-haired woman was sitting bolt upright on the edge of the settee, dressed in navy blue from her neck to her ankles, aside from a tiny lace collar, a cameo brooch at her throat and a pair of cream leather gloves. She wore a navy blue hat and navy blue lace-up shoes with a small heel. Staring at the severe expression on her wrinkled face, Henry was reminded of a Victorian photograph.

'Miss Forbes-Ellis, may I introduce the three boys who occasionally chaperone Grace when she goes to the cinema, Henry, Roger and Pip.'

They nodded one by one as she said their names.

Miss Forbes-Ellis gave them a regal nod. There was an icy silence. *She doesn't approve*, thought Henry. Just then, Molly came flying in and stopped in front of her. The old lady scowled.

'Are you the birthday lady?' Molly asked.

Grace's great-aunt shook her head, still unsmiling. Grace was looking on nervously.

Henry's mother came forward.

'This is my daughter, Molly,' she said hurriedly. 'Molly, this is the lady who's been invited to tea. It's not her birthday but . . .'

'Do you like cake?' she asked, ignoring her mother.

The woman nodded solemnly.

'Me too,' and she beamed and took hold of her hand.

To Henry's amazement Miss Forbes-Ellis allowed herself to be taken by his determined half-sister and Henry was certain he spotted the flicker of a smile.

In the dining room everyone waited until she had sat down before doing so themselves and copied Mrs Beaumont when she opened her serviette. Mrs Jeffries walked in with a pot of tea.

'I notice you have a piano,' said Miss Forbes-Ellis politely.

'My elder brother used to play it,' said Mrs Beaumont.

Miss Forbes-Ellis leaned forward as if to ask another question but then stopped. They gazed at one another.

'The Great War,' answered Mrs Beaumont to her silent question. 'I lost two brothers. And my husband.'

She gave a sympathetic nod.

'But Pip uses it now.'

'Oh, yes?' she commented, giving him a cursory glance. 'Do you have a piano teacher?'

'Yes, Miss Forbes-Ellis,' said Pip.

'A lady called Miss Bradley,' added his mother.

'Miss Bradley!' She stared at them astonished. 'Why, she's a friend of mine.'

'She's coming to the Plaza this evening to listen to Pip play in the interval.'

'But I don't understand,' she said. 'She told me it was a boy called Edward.'

'Edward is his first name but his friends call him Pip.'

'Good gracious,' she said, staring at Pip in disbelief. 'She's always singing your praises,' and with that she gave a broad smile.

Henry observed that everyone suddenly looked relieved. It looked as though Mrs Beaumont's tea party idea was going to work.

'Grace tells me you boys are learning French at your school,' she said. 'You're very lucky. It's a wonderful language and a wonderful country.'

'You've been there?' Mrs Beaumont asked.

'I used to live there. In Paris.'

'How long did you stay?' asked Mrs Jeffries.

'Years! I went there in the 1890s as a young woman, fell in love with it and refused to return home. My family were very shocked, but then everything about me shocked them.'

'But why did you leave?' Jeffries asked eagerly.

'Because the Germans were invading. And people kept insisting I go for my own safety. That was in 1940.'

'So you remained there all during the Great War?' asked Mrs Beaumont.

'Yes. But I had lots of happy times there too, mixing

with artists and film-makers, actors and cabaret artists, writers and dancers. In the summer my friends and I would eat and drink wine round a large wooden table in a garden high on a hill in a place called Montmartre, with the rest of Paris spread out below us, and we'd just talk and laugh and philosophise. I hated leaving there and I'm sorry to say I've been homesick ever since.'

'You're like Grace,' said Pip suddenly.

She laughed.

He was spot on, thought Henry. The way she waved her arms about and smiled was almost identical. And she was nowhere as frosty as they had first thought.

'That's probably why I'm the last of the aunts to have Grace stay with me. I'm a bad influence, you see,' she said with a wicked smile. 'Even at the ripe old age of eighty-three I'm still the black sheep of the family.'

'Like me,' said Grace. 'But why didn't you let me know that before?'

'I thought I might make things worse for you. And I must admit it has been a strain behaving in a *proper* manner.'

'Oh, please stop, then,' Grace begged.

'Did you ever meet the Lumière brothers?' asked Jeffries.

'No, but I saw them in the basement of the Grand Café where they used to give film shows. It was all very exciting. And I met the director Jean Renoir. That was much later of course. He had just made a film which caused a bit of a stir, *La Règle du Jeu.*'

'Can you remember any of the Lumière brothers' films?' asked Jeffries.

'Oh, yes. The one that startled everyone was a train entering a station. And there was one of a baby being fed and men playing cards.'

'We've seen those,' Henry blurted out. And then he stopped, feeling he had been rude to interrupt. But she was smiling.

'Then you're very, very lucky.' She sighed. 'I also remember the many famous singers I heard in the cafés and bars. I carried some of their records with me in a wooden case when I escaped from Paris, but alas I don't have a gramophone player.'

'I have,' said Mrs Beaumont. 'And you're quite welcome to come here and listen to them.'

'Oh, my dear!' she said happily. 'I would so love to hear them again. But for now I shall continue to enjoy this thoroughly splendid tea you've all prepared for me. And throw the severe maiden aunt out of the window. Metaphorically speaking, of course.'

After tea, Mrs Beaumont took Miss Forbes-Ellis into the sitting room while the boys cleared the table, folded it down, put it up by the wall and set out the chairs. When Henry walked into the sitting room to tell Mrs Beaumont that everything was ready, he found his sister standing beside the seated Miss Forbes-Ellis, gazing at her and stroking the side of her face. *I could hug you, Molly*, he thought.

The long red velvet curtains at the end of the study were now drawn, hiding the conservatory. Two tall lamp stands were standing in front of them, one by the piano and the other a little off to the side. They were both switched on.

'Where's Grace?' Henry asked Mrs Beaumont.

'Changing,' she whispered.

There was a slight movement from behind the curtains and Pip appeared in his tails, bowed and sat down at the piano.

Pip didn't play the Twenties' and Thirties' music he played at the Plaza. It was classical music, the kind that made you feel as though you were walking past a river but were slowed down by a sudden movement in the water so that you had to stop at the bank to stare into it. He glanced across at Miss Forbes-Ellis. She was smiling sadly as though she knew the music already.

And then it was over.

'Pip will now play the medley he will be playing this evening at the Plaza,' announced Mrs Beaumont.

Henry wondered if Miss Forbes-Ellis would approve of this kind of music. He needn't have worried. She looked as though she was about to laugh. They applauded and Mrs Beaumont drew aside the curtain.

Grace stepped into the room wearing the outfit that had been made for her for the jazz club, her hair billowing out in colossal waves. She stepped forward, glanced at Pip and sang *It's Magic*, only this time she had the proper piano accompaniment. After this she sang some swing numbers and ended with the song called *Black Coffee*. They both bowed to applause and Mrs Beaumont stood up.

'There is another reason why we have invited you here today, Miss Forbes-Ellis.'

To Henry's surprise, Mrs Beaumont appeared nervous. Perhaps she should have asked permission before taking Grace to be auditioned. Slowly she told Miss Forbes-Ellis the whole story. And then she paused.

'This week I received a letter from the school. They would not only be delighted to have Grace as a pupil but have also offered her a scholarship.'

'You mean she would be a singer?' breathed her aunt.

'Yes. But the school would give her acting and dance lessons too.'

'But that's wonderful!'

'Oh, Aunt Florence!' Grace yelled. 'You really mean it?'

'Of course I do. Oh, it's such a relief not being sensible any more.'

'For me too,' and she flung her arms around her great-aunt's neck.

Her aunt held on to her tightly.

'I always knew you were special. You should have come and stayed with me in the first place. Your other aunts are nice enough but they're a little bit, how shall I put it . . . dusty.' She turned to Mrs Beaumont. 'But you say this school is in London?'

'Where my home is,' answered Mrs Beaumont. 'I would be more than happy to have Grace stay with me there.'

'I'll miss you,' said Miss Forbes-Ellis, turning to Grace. 'That's why I kept badgering you to do your homework. I was afraid you'd be expelled again and I'd lose you.'

'Until I sell this house we can come and visit you, and afterwards you must come and visit me in London,' said Mrs Beaumont.

'And you must visit me in Paris,' she said. 'This afternoon I've realised I don't want to spend my remaining years here. After ten years I still feel like a foreigner,' and she laughed. 'I'll wait until I know Grace is settled and then I'll be off.'

'I've written to Grace's parents to tell them the news.'

'Ah. The parents.' Grace's great-aunt fell silent for a moment and then gave a determined smile. 'I'm sure they'll be delighted,' she added firmly.

That evening, Mrs Jeffries, Jeffries, Grace and Henry were allowed to stand upstairs at the back of the Plaza during the interval. The manager said that he was letting them in free because it was Pip's debut.

Henry watched the long queue of people in the aisles wanting ice creams and then the usherette's spotlight moved up to the stage area. The manager moved into the light and strode over to a microphone next to the piano. Henry could feel his mouth growing drier by the second. He prayed the audience wouldn't talk all the way through Pip's playing or jeer at him.

The manager raised his hand for silence.

'Tonight is the first time we will be presenting one of our local lads,' he announced solemnly, 'a talented boy and a pupil at Hatton Road Secondary Modern School . . .'

'They're taking all the credit,' muttered Henry.

'Ladies and gentlemen, I am pleased to present, for the first time at the Plaza cinema, Master Philip Hart.'

As soon as the manager had left the stage and Pip appeared in his tails, the audience laughed. Henry crossed his fingers.

'Don't he look sweet,' he heard a woman in front of him say.

And then Pip's fingers touched the keyboard and within seconds the laughter stopped.

They cheered when he had finished. Nearly two thousand people yelled and stamped and applauded for him to come back and take more bows.

As the titles came on to the screen for the next film, Henry heard the same woman say, 'He should be on the wireless. He'll be a star, that one. You wait and see.'

## 12. A lucky escape

HENRY STOOD IN THE RAIN OBSERVING HIS FATHER LEAVE THE station. He struggled to prevent the gusts of wind from dragging him and his umbrella across the road. As soon as his father had begun to walk up the steps towards the railway bridge, he stepped off the kerb. The wind sucked his umbrella inside out and pulled him sharply forward. Luckily there were no cars. He closed it. Better to be wet than run over.

Once he reached the pavement on the other side he stood still for a moment, almost paralysed with dread. Looking back on how excited and happy he had felt on those first meetings with his father, he was shocked at how, after such a short time, it had all gone sour. He took a deep breath and dragged himself slowly through the puddles.

His father was waiting for him at the usual place, staring into the distance, the collar of his mackintosh up, the brim of his hat pulled down. Henry placed his elbows on the wall a few paces away.

'Good film, was it?' his father asked.

Henry shrugged.

'I didn't go tonight. The ones I wanted to see are at the Savoy. I wouldn't have had time to see them and get here. It's too far away.'

'The Troxy's close.'

'I don't want to see *Jolson Sings Again*.'

'Why not? A film's a film.'

'I think it's stupid having someone white pretending to be black. There are plenty of good black performers,' he said, remembering the black musicians in the jazz club.

'Oh, yeah? Who?'

'Lena Horne. Sarah Vaughan.'

'Never heard of 'em.' There was an uncomfortable silence. 'Not long now. End of school this week, eh?'

Henry nodded. By now he was soaked.

'Everyone all right, then? That friend of yours, Grace?'

So that was it. Gran had been talking to him. He shrugged nonchalantly.

'She ever talk about our meeting?'

'No,' said Henry.

'Clever girl.'

A crowd of cinema-goers passed them, chatting and laughing. Henry envied them their happiness.

'Bring yer bag next Sunday,' his father said suddenly. 'Work starts Monday.'

'Mum wants the information about the job before then.'

'She can wait,' he snapped, and then he switched on the smile and threw his cigarette butt on the ground. 'Pick you up next week.' Before Henry could say goodbye he had already turned on his heel and walked away. He gave Henry a casual wave over his shoulder.

The cigarette butt was still alight. Henry stamped on it with his boot, twisting and turning it until the cigarette was nothing but crumbled remains. As he walked down the steps clutching his umbrella, his head bent against the wind, he wished he had never set eyes on him.

'Time to turn the old tailor's room in the bottom of the garden into a dance studio for Mrs Jeffries,' announced Mrs Beaumont. 'I've had the all clear from the solicitors so we'll clear the room upstairs at the same time. All the furniture is to go to the auctioneers and the WVS's furniture storage depot. So it's all hands on deck and not a word to Mrs Jeffries.'

With extra help from Uncle Bill and Max Beaumont it still took several days for the building at the bottom of the garden to be emptied. Henry found a narrow wooden handrail from a damaged staircase among his salvage collection.

'That can be the barre,' said Jeffries.

Henry screwed it into the wood panelled wall opposite the windows and sanded it down until it was smooth and pale. They scrubbed the filthy wooden floors while Mrs Beaumont cleaned the lavatory and little cloakroom area with its basin. After the floorboards had dried, they sanded them. During the week, Uncle Bill and Max returned with a collection of battered tins containing the remains of wood seal, and while Mrs Jeffries was busy working her way through piles of corsets in the study, they sneaked unseen round the back and put two coats on.

On Saturday morning Mrs Beaumont placed the gramophone and some records on top of the cupboard in the new dance studio. The windows were cleaned and the brass door handle polished. As soon as Mrs Jeffries returned from shopping, Mrs Beaumont snatched her bag from her.

'We have a little surprise for you, Natasha,' she said.

Mrs Morgan had raced back from her morning's cleaning at the Plaza, eager to see how she would react.

'What's going on?' Mrs Jeffries asked. 'It's not my birthday.'

She was blindfolded and Jeffries guided her through the overgrown garden.

'Is it a plant?' she said, smiling,

'No,' said Jeffries.

Henry was looking through the viewfinder of the camera. He took a photo of her.

'Henry!' she exclaimed. 'I heard that.'

'Keep walking,' urged Jeffries.

Pip was jumping up and down by the door. His mother laughed.

'You're almost there,' said Mrs Beaumont encouragingly.

'The path, I'm on the path,' said Mrs Jeffries.

'Correct,' said Jeffries.

'Careful,' said Mrs Beaumont as she approached the step.

She took hold of Mrs Jeffries' free hand and guided it to the door handle.

'It's the conservatory door. It is a plant, isn't it?'

'Turn the handle,' said Jeffries.

She opened the door and Henry slipped inside the building. He wanted to be able to see her face. He crept over to the nearest window and leaned up against it.

'You can take the blindfold off now,' said Mrs Beaumont.

As soon as it was off Mrs Jeffries gazed at the bare room and then spotted the barre.

'Your own dance studio, Natasha.'

Mrs Jeffries reddened and flung her hands over her face.

'It's beautiful. It's absolutely beautiful! All this wonderful space!' And she burst into tears. 'I'm so sorry,' she blurted out. 'I'm crying because it's so lovely.'

'Try it out, Mother,' said Jeffries.

She stood motionless for a moment as if taking it all in, and then slowly and gracefully she glided into the centre of the room, her arms outstretched. Henry was mesmerised. He had never seen a human being move with such elegance and strength. She slid her feet along the smooth floorboards as if she was moving on ice and then she began to twirl across the floor.

'Oh, I forgot,' exclaimed Mrs Beaumont, and she picked up the arm from its cradle on the gramophone and placed the needle on the record that was waiting there.

Jeffries began to leap around the room and Grace and Pip joined in. Henry snapped away, taking more photographs. And then he caught sight of Mrs Beaumont's face. She was leaning in the doorway observing Mrs Jeffries.

He quickly took one of her and she didn't notice. The music concealed the sound of the camera clicking.

The following evening Henry made for the bridge. It was deserted. His mother didn't know that this was the day he was supposed to leave for London with his father. But Uncle Bill did.

'I'm not happy about you meeting him again, let alone on your own,' he had said.

But Henry had pleaded with him. He didn't want to be treated like a child. It was important to him that he should be the one to tell his dad that he was staying in Sternsea. Man to man. Reluctantly Uncle Bill agreed to let him go. Uncle Bill couldn't have gone with Henry anyway, since he was working.

Henry leaned on the wall praying that his father wouldn't turn up. He was about to give up and go home when he heard a match being struck behind him. He swung round to find him standing in the shadows. He realised he must have been watching him for some time and it made him shiver. Neither of them spoke although Henry knew what was coming.

'Where's yer bag?' his father asked eventually.

Henry swallowed.

'At home.'

'You'd best go back and get it, then. I'll wait for you 'ere.'

'I haven't packed it.'

'What do you mean you haven't packed it?' his father whispered angrily.

'I don't want to leave here yet. I want to finish my last term at school and be around when the baby's born.'

'I've a job waiting for you. No arguments. I've given my word. And my word is my bond.'

'In the summer,' Henry began, 'when I've finished . . .'

'You have finished,' his father interrupted. 'You're fifteen. Old enough to work. You won't get an opportunity like this again.'

'I know and I should have told you earlier.'

'Told? No one *tells* me anything. If I decide something it's as good as done.'

'I'm sorry,' said Henry and he walked swiftly towards the steps.

He felt his father's hand grip him at the back of his neck. The fingers dug so hard into his skin that he was unable to move. He tried to reach up behind his shoulders to prise them off, but it was as though they had trapped a nerve in his body, making it impossible for him to struggle.

'You're coming on the train with me tonight, bag or no bag,' his father snapped. 'I should have done this weeks ago, instead of all this pussyfooting around.'

Henry tried to cry out but no sound emerged.

Suddenly he heard someone calling up to him.

'Hello there! Henry Dodge, isn't it?'

Looking up at them was a short dumpy man in an old raincoat with cropped sandy hair.

'Friend of Mr Finch's remember?' he said cheerily. 'I saw you at the Rex. *Open City*?'

His father released him. *What friend?* thought Henry. *Mr Finch had been on his own.* Henry stared at the man, speechless. Out of the corner of his eye he watched his father fly down the steps and on to the pavement.

'He pointed you out to me in the queue. Good at photography, aren't you?' he said, almost shouting.

His father turned the corner and was now out of sight.

'I like taking photographs, yes,' Henry heard himself croak.

The stranger leaned forward and looked him in the eye.

'Are you all right, sonny?'

'He bumped into me,' Henry stammered. 'He was in a hurry for the train. I must have been in his way.'

'You'd best get home.'

Henry stumbled quickly down the steps and broke into a sprint, too terrified to look behind him in case his father was hiding somewhere ready to pounce on him. He ran without stopping until he was in the hall and had closed the front door behind him. He leaned against it to catch his breath.

'Henry!'

*Oh, no!* 'Got to have my bath, Gran,' he called back on his way to the kitchen.

The tin bath, filled with the usual grubby water, was waiting for him. He shifted the kettle over to the hot plate. Gran opened the door.

'Where you bin?'

'The Plaza.'

'Nowhere else?'

'No.'

To his relief he heard his mother coming down the stairs. Gran disappeared.

'Hello, love,' she whispered, closing the door. 'Good films?'

Henry nodded.

'I've just got Molly off to sleep.'

Just then the kettle boiled. Henry grabbed the rag that was hanging at the front of the range and picked it up. He kept his back to his mother so that she couldn't see his face.


Every creak on the stair, every rattle at the window or door, every shadow across the wall convinced him that his father had broken into the house and was coming to get him.

He longed for Uncle Bill to return from work. And then he heard the key in the lock. He slipped out of bed and crept down the stairs, shivering in his pyjamas. The kitchen was empty. Sounds of running water were coming from the scullery. He padded quietly towards it. Uncle Bill was stripped to the waist, bending over the stone sink. He looked up at Henry.

He was not going to cry, he told himself. He was going to be strong.

'Henry? What is it?'

'Uncle Bill,' said Henry shakily. 'He hurt me. He really hurt me.'

## 13. Out in the open

JEFFRIES AND HIS MOTHER SAT ON THE SETTEE IN MRS Beaumont's sitting room and stared at Henry and his mother in disbelief.

'So, this man in these photographs, you say he looks like your first husband?' said Mrs Jeffries falteringly.

'No,' said Henry's mother. 'It *is* my first husband.'

'But it can't be, Maureen. We saw him being buried.'

'I've met him,' said Henry.

Jeffries gasped.

'I'm sorry,' said Mrs Jeffries, dazed, 'but I can't take this in.'

'I wanted to tell you earlier but I was afraid that if it got out, I'd be sent to prison.'

'Why would you go to prison?' asked Jeffries, looking bewildered. 'You haven't done anything wrong.'

'I'm afraid that unwittingly she has,' said Mrs Beaumont. 'She's committed bigamy. The man whose funeral you attended appears to be a Walter Briggs,' she continued. 'Mr Dodge woke up in hospital with amnesia and Mr Briggs' papers on him. It's only recently that his memory has started to come back.'

'We think Walter Briggs was the person who saved your father's life,' said Henry to Jeffries, 'not my father.'

'The police are trying to trace his relatives,' added his mother.

'The police!' exclaimed Mrs Jeffries.

'They know now. It took me a month to pluck up enough nerve to tell them.'

'You've known for a month?' said Jeffries quietly.

'Oh, my goodness!' cried Mrs Jeffries. 'You're not married to Bill!'

'No.'

'Oh, Maureen, what a mess! The children . . .' she began and then she stopped. 'So the relatives of this Mr Briggs have no idea?'

'No.'

'Where is Henry's father now?'

'London.'

'What state of mind is he in?'

'Back to his old ways, I'm afraid,' muttered Henry's mother.

'He's been to see these Army doctors,' said Henry.

'So that's why you've been so quiet!' exclaimed

Jeffries. 'I thought you'd gone back to not wanting to be friends with me and Pip.'

Henry was shocked.

'No, no! Nothing like that. I had to keep my mouth shut. For Mum's sake.'

'Maureen, what are you going to do?' asked Mrs Jeffries.

'Divorce him.'

'But you can't, Maureen! He's injured. He needs you. It might kill him.'

'If I don't divorce him, he might kill me.'

Mrs Jeffries stared at her for a moment.

'Maureen?'

'There's something else I haven't told you. When I was married to him . . .' She paused. 'I mean, before he went missing . . .'

'He hit her,' interrupted Henry fiercely. 'And me.'

'Why didn't you tell me?' said Jeffries.

'I only began to remember when Mum recognised him in the photograph. I started getting these nightmares about things that had happened a long time ago. I thought they were just bad dreams.'

'Until he told me about them,' added his mother quietly. She looked embarrassed. 'You won't think any less of me for being a divorcee, will you?'

Mrs Jeffries smiled.

'Of course not, silly. I think you're very brave. I couldn't do it.'

'Why don't you boys take yourself off somewhere,' said Mrs Beaumont. 'I think your mothers have a lot to talk about.'

Henry made his way to the door, relieved to have got the secret of his father out into the open, but worried that Jeffries might not want to speak to him again. To his surprise, he felt his friend's arm across his shoulders.

'I think you ought to tell Pip and Grace,' he said.

Henry nodded.

'That's another thing I haven't told you,' Henry said. 'Grace knows already. She found out the day we went to see *Little Women*.'

Jeffries laughed.

'She would. She doesn't miss a thing.'

The following Sunday his father was waiting for Henry on the railway bridge, only this time Henry was not alone.

'What's he doing 'ere?' he snapped, staring at Uncle Bill.

'You're lucky he turned up at all,' said Uncle Bill, 'after the way you treated him.'

'He broke his word.'

Uncle Bill held out a large envelope.

'What's this?'

'Find out.'

He snatched it from him, tore it open and peered inside.

'It's just a lot of papers,' he said angrily.

'Divorce papers. Maureen wants to divorce you.'

He flung the envelope to the ground. 'I'll deny ever receiving them.'

'You have two witnesses here.'

'Him? He wouldn't be a witness. He don't want his mum to divorce me, do you, son?'

'Yes,' said Henry.

'What did you say?'

'I remember you hitting her, Dad.'

'So. All men beat their wives. Keeps them in order.'

'She wants a divorce,' Uncle Bill said, his voice shaking with anger.

'I ain't giving her one.'

'There's something else in that envelope which might change your mind.'

'Like what?'

'Photographs.'

Henry picked up the envelope and handed it back. He watched his father's face as he took them out. He looked sharply at Henry.

'You take these?'

Henry shook his head.

'Who did, then?'

'Does it matter?' said Uncle Bill.

His father dropped the envelope, leaving the three photographs in his hands. Then he smiled. Very slowly he tore them into tiny pieces.

'All gone,' he said and laughed.

'We have the negatives,' said Uncle Bill quietly.

His father's face darkened.

'You wouldn't dare show 'em to the coppers!' he said.

Henry thought about one photograph the police had already seen, the one of his father's name on the gravestone. He must remember to keep his mouth shut about that.

'I'm warning you, I have some very unpleasant friends.'

'I'm sure you do. But you won't need to call on them. I won't be handing them to the police. Once you and Maureen are divorced you can have them.'

'Does his gran know Maureen wants to divorce me?'

'She'll be telling her now. We'd like her to leave our home a week from next Saturday. A friend of ours is getting married on that day so we'll all be out of the house. You can pick up her and her bags and take her on the train to London.'

His father picked up the envelope and stuffed it roughly into his pocket. Henry watched him amble off towards the steps. Uncle Bill made a move as if to leave.

'I want to see him get on the train,' said Henry.

They peered over the wall.

'Uncle Bill,' said Henry, spotting a familiar figure, 'you know that man who rescued me last week, the man who said he was Mr Finch's friend?'

'Yes. What of it?'

'He's sitting on the bench down there on one of the platforms reading a newspaper.'

Just then his father appeared on the same platform and the man on the bench raised the paper.

'Looks like he doesn't want to be seen,' Uncle Bill commented.

'That's a coincidence,' said Henry a few minutes later as the next train pulled out, 'he's caught the same train.'

The closer they came to their front door, the sicker Henry felt. Gran would know about the divorce by now.

'Stay there,' said Uncle Bill, 'I'll be back in a minute.'

Henry watched him head for the alley leading to the yards. Five minutes later he was back.

'Your mum's in bed with Molly. Come on.'

'Where are we going?' asked Henry, following him.

'The Plaza. I'm putting some distance between you and your gran. You can speak to her tomorrow after school. I take it you know what's on.'

'*Morning Departure*,' said Henry, running beside him. 'With John Mills.' As soon as he said his name he felt a catch in his throat. Only a few months ago he had believed his father had been like the heroic characters John Mills played.

They turned the corner and headed for one of the queues.

*

'Come in,' said Gran.

It was Monday afternoon. Henry had avoided seeing her in the morning by leaving for school before she had woken up.

'You know, don't you?' she said.

Henry nodded.

'She won't do it, you know. She says she will, but she won't. She'd never shame herself by saying what she's got to say in a court, and your father will never agree to her divorcing him. Don't you worry, he won't break up our family.'

'Do you mean Uncle Bill?'

'Of course I do. Who did you think I meant?'

'My father.'

'Don't be daft. He wants us all back together again. You, me and him.'

Henry noticed that his mother wasn't on the list.

'Molly and the baby are family too, Gran,' said Henry quietly.

'Now you know that ain't true, don't you?' And back came the smile. 'We've had a bit of a chat about that already, haven't we? Which reminds me, how is that little friend of yours? That Grace girl?'

'Very well, Gran. It was a good idea of yours to tell her great-aunt.'

She looked startled. 'How d'you mean?'

'I told Mrs Beaumont what you said and she invited

her great-aunt round for tea so she could meet us all to put her mind at rest. She said she wondered why she hadn't invited her round earlier.'

'That's nice, dear,' his gran said slowly, her face taut.

'And I've told Dad I'm not going to London this week.'

'What!'

'I want to finish my last term at school.'

'But you hate school.'

'Not this year. Mr Finch treats us as if we've got brains.'

'That's all very nice, dear,' said his gran, 'but if your father says you're to go to London, you must, and there's an end to it. He's in charge.'

'So's Mum.'

'I don't think so, dear.'

'But you'll be going back to London.'

'What you talkin' about?'

'Didn't Mum and Uncle Bill tell you?'

Gran shook her head.

'I'm not going anywhere,' she stated firmly, and she folded her arms.

'You are, Gran. Dad's going to pick you up and take you to London on Mrs Morgan's wedding day. You're always complaining about how noisy Molly is. It'll be even noisier once the baby's born. You'll be getting out in the nick of time.'

His gran looked horrified.

'But I can't! Who'd look after me?'

'Dad.'

'But he'll be out working. I'd have to do me own fire and wash me clothes and cook meals. And what about shopping and standing in all them queues? I'm not well enough to do that. There's me legs.'

'I love Molly.'

He didn't know what made him say it. The words just fell from his mouth as if they had been waiting for the right moment to pop out. His grandmother looked shocked.

'You don't mean that.'

'Yeah,' said Henry, surprised, 'yeah, I do. And you said once the baby's born, Mum won't have any time for me.'

'That's right, dear.'

'Which means she won't have much time for Molly, so Molly will need me.'

His grandmother gave a snort.

'What would a young boy like you do with a little girl?'

'I'll read her stories and make her doll's furniture and we'll go down the beach,' said Henry. 'And when she's old enough, I'll take her to the Plaza on a Saturday morning and buy her an ice cream and I'll make sure no one *ever* slaps her face again.'

'Get out!' screamed his grandmother. 'Get out of here!'

And she lunged forward, grabbed the poker and

swung it wildly at him. He moved quickly out of her way and headed for the door. As he closed it behind him he heard the wireless crackle and swoop into full volume.

# 14. Goodbye Gran

GRAN'S MOODS SWUNG FROM SCREAMING AND BANGING ON THE walls to withdrawn silences. Henry's mother ignored her, calmly continuing to cook her meals and do her washing and mending.

Henry and Molly stayed out of the house as much as possible. Molly was having a bridesmaid dress made for her by Mrs Jeffries for Mrs Morgan's wedding. Grace and a niece of Mr Hart's, who was a chocolate girl at the Plaza, were to be bridesmaids too. The dining room table at Mrs Beaumont's house was covered with old clothes and bits of old curtain material, while in the kitchen, gloves and old lace were being bleached in preparation.

Henry's mother meanwhile darned every stocking Gran possessed, sewing new buttons on old dresses and cardigans, and wrapped up her ornaments and hats. Henry felt a mixture of feelings: sadness at her leaving, anger because she had lied to him and impatience because he wanted her gone immediately. Each day she remained seemed to drag slowly.

By the time the summer term started, it was only five days away from the wedding and Pip was almost flying with excitement.

'From next week,' Mr Finch announced, while taking the register, 'Morgan will be known as Hart.'

The other pupils in the form and some of the teachers behaved differently towards Pip now, and he lapped it up. It was as though he had forgiven them without even an apology. Thanks to his performance at the Plaza, Hatton Secondary Modern had gained a reputation for being a musical school, so much so that in one of the morning assemblies the headmaster announced that the following term there would be an additional music teacher. 'And,' he continued, 'this term, the school is to have its first open day, public concert and,' he paused for dramatic effect, 'prize-giving day!'

That break time Mr Finch broke some exciting news to Henry while he and his friends were in the darkroom.

'Mr Barratt wants there to be a display of photographs from the fourth years but he wants you to take ones of them having lessons.' He handed Henry several rolls of film. 'You must treat it like a proper job.'

'Yes, sir. I will, sir. Thank you, sir!'

'I wish I had a job after leaving here,' sighed Jeffries.

'Nearly everyone's been offered apprenticeships or jobs now. Two of the boys in the greyhound racing group have been offered work, one in the stadium and the other working with a dog breeder.'

'Yes, it's good news, isn't it?' said Mr Finch. 'And the girls who did the presentation on weddings have been offered a dressmaking apprenticeship and jobs serving in the clothes department at the new C&A store. Your form is doing very well.'

'And one of the cowboy group's been offered work at a stable,' said Pip.

'Everyone except us has a job or an apprenticeship waiting for them,' said Henry.

'Early days,' said Mr Finch reassuringly.

And then it was Saturday April the twenty-second, the day of the wedding and the day Henry's grandmother was leaving for London.

Henry couldn't remember having seen his mother so confident and so firm with Gran. Once her bags were packed, he and his mother left to get changed for the wedding. She didn't want to be at home when his father arrived to pick up Gran.

Some time later, he suddenly realised that whatever Gran had said and done, she was still his gran and he wanted to say a proper goodbye to her.

He walked briskly along the road, past the Plaza and into their street. For a moment he hovered by the front window, suddenly feeling self-conscious.

'You look smart,' said a woman's voice from behind him. It was their next-door neighbour, Mrs Henson, with a bag of shopping.

Henry reddened. He waited until she had gone indoors before he opened the front door. Stepping into the hall, he was alarmed to see Gran standing on the landing. His mother's bedroom door was wide open and her hand was on the doorknob.

'Gran!' he said suddenly.

She looked startled for a moment and then gave a nervous smile.

'I wanted to ask yer mum somethin'.'

*Liar*. He held his breath and counted to ten.

'She's round at Mrs Beaumont's house,' he said quietly.

'Already? I thought she was havin' a nap. I wondered why she didn't hear me calling.'

'You must be tired out after walking up all those stairs,' he said, struggling to sound sympathetic.

'I am and that's a fact. I only hope I can get down them again.' She took one step and grabbed the banister rail as if steadying herself. 'Oh dear,' she gasped, 'it's me legs.'

'Here, Gran, let me help you.' He leapt up the stairs, held out his arm for her to take and went through the charade of guiding her back to her room.

'Why are you here?' she said, collapsing into her armchair.

By now Henry had a horrible feeling she was up to something, and the thought of her snooping around the house, prying into the rooms upstairs while the house was empty, made him feel uneasy.

'I came to say goodbye and . . .' He hesitated, racking his brains for an idea. 'And I needed to pick up a few things.'

Suddenly she looked alert.

'What things?'

He thought quickly.

'The camera.'

'That's just one thing.'

'And Molly's doll and cot.'

'She don't need them. Why does she want them?'

Henry was now even more suspicious. *Why should that bother her?*

'Mum wanted me to pick them up,' he lied.

'Oh,' she said, but he could see that she was cross.

He forced himself to kiss her cheek before racing up the stairs to his bedroom.

The camera case was still on the shelf in the wardrobe. He slung it round his neck and glanced at the raincoat. He was just thinking that he couldn't bear the thought of wearing anything given to him by her when he remembered that it was his mother and Uncle

Bill who were paying for it. He whipped it off the hanger, slung it on, picked up his Christmas umbrella and made his way to his mother's room. As soon as he stepped inside, he felt like an intruder. Closing the door gently, he placed a chair up against the door handle in case he was disturbed.

He picked up the doll's cot and placed it on the bed, trying to gather his thoughts. *What was it his gran wanted from this room? Was it money?* He headed for the chest of drawers in the alcove by the back window and quietly opened the top left-hand drawer. It was filled with his mother's underwear and stockings and a nightdress. Embarrassed, he hurriedly closed it. Inside the drawer next to it was a large cardboard box containing ration books, packets of snapshots and certificates. *Could she have been looking for Mum's old marriage certificate?* She wouldn't have a hope of finding it because it was already with the police.

He spotted the school certificate his mother had studied so hard for and Uncle Bill's two certificates and a framed wedding photograph. He noticed a neatly folded piece of newspaper. Inside was an article telling the story of a Royal Engineers railwayman who had risked his life by uncoupling a burning truck filled with munitions and had taken it to a water tower to dowse it. The name of the railwayman was Private William Carpenter.

Henry was shocked. For years he had flung the fact that his father was a hero in Uncle Bill's face, and all the time he had been living with one. Hastily he put the contents back in the box. The next drawer was filled with clothing and pieces of material, balls of wool and knitting patterns. In the bottom drawer there was a baby's shawl, nappies and bootees.

He stood in the middle of the room, his mind racing. And then he had an idea. Swiftly, he undid the bag round the doll's mattress, pulled out the tiny mattress, laid flat all the contents from the box inside the mattress cover and spread the baby clothes and shawl on top. He removed the chair from behind the door, slowly eased it open and crept along the landing. Wedged in a little box by the camp bed in his bedroom were Uncle Bill's paperbacks. *Brighton Rock* had been placed on top. He grabbed an armful of them.

He could hear his gran moving around downstairs. His heart beating, he sprinted back to his mother's room. He placed the books inside the mattress cover, did the poppers up, replaced the bottom sheet, the little pillow and doll, tucked the sheet and blanket tightly round them and laid the quilt on top. He put the raincoat on and slung the camera round his neck. He had no idea why he was removing these personal belongings. He just felt uncomfortable at them being in the house when his father entered it.

The picture books Mrs Beaumont had given Molly for Christmas were on a chair by the bed. He placed them on top of the quilt. As he did so, he spotted a pile of tiny books underneath. One he recognised immediately. It was *The Adventures of Peter Rabbit*. He sat on the bed and opened it. And suddenly a memory came back. He was cuddling up to his mother while the wind was beating against the windows and he was laughing at Mr McGregor who was chasing Peter Rabbit with a rake shouting, *Stop, thief!* And he had kept begging his mother to read the same bit over and over again.

Just then he heard footsteps in the hallway.

'Henry,' called his grandmother, 'what are you doing up there?'

'Getting some books for Molly,' he shouted back quickly.

'Books! Why does she want books?'

'Mrs Beaumont's going to read them to her,' he yelled, stuffing the little books under the cot covers. 'Just coming!' He opened the door, hooked the umbrella over his arm, picked up the doll's cot and walked out on to the landing. His gran gasped.

'Why are you wearing that new mac?' she cried.

'To look smart for the wedding,' he said, coming down the stairs, 'and Mrs Beaumont said it's going to rain.'

He was beginning to be as good a liar as his father.

'Take it off!'

'But, Gran, you gave it to me. Why don't you want me to wear it?'

'Why should you be smart for that woman?' she said, looking flustered.

'It's for the wedding guests, Mr Hart's family. That's why I've got the umbrella too.'

And then he had a horrible thought. *She wants to give it to my dad!* He forced himself to smile. 'I'll hang it up as soon as I get back.'

'But we'll be gone by then,' she burst out. And Henry could see by the expression on her face that she realised she had given the game away.

'You hardly wear it anyway,' she said sulkily.

'I'm looking after it, that's why.'

'So don't wear it, then. I'll put it away for when you're older.'

'I am older, Gran,' he said stubbornly. 'Must go now. 'See you in July.'

And before she could stop him, he stepped towards the front door, but it was closed and his arms were full.

'Gran,' he said as nicely as he could, 'could you open the door for me?'

She remained at the foot of the stairs, her arms folded.

'Please,' he added quietly.

She gave a snort, marched angrily towards it and flung it open. As Henry walked out on to the pavement he couldn't help but smile, for in that instant, he was aware that her legs had been miraculously cured of their debilitating weakness.

'Goodbye,' he yelled cheerily over his shoulder. *And good riddance.*

The wedding took place in a small church surrounded by an old graveyard, long wild grass and spring flowers. It was blustery but sunny, so Mrs Morgan was both squinting at the sun and trying to grab her veil as it rose high above her head. But it broke the ice, and Mr Hart's relatives were laughing so much as they clung on to their hats that all formality and nervousness were blown away by the gusts of wind.

Henry took four photographs and everyone hurried back to Mrs Beaumont's house to enjoy the reception before dashing off to their Saturday matinees.

'Mr Hart is going to move into Mrs Beaumont's house after he and Mum come back from their honeymoon on the Isle of Wight,' said Pip, when they arrived. 'So we can still stay here. That's good, isn't it? They're going to have the other attic room.'

Gradually Mrs Beaumont's sitting room was filled with the new Mrs Hart's relatives and friends who all worked in Sternsea cinemas as usherettes, chocolate girls, commissionaires, box-office ladies and projectionists, while Mrs Jeffries and Mrs Beaumont passed round plates of food. In the centre of the sideboard stood the wedding cake made by Mrs Jeffries from everyone's rations.

'Speech!' shouted one of the usherettes from the Savoy.

The manager of the Plaza placed Pip on a chair so that everyone could see him.

'I'm very pleased that Mum's married Mr Hart and he's going to be my dad,' he said, 'and that he's going to move in upstairs because I like it here.'

He was just about to step down when the manager said, 'Just a minute, Philip, I want to add a few words before the toasts begin. Our rewind boy will soon be called up for National Service and the Chief is very happy to offer you the job of rewind boy at the Plaza once you leave school.'

Pip looked as if he had been hit over the head with a frying pan.

'I'm going to be a projectionist!'

'Eventually. But I also want you to have time off to practise at that piano of yours so you can still play for us on Saturday nights.'

The room broke into applause.

'Also, from today, Mrs Hart won't be doing any more cleaning jobs. When she and her new husband come back from their honeymoon, there'll be a brand new usherette's uniform waiting for her.'

Pip's mother looked as though she was about to burst into tears.

'Oh, how lovely!' she whispered.

'And now,' he added, 'will everyone please raise their glasses for the happy couple.'

While the wedding cake was being cut, there was a loud knock at the front door.

'Would you answer that, Henry?' asked Mrs Beaumont. Grace followed him.

'It'll be Great-Aunt Florence,' she said.

He opened the door to a tall smartly dressed middle-aged couple. The woman had a pointed aquiline nose. She was wearing an oatmeal-coloured tweed hat perched sideways on her head and appeared to be carrying a dead fox around her shoulders. The man, who had a brick-red tan, stood erect in a green tweed suit, a bulbous nose sitting above a neatly clipped reddish moustache.

Grace gasped.

'Mother!' she cried. 'Father!'

'What letter?' stormed Grace's father.

'Could we talk about it later? I'm afraid we're a bit at sixes and sevens at the moment,' explained Mrs Beaumont hurriedly. 'As you saw, Grace has been a bridesmaid today and we're in the middle of a wedding reception.'

Mrs Forbes-Ellis glanced round and wrinkled her nose as if she had smelt something disagreeable.

'What wedding? Whose wedding?' demanded Grace's

father. 'I really think we should have been informed, Mrs Beaumont.'

'It's all in the letter,' she said brightly. 'I sent it a fortnight ago.'

'A fortnight ago we were at sea. We did tell you we were returning to this country in the spring.'

'Yes, indeed. Henry, will you show Mr and Mrs Forbes-Ellis to the study?'

Henry was astonished by their coldness. Within seconds of seeing Grace they had waved her off downstairs. If Henry's mother hadn't seen him for a week, let alone several months, she would have flung her arms around him and hugged him. Grace's parents barely looked at her.

Henry indicated the way and went ahead of them. Before he could leave the room, Mr Forbes-Ellis closed the door behind them.

*He hasn't even noticed me. I'm like an invisible servant.* He sat quietly by the fireplace.

'We can't stay long,' Mr Forbes-Ellis snapped. 'I'm being posted elsewhere and we leave next week.'

'Have you spoken to your aunt?' Mrs Beaumont asked carefully.

'No. She indicated that as I hadn't received this so-called letter you keep referring to, I should hear the news from you, Mrs Beaumont.'

'Of course.'

'How long is this wedding reception going to take?' he enquired. 'I must say I find it extraordinary that our daughter should have been allowed to be a bridesmaid, Mrs Beaumont, after her appalling behaviour at yet another school, don't you?'

Mrs Beaumont looked stumped for a moment.

'Not really. Your daughter is a delight,' she said quietly. 'And a joy to teach.'

'We've been looking at more schools,' said Grace's mother, ignoring her.

'And they won't take her,' finished Mr Forbes-Ellis for her. 'Her school reports are a millstone round our necks.'

'We've booked into an hotel on the seafront for the night,' said Mrs Forbes-Ellis. 'Dreadful place. And then we must be off to meet our sons.'

'We'll be calling at her great-aunt's when we leave here to pack Grace's clothes,' added her husband. 'We're off tomorrow and taking her with us.'

'Tomorrow!' gasped Mrs Beaumont.

'There's a school in Scotland. Very disciplinarian. If she refuses to read there, she will be severely punished.'

'Then she'll be punished all the time,' said Mrs Beaumont. 'Please, won't you sit down?'

They hesitated for a moment and then sat stiffly on two chairs.

'The problem your daughter has is not unique. Since I took over her schooling, I have heard of five cases of this very same difficulty with reading.'

'Then there's no hope,' said Mrs Forbes-Ellis.

'There never has been,' said Grace's father. 'I washed my hands of her a long time ago.'

'She has an extraordinary talent,' said Mrs Beaumont.

'Of getting away with not working,' he interrupted. 'Not even trying.'

'Trying won't change the way she sees words,' Mrs Beaumont stated.

'This is serious,' he muttered. 'Maybe some kind of mental institution would be the right place for her.'

'But think of the disgrace,' exclaimed Mrs Forbes-Ellis.

Henry froze. He glanced in desperation at Mrs Beaumont. She had to stop them taking Grace away.

'That won't be necessary,' said Mrs Beaumont steadily. 'I would be delighted to keep tutoring your daughter.'

'Very kind of you,' said Mr Forbes-Ellis brusquely, 'but not to put too fine a point on it, you're not related to us.'

'Does that matter?'

'Of course it matters.' He stood up. 'We'll pick her up in an hour and she can change out of her bridesmaid attire at her great-aunt's. You'll be relieved to have her off your hands, I am sure.'

'On the contrary. Please sit down, Mr Forbes-Ellis. I'd like to tell you what was in the letter.' He gave a sigh and sat down again. 'Your daughter has an extraordinary singing voice. Quite unique. I took it into my hands to take her to London and have her audition for one of the top stage schools in the country. They were so impressed with her that they offered her a place there.'

'A *stage* school! I'm quite sure they offered her a place. And they'll be asking me for a tidy sum to keep her there, I suppose.'

'She's been offered a scholarship.'

'A scholarship?' Mrs Forbes-Ellis repeated.

'That is correct. You won't have to pay a penny. I have a house in London and I would be more than happy to have Grace stay with me while she attends the school.'

'But this is preposterous!' he exclaimed. 'What on earth is going to a stage school going to be useful for? It's not like a finishing school.'

Henry remembered Grace saying that if her father knew she was doing something that made her happy, he would do everything in his power to stop it. Mrs Beaumont, he suspected, knew that too.

'It's very disciplined,' she said. 'She would be learning Dance, Music and, of course, Singing.'

'She's unmarriageable, you know,' stated Grace's father.

'Then perhaps it's a good idea if she learns a profession.'

'Singing?' queried her mother. 'Are you sure? Whenever I've heard her sing she has this funny low-sounding voice.'

'Alto,' said Mrs Beaumont.

'Oh, is it?' she said vaguely.

'No one in my family has ever been in the world of the Music Hall, or Variety or Entertainment of any kind. She's enough of a disgrace to the family as it is. She's going to Scotland and that is the end of the matter. As I said, we'll pick her up in an hour. Tell her she'll be staying overnight with us at the hotel.'

And with that they stood up and looked at Henry. Henry stared back, bewildered.

'The door, Henry,' said Mrs Beaumont quietly.

Henry sprang up and opened it for them.

As soon as they had left, he and Mrs Beaumont stood in the hall and gazed at one another in disbelief.

'Dungheap,' said Henry.

'It certainly is,' she agreed. 'And I'd love a diamond right now.'

'Her great-aunt?' suggested Henry wildly.

'It's worth a try,' and she moved swiftly to the telephone. 'I hope she picks up the receiver before they arrive.'

Henry stared anxiously towards the steps leading up from the kitchen, hoping that Grace wouldn't suddenly appear. He heard her burst out laughing downstairs and Molly giggling.

'Ah, hello, Florence. It's Hettie . . . They've just left . . . Not well, I'm afraid. Not well at all. I'm afraid they've rather made up their minds . . . They're on their way to your flat to pack up her clothes . . . Yes,' said Mrs

Beaumont soberly. 'Brushed it aside . . . No, I haven't told her yet . . . . Yes, of course you must . . . Goodbye.'

'What did she say?' asked Henry.

'Nothing much. She didn't have time. Grace's parents have just rung her doorbell.'

Suddenly Pip flew out of the sitting room.

'Where's Grace?' he said excitedly. 'It's time.'

'Downstairs,' Mrs Beaumont answered quietly.

'We've been rehearsing a concert for Mum and Dad,' he said. 'Can you help us, Henry?'

Just then Jeffries appeared, struggling with two chairs.

Henry was glad of something to do. There weren't enough chairs for everyone, so he and Mrs Beaumont stood at the back attempting to cover their feelings of helplessness and anger. Mr Hart and the new Mrs Hart sat in pride of place at the front.

The setting was the same as it had been for the concert for Grace's great-aunt. They switched on the two tall lamps and indicated that Mrs Beaumont should switch off the main light. Pip sat at the piano and Grace stood beside him.

'We've been rehearsing this in secret,' Grace said. 'It's a little bit of romance!'

They were all love songs and comedy numbers, mostly taken from well-known films, plus the occasional piano solo from Pip. It was after one of these solos, when Grace had begun to sing again, that

Henry heard the knock at the front door. Mrs Beaumont glanced at him and then quietly slipped out. Henry listened to Grace's rich low voice, wondering if he would ever hear it again. He remembered when he had first heard it, how he had thought there was something wrong with it simply because it was different. Now when he listened, it was breathtakingly beautiful.

He heard the front door opening and the murmur of voices. And then there were footsteps coming towards the room. *Surely they were going to let her finish singing!* Miserably he watched the door slowly open, but instead of Grace's parents it was her great-aunt. *So they had sent her to do their dirty work.*

The concert ended with applause and cheers. Mrs Beaumont showed Great-Aunt Florence to the sitting room. Henry paced up and down in the hall, dreading the moment when Grace would have to leave to join her parents. Minutes later Mrs Beaumont appeared in the hall.

'What are we going to do?' Henry asked in despair.

'Well, if we could get hold of a bottle of champagne, we could open it.'

'What do you mean?'

'Grace's great-aunt tore them off a strip,' she said, trying to suppress her laughter. 'She gave them a huge telling off. Not only that, but she sang Grace's praises, told them they didn't deserve such a delightful and talented child, and if they didn't allow Grace to go to stage school she would not only cut them out of her will but she would have a word with all the other aunts of whom it appears there are many and, it turns out, all have a soft spot for Grace.'

'So she can go?' whispered Henry.

'Yes.'

'When are you going to tell her?'

'Oh, I should think now is as good a time as any,' she said nonchalantly.

After they had waved off Mr and Mrs Hart in a car decorated with ribbons, Henry, his mother and Molly made their way home. Uncle Bill had already left for work. Henry noticed his mother was almost laughing and he knew why. No more Gran. She swung Molly's hand while Henry carried the cot and doll.

'We'll have a sitting room all to ourselves,' she said. 'And I'll be able to listen to the wireless. We'll be like royalty.'

It was when they turned the corner into their street that they saw the fire engines.

Henry started running.

'Gran!' he cried.

A fireman held him back. But Henry had managed to get close enough to the front room to see that there was no one inside. There was no furniture either. Not a stick of it. The room had been gutted well before the fire had reached it.

# PART FOUR

## Looking for the Diamond

# 1. A new life

'YOU CAN'T GO INSIDE, MRS CARPENTER,' PROTESTED THE FIREMAN.

'But I've got everything in there! Ration books, birth certificates . . .'

Before Henry could speak, Mrs Henson pushed her way through.

'My Dolly called the fire brigade. Lucky she was 'ere. She smelt the smoke and run round to the Plaza and rung from there.'

'Did you see Henry's gran leave?'

'Course I did. Couldn't miss her with that big lorry, could I? I was glad to see the back of her.' She looked awkwardly at Henry. 'I'm sorry, love, but they would've had to arrest me for murder if she'd stayed much longer.'

'Lorry?' repeated Henry's mother, bewildered.

'For the furniture, Maureen.'

'She took the furniture?'

'Well, yes, love. She explained it was all hers. I thought

that's why you let her stay with you for so long.'

Henry's mother shook her head.

'Not any of it?'

'No.'

'The lying cow! There were these three men in overalls who carried it all out. They looked like they worked for some removal firm. She was very chatty with one of them.'

*I can guess who that was*, thought Henry.

'They took everything?' Henry's mother whispered.

'Oh, yes, wardrobes, chest of drawers . . .'

'With everything inside them?'

'I dunno. I didn't look.'

'Not everything,' interrupted Henry, indicating the cot in his arms.

His mother gave a weak smile.

'That's nice. Pity you didn't get anything else out.'

'I did. I hid them in the mattress. Ration books, baby's clothes, photographs . . .'

'You mean you knew what they'd planned to do?'

'No. I came back to say goodbye to Gran and I found her snooping around on the landing. She was about to go in your room. I hid stuff in Molly's cot. I took as much as I could,' he added lamely.

'Thank you, love,' she said, her voice trembling.

'Mummy *not* cry,' demanded Molly, whose hand was still being held tight.

Henry could see that his sister was scared.

'It's the smoke making your eyes water, isn't it, Mum?'

His mother nodded.

'That's right,' but she couldn't keep up the pretence. She let go of Molly and buried her face in her hands. 'I thought this nightmare was over,' she said tearfully. 'Where am I going to have the baby? Where are we going to sleep tonight?'

'Round the corner,' said a firm voice behind her.

Henry's mother swung round. It was Mrs Beaumont.

'But you won't have any room,' she protested.

'Believe it or not, I do. You and Molly can have the room on the first landing, Henry can go in with the boys and Bill can go in the front attic bedroom.'

'But what if your sons come down?'

'There are such things as camp beds, you know. They can go in the sitting room. They're used to that sort of thing.'

Henry watched Mrs Beaumont go up to a policeman and give him her name and address. The policeman glanced over at them and walked back with her.

'Do you know what caused the fire?' his mother asked.

'Not yet I'm afraid, Mrs Carpenter,' he said gently. 'Is there a Mr Carpenter?'

'Yes. He returned to work for his afternoon shift.'

'May I have a quiet word, constable?'

It was one of the firemen. Henry watched them walk off out of hearing. He observed them, their heads bowed low as the fireman talked and the policeman listened intently, nodding at intervals and taking down notes in a small notebook. When the policeman returned, his manner was less friendly.

'Mrs Carpenter, may I ask where you and your husband have been today?'

'At a wedding and then . . .'

'There are witnesses who can confirm this?' he interrupted.

'Yes,' she replied dully. 'And after the wedding reception we had some tea and then my husband had to run off to the station.'

'So no one would have seen Mr Carpenter from the time he left you to the time he arrived at the station?'

'I've no idea. Why are you asking questions about him?'

'Hang on a minute!' broke in Mrs Henson, who had obviously been eavesdropping. 'I was 'ere and I never set eyes on Mr Carpenter.'

'You could have been indoors when he slipped round the back.'

'Are you suggesting my Bill started the fire?' cried Henry's mother, 'because if you are, it doesn't make sense. Why would he want to do that?'

'To cover the fact that he'd stolen the landlord's furniture. I have just been notified that the firemen managed to put out the fire in time to see that all the contents were missing. There is also evidence that the fire was started deliberately.'

'But some of the furniture belonged to him,' Henry's mother said angrily.

'It's an outrage!' stormed Mrs Henson. '*He* didn't take the furniture. Old Mrs Dodge did. Mrs Carpenter is upset enough as it is without you casting aspersions. And her expectin' and that. You ought to be ashamed of yourself.'

'Here, here,' said Mrs Beaumont.

By now Mrs Henson's face was crimson. 'It's not her you should be talking to. It's that evil old witch.'

'I'm taking Mrs Carpenter home with me,' Mrs Beaumont said to the policeman. 'It's quite obvious she's in shock, as are her children. If you wish to question her further, I suggest you do it there, after I have given her a hot sweet drink.'

And with that, she grasped Molly's hand, took hold of Henry's mother's arm and proceeded to walk away. 'Come on, Henry,' she commanded over her shoulder.

Dazed, Henry followed her, the doll's cot still in his arms.

'It looks a bit like a dormitory now,' said Grace, glancing around Pip and Jeffries' bedroom. They had taken apart one of the beds in the back attic bedroom, manoeuvred it in bits down the stairs, slotted it back together in their room, and put the mattress, sheets and blankets on it. 'Don't you worry,' she added, 'we'll look after you.'

'What your gran did was horrible,' said Jeffries.

'You're right,' said Pip.

Grace placed a little table beside his bed, put the camera on it and hooked his umbrella over the bedhead.

'Thanks,' he mumbled.

They headed down to the kitchen.

Henry paused outside the sitting room door. 'I'll be down in a minute,' he said. 'I just want to see how Mum is.'

His mother was lying with her feet up on the settee, browsing through the contents of the little mattress and cot. She smiled up at him.

'You never said you'd saved the exam certificates and this,' she said, lifting the newspaper cutting.

'Why didn't you tell me Uncle Bill was a hero, Mum?'

'Because you already knew. It happened when you were at your last school. But once your gran moved in, it was as if she rubbed out all your memories.'

'Mrs Henson is right. She is a witch.' He paused. 'I looked inside that Peter Rabbit book and I remembered bits.'

'The lady I used to work for gave it to me after you were born. Your dad threatened to burn it. So I used to read it to you in secret. After his funeral I borrowed the rest of the Beatrix Potter books from the library. Of course, once you could read on your own you read lots more.'

'I was reading books?'

'Don't you remember?'

'No.'

'At school they thought you knew the books off by heart you were so quick. And by the time you were in the top class, you were the best reader in the school. Your gran made you ashamed of reading. Like you were betraying your dad. Then you started pretending you didn't read until you believed it yourself. The funny thing is that soon after that you stopped making friends.'

'Yeah,' said Henry, surprised. 'That's right!'

'I think it was because you were pretending to be someone else so you didn't come across natural. And anyway, Gran preferred it if you didn't have friends. That way she could have you all to herself. She's a bully. Just like her son. There, I've said it.'

'She tried to turn me against Molly,' said Henry.

'I know, love, and it broke my heart.' She took hold of his hand. 'You saved something special for all of us. Uncle Bill's books and certificates, the photographs for me, the doll and cot for Molly, even things for the baby, but you didn't save anything for yourself.'

'I did. I've got the umbrella and the rucksack you gave me for Christmas. They're upstairs with the camera.'

'Oh, good,' she said.

'And the raincoat.'

They stared silently at one another. Henry noticed his mother's mouth twitch and then suddenly they were both laughing.

'She must have been so cross when she opened that drawer and found an empty box,' he choked. 'She didn't even want me to take Molly's cot, and it's only one of Mr Jenkins' fruit boxes.'

'Oh, stop!' cried his mother, tears streaming down her face.

'And she had no idea what I'd hidden underneath the doll. She even opened the door for me in the end.'

'She didn't, did she?'

Henry nodded his head vigorously, only able to squeak out a *yes*.

His mother collapsed back against the cushions on the settee, weeping. The sight of his mother helpless with laughter was so infectious that it made him laugh all over again, which set her off.

'No more!' she begged, 'I'm hurting!' which only made it worse.

Mrs Beaumont and Mrs Jeffries peered into the room, puzzled. Henry's mother struggled to explain but every time one indecipherable word exploded from her mouth, she and Henry collapsed again.

Suddenly Molly appeared. She stood still for a moment watching them and then gave an enormous smile. Running across the room, she flung her small arms round

Henry's mother and laid her head on her enormous belly. Henry's mother held on to her, still shaking.

'Mummy's happy,' said Molly. 'Mummy's not frighted any more.'


Henry sat on the stairs below the second landing in his pyjamas and a jersey. It was gone midnight. Mrs Beaumont was in the sitting room waiting for Uncle Bill to arrive. He heard a faint tap at the front door. Slowly he rose, crept down to the small landing below and stood outside the room where his mother and Molly were sleeping.

'She's fine,' he heard Mrs Beaumont whisper. 'They're all fine.'

'I don't know what to say,' his stepfather murmured. 'The police say it was deliberate. They were waiting for me when I finished work. I don't understand it, Mrs Beaumont. I gave her a home for years, fed and clothed her, but nothing I did made any difference. I wasn't her son and that was a crime.'

'Good job you weren't.'

'But how could she take a home away from Maureen and the kids?'

'I doubt she did it on her own. I can guess the identity of one of the three removal men.'

'Revenge,' Henry heard him mutter, 'because he couldn't have Henry to bully.'

'Come downstairs. It's warm and I've a thermos of soup waiting for you.' Henry couldn't make out what they said next and then he heard Mrs Beaumont say, 'You can stay for as long as you like.'

Henry woke to the sound of rain falling. Pip and Jeffries' beds were empty. He yawned, rubbed his eyes and hauled himself out of bed. As he padded out on to the landing and down the stairs he could hear his mother's voice in the kitchen. She sounded happy. He was about to join her when he realised someone was typing in the sitting room.

He found Jeffries hunched over Mrs Beaumont's black typewriter, pounding the metal keyboard with painstaking slowness.

'Blast!' he muttered. He swung the carriage back and attempted to type another letter over the one he had obviously not meant to type. 'It's quicker to write by hand,' he said, and he threw his hands upwards in mock despair.

'What are you writing?' Henry asked.

'A film script. That is, I'm trying but I'm not getting very far.'

Henry noticed that he was sitting on a copy of the *Sternsea Evening News*.

'What's on?' he asked.

Jeffries pulled it out from beneath him and unfolded it.

'Another of those quivering passion films at the Odeon, two romantic ones at the Savoy . . .'

'What about crime?'

'Not bad. *Appointment with Danger* at the Plaza, *Scene of the Crime* at three other cinemas, *Frankenstein Meets the Wolf Man,* with *Eyes of the Underworld*. But my mother and yours want us all to go to a film they've chosen. It's Pip and Grace's choice too.'

'Oh,' said Henry, fearing the worst.

'It's at the Troxy, which means it's not far for your mother to walk.'

'What is it?'

Jeffries cleared his throat awkwardly and raised the newspaper.

'Johnny's most savage spectacle of jungle thrills! Johnny Weissmuller as Jungle Jim in *The Lost Tribe*.'

He showed Henry the two pictures beside the announcement. One showed a man wrestling with a leopard, the other showed him carrying a woman in his arms.

'It's got animals in it, you see. Pip's missing his mother, so he needs something a bit soppy. And mine doesn't want to see anything that's going to give her nightmares. Most of the other films have got murders in them.'

'It's going to be one of those films where a woman keeps falling over every time she's running away from something dangerous, isn't it?'

'I'm afraid so,' sighed Jeffries.

That afternoon Henry sat with his mother, Mrs Jeffries and his friends in a packed and noisy Troxy, while Molly stayed behind with Mrs Beaumont. Throughout the film he kept glancing at his mother to make sure she was all right. She was smiling and seemed relaxed so he was taken by surprise when she rose to leave before the Laurel and Hardy comedy.

'Don't look so worried, love,' she whispered, 'I'm just a bit tired, that's all.'

In spite of having laughed at Laurel and Hardy's antics, Henry still felt a sense of unease when he left the Troxy and passed the road leading to the railway bridge. His friends stayed close, as if forming a protective ring. Without saying a word, they crossed the road and headed for the black shell with its boarded-up front door that had once been his home. On either side of it, lights from the other houses spilled out on to the pavements, giving it a sinister air. He peered into the front room where his gran had sat day after day. Above the empty mantelpiece was a mirror-shaped space in the grubby wallpaper. Even the light bulb in the light fitting had been taken. The others followed him silently down the alley alongside Number 18 and along the back of the yards. Henry opened the door into his yard and stood motionless in the dusk, staring through the window into the empty kitchen. It was as if no one had ever lived there. He peered into the air-raid shelter. Everything was there, untouched, including the wheelbarrow, the piles of misshapen pieces of wood he had salvaged from crumbling bombsites and the beach, and the wood delivered by the railway. He gathered some of it up and the others started to help him.

'Gotcha!' yelled an angry voice, and before Henry could swing round, a strong hand grabbed him firmly by the shirt and dragged him outside. Grace screamed. Henry looked up to find himself staring up at a tall burly man, a rough cap pulled over his balding head.

'Mr Henson,' gasped Henry with relief.

'Henry! I thought you was a looter. You'd never believe how many people have been trying to break into the house.'

'I wanted to take the wood I collected to Mrs Beaumont's house,' he explained.

'I'll give you a hand.'

Between them they filled one wheelbarrow and carried a long plank into the alley behind the yards.

'Where are we going to put it all?' asked Jeffries. 'Mrs Beaumont doesn't have a shed or an air-raid shelter.'

'And you mustn't put it in the dance studio,' protested Grace.

'In the basement,' said Pip. 'There's a place for coal there.'

Once they reached Mrs Beaumont's overgrown front garden, Mr Henson helped them stack the wood by the steps leading to the basement.

'I'll take the wheelbarrow back and load it up again,' he said. 'One more trip and that should do it.'

'I have a feeling we won't be able to make a second journey.'

'Of course, it's Sunday,' commented Mr Henson. 'Bath night.'

They all nodded.

'Don't you worry, I'll bring it round 'ere for you.'

It was late and they all had to get indoors for their baths. After they had said their goodbyes to Grace in the porch and opened the hall door, Henry heard a loud cry from his mother's bedroom.

'Mum!' he yelled and made for the stairs.

'Henry!'

He swung round. Uncle Bill was standing in the sitting room doorway.

'Wait down here,' he said. 'If you want to go to the toilet, you must use the one outside in the studio.'

'Why? What's happening?'

'The district nurse is up there. Your mother's in labour.'

Molly was wrapped up, her head on a pillow on the settee. Mrs Beaumont was sitting beside her, stroking her hair. Henry could see Molly had been crying. Her eyelids were fluttering as if she was fighting sleep but losing the battle.

'She didn't understand why she wasn't allowed to go upstairs,' Mrs Beaumont whispered. 'She thought your mother was ill and she wanted to make her better.'

'But she was only with us a little while ago. She never said anything,' he exclaimed.

'It all started very quickly, that's why she had to leave the cinema.'

'Where's everyone else?' he asked.

'In the kitchen. They didn't want to disturb your mother by going upstairs.'

He glanced across at Uncle Bill. He was sitting on the edge of a chair, staring anxiously down at the floor, his fists clenched. Suddenly his head shot up and he sprang to his feet. A baby was crying. He bolted out of the room and Henry quickly followed him. Together they stood helplessly at the foot of the stairs. After what seemed like hours, the district nurse appeared on the landing.

'A little boy,' she said matter of factly.

'And Maureen?' asked Uncle Bill.

'Mother and baby are doing well. But she's not to get out of bed for three days. She's to have meals brought up to her. She must have all the rest she can get.'

'There are two other women in the house,' said Mrs Jeffries from the kitchen steps. Jeffries was standing excitedly behind her.

'Three when Mrs Hart returns from her honeymoon. We'll all make sure she stays in bed.'

'I'm glad to hear that,' the nurse said brusquely. 'This fire business is shocking, I know, but I'm relieved she can be somewhere where she can be looked after properly.' And she scowled at Uncle Bill as if he was the cause of all his wife's problems.

By now Pip and Mrs Beaumont had joined them in the hall. Henry's stepfather began to walk up the stairs. The nurse pursed her lips.

'Two at a time is plenty,' she said. 'And a cup of tea, toast and scrambled egg wouldn't go amiss for the new mother,' and with that she turned on the heels of her heavy lace-up shoes and strode back into the bedroom.

Henry followed Uncle Bill.

His mother was sitting propped up against plumped-up pillows, wearing a cardigan over her nightdress, her hair damp and tangled. She looked tired but as pretty as a film star, thought Henry. He glanced at the bundle in her arms and recognised the shawl he had rescued. He and Uncle Bill leaned towards it together. She beamed up at them.

'I can't let go of him,' she said.

She moved the shawl to one side. A tiny red-faced baby was lying there asleep.

'He's out for the count,' observed Henry.

'You make him sound as if he's just done twenty rounds in a boxing ring!' said his mother. She patted the side of the bed. 'Come and sit beside me, both of you.'

From the other side of the room Henry heard tut-tuttings from the nurse.

'My three men,' she said, gazing happily at them. The baby gave a sudden snuffling noise as if taking a breath in his sleep.

*This is my brother*, thought Henry, and he felt a catch in his throat.

'Oh, Bill,' laughed his mother.

'I'm sorry, I can't help it,' he said, tears running down his face.

Henry was startled. He had never seen a man cry.

'Do you want to hold him, Bill?' she asked.

Before the nurse could protest, she handed him over. The baby looked even tinier in his stepfather's arms and Henry knew immediately what he had to do.

'Wait there,' he said and ran for the door.

He heard his mother laugh.

'I wasn't planning on going anywhere just yet, love.'

Alone in his bedroom Henry stood still for a moment, trembling. He dragged his arm roughly across his blurred eyes, pulled the camera out of its case and headed for the landing.

'Don't pose,' he said in his mother's bedroom. 'Ignore me,' and he quickly took a photograph of the scowling district nurse. As his mother laughed at her outraged face, Henry took one of her.

An hour later, Molly woke up with a start.

'Mummy!' she cried.

Mrs Beaumont pulled her gently on to her lap.

'Mummy's asleep. And so is your baby brother. Would you like to see him?'

She nodded.

'You have to be very quiet, though,' and she pressed a finger to her lips.

Henry watched them walk hand in hand out of the sitting room. Pip and Jeffries had already gone to bed, but he had been too excited to sleep. He was sitting with a mug of cocoa warming his hands.

When they returned, Mrs Beaumont sat Molly back on the settee.

'Would you like to sleep with me tonight?'

'And Dolly?'

'Of course. There's somebody else who can come too,' she said and she produced a parcel from behind an armchair.

'This is for you. It's a special present so you can remember the day your little brother was born.'

Molly tore off the wrapping and gave a squeal. Inside was a floppy dog.

'He's a rather special dog,' said Mrs Beaumont. 'He has a secret. Look.'

She turned it over, undid some buttons hidden under a flap of fur and put her hand inside. 'It's for you to keep your nightdress inside. Do you like him?'

Molly hugged the dog tightly, nodding.

Mrs Beaumont turned to Henry.

'You have a present too,' she said, 'so you won't forget today either. It's in a leather case upstairs. And this goes with it,' and she held out half a dozen new boxes of film.

Henry couldn't believe it.

'The camera?' he whispered.

She nodded, smiling.

'Thank you,' and he quickly stuck his nose in his cup, his hands shaking with excitement.

'Drink up,' she said. 'We could all do with some sleep.'

Henry didn't want to go to the cinema that week. He was mesmerised by baby Laurence. He and Molly, his mother and stepfather settled in very quickly at Mrs Beaumont's house. It was as though the baby glued them all together. Within a week, Henry found that he had begun to forget the misery his father and grandmother had brought to their lives, and by the following Saturday, he and his friends were back to the familiar routine of looking through the *Sternsea Evening News*.

'*She Wore a Yellow Ribbon*,' Jeffries announced.

'Sounds like a girl's film,' said Henry.

'And what's a girl's film?' Grace said hotly.

'Oh, no, it isn't,' Jeffries continued. 'It's got John Wayne and Indians in it.'

'What's with it?' asked Henry.

'Er, *Bride for Sale*, but it says it's a comedy.'

'M'm,' said Henry doubtfully. 'What else?'

'There's a musical at three cinemas,' said Jeffries. 'Irving Berlin's *On the Avenue*. Oh.'

'Oh, what?' said Grace. 'The film with it is an A?'

'No. Another U. It's called *Mother Knows Best* – a romantic frolic.'

'I don't know why you're all staring at me,' Grace protested. 'I'm not interested in a romantic frolic either.'

'That's a relief,' said Jeffries and he returned to the paper.

'What have they got there from Monday?' asked Pip.

'*Rebecca*.'

'*Rebecca!*' exclaimed Mrs Beaumont, who up till then had been quietly scrubbing potatoes with her back to them. 'I'd love to see that again.'

'"What was the dark intangible shadow that hung over these two human lives?"' read Jeffries dramatically.

'It's got Laurence Olivier in it,' she added.

'Is it a love story?' asked Jeffries.

'It's more of a thriller really. Very atmospheric. There's this sinister housekeeper called Mrs Danvers . . .' She stopped. 'I don't want to tell you too much. It'll spoil it. I bet it has a western with it.'

'It has!' said Jeffries. '*Wagon Wheels Westward*.'

'Oh, let's go and see that with *Rebecca*,' said Grace.

'Hands up for yes,' said Jeffries.

They all raised their arms.

'Carried unanimously.'

It was decided to see *She Wore a Yellow Ribbon* the next day and *Rebecca* on Wednesday.

'And I am going to treat you all to *The Happiest Days of Your Life* on Friday,' said Mrs Beaumont as Mrs Jeffries walked into the kitchen. 'It's all about a girls' boarding school which is billeted on a boys' boarding school and there are some very funny people in it. You too, Natasha.'

'Hettie, I really can't allow you . . .' Mrs Jeffries protested.

'And then Maureen and Bill can have the house to themselves for one evening.'

Mrs Jeffries smiled.

'Well, if you put it like that . . .'

'I do.'

And so it was settled.

On Sunday evening, after *She Wore a Yellow Ribbon*, Henry walked out of the cinema in a daze, his head filled with earth-red rocks jagged against the skyline, lines of soldiers on horseback, a dead postmaster slumped across the doorway of a stagecoach, deserts and buffaloes, a lone cavalry man trapped by a small ravine and his heroic leap over it as he fled from Indians. Just staring up at the huge landscape on the screen had made Henry feel he had more room to breathe. He was remembering the tall drawling John Wayne, his black silhouette on horseback against a fiery orange sky, when he heard Mrs Beaumont say, 'Not too soppily romantic, then?'

'A bit, but the filming was . . . *spectacular*!'

'What about you, Roger?'

'I liked it. But it wasn't as good as *Fort Apache*.'

Grace groaned.

'You're too fussy,' she said, giving him a playful punch.

*Rebecca* couldn't have been more different. It was set in Manderley, a huge house in Cornwall and everyone spoke in posh clipped English accents. With its vast rooms and sudden shafts of light flooding the long dark corridors, it was like a foreign country to Henry, a world where one of the many servants would light a blazing fire in a massive fireplace in the morning room and light another one later in the afternoon room. And everywhere there were signs of the mysterious Rebecca, who had drowned and had been worshipped by the sinister housekeeper, Mrs Danvers.

'I'd tell that Mrs Danvers to take a running jump,' he whispered to Jeffries, when she tried to persuade the new wife of Rebecca's husband to throw herself out of a window.

'She's the best thing in it,' said Jeffries thoughtfully.

'Yeah,' agreed Henry. He gazed up at the actress playing Mrs Danvers, standing upright in her black dress, watchful, silent and unsmiling, as the ceiling-high curtains billowed violently beside the towering windows, the sea crashing on the cliffs below.

On Friday, Grace's Great-Aunt Florence came with

them to see *The Happiest Days of Your Life*, and as they stepped outside the cinema after seeing it into a deluge of torrential rain, they were still laughing.

'What about that bit where the boys ran into the dormitory and had a pillow fight with the girls,' Grace said.

'And there were feathers flying everywhere,' Pip added.

'I liked the scene when the caretaker and his assistant had to keep changing the lacrosse net to rugby posts and then back again all the time,' said Jeffries.

'Call me sausage!' Great-Aunt Florence sang out, pretending to be the gawky sports teacher, and she gave Grace a hug.

'I haven't enjoyed anything so much for ages,' said Mrs Jeffries. 'That look on the Math's teacher's face when she gushed all over him and told him how much she had enjoyed censoring the pupils' letters with him!'

Once they reached Mrs Beaumont's house, they said their goodbyes to Grace and her great-aunt, ran up the steps past the storm door and left their umbrellas dripping all over the porch floor. Mrs Beaumont closed the storm door and pushed open the hall door. Whispering and attempting to smother their laughter, they crept down to the kitchen so that they wouldn't wake Molly or the baby.

Uncle Bill was in the kitchen, reading.

'Maureen's just giving Laurence a feed,' he said.

Henry still couldn't get used to a baby being called

Laurence. It seemed too big a name for someone so small. His mother had named him after the actor Laurence Olivier. But Henry had already begun calling him Larry.

'Good film?' asked Uncle Bill.

'Wonderful!' chorused Mrs Beaumont and Mrs Jeffries.

'You and Maureen must see it,' added Mrs Beaumont. She turned to Henry and the others. 'Let's go again tomorrow night. The audience were laughing so much in places that I missed bits. What do you say? On me, of course.'

Henry grinned. This was like Christmas.

'We'll do some jobs for you,' said Jeffries.

'I can't come,' said Pip. 'I'm playing the piano at the Plaza.'

'You can come with me and Mrs Carpenter if they show it again,' said Uncle Bill. And then he frowned. 'Although I suppose I can't do that till after the . . .'

And he stopped. *After the divorce*, thought Henry, which was going to be difficult because the police still hadn't been able to find the whereabouts of his grandmother. And wherever she was living, that's where his dad would be.

'I'll come with you, Pip,' said Mrs Beaumont. 'I don't think I'll mind seeing it a third or even a fourth time. It's so nice to see a film that makes you feel happy. Now, let's get the kettle on.' There was a loud knocking from upstairs. 'Would one of you boys answer that? It'll be Grace. She's probably forgotten something.'

Henry shot up the steps to the hall and flung open the door to the porch. He was still smiling over one of the scenes in *The Happiest Days of Your Life* when he unlocked the storm door.

But it wasn't Grace. Standing outside on the steps were two men in raincoats and sodden hats.

'We're police officers,' said one of the men. 'We've come to speak to your mother and Mrs Jeffries.'

## 2. Digging up the truth

'HENRY!'

Mrs Beaumont had come up to see what was happening. Henry was staring speechless at the policemen.

'Yes, Mrs Beaumont?' he said, dazed.

'Show these gentlemen into the sitting room. I'll close the storm door. It's like Noah's Flood out there.'

Although her voice was light, Henry could tell she was worried.

The policemen hung their dripping raincoats and hats on the pegs in the porch.

'I'm Detective Constable Blakely and this is Detective Constable Adams,' said the older man.

Henry recognised both of them. Detective Constable Blakely was the man who had chatted to him at the police station the day his mother was interviewed, but he couldn't remember where he had seen the other detective.

'Is it about the fire?' Henry asked.

'It's about quite a few matters,' said DC Blakely. He glanced at Mrs Beaumont. 'Some tea might be in order,' he added quietly.

They gathered in the sitting room. Uncle Bill and his mother sat on the settee, clutching hands, Mrs Jeffries sat beside them with Jeffries perched on the arm next to her.

The policemen sat in the armchairs, while Henry sat cross-legged on the floor.

'Please stay,' begged Mrs Jeffries as Mrs Beaumont made to leave.

She sat down, giving Mrs Jeffries and Henry's mother a reassuring look. It was then that Detective Constable Blakely spoke.

'It might be wise if the boys left the room.'

'I want to know what's going on,' Henry protested.

'I think Henry's had enough secrets kept from him,' said Uncle Bill. 'I'd like him to stay. Maureen?'

She nodded.

'And I'd like Roger to stay too,' said Mrs Jeffries.

The policemen looked at one another uneasily. DC Blakely cleared his throat.

'What we have to tell you will come as a great shock. We'll start with the photographs.'

'Photographs?' interrupted Henry's mother. 'But we only showed you one. The gravestone.'

'We're talking about the ones taken in the warehouse with the suitcases of petrol coupons stored in it.'

Henry's mother gasped.

'How do you know about them?'

'Yes. And how did you get hold of them?' said Mrs Beaumont.

'You know about them, Mrs Beaumont?' asked DC Blakely slowly.

'Yes. And I have the negatives.'

'A concerned member of the public brought them to our attention. He managed to enlarge certain areas for us to help with identification . . .'

'Mr Finch!' blurted out Henry. 'That's why the darkroom still felt warm when I returned for the negatives. He must have looked at my prints after I'd gone and spent all night making new ones. He was the one who touched the enlarger. Not me!'

'We are not at liberty to say who this member of the public might be. I would also like to point out, madam, that withholding evidence from the police is a very serious matter.'

'I intended to show them to you at a later date,' said Mrs Beaumont, 'which is why I took details of the address of the warehouse from the man who took the photographs.'

DC Blakely was immediately alert.

'You mean Henry didn't take the photographs?'

'No. A friend of my younger son did, a professional

photographer called Jim MacTavish. What Henry did was to have a young man called Charlie tail his father up to London, where Mr MacTavish was waiting for him at Waterloo Station. After being given the nod by Charlie as to which man he needed to follow, he did so, hid in a warehouse and took the photographs. He then hared back to Waterloo, took the milk train down to Hatton Station and delivered the rucksack with the camera in it to me. The rest you know.'

'I don't understand,' said Mrs Jeffries.

'We didn't tell you everything,' said Henry's mother, turning to Mrs Jeffries.

'We thought the less people knew about it, the better,' added Uncle Bill.

'You see, my husband not only refused to divorce me but said that if I didn't let Henry go to London, he would move back in with me and have Molly and the baby adopted.'

'Oh, Maureen!' cried Mrs Jeffries. 'That's awful!'

'I suspected he wanted Henry to get involved in something criminal,' said Uncle Bill, 'where his face wouldn't be recognised.'

'On that we agree,' said DC Adams, 'which is why this member of the public contacted us. He too was concerned that your son was mixing with some very shady characters. And for what Mr Dodge had planned, he did need an unknown face. And quickly. It's the end of petrol rationing this May. No one will need to break the law and buy extra coupons after then.'

'Of course!' exclaimed Mrs Beaumont.

'We suspect that a gang, led by our Mr Dodge, needed Henry to be the front man, selling the coupons, though in this case, forged coupons. It's a lucrative business. These people can get as much as forty guineas for a thousand of them.'

'But why do you want to speak to me?' Mrs Jeffries interrupted. And then her face fell. 'Oh, my goodness! You don't think my son is caught up in this too, do you?'

'No.'

'Then why?'

'We'll be coming to that, Mrs Jeffries,' he answered gently. He looked back at Henry's mother. 'As soon as we saw these photographs we sent them to the Metropolitan Police. Not long afterwards, you visited the police station with the photograph of your husband's gravestone. When we spotted the name Dodge, we were immediately alerted because we were led to believe that the other photographs which were brought to us . . .'

'By Mr Finch,' added Henry.

'Had been taken by a Master Henry Dodge.'

'That's why you were talking to me. Because you wanted information from me.'

'That is correct.'

'And we grew more suspicious when you didn't

mention the other photographs,' said DC Adams, 'which is why we had you followed.'

'You're the man who called out my name the night my dad tried to take me to London!' Henry exclaimed, suddenly remembering where he had seen him.

'We thought you might lead us to the gang.' He turned back to Henry's mother. 'Do you remember we asked you to bring in your first marriage certificate?'

'Yes.'

'There was a very good reason for that.' He paused. 'This is going to be difficult for you, Mrs Carpenter. You see, like us, when the police officers at the Met saw the three photographs, they recognised the machine in the background as one used for forging petrol coupons. But what really got them interested was the man Mr Dodge was seen talking to. In fact the Met have been keeping an eye on him for some time because they know he's involved in money forging with a criminal set in the Netherlands. And they would love to know where that warehouse is,' he added, glancing at Mrs Beaumont. 'But his brother is also well known to the police. He specialises in forgeries of a different nature – that of legal documents, which is why we sent your marriage certificate to London for their experts to examine.'

'Oh, no!' she cried.

'And it *is* a forgery, Mrs Carpenter. You were never at any time married to a Mr Alfred Dodge. We suspect this wasn't the first time, and that he was married to someone else already. Can you tell me where this ceremony took place? I doubt it was at a Town Hall.'

'No,' she whispered. 'It was an office.'

'I'm so sorry but . . .'

By now Henry's ears had begun to fill up and he felt sick. He didn't hear what else the detective said but it didn't matter because he could guess.

'You mean,' he heard his mother say, 'you mean I was an unmarried mother!'

'Until you married Mr Carpenter, yes.'

She turned to his stepfather.

'Oh, Bill, how can I ever look you in the face again?'

But he was smiling.

'Don't you see, Maureen? You're not a bigamist. And you'll never have to be a divorcee. We're legally married. That's right, isn't it, Detective Constable?'

'That is correct.'

Henry sat with his head bowed while the room began to swim around him. *But I'm illegitimate.*

Something in the manner of DC Adam's voice pulled him up short. He had turned his attention to Mrs Jeffries.

'I'm afraid I have some more distressing news which concerns you,' he was saying.

Mrs Jeffries looked shocked. She sprang to her feet. 'It's about my husband, isn't it? Has he been seen?'

The detective fell silent.

Mrs Beaumont beckoned her over to sit next to her.

'I'm sorry,' said Mrs Jeffries, looking flustered, 'I interrupted you. Please go on.'

'We obtained permission to exhume the body of this Walter Briggs, the man who was buried as Mr Dodge,' he said.

'But what has that to do with me?' she asked, bewildered.

The atmosphere in the room had become chilled. Henry couldn't take his eyes off the detective.

'Because there have been so many sightings of your husband,' he began.

'All lies,' she said.

'Yes. We know that now.'

She stared at him.

'What do you mean?'

'As I said, because of these sightings, the Army kept his dental records.'

No one moved.

'I'm sorry to have to tell you this, Mrs Jeffries, but we can now confirm, from the dental examination carried out on the man we exhumed, that the deceased was not Walter Briggs but your husband, Private Jeffries.'

'No!' shrieked Mrs Jeffries. 'No! No! No!'

'We knew he wasn't a deserter,' yelled Jeffries. 'We knew! I want all those people who threw us out into the streets to know that now!'

'He's not coming back!' cried his mother. 'He's not coming back! I was at his funeral and I didn't know it! I didn't know!'

Mrs Beaumont threw her arms around her.

'I'm afraid there's more,' the detective said gravely. He turned back to Henry's mother, who was staring, eyes glazed, at Mrs Jeffries. 'Mr Alfred Dodge never reported back to his unit once his memory came back. And never at any time did he meet any medical staff.'

'He's a deserter,' Henry said quietly. 'I'm the son of a deserter.'

No one would want to live under the same roof as him now. No one would go anywhere near him except to call him names. No one would give him a job. Living with his mother would only remind her that he was illegitimate, and Molly and Larry would spend the rest of their lives being jeered at or being given the cold shoulder. He leapt up and fled from the room. His mother called out to him. Ignoring her, he flung open the two front doors and stepped out into the driving rain.

As soon as his feet hit the flooded pavement he began to run. He had to get away from all of them. He never wanted to see Mrs Beaumont again. He never wanted to hear her go on about looking for the diamond in the dungheap. It was all right for her. For some people there weren't any diamonds. Sometimes it was all dung. It was almost as if he was being punished for all the years he had avoided Pip and Jeffries. He wanted to be free of all this pain. He wanted to be dead.

He took the side streets in case he was followed, headed for the road where Jeffries and his mother used to live, and stumbled across the bombed houses, past the council garden built on ruins in Disraeli Road and towards the common. He didn't care about the rain. He just wanted peace and he knew there was only one place he would find it. He pushed himself on and on, ignoring the pain in his chest. Beyond him was the fairground, but the front was deserted. The rain had swept all of Sternsea's inhabitants and visitors inside. He drove himself towards the cracked pavement and on to the beach. Gasping for breath, he stared out at the sea.

The sound of pebbles moving behind him startled him and he swung round. Standing there, as soaked as Henry, was Uncle Bill.

'Go away!' Henry shouted. 'Leave me alone!'

'I've come to take you home,' yelled his stepfather, the wind and rain half drowning his voice.

'We don't have one. My father burnt it down. Remember?'

'It's where your family is. That's home.'

'I don't have a family. Molly and Larry won't want a brother who's a bastard. It's better if I'm dead! If I live with them they'll be tarred with the same brush.'

'Those are your gran's words, not mine.'

'I'm rubbish. That's what I am. Like father, like son.'

'That's not true!'

'Mr Jenkins threw me out because I was friends with Jeffries. If he'd known what I was, he would never have given me a job in the first place.'

'That's his loss.'

'Words! Words! Words!' yelled Henry. 'They won't change anything.'

'All right then, let's look at *like father, like son*. What fathering have you had from your dad? Precious little when he was around, except when he was drunk, and that was the sort of fathering you didn't need. From the moment I met your mum I wanted to marry her and be a dad to you. I wanted to adopt you. Remember? I didn't just love *her*. If anyone's fathered you, it's been me. *I'm* your father. Forget all about the blood business.'

'But Mum won't want to know me now she knows I'm *born on the wrong side of the blanket*,' Henry spat out.

'Your mother's changed. A year ago, the very thought of being a divorcee would have finished her. Now she has a friend who was an unmarried mother and one she thought was the wife of a deserter. And do you think those friends won't want to have anything more to do with you now? Do you?'

'I'm not listening to this!' And he pressed his hands to his ears.

'And she loves you.'

Henry turned his back on him and walked away. His stepfather grabbed his shoulder and swung him round.

'She was terrified of your dad. She couldn't have stood up to him before. But she has now. And she did it with your help. She fought back. And he's a man who fights dirty.'

'But don't you see, that makes me dirty too.'

'You're not just *his* son. You're your mother's son too. You have her brain for a start, and I'm proud of you. I'm sticking by you, no matter what. And I still want to adopt you.'

'Can't you see? It's better for everyone if I'm not around any more. It's better if I'm dead.'

By now the wind was growing stronger so that the force of the rain was like a whiplash across his face.

'How do you think your mother would feel?' said his stepfather, gripping him by the arms. 'How do you think Molly would feel if the brother she worships left her for ever? And what about me, Henry? How do you think I'd feel? I want to watch you grow up. I want to be able to walk into a cinema one day and see your name on the credits.'

'Molly and Larry are your children. I'm not,' Henry snapped and he struck out determinedly for the sea.

The next thing he knew, Uncle Bill gripped him from

behind and hurled him back on to the shingle. Henry leapt to his feet and swung wildly at him, but he caught Henry by the wrist and placed his other hand on Henry's forehead, standing calmly like a rock while Henry thrashed around waving his arms and fists, unable to reach him.

When Henry tried to break away and dash towards the sea, Uncle Bill threw him back on to the beach, and as fast as Henry struggled to his feet and started running, he felt his hands dragging him back again and again and again.

After a while he began to stumble with fatigue. Reeling with exhaustion, he glared angrily at his stepfather, who stared back at him, an immovable mountain. And then it hit him. This man he had called Uncle Bill for five years was fighting for his life. Suddenly he began to sob, like he had done after seeing *The Bicycle Thieves,* only this time he was crying because he realised that for years he had had the chance of having a father and he had lost out because of his grandmother's jealousy.

'It's too late!' he cried out.

'No, it's not,' yelled his stepfather, 'we've got years.' And he heard the catch in his throat. 'I'll be your dad till the day I die.'

Henry had no idea who stepped forward first. In his stupor all he was aware of was the two of them hugging each other fiercely, and of the rain drumming mercilessly on their sodden clothes and the crashing of the sea.

## 3. Shedding an old skin

A POLICE CAR WAS WAITING FOR THEM BY A DESERTED candyfloss stall. DC Blakely opened the back door and Uncle Bill gently pushed Henry in. The hammering from the rain on the car roof was deafening. Henry leaned back, staring vacantly out of the window while his body shook with the cold and his face burned.

When they reached Mrs Beaumont's house, Henry dragged himself up the steps. He listened out for voices in the hall but there was only silence. His mother was waiting for them in the kitchen, pyjamas draped in front of the range. She put her arms round him and held him.

'Don't you ever go scaring me like that again,' she said softly.

Shivering violently he somehow managed to get undressed and into bed upstairs where he lay clinging to a hot-water bottle.

Hours later he woke up sweating, his pyjamas and

sheets sticking to his skin. He was vaguely aware of a cup being held to his lips and his temperature being taken by Mrs Beaumont.

'Your mother's feeding the baby,' she whispered.

The next morning when he opened his eyes there was a white-haired man talking to his mother in the doorway and he heard the word influenza and his mother crying, and then he fell asleep again.

The days drifted one into the other. People came and went with towels, stripping the bed of the wet sheets and replacing them with dry ones, and his bouts of shivering followed by periods of sweating continued. He heard talk of freak weather from outside which seemed to mirror his state, one moment spring-like, the next a return to winter. One day he was lying on top of the bedclothes gazing at snow billowing into the room through the open windows while he lay streaming with perspiration. And then there were the aches, which penetrated every bone in his body. Those he didn't mind. It was the intense sick feeling which was unbearable. Sometimes he woke to find Uncle Bill sitting beside him reading a book, and at other times he would be thrown into a half dream where he was back at school trying to develop photographs over and over again till he felt exhausted. One morning Mr Hart and Mrs Beaumont carried a large dark brown wireless into the room, the kind which plugged into a socket in the wall, and Henry was glad of the company as he lay and listened to the voices from it, drifting in and out of sleep.

One afternoon, Mr Finch visited him.

'I know everything,' he announced.

Immediately, Henry felt again that his life was over.

'And being the illegitimate son of a deserter doesn't make a jot of difference to the photographs you've taken,' he stated. 'So don't be so dramatic, lad,' and he spread the photos out on the eiderdown and began to chat about what ones to put together for a display in the school hall. As he left he casually chucked a large colourful comic called *The Eagle* at Henry. 'It's just come out. The school was sent some free copies. There's a real-life story in there. *School for Spies*, it's called. Tell me what you think.'

A few days after this visit Henry woke to find Pip, Jeffries and Grace sitting round his bed, staring intently at him. Grace sprang to her feet and ran out on to the landing.

'He's awake!' she yelled.

Moments later there were footsteps, his mother appeared and the next thing he knew she was plumping up his pillows so that he could sit up comfortably.

'Tea,' she asked, 'and a bit of toast?'

Henry nodded, although eating was the last thing on his mind.

'You've got some colour now,' she said, smiling.

'You looked grey before,' said Jeffries, 'like a gravestone.'

'Roger, your mother asked me to tell you that Captain Wilkins has arrived. He's downstairs talking to her.'

'Not again!' he snapped. 'I don't know why she lets him into the house.'

'You know why. He wants to talk about your father's funeral.'

'Well, I don't, and anyway it's none of his business. And no, I still don't want to see him.'

She gave a brief nod and left the room.

'Who's Captain Wilkins?' Henry asked.

'Oh, some man the Army sent to visit us because my father died. He's supposed to *comfort* us for our loss,' Jeffries added sarcastically. 'Bit late now.'

'They're giving your father back his rank, though,' said Grace gently.

'Which they took away in the first place because he *deserted*.'

'I didn't know that,' said Henry, surprised. 'What rank was he?'

'Corporal. Look, can we change the subject, please?'

'Good idea,' said Pip, who looked as though he was about to explode.

'Yes, of course,' said Grace quickly. 'The reason we came up here, you see, is because we have some wonderful news.'

At this point Pip sprang to his feet and started to do one of his strange whirling dances.

'Tell him!' he said.

'Tell me what?' asked Henry, still feeling as though someone had stuffed cotton wool in his ears.

'Mrs Beaumont has been in touch with Mr Hale,' said Jeffries.

'Who's Mr Hale?'

'The publisher, remember?'

'Oh, yeah, I remember.' He was the man who had sat at their kitchen table beaming at Mrs Beaumont the night she had returned the photographs.

'Well, actually,' said Grace, 'she didn't exactly get in touch with him. He's been writing letters to her and phoning every day.'

'How do you know?' asked Jeffries.

'I'm here when the post arrives. Sometimes she gets a letter from him in the first post *and* the second post.'

'Are you going to let me tell him?' Jeffries asked.

'Of course. Only do get on with it.'

Jeffries cast his eyes up to the ceiling.

'As I was saying, Mrs Beaumont got in touch with Mr Hale,' and he glared at Grace as if daring her to interrupt him again, 'and he's offered me a job at the publishers as a tea and errand boy, and he's going to find out about evening classes for me and I'm going to learn how to type properly.'

'But that's not all,' interrupted Grace.

By now Pip was jumping up and down.

'Pip!' protested Jeffries.

'Sorry,' said Pip and he joined them by the bed.

'Daniel has a friend who's started a small film archive,' said Jeffries. 'Daniel is giving him his films and they need to be put in order and he's asked me if I'd like to help him. That'll probably be in the evenings and at weekends. I've been offered *two* jobs! So we'll be moving to London.'

'To Mrs Beaumont's house,' added Grace. 'So he and Mrs Jeffries will be living with me and Mrs Beaumont.'

'And Mum says I can come up and stay sometimes,' said Pip cheerfully.

Henry tried to smile. He was genuinely pleased for Jeffries but it made him feel like an outsider all over again. He wondered if he was going to feel like this for the rest of his life, watching people but never quite being with them. He was now the only one who had nowhere to go after he had finished school. He noticed that Jeffries was beaming at him.

'That's good,' Henry croaked, closing his eyes.

When he opened them again they were gone and he wondered if he had dreamt it all.

The next morning he was neither sweating nor shivering and for the first time in what seemed like weeks he was aware of a new feeling. Hunger. An image of baked beans on toast swam into his head. He slipped out of bed and leaned against it for a moment to steady himself and stumbled out of the room on to the landing. Gripping the banister rail, he moved with concentration down the stairs.

As he approached the steps from the hall he could hear Molly asking Mrs Beaumont questions in the kitchen. He swung open the door to find his mother sitting in a wicker chair breast-feeding his baby brother. He reddened and looked away. Mrs Beaumont took down a tin of baked beans from the cupboard.

'How did you know?' Henry asked in astonishment.

'Intuition,' she said. 'I'm right, aren't I?'

He nodded and sat at the table.

'I'm missing school,' he said to his mother.

'We had noticed.' She gave him a smile. 'But you won't be going back for a while. The doctor says you're to have another week off to convalesce.'

'How long have I been ill?'

'Ten days.'

'Is that all? It seems longer.'

It was during his week of convalescence that Henry discovered more about Pip and Jeffries.

The first surprise was when he woke at dawn to find that Pip's bed was empty and he went to look for him. From the top of the first flight of stairs he could hear the piano being played in the study. He crept down to the bottom step and sat down to listen. The music mesmerised him. It was as though he was watching a film inside his head. In the film there was a lone youth running, but he was not in any danger. He seemed to be heading towards something rather than fleeing from it. Henry could see him sprinting past deserted fields and then hurling himself into some woods, the wind gusting through the branches above his head. Then he was out into the sunlight on a steep narrow road. The music took him effortlessly to the top of a hill. On the other side lay the sea. He kept on running until he came towards a path high above the rocks and slid down an opening, scrambling down rough steps to a small inlet. And then suddenly he was barefoot, standing on the sand gazing out at a boat in the distance. It was then Henry realised that he was the boy and that he wanted to be with the people on the boat. He wanted to be one of the crew.

And then the music stopped. Before Henry could creep back upstairs, Pip had opened the door. He stood in the hall in his pyjamas and smiled at him, almost as if he had expected him to be there.

'I'd like to play it at the cinema,' he said matter-of-factly, 'but it's too long. I think Grace's great-aunt will like it though, don't you?'

Henry nodded.

'I've written something of my own. Can I play it for you?'

There was no need for Henry to reply. He followed him willingly into the study.

*

It was on the day of Corporal Jeffries' funeral that Henry discovered more about Jeffries.

From outside the bedroom he could hear strangers arriving downstairs in the hall. He hovered on the landing and eavesdropped as Mrs Beaumont ushered them into the sitting room. He hadn't been allowed to go to the funeral service. *Doctor's orders*, his mother had said.

There was a loud knock at the front door and there were male voices coming from the porch, well spoken and solemn.

'Roger!' called Mrs Beaumont.

Footsteps came up the steps from the kitchen.

'It's the undertakers,' she said, 'and the military.'

'Come to arrest him, have they?' he heard Jeffries say angrily. 'Are they going to court martial his bones, then?'

'I think it's their way of apologising and recognising that your father was a good man,' Mrs Beaumont said softly.

'They insulted him and they insulted my mother. And all these aunts and uncles who've turned up should have stayed away like they have done for years. And that goes for my grandfather too. I don't know him and I don't want to know him. They should be ashamed!'

'They are ashamed, Roger.'

'Even if my father had been a deserter, they should have helped my mother.'

Henry slipped back into the bedroom and gently closed the door. He crossed over to the window and peered out from behind the curtains. Outside, a small crowd of people had gathered in the street. As Jeffries and his mother walked down the path towards a large black car, a smartly dressed corporal appeared and opened the door for them. It looked as though Corporal Jeffries was being given a hero's send-off. Jeffries and his mother sat in the back seat, their heads bowed.

Henry stared down at the hearse. The coffin was draped with a Union Jack. Nestling in pride of place on a neatly folded webbing belt was a bayonet, on top of which was a brown peaked regimental cap.

And Henry was glad. This recognition of a kind man, this desire to make something good out of something bad, helped console him for the guilt he felt over his father's unforgivable crime.

'You didn't win,' Henry whispered. And the message was also for his grandmother.

He knew Jeffries would be out for most of the day, as the funeral reception was being held in one of the hotels on the seafront, and he felt at a loss as to what to do. He wished that he were with Jeffries. He picked up the large envelope on the bottom shelf containing the novel Jeffries had written and eased out the neatly typed pages. From the moment he read the opening sentence he found himself flung into a world filled with sadistic rulers and poverty-stricken, terrified slaves, strange land-scapes, and underground caves where men, women and children fled and lived among monstrous machines. The anger and fear which surged off the pages stunned him, and the way Jeffries described terrifying scenes made Henry forget that he was reading words. It was as though he was watching a film as powerful as *Battleship Potemkin*.

Late that afternoon, moments after he had finished reading the final chapter, he heard a creak on the stairs. He slipped the papers back into the envelope and had only just returned it to the shelf when Jeffries walked into the room.

He was still wearing his smart clothes with a black armband. Henry wanted to ask him about the funeral but all he could do was to stare at him, feeling bad that he hadn't been with him.

'We drove past all these people waiting on the pave-ments,' Jeffries blurted out. 'They crossed themselves when they saw my father's coffin and the men took off their hats. And any soldiers or airmen or naval ratings we passed stood to attention and saluted. And at the church there were all these corporals waiting for him. And they carried him in. They treated him really well.' He cleared his throat hurriedly. 'I've got to go back downstairs. There are loads of relatives down there. I don't want to talk to them but I don't want to leave Mother on her own. Do you want to join us?'

After what his father had done, Henry couldn't face it. He shook his head.

'Doctor's orders again, eh?' said Jeffries.

Henry nodded.

'See you after they've gone,' and he went to leave the room.

'Jeffries.'

He swung round.

'Yes?'

'I read your story.'

He looked shocked.

'My novel?'

'It'd make a really good film,' Henry added quickly.

A look of suspicion came over Jeffries' face.

'You're not just saying that?'

Henry shook his head.

'I couldn't stop reading it.'

Jeffries gave a bashful smile.

'I'm going to be a writer one day.'

'I know,' said Henry.

'And do what my father did before he was called up.'

'Teach music?'

'No. Films. One day I'm going to tell people about great films, like great music.'

'I want to *make* them,' Henry blurted out. 'I want to be a camera operator.'

Jeffries grinned.

'Then I'll show your films. And Pip will be the projectionist,' he declared. 'I'd better go now,' he added awkwardly, 'Mother's waiting for me.'

Left on his own, Henry thought about what Jeffries had said. He had the feeling that Pip would be more than a projectionist, that he would be the one who would surprise everyone. He heard footsteps coming back up the stairs again. Jeffries put his head round the door.

'I've just realised what you said. You *read* my novel. You read a book!'

## 4. First date

IT WAS THE BEGINNING OF A MONTH OF PREPARATION FOR THE open day and concert. Everything Henry had made had been taken from his home: the clothes horse, the little foot stool, the bookends and a cutlery divider, so when he wasn't in the darkroom he used any spare time he had left in the woodwork room, putting the finishing touches to a new pair of bookends and a birthday present for his mother.

Pip told Mr Finch about Great-Aunt Florence's gramophone collection and asked if he could perform two of the songs.

'They're Twenties' and Thirties' French café songs,' said Pip.

Mr Finch looked surprised, 'You can do that?'

'Yes, sir.'

Jane and Margaret asked if they could join in and dress up as 1920s' French ladies and pretend to be in a café listening to the songs. Pip took them round to Great-Aunt Florence who produced some silky dresses for them to borrow.

'You could play the waiter,' said Jeffries to Henry.

'Oh, no,' said Henry, protesting.

'Oh, go on,' cried the girls.

'We need a waiter and you're good at French,' Jeffries added.

Henry groaned and gave in.

The cinemas were full of crime films that week, including a Humphrey Bogart film, *Call it Murder*, but the biggest topic of conversation among the boys in his class was a young blonde English actress called Diana Dors. She was in *Dance Hall*. The film with it was *The Overlanders*, a film set in the Australian outback and it was in the queue for this programme that Henry spotted Jane and Margaret desperately looking for an adult to take them in. He and the others didn't have to bother because Mrs Jeffries was with them.

'Geraldo and his Orchestra are in it,' she had said, 'I don't want to miss them.'

Jeffries waved at them to join them and immediately started to talk to Margaret, who was another bookworm. As Pip and Grace were busy chatting to one another, Henry and Jane were thrown together.

For a while neither of them said anything. It was strange. Even though they had been in the same form for years, he felt stupid and tongue-tied.

'It was nice of you to give Jack the railway job,' she said after a while.

'I didn't exactly give it to him.'

'The driver who put in a good word for him, isn't he your stepfather?'

'Yes.'

'How did he know how badly Jack wanted to be a train driver?'

'I told him.'

'There you are, then,' she said.

There was another awkward silence.

'Do you still want to be a nurse?' he asked politely.

'Definitely. One of the nurses who helped me with my research for the presentation has told me I can write to her if I like. She's going to give me advice.'

'That's good.'

'Do you know what you want to do yet?'

He was about to shrug it off but something made him want to tell her.

'You know, don't you?'

'Yes.'

'Tell me. I won't laugh if that's what's worrying you. You didn't laugh at me when I told you I wanted to be a nurse.'

He lowered his voice. 'I want to be a camera operator. It's a long apprenticeship. You have to start out as a clapper boy first.'

'Do you mean a film cameraman?' she whispered.

He nodded.

'You'd be good at that.'

Henry felt ten feet high.

During the interval, after *The Overlanders*, Henry watched people race up the aisle for ice creams.

'Look,' said Pip excitedly. 'There's Mum!'

She was standing by one of the exits in the smart brown uniform of the Plaza with the gold buttons, starched white collar, brown pill-box hat and white gloves. She gave Pip a wave.

'She seems really nice,' said Jane.

'She is,' said Henry. 'So's Mr Hart.'

'Pip's lucky. I can't wait to get away from my parents. This woman I told you about says that if I'm serious about being a nurse, I could train in a hospital and live in nurses' quarters. I'd love that. No more rows. No more Dad coming home drunk.' She stopped. 'Don't tell anyone about that, will you?'

'No, course not.'

'As soon as I walk out of our lodgings, I feel so relieved I could take off and fly. That's why I don't want school to end. I like learning. And I'm going to miss everyone.'

It was time for *Dance Hall*. On the screen, four factory girls were getting ready to go out to the Palais.

'Bit posh for factory girls,' Jane whispered.

They smiled at one another and then turned their attention back to the screen.

Henry could see what the boys meant about Diana Dors. She had enormous lips, a very curvy body and a smile that made you melt. He glanced quickly at Jane. Diana Dors was all right, he thought, but Jane was much prettier.

'We're going to see *On the Town* on Friday,' he whispered. 'It's a new American musical. Want to come with us?'

From the moment the music pounded into the auditorium and a dockyard worker walked along the New York docks at dawn, Henry knew that this was a different kind of musical. As he turned to glance at Jane she was beaming back at him. On the screen hordes of American sailors poured down the gangway and a trio of friends stood enthusiastically determined to take New York by storm in their twenty-four-hour's leave. Before long, two of the sailors had been swept off their feet by girls, and the third sailor began a search for the dream girl he had seen on a subway poster.

'Even the romantic bits were funny,' said Henry when they walked out through the foyer.

'I liked it when they sang and danced in the museum by the skeleton of the dinosaur!' said Pip.

'And when they were dancing in the streets,' added Grace.

'The story went at such a lick,' Jeffries exclaimed. 'It was so *exhilarating*. So powerful!'

Henry couldn't have put it like Jeffries. But he was right. The whole film took your breath away. And he knew he would have to see it again.

The audience came flooding out of the cinema into the summer night, bubbling. Henry felt so excited he wanted to leap around. As soon as they had broken away from the crowd, Grace and Pip flung their arms across each other's shoulders and sang, '*New York! New York!*' Jeffries and Margaret did the same and as Henry put his arm round Jane's shoulders, she was putting her arm around his and they added the third '*New York! New York!*' The six of them strode down the street together towards a flattened bombsite singing, '*It's a Wonderful Town!*' just as the three sailors and their girlfriends in the film had done.

That night Henry couldn't sleep. He kept going over and over the memory of the six of them singing, their arms across each other's shoulders, his arm around Jane. She felt so soft and warm he wanted to bury himself in her. He would have to wait until Monday morning till he saw her again and it seemed a long time away.

'Henry,' he heard Jeffries say from his bed, 'I can't sleep. I keep thinking about tonight.'

'Me too,' Henry whispered back.

*

'You'll have to wait until open day on Monday before you see the present I've made for you,' said Henry, handing his mother a birthday card the next morning. 'It's in the woodwork display.'

Although it was Saturday, he had agreed to go into school to help Mr Finch put the finishing touches to the photographic display. He planned to drop in at the railway station on the way to take the last two photographs on his film. He was looking forward to being back in the darkroom, developing the used film and putting in a new roll.

'Would you drop Molly off at Mrs Henson's?' asked Mrs Beaumont. 'Your mother's packed everything she needs for the afternoon in your rucksack. It means she won't be under our feet when Mrs Jeffries and I prepare the birthday tea.'

Before leaving, Henry took a quick glimpse at the *Sternsea Evening News* to see what was on. The new film of *Treasure Island* was opening at the Odeon. There had been mixed publicity about it and, having just read the book, Henry was keen to see the film and make up his own mind.

Molly was standing impatiently in the hall, hugging her floppy dog, with his mother and baby Larry. Henry slung his rucksack with her potty and a change of clothes over his shoulder and took her hand. His mother kissed her and gave him a clumsy hug while hanging on to his half-brother.

He checked that the new roll of film was in his trouser pocket and started walking down the path. Mrs Beaumont came running after him with a man's jacket and the Peter Rabbit book. She slipped the book into one of the pockets.

'It's July,' he protested.

'Tell that to the sky.'

He groaned, took off his rucksack and slipped the jacket on while Mrs Beaumont held Molly's hand. A gust of wind blew across the path. 'Told you so,' she said. 'Now, don't be late. Tea Party is at five o'clock.'

'I won't be,' he said. 'Wave to Mrs Beaumont,' he told Molly.

'Bye bye, Auntie Henni,' she said.

'Hettie!' he exclaimed as they walked towards the wooden gate.

'Tetti,' she said.

They had only walked a couple of yards when a car drew up alongside them. A tubby man with greased-back hair and a thin moustache leaned out of the window. He was holding a map.

'We're lost,' he said, indicating the man in the driver's seat, a burly bald-headed man. 'We don't know this town too well. Can you help us?'

The man opened the door and held out the map for Henry to see. Henry was puzzled.

'You need a street map,' he said. 'This is a map of southern England.'

The driver climbed out. The next thing Henry knew, Molly was pulled from his hand and thrown into the back seat. She gave a frightened scream.

'Molly!' he yelled.

As Henry leaned in to grab her, a pair of strong arms shoved him violently into the car and the door was slammed behind him. By the time he had sat up, the car was speeding down the road.

## 5. Ted and Percy

MOLLY WAS SOBBING UNCONTROLLABLY. THE MAN WHO HAD showed Henry the map turned round and glared at him.

'If you don't shut her up, I will,' he said. He swung round to the driver. 'You should have left her on the pavement.'

'No time. He would have been out like a shot. And someone might have noticed. Anyways, it did the trick, didn't it?'

'You've got the wrong person,' Henry began. 'I don't know you.'

'What's yer name?' asked the passenger-seat man.

'Use yer loaf,' said the driver. 'We know who he is.'

'What if we've been following the wrong boy?'

The driver gave a sigh.

'Tell him your name, sonny.'

'Henry Dodge.'

'There you are, then,' he said, slamming the palms

of his hands forcefully on to the wheel.

Henry was stunned.

'But why?' he began.

'Stop askin' questions. You'll find out tomorrow morning.'

He wrapped his arms tightly round Molly. He remembered Mrs Henson. Would she pop round to Mrs Beaumont's house when they hadn't turned up, or would she think they had changed their minds? And what about Mr Finch? He might think Henry had let him down. And his mother wouldn't miss him for hours. They could be miles away by then.

'Where are you taking us?' he asked.

'What have I said about asking questions?' the driver roared.

Henry felt Molly jump and clutch at his arms. Once they left Sternsea, they slowed down. Henry stared out the window, keeping his eye out for signposts.

They must have been in the car for well over an hour when he realised they were heading for London.

'Wanta wee-wee,' whispered Molly.

The man in the passenger seat whirled round, alarmed.

'Don't you wet that car seat or I'll be in trouble.'

'We need to stop,' said Henry.

'There ain't no little boy's rooms round 'ere, sonny,' said the driver, glancing out at streets and houses.

'I've got her pot in my rucksack. If you stop by some trees, I could take her with me.'

'And make a run for it,' added the driver over his shoulder.

'How can I? I've got her with me.'

'You could carry her,' said the man in the passenger seat.

'Don't give him ideas,' said the driver.

'Wanta wee-wee!' cried Molly piteously.

'We got to stop!' urged the man in the passenger seat.

They pulled up by a field. Henry looked swiftly round for someone he could call out to but there wasn't a house in sight. As Henry climbed out of the back with Molly he heard the driver mutter something about ditching her. The thought of her being abandoned in the middle of nowhere horrified Henry.

As soon as she had finished, he pushed the emptied pot quickly into the paper bag his mother had packed it in, his eyes fixed on her. He was acutely aware of the driver standing near them as he wedged it back in the top of the rucksack. 'Hang on to me very tight,' he whispered, lifting her. 'I'll hold doggie. You hold me.'

The driver stared at them. Henry slid on to the seat, slammed the door shut, and gripped her firmly with his legs.

As soon as they hit London, Henry peered out of the window searching for a policeman, ready to signal to him, but the only one he spotted was a traffic policeman. He waved to him as they passed but he didn't even glance in their direction. He looked out for a clock to see if it was five o'clock yet.

The car drew further into London but it was not the London Mrs Beaumont had shown him. Her London was a world of bookshops and cinemas, theatres and jazz clubs. This part of London was run down and obliterated. He was familiar with heavily bombed streets, having grown up among rubble. But the streets he now looked out on were even more decimated. He suddenly became aware of missing things he had taken for granted in Sternsea – the lighter colour of the sky because it was near the sea and the sound of seagulls, although the streets still had the odd cinema standing, he noted. He peered out of the window at the roads, teeming with people, buses, bicycles and cars. *No one will find us here*, he thought. It would be like looking for a needle in a haystack.

Molly had fallen asleep, her face grubby from crying and rubbing her eyes. The heat was oppressive. Outside, the sky was grey, like a dark umbrella that kept stale air from escaping and stopped fresh air from blowing in. He tried to remember everything in case it might come in useful later but all he could see among the crowds were the familiar queues of women waiting outside shops. There was a rumble of thunder in the sky. Henry was sweating in the jacket Mrs Beaumont had insisted on making him wear. And then he remembered the roll of film. He moved his hand slowly to check that it hadn't fallen out of his pocket. It was still there. He was sure his pockets would be searched for money when he reached their destination and if they found the film, they'd know he had a camera, start poking around in the rucksack and nick it. And then he had an idea. Very slowly he moved the dog Molly was clutching and painstakingly unbuttoned the back flap of fur. He tucked the small box of film behind her nightdress and did up the buttons.

By now the car was beginning to slow down. They turned into a street of small houses and then slipped into a back street, which had only five houses left standing on it. The car stopped outside one, the top half of which had been blown away.

'You get them out 'ere, Percy,' said the driver. 'I'll take the car back to his highness and come back later. Too tricky parking it round 'ere. Some nosy parker will only spot it and nick the tyres.' He turned to face Henry. 'You wait there till he unlocks the front door. Got that?'

Henry nodded.

He watched the one called Percy ease his roly-poly frame out of the car. He could easily have made a dash for it if he had been on his own. With Molly it would be too risky.

'Unlocked and all clear, Ted,' said Percy with a slight swagger. 'Out you get,' he ordered, glaring at Henry.

Molly was rubbing her eyes.

'Molly want Mummy,' she said crossly.

'You want a good slap around the chops, that's what you want,' said Percy.

'Wanta wee-wee.'

Henry saw a trickle flowing down the inside of one of her legs.

'Oh no!' bellowed Percy. 'Get her inside. Now!'

Henry looked quickly down the street but before he could make a move Percy moved towards them.

What remained of the house they entered was a hall, a flight of stairs that disappeared on to a jagged floor, a broken wall and the sky, a cupboard door under the stairs and two other doors leading off. Percy opened the back door which led into a small kitchen where there was a table, a collection of assorted chairs, a large black kettle, teapot, frying pan and saucepan, which Henry recognised as belonging to Uncle Bill and his mother. Two of her tea towels hung from a piece of string above the range.

And it all became clear. This was all his father's doing. He suddenly remembered how he had held him in a vice-like grip the night he had tried to force Henry to go to London with him, and he shuddered.

He squeezed Molly's hand and headed for the door by a filthy window.

'Where do you think you're going?

'To the scullery.'

'There ain't one.'

'I've got clean knickers for her,' he said, unpacking his rucksack. He took out the bag with the tin chamber pot in it.

'Sort her out,' Percy said roughly. 'I'll wait outside but don't try no funny business cos you won't get far.'

'Where's the nearest tap? I need to wash these,' said Henry, holding up the wet knickers.

Percy stepped back sharply.

'There's a tap in the alley across the yard but you ain't going anywhere near it, sonny.'

'Can you get some water, then?' he asked, sitting Molly on the pot.

Percy picked up a tin bucket by the door and waved a key at him.

'Just in case you've got any plans to run away.'

Henry heard him lock the back door. He rubbed some of the grime from the window to let some light in. Outside was a scrubby little yard with a broken wall. He could see Percy in the alley, filling the bucket from a standpipe tap and panting with the weight of it as he returned. Henry withdrew quickly.

As soon as Percy had dumped the bucket down on the floor, Henry carried the kettle and a saucepan towards it and filled them.

'Now what are you doing?' Percy snapped.

'For drinking water,' Henry explained.

'Oh,' he said, 'that's all right, then.'

'Can you empty this?' Henry asked, presenting the filled chamber pot.

'Oh, no,' he said, waving his arms. 'I'm not going anywhere near that. You can empty that in the privy outside.'

Henry made for the door.

'Oh, no you don't. Give it 'ere!'

Henry watched him as he held the pot at arm's length and walked gingerly towards the back door. Grabbing the tea towels, Henry dipped one in the bucket of water, wrung it out, wiped Molly down, dried her with the other tea towel and put her dry knickers on.

'That'll need rinsing,' said Henry when Percy brought back the empty chamber pot. 'It'll smell otherwise.'

'Let it smell then,' he said, thrusting it into Henry's hands.

Henry slipped it back in the paper bag and into his rucksack.

'Firsty,' announced Molly.

He picked up a cup from the shelf and poured some water from the kettle into it. Molly gulped it down.

'Got any soap?' Henry asked.

'What do you think this is? A ruddy hotel?'

'I need to wash her knickers.'

Percy stared angrily down at her and Henry realised he would have to get on with it, otherwise Molly would be seen as a nuisance and they'd dump her.

'I'll wash them in the bucket,' he said hastily.

He rinsed and wrung them out with the wet tea towel, and hung them dripping over the string.

'Are we staying here?' he asked.

'You're full of questions, ain't you?'

'I was taking Molly round to a friend of my mum's this afternoon. She'll be wondering where she is.'

'Well, she can keep wondering, can't she? You're stayin' the night. After that, I don't know.'

'Do you want me to light the range?'

The man stared at him as if he had gone to the moon.

'You know how to light a range?'

'Yeah. So if you got any old newspapers, bits of wood, coal, matches, I can get started, if you want. You're in charge.'

'Yeah, that's right,' said Percy, looking pleased. 'And don't you forget it.'

By the time Ted arrived, the range was lit and Molly was sitting at the table with the crayons and pieces of paper his mother had also packed in the rucksack. He stood in the doorway, staring at the range.

'I told him to do it,' said Percy, boasting.

'We can have a cuppa then,' he said, slamming down a pile of chips wrapped in newspaper on the table. Henry noticed him glance at his rucksack.

'Had a look in his bag?' he grunted.

'Nah.'

'Why not?' and he shook his head with impatience, picked it up and undid the straps. Henry's heart sank. He'd find the camera now. He flung it open and came face to face with the bag containing the pot.

'Ugh!' he said, chucking it to one side.

'That's why not,' stated Percy.

After chips and a cup of tea, Henry noticed it was growing dark outside. He wondered when his father would be turning up, but from the behaviour of his captors, it didn't look as if they were expecting him that night. Ted produced some bottles of beer. Henry sat Molly on his lap, took a deep breath and opened *The Adventures of Peter Rabbit*. It seemed a bit strange reading about the goings-on of a rabbit in front of two beer-swilling kidnappers, especially as they appeared to be listening to the story as well.

'We're sleeping in the front room,' Ted announced, when Henry had finished, 'so we can keep an eye on you. And I have the key.'

The front room was small with an old settee in it which faced the window. It was covered in cushions and an old blanket. A pair of grubby curtains hid the view. It looked as if they would all be sleeping side by side.

'Dirty room,' Molly said. 'Want to go home.'

Percy took the end by the fireplace, Ted sat in the middle and Henry sat at the other end with Molly on his lap. Henry's brain was whirling too much to drop off, but he closed his eyes because Percy and Ted were taking it in turns to watch him while the other slept. Eventually Molly cried herself to sleep. Sitting there, with her slumped on his lap, Henry watched the first hint of dawn lighten the curtains. It was then that he noticed that both Ted and Percy were asleep. A little chink of light hit the wall behind them through a tiny gap. He knew immediately what he had to do. The first hurdle was how to get out from under Molly without waking her and the two men.

He held her firmly and leaned forward. Using all his strength, he slowly pulled himself to his feet. Hardly daring to breathe and sweating with adrenalin, he stood still for a moment. The men did not stir. He lowered Molly back on to the settee beside Ted, crept towards his rucksack and undid the straps. As he pulled out the bag containing the pot, the paper rustled. Ted moved and gave a grunt. Henry froze. He stared at Ted for a moment, put the bag on the floor and reached for the camera case underneath Molly's cardigan at the bottom of the rucksack. Once he had the camera out of its case, he held it inside the rucksack to muffle the click of the bellows releasing. Neither of the men stirred. With painstaking slowness he moved towards the window and pulled the curtains a little to the side. A shaft of light hit Molly and her guards.

By now Henry's mouth was so dry that he had a tickle

in his throat and he noticed that his hands were shaking. He was terrified he would cough and be caught in the act. He willed himself to remain calm, peered through the viewfinder and pressed the button. The shutter clicked noisily into action. And still they slept.

He moved closer, winding the film on and changing the distance to four feet, stepped a little to one side so that he didn't block the light from the window and took the last photograph on the roll of film. Swiftly he moved back to his rucksack, folded the bellows and snapped the camera shut, slipped it into the leather case and placed Molly's cardigan over it. He was just about to put the pot back in when Molly's eyes suddenly sprang open and she gave a scream. Henry pulled her pot out of the bag and picked her up. By now Ted was awake.

'What are you up to?' he demanded.

'I'm getting her pot out,' he explained.

'Wanta wee-wee,' Molly said, and Henry could have hugged her.

He plonked her on top of it.

'Do you have to do that in 'ere,' Ted grumbled, rubbing the dark stubble on his jaw.

'I'll need to empty it,' said Henry.

'Oh, no you don't. I was told you were a clever tyke.'

'Then you'll have to empty it.'

'Oh, no. Not me,' he said, moving away. 'Percy!'

Percy gave a groan.

'Percy, wake up, will you?'

But Percy kept sleeping.

Ted struggled to his feet and stumbled over to the window. He peered out at the damaged landscape, scratching his head and yawning. He didn't seem to notice that the curtains had been moved.

'Okeydoke. You do it, then,' he said over his shoulder. 'But the girl stays with me. If you try and escape, well, I don't need to go into details, do I?'

'No, sir,' said Henry.

Ted swung round and stared at him.

'Sir? I like that.'

Henry hated leaving Molly and the exposed rucksack but as he walked through the kitchen carrying her pot, he suddenly realised that he was bursting. Standing in the outside privy, he relieved himself but he seemed to have a river inside him, and all the time he stood there urinating, he kept picturing Ted searching the rucksack, knowing that the camera was only concealed by a tiny cardigan.

By the time he returned to the kitchen he could hear Molly crying. He began running.

'What have you done to her?' he yelled as he scooped her up into his arms.

'I ain't done nothin'. She was trying to get away! And when I tried to stop her, the little so-and-so only kicked me in the shins!'

Percy was wide awake now and Molly was clinging

tightly to Henry. He knew he had to get her pot back into the rucksack quickly. He knelt down, her arms and her dog wrapped round his neck, shoved the pot into the paper bag and thrust it inside.

'Nearly there,' he said, trying to reassure her.

'We got to go out,' Ted said to Henry. 'Get in the hall.'

He pointed at the cupboard door.

'Open it.'

Henry did so and found himself being pushed with Molly into a cellar, with such force that he had to grip Molly hard to stop her from falling down the stairs.

'I need her pot,' Henry yelled.

Within seconds the rucksack was dumped on the top step, the door slammed and he and Molly were plunged into darkness. They listened to the sound of the key turning in the lock, the slam of the front door and silence.

'Let's sit on the stairs, Molly,' said Henry.

As he gently pulled her down he could feel her shaking. He touched the wall and his hand came back wet.

'Molly cold,' she whimpered.

'I'll get your cardigan out for you,' he said.

Fumbling, he felt his way round the rucksack, searching for the straps. He pulled out the pot but it slipped and he heard it clatter down the stairs. And then his fingers touched the little garment he had watched his mother knit for her.

'Still cold,' she whimpered after he had buttoned it up for her.

'You can wear my jacket,' he whispered, though why he was whispering was a mystery since there was only him and Molly in the house. He pulled off the jacket, wrapped it round her and did it up. She giggled. He put his arm round her and tried to think of how they could pass the time in a cellar that was so devoid of light that they were unable even to see their hands in front of their faces. It was even darker than . . . Suddenly he sat bolt upright.

'A darkroom,' he finished.

'Yes, it is,' agreed Molly.

Not that he needed such pitch blackness to take the film out of the camera, but it gave him privacy, not only from Ted and Percy but also from Molly.

He pulled the camera out of the leather case and then hesitated. Molly was sharp. She didn't miss a thing. If she heard him opening it she might guess what he was doing and blurt it out in front of Percy and Ted.

'Is doggie nice and soft?' he asked loudly.

'Yes,' she said but her voice was trembling.

'You're a very brave girl looking after him.'

'Yes,' she whispered, and he heard her stifle a sob.

With the camera in his hands, he felt for the knob at the side and turned it till it felt loose in his hand. To cover the sound of opening the camera he gave a loud cough.

He touched the round circular piece at the top with his fingers and levered it upwards, releasing the spool of film. *Lick the sticky band at the end and seal it*, he told himself, feeling for it with his fingers.

Now he needed somewhere to hide it. He was still convinced that his rucksack would eventually be searched and that the camera would be discovered. Whoever opened it would smell a rat if they found it empty. He needed to put the new roll of film in to throw them off the scent.

He slid the used roll into the right hand pocket of his trousers.

'Molly,' he said, 'would you let me give doggie a cuddle too?'

'Why?'

'I think it would make me feel better as well.'

'All right,' he heard her mumble reluctantly.

He fumbled for the dog. Once he had it in his arms he unbuttoned the back, took out the small Kodak box, opened it and removed the cylindrical container, which had the new roll of film inside it. He prised open the lid and carefully emptied out the new film into the palm of his hand. He hesitated for a moment. He mustn't get the two films mixed up. He put the new film into the empty box and slipped it into his left pocket. Taking the used film from his right pocket he slid it into the empty cylindrical case, snapped the lid over it, tucked it behind the nightdress and carefully buttoned up the dog. He touched Molly and handed the dog back to her.

'Thank you, Molly,' he said.

'All better now,' came a matter-of-fact voice from the darkness.

'Yes. Much better.'

The next hurdle was to put the new roll of film into the camera. He felt for the empty spool at the bottom of the camera, released it, clicked it in place at the top and turned it round until he could feel the slit with his thumbnail.

Taking the new roll of film out of the box, he groped around inside the camera, his heart thumping. He levered the pin out, wedged the film firmly into place, broke the seal and gently pulled the tab at the end of it towards the empty spool, easing it into the slit. As he turned the knob at the side he could feel with his fingers that the film was taut. He coughed again to cover the click of the camera as he closed it. He would have to guess how far the film had moved round the spool as he turned the knob. It wouldn't matter if he wound it on past number one. Now all he had to do was to make it look as if he had been taking photographs. An unused roll might make them suspect it had only recently been put it in and they'd search for the used roll.

'Sing me a song, Molly,' he said loudly, releasing

the bellows. 'A friendly song. For doggie.'

'Don't know a doggie song,' he heard her say miserably.

'*How much is that doggie in the window,*' he sang, taking a photograph of the dark and winding it on, '*the one with the waggly tail,*' he bellowed, taking two more pictures.

He closed the camera, slid it into the camera case and put it back in the rucksack. '*Where is that potty in the cellar, the one with the broken green rim? Oh, where is that potty in the cellar? I think we had better find him.*'

To Henry's relief, she laughed.

'Do you think if we went down the stairs together on our bottoms we could find it?'

There was silence.

'Molly?'

'Molly nodded,' she said.

He moved close to her and they moved down to the next step. They found the potty wedged in a corner on the seventh one. One by one they manoeuvred themselves upwards back to the top step. Henry shoved the pot into the rucksack. Once the straps were tied, he put his arms round Molly and drew her close. It was then he remembered the empty Kodak box the new film had come in. He had to get rid of it.

'Tell me the story of *The Fierce Bad Rabbit* again,' he said.

As she did so in her garbled way, Henry took the box

out of his pocket, slowly chewed his way through it and swallowed it.

They were in the middle of yet another re-telling of Mr McGregor yelling, 'Stop, thief!' when the sound of voices in the hall silenced them. He recognised them only too clearly. His father's. And Gran!

'What's this?' he heard her ask loudly.

'Wet knickers,' Percy said. 'They belong to the little girl.'

'What little girl?' interrupted his father.

'His sister,' said Ted.

'His sister! His sister's here?'

He was yelling now.

Henry could feel Molly trembling.

'You stupid cretins!' he screamed. 'Every policeman for miles will be looking for her now!'

And then Henry heard something which sent a chill through his body.

'We'll have to get rid of her and quick!'

# 6. Molly

AS SOON AS HENRY HEARD THE KEY IN THE LOCK, HE HELPED Molly to her feet and slung the rucksack over his shoulder. The door swung open. His father was standing next to Ted, whose large bulky body made his father seem puny. Suddenly his father's moustache made him look ridiculous. He hated him.

'I'm sorry about you being locked up like this,' he said, smiling. 'There's been a bit of a misunderstanding.'

*Liar*, thought Henry. Did he think he was deaf?

Henry stepped into the hallway, his arm firmly round Molly. He noticed that the curtains in the front room had been drawn back tightly across the windows.

'Gran's waiting for you,' said his father.

Together he and Molly walked into the kitchen. His grandmother sat slumped in one of the chairs, her face flushed. As soon as Molly spotted her she said, 'Auntie's cross.'

'Auntie's tired,' he said quickly.

There was a bag of shopping on the table. His grand-mother scowled at Molly. Henry forced himself to smile.

'Like a cuppa, Gran?' She pointed helplessly at the cold range. 'I'll light that,' he said.

He settled Molly at the table, quickly drew a picture of a large tree, the sun, a field, a pig and a cat and told her to colour them in.

'You go in the other room and put your feet up.'

His gran rose wearily to her feet.

'There's potatoes to peel too,' she grumbled.

'I'll do those.'

'I was going to do mashed potatoes and sausage.'

'Leave it to me, Gran.'

'That's for three of us.' She glared at Molly. 'Four of us now.'

As soon as she was out of the room he moved towards the door to listen to Ted and Percy talking to his father.

'I'll be off soon,' said his father. 'And back Tuesday afternoon. Then you two can deal with the girl.' And then Henry heard the words he had been dreading.

'What's in the rucksack?'

'Stuff for the little girl,' he heard Ted answer.

'You empty it out, then?'

Henry raced back to the range and shoved in handfuls of paper, bits of wood and old coal. He was just laying new pieces of coal on top when he heard his father stride into the kitchen. There was a thud as his rucksack was slammed on to the table. Molly jumped off the chair and ran over to him. Out of the corner of his eye he watched his father pull out the contents. He noticed that Ted was also in the room. There would be no cardigan concealing the camera now.

'What have we here?' his father said, pulling out the camera case. He held it up and pushed it in Ted's face. 'Know what this is?'

Ted shook his head nervously.

'A camera. A very nice camera as it happens. Now I wonder why my son wanted to keep it a secret?' And he glanced across at Henry. 'Like to tell us why, Henry?'

Henry knew it was important to say the right thing but he couldn't think what the right thing was and remained silent.

'Quiet, ain't he? I hope he ain't been taking any photographs.' He turned to face Ted. 'You was watching him the whole time last night, I hope. No dropping off to sleep?'

'Nah, course not,' stammered Ted.

'Well, just to be sure,' he said, swinging round to Henry, 'I'll take a look.' He pulled the camera out of the case and slid the cover up in front of the tiny window at the side. 'He's taken five photographs, it says.'

Henry almost smiled with relief. He must have wound it on further than he had thought. His father opened the camera, hauled the film out and flung it to the floor. 'All gone,' he said calmly. 'Nice camera. Could fetch a tidy sum. These are anything between twenty and thirty quid new.'

'That's mine,' said Henry hotly. 'It was given to me as a present.'

'Not any more, sunshine. And let me remind you, you're not too old to get a hiding.'

Henry could feel Molly trembling as she clutched his trouser leg.

His father swung round to Percy and Ted.

'You can go. I'll deal with him now.'

They passed Gran in the doorway on their way out.

'Why are you doing this to me?' Henry blurted out.

'You're his son,' she stated. 'You do what he says.'

'But why couldn't you wait till I'd finished school? I only had three days to go.'

'I did it so you couldn't finish school,' said his father.

'Why?' asked Henry, bewildered.

'Because you wanted to, and I can't have that, see?'

Henry stared at him. He didn't know whether his father was evil or mad. He turned away, took a match from the matchbox and lit the fire in the range. He noticed that his hand was shaking.

'Help me blow on it, Molly,' he said gently.

Later, after sausage and mash, his father told his gran that when he returned on Tuesday he would be bringing the papers.

'I was hoping it'd just be me and Henry,' she complained, giving Molly a hostile stare.

'You'll only have to put up with her for two days,' he said.

'Five minutes is too much,' she muttered.

'Not long now, Mum,' he said, kissing Gran on the forehead and handing her a key. 'If you get any nonsense from him, the cellar's a good place for calming him down.'

Henry gave a shudder as he spotted her glancing at Molly.

He watched Gran follow his father out into the hall, where they were whispering about going to see some man. He had just heard the man's name when Molly burst into tears. By the time he had put his arms round her to comfort her, the name had gone out of his head. He listened to the front door being locked and his gran huffing and puffing as she returned to the kitchen. She stood red-faced in the doorway.

'You go and put your feet up,' said Henry.

The strain of keeping Molly occupied and his gran cheerful was exhausting. His mind racing, he knew he had to find a way of getting Molly to safety before Ted and Percy returned. In the evening he took a pillow and a cushion from the sitting room, made up a little bed for Molly on the kitchen floor and went through as much as he could remember of her bedtime routine, even making her clean her teeth with a finger dipped in water. He read her *The Adventures of Peter Rabbit* until she had fallen asleep, and covered her with his jacket. Then he took his gran another cup of tea.

'At last,' she said, with satisfaction. 'We can be alone now. Just the two of us, eh?'

'How are your legs?' Henry asked sympathetically.

'Not good. Not good at all. And I've got to queue again tomorrow,' she complained.

'I can do that, Gran.'

'I'm to lock you in the house,' she said firmly.

'But how are you going to carry it all?'

'Exactly.'

'There is a way,' he said slowly. 'If me and Molly come with you, you could still keep an eye on us, couldn't you?'

She looked at him, puzzled. 'How do I know you won't run off?'

'Why would I want to do that, Gran? All I wanted to do was to finish school and that'll be over by Wednesday. Now I can help you find somewhere better to stay.'

'Your father's already done that.'

'He's got another place for us to go to?'

'Another country more like,' she said, looking secretive.

'Another country?' repeated Henry, fighting to sound casual.

'Now, you're not to let on I told you, though you'll know soon enough when we catch the boat.'

'When's that?'

'Tuesday, of course.'

He fell silent, watching her in disgust as she slurped her tea.

'This is just like old times, ain't it, dear?'

'Yes,' said Henry, feeling sick. And then he had an idea. 'It'd be nice if we had more time to spend together tomorrow too, wouldn't it?'

'You mean lock her in the cellar and leave her there?' And she began laughing.

'I wasn't thinking of that,' he said, struggling to control his anger. 'What would make me very happy, Gran, is if I knew Molly was going to be safe.'

'All arranged, dear. Those two men are going to leave her outside a church.'

'But she might wander off and get run over by a car. I've got a better idea.'

'Oh, yes?'

'And then if things go wrong . . .'

'What do you mean, if things go wrong?'

'Ted and Percy might get caught.' His grandmother looked alarmed. 'And they might tell the police about you and Dad.' She began to look worried. *Take it slowly,* he told himself.

'Suppose we all go out to the shops and I go to a telephone box.'

'You what!' she exclaimed. 'I'm not listening to this.'

'Wait a minute, Gran. Let me explain.'

'You ain't making no phone call.'

'You'll be with me listening to everything I say. That way if anything goes wrong, you'll be in a good light.'

'What d'you mean, a good light?'

'We *all* go to the phone box,' he repeated, 'and I ring the police.'

'Over my dead body!'

'If I say anything you don't want me to say, you can stop the call.'

'I don't like what I'm hearing,' she protested.

'I ring the police,' repeated Henry carefully. 'I tell them that they can find the missing girl, Molly Carpenter, holding her dog in the phone box.'

'No. I don't like this,' she said, shaking her head. 'I don't like this at all.'

'I make out it's like a game. I tell her that if she waits there, she'll have a lovely drive in a police car and they'll take her home to Mummy and Daddy. We watch her from somewhere nearby so she doesn't run away, or a stranger doesn't go off with her. Once she's picked up by the police there'll just be the two of us.'

'Don't be daft,' she said. 'It's too dangerous.'

'It'll be more dangerous if she stays here and something happens to her.'

'Nothing's going to happen to her. Your dad's a clever man. He's got it all worked out.'

Henry began to think quickly of every British thriller he had seen.

'I know that, Gran. But Ted and Percy aren't as clever and I overheard them say they're going to get rid of her. If you help her to safety, you'll have saved her life, which means that if you're caught, the judge will be more lenient with you.'

'Judge?' she said, looking alarmed.

'You wouldn't want to be *hanged*, would you, Gran?'

Her hands flew up to her throat.

'Don't say such things. They wouldn't hang me.'

'They would if you were an accomplice to *murder*.'

She shook her head wildly.

'It'd be either that or life imprisonment,' he added.

She gave a small moan.

'And like I told you, once she's being looked after by someone else, it'll be just the two of us and I can look after you properly.'

She nodded.

'When do you think we should do it?' she asked fearfully.

'First thing tomorrow morning, good and early, before it's too crowded.'

'I hate all that queuing,' she said, 'and your dad's got me registered as Walter Briggs's wife and it makes me feel peculiar.'

*

Henry sat at the table, his eyes on the kitchen window, waiting for daylight. Eventually Molly opened her eyes and burst into tears. She ran over to him and flung her arms round him. 'Want Mummy,' she sobbed, 'want Daddy.'

'You'll see them soon,' he said reassuringly. 'We're going to take you to a special box with a telephone in it and a nice policeman is going to pick you up.'

She clung on to him. 'Henry come too.'

'Yeah. Course I will. Later. There won't be enough room in the car, see? They'll come and pick me up after you've got home. All right?'

She nodded.

'And you've got to look after doggie,' he said firmly.

'And you promise you won't run off and leave me,' Gran asked.

Henry swallowed. He had never broken a promise ever. But if he didn't do what she asked, he knew she wouldn't agree to his plan.

'I promise, Gran.'

'That's all right, then,' she said as they set off down a side street. 'But I'm still not sure we're doing the right thing.'

'I don't want you to be punished for something you didn't do, Gran.'

'No,' said Gran, her voice trembling, 'neither do I.'

Henry recognised a little row of shops he had seen

out of the car window and he remembered there was a telephone box nearby. He spotted it opposite a café. Perfect.

'We can watch from the café window and I can get you a cooked breakfast.'

He put his hands in his pocket and gazed at the coins, his Odeon ticket to *Treasure Island*. Luckily his father hadn't searched him.

'That'd be nice,' she said.

Molly was still gripping his hand. He had placed the Peter Rabbit book in his jacket pocket while she walked with her other arm wrapped tightly round the dog. Every now and then, he gave her fingers a squeeze.

'Look, Molly,' he said in the brightest voice he could muster, 'look at the nice telephone box. That's where we're going.'

They crossed the road. Henry's legs were shaking by now and the roof of his mouth seemed to have lost all moisture. He began to sweat. *Keep calm*, he told himself. He pulled open the door. They squeezed into the box but the door wouldn't close properly and his gran was beginning to look flustered.

'Here goes,' he said cheerfully and he lifted the receiver. He dialled the first nine and watched the silver dial crawl with painstaking slowness back to zero. He dialled the second nine. His mouth was growing even drier and the calm smile he was struggling to keep on his face was making it twitch. And then he was dialling the third nine.

'I dunno,' said Gran, moving nearer to the phone.

He grinned even harder as the dial returned to zero for the last time. The phone was ringing. It rang and rang for a lifetime. And then a female voice said, 'Which service do you require? Fire, Police or Ambulance?'

'Police,' he said croakily.

His gran held her hand over her mouth.

'Your name?' said the voice.

'John Smith.'

'And where are you phoning from?'

Henry had seen enough films to know that this was what they would ask and he had taken a good look as they were crossing the road.

'A telephone box in Arthur Street,' and he gave the woman his number. 'Opposite the Mayflower café, outside Pearson's hardware store.'

There was a click and then a man said, 'John Smith?'

'Yes, sir.'

'What seems to be the matter?'

'I know the whereabouts of the missing girl, Molly Carpenter.'

'Oh, yes?' said the policeman slowly. 'Where is she, sonny?'

'She's in the telephone box beside me holding her dog.'

'Is this a joke?'

'No, sir,' said Henry, his voice trembling. He turned to

his sister. 'Molly, say hello to the nice policeman,' and he held the phone to her ear.

'Hello,' she said. There was a long pause. 'Molly,' she said eventually. 'Auntie cross.'

Henry snatched the phone back.

'That's it!' snapped his gran. 'Why should we help the little horror?'

'Hello,' said Henry quickly.

'I heard your companion,' said the man quietly. 'Are you her half-brother, Henry?'

'What's he sayin'?' Gran asked.

'I take it you can't say much,' said the policeman.

'That's right,' answered Henry. 'In Arthur Street.' He then turned to his gran, holding the receiver but acting as though the call was finished so that the policeman would be able to hear him at the other end.

'That's done now, Gran. You go and wait in the café opposite and save us a seat. There's still a table free in the window.'

'Oh, no,' she protested. 'I promised yer dad I'd keep an eye on you all the time. It's more than my life's worth if you got away.'

'After the police pick Molly up and you have a nice breakfast, I'll help you with the shopping and then we can go back to that bombed house.'

'Lovely,' she said. 'Are you glad you're with me and yer dad now?'

'Yes,' he lied.

'You need a few edges knocked off you, though. You've been getting a little bit lah di dah, you know, a bit above yourself. I know you're disappointed about that job you wanted but all boys have silly ideas about what they want to do, and then they have to grow up and do what their dad tells them.'

'Yeah.'

'Ain't you goin' to hang up?'

Henry nodded and put the receiver down.

He took the little book from his pocket and handed it to Molly.

'Read it to Molly tonight?' she said, looking up at him.

Henry nodded. He was afraid that if he spoke, his voice might betray the pain he was feeling. If the police didn't find him before he left the country, he might never see her again.

'Molly,' he said steadily, 'we're going to play that game I told you about now. And if you're good at it you'll have that drive in the police car.'

Suddenly she hung on to him.

'You come,' she pleaded.

'Later. I'll be watching you from over there.' He could see she was frightened. 'If you're good, the policeman will give you an ice cream. You'd like that, wouldn't you?'

She nodded vigorously.

'You're a clever girl,' he said.

He hated letting go of her. He gave her a quick kiss on the cheek.

'Look after doggie,' he whispered.

'You come soon?'

'Very soon.'

As he walked away from the telephone box, he felt a lump so large in his throat that he thought he would be sick. He prayed she wouldn't follow him. As if reading his thoughts, Gran said, 'If she comes after us, we'll have to take her straight back to the house.'

The table by the café window was still empty. Henry stared out at Molly standing in the telephone box, small, frightened and alone, while his gran wittered on about her shoes hurting her. He sat and watched and waited, willing the police to arrive soon. Suddenly Molly spotted him and pushed against the door.

'*No, no, no,*' he whispered inside his head.

And then a police car arrived and within seconds a policeman was beaming down at her. As he picked her up in his arms Henry watched the dog fall to the ground and then he was gone.

'She's dropped her dog,' he said, standing up.

Gran gripped his arm fiercely.

'Sit down,' she hissed.

'She won't sleep without her dog.'

'Let her stay awake, then. She won't be disturbing us, will she?'

Henry watched the police car drive away. He gazed despondently out of the window, unable to look at her in case he betrayed his feelings. No one would ever see the photographs of Ted and Percy now. A woman with a little boy opened the door to the telephone box. Immediately the boy gave an excited cry and picked up the dog. Henry could only look on helplessly.

As if from nowhere, another policeman appeared, threw open the door and spoke to the mother. He saw the woman say something to the boy. The little boy handed the dog up to him and the policeman walked off and out of sight.

Henry almost cried with relief.

# 7. Facing the consequences

NO POLICE CAME TO THE CAFÉ TO PICK THEM UP. AS HIS grandmother ate her way noisily through her breakfast, Henry kept glancing out of the window, but it was as though he had been abandoned. He couldn't understand it. He knew the policeman he had spoken to had overheard where he and his gran would be sitting, so why didn't they come? When it was time for them to leave, Henry cursed himself for the promise he had made not to run away from her. But if he hadn't made it, he reminded himself, Molly wouldn't be safe.

For the rest of the day, he waited hand and foot on Gran in the bombed house while she talked about the old times or complained about her legs. And as Henry listened, smiling and nodding, he knew there would be trouble. His father was a violent man and expected to be obeyed.

By the time she had gone to bed he felt sure that the

film would have been discovered. In spite of his promise to her, as soon as he heard her breathing deeply he tried to open the kitchen window, but it was stuck. Even if he had managed to break the glass without waking her, he still wouldn't have been able to climb through. It suddenly occurred to him that not only had the house been carefully chosen, it had also been prepared for his captivity. He crept past the sitting room, moved slowly up the staircase on to the jagged landing and stared at the exposed sky. He could have jumped but it was a long fall and if he had broken an ankle he would be even more at the mercy of his father.

The landing began to shudder under his weight and he retreated and sat for a while at the foot of the stairs, thinking. Eventually he returned to the kitchen, made a rough bed for himself on the stone floor and attempted to fall asleep, but every time he closed his eyes he found himself trying to work out where his father might be taking them. It couldn't be France, otherwise his gran wouldn't have said that learning French was a waste of time. He had tried to worm more information out of her earlier that evening but she had refused to give anything else away.

The only thing she had told him was that it wasn't worth lighting the range in the morning, as his father would be coming to collect them early. It was then that Henry realised that Molly would have been left on her own, locked up in the house until the afternoon, when Ted and Percy came to pick her up. He had done the right thing, whatever the consequences.

Once daylight fought its way through the grimy window, he began to feel sick with dread. He jumped. The key was being turned in the front door. He pulled his jacket up to his nose and pretended to be asleep. Footsteps moved across the hall.

'Time to get up, Mum,' his father said, and then he heard the feet come stamping into the kitchen.

'Get up, you little tyke!' he shouted, and the jacket was flung off him.

As Henry hauled himself to his feet, his grandmother shuffled into the room. His father slammed some official-looking papers and passports on to the table.

'When did Ted and Percy come, then?' he asked Gran.

She stared at him and then glanced at Henry.

'Ted and Percy?' she repeated faintly.

'They come last night or this morning? I told them to come this afternoon for the girl. I got to give them some instructions. Why'd they come for her early?'

'They haven't been yet,' whispered Gran.

'Where is she, then? You didn't lock her in the cellar, did you?'

'No.'

'Where is she, Mum?' he asked with unnerving quietness.

'Gone.'

'I can see that. Gone where?'

His gran pointed to Henry.

'He heard Ted and Percy say they was going to get rid of her.'

'So?'

'Murder her.'

'Where is she, Mum?'

'In a church. I did what you wanted them to do before they got their hands on her.'

'When did you leave her there?' he asked sharply.

'Yesterday morning.'

'Yesterday morning!' He paused. 'Hang on a minute, what church?'

'The one near that café.'

'What church near the café?'

'I don't know what it's called. Can you remember, Henry?'

'Saint something. Saint er . . .' He thought wildly and then he remembered the film with Ingrid Bergman in it. 'Joan. Saint Joan.'

'That's what you wanted, wasn't it, Alfred?'

He gave a brief nod.

'And you locked Henry up in 'ere?'

'Not exactly,' she faltered.

'Molly wouldn't have gone without me,' said Henry quickly. 'I told her to sit in a pew and wait till she saw a man wearing a white collar back to front.'

'You went out with him and the girl, Mum?' exclaimed his father. 'You might have been seen.'

'We went early,' said Henry.

'That's right,' added his gran.

'If she's been picked up, she'll have been taken to a police station. The police will know she must have been hidden somewhere round 'ere. It's a wonder the place isn't crawling with cops. We'd better scarper. I was going to leave you 'ere for a couple of hours while I went and had a chat with Ted and Percy but you'll both have to come with me now.'

Henry stared at them, hardly able to breathe. The thought of being stuck with them for years made him feel desperate.

'I'll just have a quick dekko in the other room,' said his father, 'make sure we haven't left anything we wouldn't want the police to find.'

Henry watched him leave the room. His gran quietly closed the door after him. She was beaming at him.

'It'll just be the three of us,' she whispered. 'I'm glad you changed your mind about coming with us. You and your father can look after me in me old age,' and she took hold of his arm and squeezed it.

And then Henry saw the most extraordinary diamond, a diamond which a few months ago he would have considered a dungheap.

'And you don't mind that I'm illegitimate?' he asked.

His grandmother gasped and let go of his arm.

'That's a terrible thing to say. How could you?'

'I didn't want to tell you, Gran, but I know you always like me to tell you the truth.' He could see that she was trembling. 'Mum and Dad weren't married.'

'Wash yer mouth out! I was at the marriage ceremony.'

'Which was where, Gran?'

'In this smart building, of course.'

'The man who married Mum and Dad was a fake. The marriage certificate was a forgery.'

'How can you say such dreadful things? You better not let your dad hear you. I don't know what's got into you.'

'It's what I was told.'

'Who by?'

Henry paused.

'The police. They told Mum to bring in her marriage certificate. Turns out she isn't a bigamist at all. Turns out her marriage certificate was forged by a mate of Dad's. His brother and Dad were standing together in the photograph. That's what made the police suspect.'

'What photograph?'

Henry could have kicked himself. He knew he was treading on very dangerous ground. He heard the door open behind him. Neither he nor his grandmother turned round. Instead, they stared at each other in silence.

'Ready, then?' said his father to Gran.

Neither of them moved.

'Come on,' snapped his father. 'We need to get out of here.'

'Henry's been saying some terrible things,' his grandmother said huskily.

'Oh, yeah? We can sort him out later. Let's get a move on!'

Still Gran didn't move.

'What's the matter with you two?'

Gran turned slowly to face his father.

'He says he's . . . he says . . .'

Henry could see that she couldn't even bring herself to say the word.

'Illegitimate,' finished Henry for her.

'Do we have to talk about that now?' his father snapped.

'Yes, Alfie, we do. He says your marriage certificate's a forgery, done by a mate of yours.'

'Says who?' yelled his father and he rushed at Henry, grabbed him by the collar and flung him against the wall. Henry stared back directly into his eyes, all hatred of the man now out in the open.

'Says the police,' said his gran.

Henry felt his father's grip on him relax.

'The police?' he said, alarmed.

Henry listened as his grandmother spilled out everything he had told her. His dad let go of him and leaned on the table facing her.

'I couldn't tell you, Mum,' his dad said pleadingly. 'I found out after Henry was born. I couldn't tell Maureen. It would have killed her.'

'The police think you were married to someone else,' Henry yelled angrily. 'Is that why you couldn't marry her? Is that why you lied to her?'

His father grabbed him again.

'Did I ask you to speak?'

'So it's true,' said Gran quietly. 'I've been living with a . . . I've eaten at the same table. I've . . .' She began waving her hands frantically in front of her face as though trying to fight off an invasion of flies.

'I'm not going anywhere near him,' she shrieked. 'I don't want him anywhere near me!'

'But I'm the same person, Gran.'

'Oh, no, you're not. I don't know you. I don't want to be in the same room as you.'

His father glared at Henry.

'What else do the police know?' And then Henry could see the penny dropping in his father's eyes. 'The photograph! They must have seen the others. They must know about the petrol coupons.'

Henry nodded.

'No skin off my nose,' he said, shrugging. 'Too late, ain't it? So your little plan failed.'

'What little plan?'

'Showing them to the police.'

'I didn't. It was Mr Finch, my teacher. He did it behind my back.'

'The *beloved* Mr Finch, eh?' snapped his father sarcastically. 'The one who wanted you to finish school?'

'It was me who wanted to finish.'

'Well, you won't now, will you?'

'You heard Gran. She doesn't want me around.'

'Never a truer word spoken,' she muttered.

'We'll be off, then,' his dad said. 'And leaving you behind,' and he tore up Henry's ticket, threw it on to the table and gave a slow smile. 'Locked up in 'ere.'

'But why?' asked Henry, bewildered.

He shrugged.

'Why not?' He turned to Gran, 'Come on, we've a boat waiting for us.'

'I feel sick,' she murmured. 'All these years and I never knew he was like that.'

Henry had nothing to lose now.

'And the son of a deserter, Gran. Don't forget that.'

She swung round, the spittle gathering in the corner of her mouth.

'You liar!'

'Ask Dad. Ask him about the doctors he never saw and the unit he never reported back to. Ask him about the letter Private Jeffries wrote saying Dad had saved his life.'

'He thought he *had* saved his life. He can't have known it was Walter Briggs what done it. He just got the two of them mixed up. That's not your dad's fault.'

'How could Private Jeffries have written the letter if he was dead, Gran?'

'That's enough,' warned his father.

Henry dived behind the table, his father moving rapidly after him.

'Dead?' repeated his grandmother. 'Of course he's not dead. He's a deserter!'

'He was dug up, Gran. And the police got these dentists to look at his teeth. And guess what? It turns out that the Army hung on to his medical records because they thought he were still alive. And why? Because you were always telling the police you'd seen him. If you'd kept your mouth shut, they would have been destroyed and the police would never have found out. Gran, the body under Dad's gravestone is Private Jeffries!'

'You're lyin'! He's a deserter!'

'He's dead, Gran. Dead! Dead! Dead! He's been dead for ten years.'

His father gave him an almighty push, which sent Henry flying against the wall, winding him. By the time he had struggled to his feet his father had grabbed him and pushed him towards the cellar door. Henry fought wildly but his father elbowed him in the stomach. The next thing he knew he was in the dark and the door was closed behind him.

On the way in, Henry's back had banged against

something hard sticking out of the wall. He moved his fingers along the plaster. As soon as he touched the smooth rounded object he knew immediately what it was. A light switch. He felt a fool for not looking for one while he was locked in with Molly. He switched it on. To his surprise, what he had believed was a coal cellar was a basement. He moved swiftly down the stairs. There was a window with two short planks nailed over a blacked-out window. He tugged at the wood, trying to prise them away but it was hopeless. Someone had made a good job of boarding it up.

Looking around there was nothing he could use to remove them. The place was empty, its walls black with filth. He ran back up the stairs and tried to open the door.

Eventually he slid down and sat on the top step. There was no way of getting out. Even if the roll of film was discovered, the photographs wouldn't tell them where to find him. He leaned back against the door.

'Dungheap,' he whispered.

He had no idea how long he had dozed off for, or whether it was day or night. All he knew was that something had woken him. He jumped to his feet and hammered on the door. Within seconds the key was turning in the lock and the door was opened. But his relief was short-lived. Standing in front of him, legs astride, were Ted and Percy and they did not look happy.

'No need to have knocked, my son,' said Ted. 'We was given our orders as to where we might find you. You've been a bit of a naughty boy, haven't you?'

'Bit of a squealer, ain't you?' added Percy. 'Been a bit too pally with our flat-footed friends, 'aven't you?'

Henry had a sick feeling in the pit of his stomach and a suspicion that he was about to receive the treatment Molly had missed out on.

They dragged him out of the cellar into the hall and slammed the door behind him.

'Can you swim?' whispered Percy, leaning towards him.

'A bit,' stammered Henry.

'What he means is,' said Ted, 'can you swim with these tied to your ankles?' And they produced bricks from their pockets.

*Diamond, diamond, diamond*, Henry kept pleading inside his head as he backed, sweating, against the door. And then he felt the key digging into him. He put his hands behind his back and managed to get his fingers around it.

'That's murder!' he yelled, hiding the sound of pulling it out of the lock. He gripped it tightly.

'You don't say,' said Percy.

'I won't go to the police.'

'That's true,' said Ted.

'Why would I want to?'

'I don't know. You tell me,' said Percy, pushing his

foul-smelling mouth up against Henry's face.

'Aren't you leaving the country too?'

At that they broke away.

'What do you mean, leaving the country?' said Percy.

'My dad and gran, they've got special papers.'

'I don't believe you,' said Ted.

'This is one of your fancy tricks, like keeping that camera a secret,' said Percy.

'They tore mine up. They're on the kitchen table. Look if you don't believe me.'

The men glanced at each other.

'You go,' said Ted, 'I'll stay 'ere and keep an eye on him.'

Henry was so wet with perspiration that he was praying the key wouldn't slide out of his fingers. Suddenly he heard Percy yell.

'The double-crosser!'

'Wait there,' said Ted.

As soon as he ran into the kitchen, Henry opened the cellar door, slipped in, closed it swiftly behind him and locked it. The basement was now his refuge. Within seconds there was a loud hammering on the door and shouting. This was followed by a brief silence and muttering. A loud smash followed, as if furniture was being flung against it. Henry backed down the stairs, his eyes fixed to the jiggling door handle. He heard the word *brick*. To his alarm, one of the panels at the top of the door splintered, leaving a long gap. He could hear Ted cursing furiously. A large muscular arm forced its way through the hole.

'The key!' he whispered to himself.

He raced up the steps and pulled it out of the lock. Ted's hand scrabbled around the doorknob, groping round the keyhole. There was a roar of anger. The arm disappeared and the brick was hammering at the door again. It whisked past Henry, narrowly missing him. Ted was now hurling insults at Percy. Henry scrambled down the stairs and picked it up. At least he had a weapon now. He ran over to the window and began to hack away at the wood. As he listened to the door being smashed above him, he managed to prise off one beam and pull it away from the window. The blackout was on a frame, which had been slotted in behind the glass. He returned to the foot of the stairs and glanced up. All four panels had been smashed open now. Rushing back to the window, he concentrated on the second beam, knowing that the men wouldn't dare hurl themselves at the door. If they did, they would topple down the stairs.

And then his heart sank as he heard the clatter of the lock hitting the ground, and a voice screamed out, 'Yer little bastard!'

'Correct,' he muttered to himself, pulling off the beam with all his strength. The blackout frame came out easily, but he could hear footsteps thundering down the stairs, and as he looked outside into the early evening he could see the ground level halfway up the window. He was about to open it when he felt two pairs of arms seize him from behind and his feet leave the ground. As they hauled him away a light from a torch outside flashed into his eyes, blinding him. He could sense the two men jump.

'Get him away from the window!' ordered Ted.

'Too late!' yelled Percy.

There was a loud hammering at the front door. Ted and Percy threw him to the floor and raced up the stairs. Henry stumbled to his feet.

'It's the men in the photographs,' he heard a man yell.

'Oh, no you don't,' said another voice. 'You're going nowhere.'

Henry was halfway up the stairs when a policeman appeared in the broken doorway.

'Are you Henry?' he asked.

'That's right,' and he grinned. 'Henry Carpenter.'

# 8. The final reel

'MOLLY'S ASLEEP,' SAID HENRY'S MOTHER, STEPPING INTO MRS Beaumont's sitting room.

'*Now* will you tell us?' asked Grace.

It was later that night. The police had driven Henry at breakneck speed down to Sternsea. Once back at Mrs Beaumont's house, a bath had been run for him while his mother and Uncle Bill hugged him on the landing outside and his friends waited in the sitting room.

'There's a nice young girl down there who's been worried frantic about you,' his mother told him quietly. 'She came with her friend.' And she kissed him on the cheek. 'My lovely boy.'

'I'll get back to the station,' said Uncle Bill. 'Now I know you're safe, I'll be off and tell them the good news.'

'The other drivers,' explained his mother. 'They've been covering for him.'

By the time Henry had sat down in his pyjamas with

dried scrambled eggs on toast, and his mother had settled the baby, Grace was almost crawling up the wall with impatience.

'If you don't tell us soon, Great-Aunt Florence will be reporting me missing as well.'

Pip and Jeffries, Grace, Jane and Margaret, Mrs Jeffries, his mother and Mrs Beaumont surrounded him.

'I take it you know that Henry managed to have Molly rescued?' began Mrs Beaumont.

'Yes, yes, we know all that,' interrupted Grace.

'Wait a minute,' said Jane. 'Me and Margaret don't know.'

'Well, the police knew Molly and Henry were missing quite early on,' explained Mrs Beaumont quickly. 'Mr Finch rang here wanting to know why Henry hadn't turned up, and just around then Mrs Henson knocked on the door asking if Molly had been taken ill. We thought they might have had some kind of accident so we rang the police and they contacted the hospital but no one matching their description had been brought there with any injuries. When they hadn't turned up for the birthday party, we phoned the police again and they contacted the police in London.'

'Why London?' asked Jane, puzzled.

Mrs Beaumont glanced at Henry as if asking for his permission to go on. Henry nodded.

'They knew that Henry had refused to get involved in criminal activities there.'

Jane stared at him in awe.

'I'll tell you more later,' said Henry.

'So the police suspected that the criminals had decided not to take no for an answer,' continued Mrs Beaumont. 'I went up to my house in London and gave them my phone number and address there.'

'And I stayed here so I could be near the phone should the police ring here,' said Henry's mother. 'They popped round on Monday, told me that the London police had received a phone call from Henry telling them where to find Molly, and that they'd picked her up and she was safe.'

'But exhausted,' added Mrs Beaumont, 'so after Molly had insisted that the police give her an ice cream, they brought her to me.'

Henry was aware that Jane was staring at him.

'But how did they find Henry?' cried Grace, exasperated.

'When Henry called them he pretended that the call was over but didn't put the receiver down, so the police were able to overhear that Henry and the woman he was with would be watching from a café window opposite.'

'But why didn't they rescue him then?' asked Jeffries.

'Because they wanted to follow him and catch the whole gang.'

'They just made it,' said Henry.

'Though they didn't manage to find everyone,' Mrs Beaumont said quietly. 'But I forgot to tell you about the photographs.'

'What photographs?' asked Pip.

'Henry?'

Henry nodded and told them what he knew up till leaving Molly.

'So who found the film?' Pip asked.

'I did,' said Mrs Beaumont. 'When the police brought Molly round to my place that morning, I could see that what she needed was a warm bath and a nap while I washed her clothes. They were filthy. I hoped her nightdress was in the dog because I had nothing else she could wear while they were drying. So I unbuttoned the dog . . .'

'And that's when you found the roll of film?' said Jeffries.

'Yes. I didn't realise how important it was then, but I knew Henry wanted to develop it for the photographic display and I wanted to carry on as though he was still going to make it to the last day at school. The police told me they were going to pick us up later, so I called Jim MacTavish, Max's photographer friend. He picked it up and whisked it off to some lab to develop it. Well, as soon as he saw the pictures of Molly asleep on the settee next to those two crooks he recognised her from having seen her at my place. We called the police immediately and they were delighted. They've been trying to get evidence which will stick with these two characters for some time. And there's no denying they had something to do with her kidnap, with Molly lying there beside them.'

'It's a pity you can't remember where your father said he and your gran were going,' said Henry's mother. 'Not knowing where they are gives me the creeps.'

'Your father!' chorused Jane and Margaret.

'The police are on the coast keeping an eye out for them,' said Mrs Beaumont, 'but they've probably left the country by now.'

'And you can't remember anything at all?' Pip asked Henry.

'Yes, but nothing useful. I know they were off to meet some man.'

'What was his name?' asked Pip.

'That's just it, I can't remember. It was a name like Cedric, like that actor in *The Man in Black*.'

'Valentine Dyall?'

'No. His second name is like a first name, John or James. It was the one who pretended he'd died and disguised himself as a drunk boatkeeper so he could catch those people plotting against his daughter. He was in *The Small Back Room*, too,' he said, turning to Jeffries, 'remember? He was the barkeeper.'

'Well, while you're chewing that over there's something Uncle Bill picked up from your school,' said

Mrs Beaumont, pointing to his mother.

'Mum's birthday present!'

'Made by you.' And she lifted it up from behind the settee.

It was a small low table.

'Oh, Henry!' his mother cried.

'It's a coffee table.'

'It's the latest thing,' said Jane. 'I saw a picture of one in *Woman*.'

'It's beautiful.'

'It's made of oak,' said Henry. 'The woodwork teacher had some left over.'

'John Cedric?' Jeffries interrupted, still thinking about the previous conversation. 'James Cedric?'

'Other way round. Cedric John or Cedric James,' and then Henry remembered. 'Sid James!'

'They were meeting the actor Sid James?' said Grace.

'No, the name of the man they were meeting was Sidney.'

'Are you sure that's not where they were going?' asked Margaret.

'Going to Sidney?'

'Sydney, Australia!' chorused the girls.

'Good Lord!' exclaimed Mrs Beaumont. 'I'll phone the police.'

She had hardly reached the door when the telephone rang.

'That's probably them now.'

From the sitting room they could hear her talking in the hallway.

'Certainly,' she said. 'I'll go and get him.'

She poked her head round the door.

'It's for you, Henry.'

'Is it the police?'

'No.'

'Who is it?'

'Come and find out.'

Mystified, Henry headed for the hall and picked up the receiver.

'Hello.'

'Hello,' said a man's voice, 'I take it you're Henry.'

'Yes.'

The man had a slight country accent.

'I'm Max's friend, Jim MacTavish. I developed your roll of film.'

'Thank you, Mr MacTavish!'

'I hope you don't mind but I made some copies and showed them to a friend of mine who's a camera operator. He's just about to start a job on a new film in London but his clapper boy's got his call-up papers for National Service. It's a responsible job. Clapping the clapperboard is the easiest part, that and making sure the crew have gallons of tea. What I'm saying is, the job's yours if you want it. Interested?'

*

The headmaster stood solemnly on stage in front of a table which was covered with cups, books and shields. He was wearing a black gown and looking very pleased with himself.

'Ladies and gentlemen,' he began, 'as you know, this is the second year we have had a fourth form. And what a year it has been for our boys and girls! Those of you who have seen what they have achieved, from needlework to woodwork, from pottery to cookery, cannot but be impressed by their endeavours, and for this I must also thank my staff for their hard work.'

Henry sat with his friends on the right side of the hall. The parents were sitting to the left of the aisle. All the women were wearing hats and gloves and the men were in suits. Henry glanced at the walls where his photographs were on display. He turned round and saw Mrs Beaumont and Grace sitting in the back row. They waved to him.

'You've seen our gymnasts, heard our pupils sing English folk songs, listened to them speak French and heard one of them play the pianoforte.'

This was greeted with a murmur of appreciation. Henry spotted one of the women waking her husband.

'In the first term of this, their final year, we introduced some new educational experiments to the fourth formers. The boys can now clean and cook and the girls can put up a shelf.

'And now to the History presentations. This has been an enormous success and has shown that although we may not have the academic accolades of the grammar school, we have some remarkably resourceful pupils, and who knows, perhaps one or two may go on to take up further studies.'

Nervously Henry listened to him call each group to come up on stage to receive a cup or book.

'And now for our last trio,' he announced. 'Philip Hart, Roger Jeffries and Henry . . .' He paused, looking awkward for a moment and then he smiled. 'Just Henry.'

They headed for the steps at the side and walked up on to the stage.

'Philip Hart is to receive the music cup. Philip begins work as a rewind boy at the Plaza cinema where he can be heard playing the pianoforte on Saturday nights during the Intermission.'

The headmaster presented the cup to Pip and shook his hand among tumultuous applause.

'Roger Jeffries is to receive the English cup for his wonderful H. G. Wells-inspired stories. He will be leaving us to begin work in London at a publishers and to help form a film archive.'

Henry watched Jeffries shake hands and walk down the steps to more applause.

'And now for the third member of the film group. Most

people will know him as Henry Dodge but he is about to be adopted by his stepfather, Mr William Carpenter.' He paused. 'I think many pupils and parents will have heard of the recent exploits of this young man. Finding himself kidnapped with his young sister, he managed to save her life by using his wits and, through his photographic skills, which many of you will have had the pleasure of seeing here on the walls, he has helped to put away two very unpleasant characters.'

Someone began to clap. The head put up his hand for silence and picked up the last cup.

'Henry is to receive the photography cup and I am delighted to announce that after leaving Hatton Secondary Modern School, this young man is to begin an apprenticeship in the moving picture industry as a clapper boy.'

And he held his hand out for Henry to shake.

There was a gasp from the hall and above the applause came cheers. Henry looked down and saw Uncle Bill and his mother clapping vigorously. When he returned to his chair he noticed Jane smiling.

'And now, ladies and gentlemen, boys and girls,' announced the headmaster grandly, 'will you all now rise for our new school song, *Let us stride forth and let our young hearts sing.*' And with that he made a flamboyant gesture towards the piano. 'Take it away, Miss Plimsoll!'

And everyone rose to a crescendo of crashing chords.

# Postscript: London

HENRY AND JEFFRIES GRINNED AT ONE ANOTHER OVER THE TABLE in the basement kitchen, Jeffries in his pyjamas, Henry wearing a jacket, flannels, shirt and tie. Through the back windows the dawn light had only just begun to stream into the scrubby back garden. For both of them it was their first day at work. Jeffries would be leaving later than Henry. Work for Henry at the studio began early.

'Imagine being picked up by a car!' said Grace. She was sitting at the end of the table in her nightdress, watching Henry eat his breakfast. 'Now don't forget, you both have to tell me every single detail when you get back so that I can tell Pip when I phone him.'

'We can tell him ourselves,' said Jeffries.

'No, you can't. He'll be busy rewinding films in the projection box when you get back. And you'll be at work when he's at home.'

Jeffries caught Henry's eye. It was obvious that

Grace wanted to be the first to tell him.

They had all been living in Mrs Beaumont's London house for a week now, Jeffries and Henry sharing one of the two attic bedrooms.

'You've got to eat more than that,' exclaimed Henry's mother, looking at the half-eaten piece of toast on Henry's plate. 'You've a long day ahead of you.'

'What time is it?' he asked.

'Five minutes later than the last time you asked,' answered Mrs Beaumont, popping her head round the door.

The waiting was unbearable. Once Henry knew he had the job of clapper boy, he wanted to start work the very next day. Now it was the actual day and he still had to wait.

The doorbell rang. Henry jumped, almost spilling tea over his clean shirt. He pushed back his chair and sprang to his feet. His mother flung her arms round him.

'Have a lovely day,' she said proudly.

Upstairs Henry could hear footsteps. His mother let go of him and Henry shot up the stairs towards the ground floor. He met Uncle Bill in the hall.

'It's here,' he said, smiling.

Through the open door Henry saw the car waiting outside.

By now Jeffries and Grace had run into the dance studio and were peering out of the window, with Mrs Jeffries.

'It's like being a film star,' said Grace excitedly.

Henry ran down the steps. He didn't look behind him. He knew that by now his mother and Mrs Beaumont would have joined his friends and Uncle Bill at the front window. The driver, who was wearing a tweed cap at an angle, leaned towards the open car window.

'Henry?' he asked. 'Pinewood?'

'Yeah. Please,' said Henry, suddenly feeling a lump in his throat.

It was only when the car drew away that he looked up at the window and waved.

'This way.'

A tall youth with thick black hair and glasses was waiting for him at the entrance to the studio. He was the clapper boy who was leaving.

'I'll take you to the camera room,' he said.

Henry followed him down a long corridor.

'I'm Alan. I'll be showing you the ropes over the next fortnight,' he explained. 'In here.'

They walked into a room where black boxes of varying sizes were stored.

'We need to carry these into the studio and unpack them.'

Henry stared at the largest of the boxes. It was the size of three coffins stacked on top of one another. *How are we going to carry that?* he thought.

'Don't panic,' laughed Alan. 'The grip usually helps us with that.'

They lifted up a heavy rectangular box and took it out of the room and along a corridor towards a studio.

'This has film magazines in it,' Alan said. 'And they're not the kind you read.'

Entering the studio, Henry noticed a set which resembled a down-at-heel newspaper office. They hurried back to the camera room and picked up another black box.

'What's in here?' Henry asked.

'Put it down. I'll show you.' Alan unclipped the lid and raised it. The box was lined with red velvet and sectioned off into separate velvet compartments. Inside the compartments were different-sized lenses. 'There's a lot to learn but you'll soon pick it up. It'll probably be a couple of months, though, before they let you loose in the darkroom. Sid will have to do it until then.'

'Who's Sid?'

'Focus puller. Also known as assistant cameraman. He makes sure the actors and actresses stay in focus.'

'I didn't know clapper boys had to develop the film.'

'They don't. The laboratories do that. They pick up the cans of exposed film at the end of the day.'

'So why will I have to go into the darkroom?'

'To unload the exposed film from the magazine at the back of the camera, put it in a can for the laboratory and seal it up. Tricky in the dark, I can tell you. If you mess it up, hours of film and lots of money will be lost and you'll be out of a job!'

'Hurry up, you two!' said a voice behind them. 'We have to be up and running by eight thirty!'

A young stocky man with a mass of sandy hair was heading for the gargantuan black box.

'Sid,' whispered Alan. Henry watched Alan clip the lid of the box down. 'Never, never, never leave this unclipped. You could get fired for that. The lenses in here are so expensive. If someone knocked the box over and the lid flew open . . .' He gave a dramatic pause. '. . . Too horrible to think about.' He lifted the end of the box. 'Come on, we need to get a move on.'

Carrying it into the studio, Henry noticed a man on the set smoking a cigarette. A woman was sitting on the edge of the desk reading a newspaper.

'They're stand-ins,' Alan explained as they lowered the box. 'They'll do the actor's and actress's moves so the scene can be lit while they're being made up. It means all the lighting will be sorted out when they're called on set. The boss man decides how that's done.'

*Boss man*? He couldn't remember reading about him in the bookshop.

'Director of photography, otherwise known as lighting cameraman. Sir, to you.'

'Is he the man who gave me my job?'

'Don't you know?' asked Alan, surprised. 'I thought it was your father. That's how I got mine. He put in a good word for me with the camera operator. He's the one who chooses the crew. Is he a relative of yours?'

'No. I don't know anyone here.'

'So how did you get this job?'

'It's a long story.'

On their way back to the camera room, Henry could hear voices. There was something familiar about one of them. When he walked into the room, standing beside the last box in jacket and tie, was Mrs Beaumont's youngest son.

'Max!'

'He's the camera operator,' said Alan. 'I thought you said you didn't know anyone.'

'He's the son of a lady I know.'

'Not such a long story, then,' said Alan drily.

Among much laughing and joking, Henry, Max, Sid and a wiry middle-aged man called Fred, who Henry discovered was the grip, hauled the massive box out of the room, down the corridor and into the studio, where they unclipped it. Inside was an enormous movie camera, the kind you had to sit up high behind. Henry had seen ones like it in opening shots of newsreels in the cinema, like Pathé News. He stared up at it in awe. *One day that's where I'm going to be,* he thought.

'I've got to show you the negative report sheet now,'

said Alan. He walked over to a table where Henry saw a large paperback book, the pages of which were the same size as the ones his mother put into a typewriter.

'On this top page,' Alan said, opening the book, 'you write all the details of which scenes are filmed each day and how many takes there were for each scene. When the director tells you which ones he wants the lab to print, you draw a circle round them. OK?'

Henry nodded.

'Each top sheet needs to be torn off,' Alan said, lifting it up, 'because it has to be sent off to the laboratory with the cans of exposed film.'

'Exposed. That means the film which has been used.'

'Yes.'

'Is that carbon paper?' Henry asked, spotting the shiny dark blue paper underneath.

'Yes. You've seen this before?'

'My mum types. She uses it when she wants to make copies.'

'That's why it's here,' said Alan. 'Under it are four other sheets of paper. You'll have to press really hard with the pencil for your writing to go through to the bottom copy. The camera crew get that one. Sometimes it comes out so faint you can hardly read it.' He tucked a round metal container under his arm. 'I need to load some film in the darkroom. If you want to help, you can get those boxes out of the way.'

Henry checked that the lids were clipped down and pushed the boxes to the side of the studio. Eventually Alan reappeared from the darkroom and Henry watched him fix a loaded magazine above the camera at the front.

'Will I have to do that too?' Henry asked.

'Yes. Hang on a bit while I put film into two more magazines,' and he disappeared back into the darkroom.

Henry was trembling with adrenalin. He wanted to leap into the air with joy, yet he felt solid too because even though he knew there were a lot of new things to take in, he felt completely at home. He was watching Sid checking the camera when Alan returned with a loaded magazine under each arm.

'It's always a good idea to have them ready for later,' he explained, placing them on the table.

'How long are the reels inside?'

'A thousand feet. That's about ten minutes of filming. We usually get through about six reels a day.'

'Sixty minutes!'

'Yes, but only about a sixteenth of that will be used.' He stuck his pencil behind his ear and walked over to the camera. 'Come and take a look,' he said over his shoulder.

Eagerly Henry watched the loaded magazine at the front move slowly round as Sid threaded the film from it down through the mechanism of the camera and up towards the empty magazine at the back. He noticed Sid glancing over at Fred, who was listening to a man with a beard. Fred caught Sid's eye, gave him a nod and he walked over to construct what appeared to be a small railway track on the floor in front of the camera. It led to a table with a telephone on it.

'That's so Max can get a closer shot of the scene by the telephone later on,' explained Alan. 'Fred will push him along the track.'

A tall man with curly red hair appeared behind the camera holding a long pole with a microphone attached to it.

'Is that the boom?' asked Henry.

'Yes. It picks up the sound.'

'I've read a bit about it in this book and seen photographs, but I never knew you could see inside the camera.'

'That's because it's not covered by the blimp.'

'What's a blimp?'

'The curved metal case above the magazines. It's only shut when everything is ready to shoot. The film makes a hell of a racket when it's moving round. The blimp muffles the sound. Look.' Sid was pulling down the metal case tightly round the camera, hiding the mechanisms. 'That means Sid's finished checking the magazines.' Alan grabbed the clapperboard from the table. This will be your next job.'

Henry watched him chalk up the name of the studio,

the director, the cameraman, the date and the name of the film, *Deadline Dues,* Scene 8, Take 1.

'I thought this was the first day,' said Henry.

'It is.'

'Why have you put scene 8, then?'

'The scenes aren't shot in order. They're spliced and joined up in the right order later. There's one more thing I need to show you.' Alan beckoned him over to the second box they had carried into the studio.

As he swung back the lid, Henry stared again at all the different-sized lenses.

'It looks harder than it is,' said Alan reassuringly. 'But usually only three of these are used. For a close-up you'll need a three inch lens or a 75 mill,' he began.

'Mill?'

'Millimetres. That's what the American lenses are called,' and he continued to show Henry which lens was which.

It took a good half an hour for the camera to be ready and nearly all morning to do the lighting. Later, two members of the cast were called. Henry observed a plump woman standing in front of a smartly dressed actress wearing a suit, pressing what looked like blotting paper against the make-up on her face. An actor was standing on a mark on the floor of the set, wearing a long raincoat and trilby. The raincoat was identical to the one Henry had been given at Christmas.

It was covered in damp patches, as though the character the actor was playing had just come in from the rain. A thin young woman wearing spectacles was peering at the damp patches and taking notes.

'She's the continuity girl,' said Alan. 'Because each scene is filmed in bits and sometimes over several days, she's got to make sure that everything looks the same.'

Henry returned to watching the actress. The hat she was wearing tilted to one side and he heard the director telling the man with the beard that when she was on the telephone he wanted it to cast a shadow across her face.

There was a relaxed concentration as each part of the scene was rehearsed and filmed over and over again. Henry watched Max peering intently through the viewfinder at the side of the camera.

'Why don't you go to the canteen and get a cuppa for everyone?' said Alan. 'That's one of the jobs you can do today. Just pick up a tray.'

'How will I get everyone's cup on one tray?'

Alan laughed.

'Sorry. You don't get tea for everyone in the studio. Just the camera crew. We all work in fours. That's me, the boss, Max, Sid, and you of course.'

Henry decided to get tea for the grip as well. When he returned with six cups he wondered if Jeffries was doing the same thing at the publishing house. The studio was now in a fog of cigarette smoke and Alan was nowhere to be seen. He guessed he must be in the darkroom again. He glanced up at Max.

'Ah, lovely!' he said, stepping down and eagerly taking a cup like a man in a desert reaching an oasis. He gave Henry a friendly wink and Henry headed towards the boss, grip and Sid. On the way back he saw Alan with a sealed can. The top sheet of the negative report sheet had been attached to it.

*Another thing to remember*, and he watched Alan replace the blue carbon paper under a new top sheet and take a loaded magazine over to the front of the camera.

They were allowed three-quarters of an hour in the middle of the day for a bite to eat. Grabbing some sandwiches, Alan beckoned Henry to follow him. He took him to a small room, carrying a magazine of leftover film and one of the flat empty cans.

'There's about two hundred feet of film in here,' he said. 'It's for you to practise on.' He opened the magazine. 'This magazine has to be opened in the dark. See that small circle of bakelite in the centre of the reel?' he said, pointing to a circular brown object. 'You have to make sure that you take the reel out flat, without that falling out. Then you have to transfer it to the can.'

'In the dark?'

'Yes. And it's really dark, not like a photographic darkroom. If that middle falls out, it's murder to get it back in again.'

'But how will I see what I'm doing?'

'You don't. You have to do it by feel. That's why you need to practise. Once you can do that, you'll be a clapper unloader as well as a clapper loader. Try it.'

With the utmost concentration Henry picked up the reel. To his horror the middle fell out and the reel went everywhere.

'You need to be gentle. You have to put your hand flat underneath it first. You can try again tomorrow. Keep practising every time we take a break. Then try it with your eyes shut. That's the way to do it. Now eat your sandwich. We have to get back to the studio pronto.'

By the time the fourth reel of film was sealed in a can and stacked with the other cans ready to be picked up by a man from the laboratory, it was half past seven and they had gone into overtime. The camera, magazines and lenses were packed up into the black boxes and returned to the camera room ready to be unpacked again the next morning.

'I'm sorry I haven't spoken to you much today,' said Max as they walked down the corridor. 'I hope Alan's been explaining things. We're off for some fish and chips now and then going into one of the small studios to see a film.'

'Oh,' said Henry, disappointed. He had hoped to have some company on the way home. 'I'll go and get the bus, then.'

'Aren't you coming with us?' said Max, surprised.

'You mean I can?'

'Of course. You're one of us now. And don't worry about a bus. A studio car takes you home as well as picks you up.'

When Henry arrived back at Mrs Beaumont's house, he found Uncle Bill sitting at the foot of the steps in the hall, his nose deep in a book, a pile of paperbacks and a thermos beside him. He poured cocoa from the thermos into a mug and held it out for Henry to take.

'Your mum's asleep. I promised to wake her as soon as you got back.'

'The camera crew asked me to join them after work,' Henry explained.

'I know,' said Uncle Bill. 'Max telephoned us in case your mother was worried.'

Henry glanced at the book. On the cover there was an outline of a ship on a stormy sea. Above the ship in huge lettering were the words *SEA CHANGE*.

'*A novel for boys by Richard Armstrong*,' read Henry.

'I got it from the library for you. I've heard a lot of good things about this writer. But then I started reading it and couldn't put it down. There's another of his books here,' he added, handing him one from the top of the pile. '*Sabotage at the Forge*.'

In the middle of the red cover was a grinning boy

wearing a cap. He was holding an oil can. Behind him was an old building with smoke coming out of tall chimneys.

'*A story for boys set in a Tyneside steelworks*,' said Henry.

'It's a detective story.'

'It looks good. Thanks. A bit different from *Ballet Shoes*, then.'

'And what's wrong with *Ballet Shoes*?' said an indignant voice above them. 'It only happens to be the best book ever.'

It was Grace in her nightdress. Jeffries was standing beside her in his pyjamas.

'We've been waiting for you for ages,' she said impatiently.

'So how was it? Did you get to use the clapperboard?' asked Jeffries.

'No. Tomorrow I will. The camera operator who chose me is Max. Did you know?'

'Only after you'd left. Mrs Beaumont wanted it to be a surprise. What's it like?'

'There's four of us in the camera crew, same as the sound crew and the sparks.'

'Sparks?' said Grace.

'Electricians. Max said I'm one of them now but I won't feel like a real member of the crew till I'm a clapper unloader.' And he yawned.

'What's a clapper unloader?' asked Jeffries.

'Tell him tomorrow,' said Uncle Bill. 'You need some sleep.'

'Sleep!' exclaimed Grace. 'I can't go to sleep until I know *everything*, and after that I have to tell Henry what happened to Roger at the publishers.'

As they walked up the stairs Henry glanced at Jeffries over Grace's head. It seemed as though nothing had changed.

'Well,' Henry began, 'do you know why you need a clapperboard?'

'To number the scenes?' said Grace.

'Yeah. And to synchronise the sound. It's a signal for the sound people.'

'Go on. What else?'

Henry took the magazine of used film into the darkroom. It was his first time. For seven weeks he had heard darkroom horror stories, which Grace had eagerly lapped up to pass on to Pip. One clapper boy had put the wrong reel into the can and another had been so used to practising with his eyes shut that he did it in the darkroom without checking that the light had been switched off first. Both boys had destroyed hours of work. *I am not going to make the same mistake*, Henry told himself.

He slid the palm of his hand under the exposed reel and eased it gently into a can. *So far so good,* he thought.

*The middle hasn't fallen out.* Groping around for the lid, he screwed it down firmly, remembering to keep the magazine to one side and the can on the other so that he wouldn't get them mixed up. He felt for the reel of sticky tape in the dark, clawed at it with his fingernails and wound it round where the lid overlapped the bottom of the can.

*And twice for luck*, he decided. *Now what?* And then he remembered. *Laboratory label!*

Once the label and top sheet from the negative report book were stuck to the can, he stepped out of the darkroom with it under his arm, aware that he was sweating.

*Place it on the table and pick up the loaded magazine of unexposed film ready for the next scene*, he told himself. Now he was back on familiar territory. As usual, he fixed it in place at the front, ready for the focus puller to thread it through to the empty magazine at the back.

*Carbon paper under a new top sheet next.* Once he had done that, he stuck his pencil behind his ear and picked up the clapperboard. It was oily from the constant rubbing off of numbers throughout the day, so he had to press the chalk firmly with his blue stained fingers to make the numbers visible.

*Nearly there.* He stood still for a moment to catch his breath. *I've done it! I have just unloaded my first reel of film negative in the darkroom. I can call myself a real clapper unloader now.*

The blimp had been closed. He glanced up at Max sitting high behind the camera. He gave Henry a thumbs-up sign. Henry grinned and stood in front of the camera. The director nodded and Henry opened the clapper.

'Scene five eight four. Take one,' Henry said loudly, slammed the clapperboard down and stepped out of the way of the lens.

And then the director yelled a word Henry had heard a hundred or more times over the past few weeks, a word he knew he would never grow tired of hearing.

'ACTION!'

## Author Acknowledgements

Colindale Newspaper Library, Beaver Booksearch, John Budd, Roy Barrow, Sylvia Brooks Ingham, Mary Rutter Kelsey, Lewis Rudd MBE, John Wiles, John McCallum, Philip Ower, Matty O'Kelly, Mary and David Austin, Peter Marshall, Sir Sydney Samuelson CBE, Barry Wilson, Maggie Cooper, Portsmouth Museum, Ken Penry, Lt Col (Retired) Mike Boocock, Police Inspector Gladys Howard (Retired), The authors of *The Cinemas of Portsmouth* (J. Barker, R. Brown and W. Greer).

And a special thanks to the pupils of Petersfield Secondary Modern School who very kindly shared their reunion with me.

Description of Waterloo Station in 1949 inspired by the watercolour painting: *Waterloo Station – Peace* by Helen McKie, 1948.

*It's Magic* – Music by Jule Styne, Lyrics by Sammy Cahn. Warner Chappell Music Ltd.

The author has tried her best to obtain permission to quote from this song.